The Rogue world evolves, and we see how Portia's motivation, decisions, struggles, and selfless heart mold and equip her for more than she ever thought she was capable of. But doing the right thing might cost her everything. This thought-provoking story gripped my heart with every turn of the page.

- Joann Claypoole
  www.joannclaypoole.com

I enjoyed this wild adventure with moral principles and truths sprinkled throughout. I love how Hogrefe intertwines historical events and people from the 1700s and ties into a futuristic world. This makes her stories all the more unique and entertaining.

- Becky Van Daniker
  www.reviewsbyvandaniker.wordpress.com

Hogrefe mixes suspense, espionage, angst, pain, and anxiety into the pages, along with a hint, and sometimes more than a hint of romance. Her characters are real and flawed. They fit smoothly into the story line; well balanced and fully told.

- Betty Thomason Owens
  www.bettythomasonowens.com

Talk about a page-turner! Make sure you give yourself plenty of time to read this book because you won't want to put it down.

- Phyllis
  www.amongthereads.net

Kristen Hogrefe has done an extraordinary job of creating a memorably suspenseful, thought-provoking, and genuinely fascinating dystopian world.

- Jennifer
  www.carpediem.fyi

THE REACTIONARY

by

KRISTEN HOGREFE

W

Write Integrity Press

The Reactionary
© 2019 Kristen Hogrefe

ISBN-13: 978-1-944120-77-1

This book is a work of fiction. The author discovered a good deal of fascinating historical information during her research, and to the best of her knowledge and belief, she represented actual historical facts with integrity. Aside from the historical characters and events, the names, characters, places, and incidents are either products of the author's imagination or used fictitiously. Any similarity to actual people and/or events is purely coincidental.

All quoted Scripture passages are taken from the KING JAMES VERSION (KJV): KING JAMES VERSION, public domain.

 Published by Write Integrity Press
PO Box 702852
Dallas, TX 75370

Find out more about the author, **Kristen Hogrefe,** at her website, **www.KristenHogrefe.com** or on her author page at
www.WriteIntegrity.com

Printed in the United States of America.

CONTENTS

PART ONE: THE PLAGUES

PART TWO: THE SUMMIT

"I am not bound to win, but I am bound to be true. I am not bound to succeed, but I am bound to live up to what light I have."

Abraham Lincoln

PART ONE THE PLAGUES

CHAPTER 1

~ Portia ~

Friday, 6.26.2150
Crystal

All the banging in the world won't make the stationmaster answer his door faster. I press my body against the frame of his booth as the late June gale unleashes another wave of icy rain. My coat clings to me like a second skin.

"You shouldn't go," my brother Darius had said. "Luther can take care of himself and will come back when he's ready."

But Luther hadn't even sent a message over the wire to tell me he reached Chrysoprase safely. And he's been gone over a week.

Anything could have happened to him. Gages loyal to Felix could have captured him on their retreat to the northern Black Tundra. His train could have been seized. His parents might already have left, and his stubborn insistence on traveling during a civil insurrection would be a waste of time.

The booth door groans open to reveal the stationmaster's scowling face. "What do you want?"

"Please." I have to shout above the wind's roar. "When is the next train from 'Prase?"

"Don't know. No one's going anywhere in this weather." He pulls the door tighter. "Besides, it's getting dark. Go home before this gets worse."

"But…"

The door clicks closed. There's no use standing in a freezing downpour.

I stagger through the gusting wind, across the station platform, and toward the entrance of the Crystal Globe. Located in the heart of our capital cube Crystal, it used to be the most elite university among our thirteen squares. And the draft board had once chosen me to train there.

Now, the Crystal Globe isn't much of anything. What is a university without students? The candidates have fled, the classrooms sit silent, and the ghost-town-like dorms house only homeless Rogues like me.

The marble steps to its prestigious library are as vacant as the ruins of the one in Cube 1776. Last year, when I was enrolled here, exploring the remnants of the past civilization had seemed like a fun adventure. Now, the eerie stillness of my own world makes me wonder if the ASU might soon join the annals of history and be forgotten.

No, I can't think that way.

The wind catches the thick library door, slamming it against its frame with a loud bang that echoes inside the empty space. I shove it closed and step into the plush interior.

But my mind plays tricks. Where my boots press into the groomed carpet, I imagine the cracked tiles of the lost library. It's as if I'm seeing reality half as it is and half through a black and white, shattered nightmare.

I run toward the stairwell, only to meet another ghost of the past. Juliana Caesura's portrait stares at me from the collection of framed leaders. The deceased Friend's haunting gray eyes seem to follow my movements, but of course, it's my imagination, my horrible imagination.

Next to her frame is an empty one. Revolution had swept through the land so quickly that her son Felix had no time to arrange a formal inauguration for himself. He, the bulk of the Crystal Gage taskforce, and his other loyalists retreated to the Deadwood fortress to regroup. There was no telling when he would make his next move.

But we have to be ready when he does.

Almost three weeks ago, we had the element of surprise on our side, but now, can our threadbare leadership team hold together the disunified squares?

I push past the gallery of Friends' portraits and grip the stairwell railing. At the top, I enter Felix's code, the year 2150, in the keypad to access the archives.

As I do, my stomach churns. This year will decide if he reclaims the ASU for the Rosh League and secures his own position or if our Brotherhood can liberate the land once and for all.

Revolution looks easy next to the tall order of "securing the blessings of liberty" to a divided people.

My boots against the metal stairwell echo into the archive void. The lights are off, so I grip the cool railing and descend toward the portal door in the dark.

There's a faint glow underneath the door. The meeting has already started, and I'm late.

I enter the code again and step inside. The room remains unchanged with its plush, theater-like seating and wide screen. It was originally designed to provide private Translation sessions for the ruling elite.

The first time I had entered the portal had been to plant a virus that would allow the Brotherhood to spy on the Friend and Dome leadership. The mission had cost my career, any hope of a future with Luther, and worst of all, my father.

True, I had escaped the satellite and picked up the broken pieces of Luther's and my relationship, but nothing in this life is guaranteed.

What will this new mission cost me?

Darius swivels his seat by the podium while Lydia and Alexis glance at me from the front row. My heart drops that Fox, Jael, and the others can't be here, but then, our core team is spread thin. Still, someone I expect is missing. My gut twists. I hope Deidra hasn't taken a turn for the worse.

"Sorry I'm late," I mumble and drop into a seat beside Lydia. My former roommate is as slender and pale as ever, but there's a quiet confidence about her. The pressure of her rotten internship had only helped bring to the surface her hidden strength.

"You're all wet! You must be freezing." Alexis furrows her brow in concern, and she seems to shiver, just looking at me. Our lives now are a far stretch from her once cozy life in the upper management of the ASU.

I warm at her sympathy but shrug. "I didn't have time to change." Having survived Warren's freezing winter, I don't notice the cold's discomfort as much anymore.

Lydia squeezes my arm. "Did you learn anything?"

I shake my head. "The stationmaster said no trains will run until this storm passes."

Darius grunts and rubs the reddish-brown stubble he calls a beard. "I could have told you the same thing and saved you a soaking."

I clench my fist in frustration. "Luther's been gone a week. Am I the only one who's worried?"

My brother's brown eyes flicker with compassion. "I'm sorry, Portia, but Luther can handle himself. Right now, we have bigger problems—like trying to protect a nation without any defenses."

Alexis switches out of motherly concern mode and into her no-nonsense political role, one she's honed for decades. "That's why we need international allies."

"Allies?" I repeat, testing the word. The ASU has been alone, like a silent island, for all its existence. Why would any other nation across the ocean take interest in us now?

Darius drums his fingers on the podium. "We need to live in reality, Alexis. Most other countries, assuming they still exist, don't know we're here or if they do, could care less. We're on our own."

Alexis pushes a wayward bobby pin to hold back her cropped gray hair. The ex-Dome representative gives Darius an even stare. "News flash, they do. And we can't dismiss them all. Though I rarely engaged in international communications, I did attend a virtual summit last year."

"What kind of summit?" Lydia asks.

"The Rosh League holds periodic summits to keep its territories accountable," Alexis says. "These meetings are a big deal, because all ten of the Rosh League council members converge in a secret location to discuss their own matters and then translate in territory leaders to give an account."

Alexis's eyes take on a faraway look. "The incidents of missing and vandalized equipment happening in 'Prase at the time caught their attention, and as a Tooler representative, I was chosen to explain."

I nod and remember Dad mentioning that there had been problems in the shipyard where he worked. People blamed the Rogues. At that time, I didn't know what the name meant. Now, I suspect Dad or Darius might have been behind the incidents.

Alexis frowns at the memory. "Viceroy Plume, the lackey overseeing the ASU and rumored to report to the chairman himself, demanded to know if we suspected the Rogues having a connection to the Orvieto Confederation. I asked him what he meant and who Orvieto was. He told me if I didn't know, it didn't matter."

Darius rubs his temples. "What does any of this have to do with your proposal for an international ally?"

"I'm getting there. Don't interrupt."

Alexis might be the only woman I know who can get away with lecturing my brother. But then, she's old enough to be our mother.

Darius doesn't argue, but his frown deepens, and his crossed arms suggest he's no longer interested.

Alexis arches an eye at him and focuses on Lydia and me. "The viceroy fined us for misappropriation of equipment and warned us to handle nuisance rebels before they cause more problems. His censure felt like a slap on the wrist, which made my report to the Friend and Commanding Gage an easier job to deliver. When the council excused me and ended my Translation session, I had a few hours before I needed to brief my superiors, but first, I made a trip to the archives."

I grin. Alexis and I have more in common than she knows. The archives had held such an allure to me during my first semester as a candidate. Now, I just wish I had time and leisure to explore them more.

Lydia pinches the end of her sandy brown braid and leans forward. "What did you find?"

Alexis sighs. "Not much. Orvieto is a small city in a country called Italy, but I couldn't find any information about a Confederation or why the chairman suspected ties to the Rogues."

Darius uncrosses his arms. "In other words, it was a dead end. This is interesting, Alexis, but we have serious problems to talk about. Perhaps you can save your stories for later."

Her nostrils flare. "If our country has any hope of surviving against Felix's forces, we need assistance, and Orvieto might be our only option."

"But you said you know next to nothing about the place," Darius shoots back.

Lydia reaches for Darius and rests a calming hand on his shoulder. "Let her finish."

He huffs and holds his peace.

"Go on," I coax Alexis. She's not a person Darius can rush. She needs to tell her story in order, and no amount of prodding will make her jump to the bottom line.

She takes a deep breath. "I delivered my report as required, and Gage Eliab dismissed me. He didn't want or need my help to tighten his search for the Rogue threat, but I determined to learn more about Orvieto. If they were helping the Rogues, that would be intel the CGA would need to…" She stops short and blushes. "I'm sorry, but at that time, I thought you Rogues were the bad guys."

I nod. There was a time I didn't know what Rogues were either. The Crystal Gage Association branded them as insurgents and traitors, and no one was wiser to suspect they were in fact trying to help the people shrug off a government that ran on deception and civilian blood.

Alexis clears her throat. "As a Dome rep, I had access to the equipment for exploring historical Simulations as well as hosting real-time Translations. I rarely used it, but I decided to do some investigating of my own. To my surprise, Orvieto showed Translation capabilities, but there was a block on it. That made me even more curious. Simulations weren't blocked, so I clicked on every date available and spent the rest of my day reliving past accounts."

I perch on the edge of my seat. "What did you find?"

"More than I can relate now, but here's the main thing I learned."

Darius rolls his eyes as if to say, *Finally, she's getting to the point.*

"In the year 2013, Orvieto started an event called Orvieto Forever," she says. "It celebrates Italy's role in American Independence and champions the ideal of a global brotherhood, based on the ideals outlined in the Declaration of Independence."

I bounce to my feet in excitement. "Really? That's incredible! You mean other countries valued American liberties and wanted the world to embrace them?"

"Yes, that's what I gathered. I think there are—or were—other countries that offered similar liberties. I can't say that's the case now."

"But maybe Orvieto is still holding out from the Rosh League," I say. "Maybe there are other places who would ally themselves with us."

Darius grins at my enthusiasm but gives me a warning look. "Don't get too excited. These are all big ifs. Does Orvieto even exist anymore, or has the Rosh League eliminated them? And for the love of Pete, where is Italy? Would they have the means to help us, and would they even want to?"

My shoulders sag. Darius is ever the realist, and I hate that he's probably right. If we don't have a clue where Italy is, how can they know about us? The thirteen squares that form our country have only interested the Rosh League because of our resources. After all, they had named each one after the precious foundation stones of a legendary city. Why should anyone else care about us unless they had another selfish reason?

Alexis ignores him. "Italy is—or was—located across the Atlantic Ocean and is a boot-shaped peninsula on the Mediterranean Sea."

Darius heaves an exaggerated sigh. "You do realize your geography lesson doesn't mean anything to us, and frankly, it doesn't matter. The chances of Orvieto becoming our ally are zero to none."

She juts out her chin. "The way to find out is to unblock that Translation connection."

I hold my breath. Darius is the one person I know who has the smarts to do that. I shoot him a pleading look.

He runs a hand through his reddish-brown hair, now speckled with gray. "Don't give me those big blues of yours, Portia."

"Would you at least try?" I ask.

Darius sighs again. "Sure, in my spare time when I'm not trying to hack into and decode Felix's communications about destroying us, or stretch our maxed resources to help satellite survivors, or organize teams of militia to help quell confused, rioting civilians."

Militia. It's funny how Darius had adopted the term used in the Revolutionary War to refer to fighting members of the Brotherhood.

But there's nothing funny about our situation. We're at a breaking point. If we can't organize our defense soon, there won't be anything to stop Felix's Gage Army from reclaiming the ground he lost.

Darius scans our faces. "And even if we were able to contact Orvieto, what do you plan to offer them in return for their help? Alliances are mutually beneficial. No one wants to take on a leech, and we blew up our natural resource operations to destroy the satellites."

I hate that he's right.

Darius must notice me sink lower in my seat and pauses his vent. "I'm sorry, sis, but we can't waste time on what-ifs now."

The portal door clicks open, and a dark figure all but fills the entrance with his hulking build. I rush toward him for a bear hug.

Gath's skin bronzes in a blush. "Whoa, little sister! What's that for?"

"That's for Deidra." I hug him again. "And that's for you." On the other side of almost losing Gath and Deidra forever, I'm not taking them for granted. They aren't just friends. They're family.

Gath laughs, a deep, rippling sound that starts in his chest and reverberates like an earthquake. "It's good to see you, too."

I pull back and search his face. "How is she?"

"Resting." His silvery eyes hold the same fatigue as the rest of ours, but there's a sparkle to them I'm beginning to understand.

Darius nods at him in welcome. "Any news from the perimeter?"

"The perimeter's still quiet, but..." Gath rests a hand on my shoulder as if grounding me for what's coming next. "We have another problem."

"What do you mean?" Darius asks.

"Can you spare a few hours?" Gath adjusts the rifle slung over his shoulder.

"That depends if we want to sleep tonight."

"Sleep or investigate a matter of national security."

Darius arches a brow and rises. "I'm listening."

Gath shakes his head. "You'll have to see this to believe it."

Kristen Hogrefe

CHAPTER 2

~ Portia ~

Friday, 6.26.2150
Crystal

"What's wrong?" I pant for breath. Keeping up with Gath's long strides might as well count as running.

He leads the way up the stairwell and into the cavernous space of the library but doesn't answer my question. Darius mutters something to Lydia behind me, while Alexis brings up the rear.

When we push open the glass doors, a gust of wind fights us, but the rain has stopped. In its place, low-hanging clouds darken the evening sky. I can't tell if they're actual rain clouds or thick patches of fog.

"Where are we going?" I ask.

"Train station," he says. "I'm taking you to Cube 1776."

Darius digs his heels into the pavement. "Whoa, what are you talking about? I don't have time for a trip, not when there's so much to do here."

I hug my faded brown jacket tighter, though it's still wet from my last excursion. "Besides, the trains are down."

Gath stops long enough to glance between Darius and me. "Not this train. It's leaving tonight. Half a dozen militia and I are going to be on it."

Darius grabs Gath's shoulder to keep him from marching ahead. "Get a grip, man. Tell me what's wrong. Then, we can decide how to throw around what few resources we have."

Gath sets his jaw. "My man reported seeing what he calls a phantom ship about to enter the Potomac. He also reported a dark shadow in the nearby waters. Word came half an hour ago while I was visiting Deidra in the infirmary. Do you want to take his word for it?"

Darius stiffens. "What do you mean—dark shadow?" He cuts his eyes toward me and back to Gath. Why does he look nervous, almost guilty?

"I told you all I know," Gath says.

Darius releases his shoulder. "What time is the train leaving?"

"One hour."

"I'll be there." Darius turns to Lydia, Alexis, and me. "You three should stay here. There's no need for all of us to jump into harm's way."

"I'll stay," Alexis says quickly and pulls the collar of her jacket higher around her neck.

Lydia meets Darius's gaze with an anxious smile. "Send word over the wire if you need me to mobilize anyone else." My brother offers her a subtle smile in return.

Interesting.

"I'd like to come," I say. "Luther hasn't returned, and having something else to think about will help."

Darius's smile fades to a frown. "It would be safer if you stayed here."

I fold my arms. "Safer? Than what? If Felix decides to let

loose his antics over the ASU, he's going to start with the Crystal Globe because we have so much technology here. Traveling to Cube 1776 almost seems like the safer option."

Gath grins at me. "Let her come, Darius. She knows how to keep up. She's also a good shot now, from what I hear."

Darius hedges. "Sounds like you have enough good shots already."

"It makes more sense for me to go than you." I challenge him. "You just said you don't have time for a trip. If Gath wants help verifying these reports, I'm the better choice. You could stay and keep working the intel angle on Felix's movements."

"And help me with that Translation connection," Alexis adds.

Darius colors in frustration, but Lydia places a gentle hand on his arm. "They're right. The Brotherhood is no longer a small band of rebels. We're trying to hold a country together, and you're the one everyone is looking to for direction. Instead of running off to save the day, maybe it's better if you organize home base."

Gath slowly nods. "I agree. I was wrong to pull you away. You have enough to do here."

"We really need to sit down and talk about a new government structure," Alexis says. "I've been doing some more research on the past civilization, and their model might not be such a bad one to adopt."

From the tight expression on Darius's face, another portal chat is the last thing my brother wants right now. He's a man of action, not organization.

Catching his glare, Alexis hurriedly adds, "Of course, that can wait until Gath and Portia return."

Darius shifts his weight and moves back toward the library

doors. "All right, you two go, but send a line through Red the minute you learn anything."

"Affirmative," Gath says and waves at me to follow him.

I glance once more at Darius to discern the glint in his eye. Again, his gaze suggests guilt or maybe fear? Is he worried about me?

I offer a brave smile and hurry down the library's marble steps after Gath. He waits for me on the walkway at the bottom. "Grab your go-bag," he says. "Don't know how long this trip will take. Meet me at the track in 45 minutes. I want everyone there early for a quick debrief."

"Does Deidra know you're leaving?" I ask.

He frowns, causing the recovering hollows in his cheeks to reappear. He still has fifty pounds to go before he regains his healthy bulk, but thanks to Deidra, he wasn't nearly as emaciated as most prisoners on VW Day—or Victory in Warren Day as we called the satellite liberation.

"I just came from visiting her, but no, she doesn't," he says. "I'll have to send her a line once we reach Red's hostel."

"I could check on her before I meet you," I offer. "My bag's always packed and ready. Besides, I found something in the archives I want to give her."

He grins. "A good book?"

"A very good one."

He flashes a hopeful smile. "Thanks—if you can get her to read it. I'll see you at 19:45 hours."

I dart across the pavement and jog toward my dorm room. It's not the same room I had when I first came to the Crystal Globe as a Revisionary candidate. All the Brotherhood members on campus stay in the dorm between the cafeteria and the one being used as an infirmary. I haven't had time to even visit my old room and retrieve my school bag and tablet. The darn thing is probably still stashed in the Ottoman. Not that I need it now.

After retrieving my go-bag, I enter the infirmary dorm where a former Gage stands guard out front. I don't know what we'd have done if the CGA hadn't been divided by the news that satellites were nothing more than slave camps, killing innocent prisoners. The Brotherhood primed the rumor mill with stories about the satellites as soon as the first explosion at Warren rocked the ground, and soon, some Gages were questioning Felix's intentions and the suspicious circumstances of his mother's death. Then, when Gath appeared on the scene, many jumped ship to rejoin Gath, their former leader who had been second only to Eliab. Unfortunately, many also chose to take their chances with Felix.

The Gage sees me and tips his chin in acknowledgment.

"Evening," I say. "I'm checking on Deidra."

"Go ahead."

The bottom lounge floor resembles a make-shift storage room, holding all the medical supplies we managed to rummage together from around campus. Half a dozen wheel chairs and crutches have been stacked in one corner while mounds of fresh linen cover coffee tables and couches.

A light from the hallway peeps through a pair of double doors. I push through them and enter what used to be a rec room. Now, the pool tables store medical supplies, and the large panel that used to be an entertainment screen offers two patients some privacy.

I nod at two Healers on duty. They buzz between patient cots like overworked bees. Although the numbers in the infirmary have gone down since the initial influx of wounded satellite survivors, many of the remaining ones won't be leaving anytime soon—or ever.

I tiptoe up to the lime green shower-rod curtain serving as Deidra's privacy screen and slide past it. She's asleep. Next to her is an overturned bucket Gath must have been using as a stool. Thinking about that lanky giant trying to sit on the thing makes me smile.

Her wavy dark brown hair falls past her shoulders across the stiff white sheet. Thick lashes flutter in fitful sleep. Maybe I'll just leave what I brought her and not wake her.

But there's something tragic about her sleeping beauty that bids me to stay. I brush a strand of hair away from her eyes and slide onto the bucket to study her face. Her once creamy caramel skin tone still holds an ashy hue. After Gage Eliab had caught me inside the Warren barrack, he marched me past the transport vehicle Deidra and I used to enter the satellite. Our armed escort lay shot on the ground, but Deidra hadn't been anywhere in sight.

As Gath tells the story, that's because she was lying on the floor under the steering wheel and out of my line of vision.

When the escort outside the truck had been shot, the bullet penetrated the cab and also sliced through her thigh. As more shots shattered the windshield, she slid low underneath the steering wheel and stuffed herself under the seat, which had a hidden crawl space leading to the back of the truck. It led to a man-sized crate, stacked beneath other storage containers.

There, she held her breath while Eliab's men loaded his own crates with the new explosive vests and mind-manipulation technology while they corralled the other prisoners and me inside.

Little did I know that she was slowly bleeding out feet away from me.

When we reached the mine, she overheard everything that happened—from Eliab's cruel demonstration to my arguments. However, she started losing consciousness from loss of blood and lack of fresh air. When our voices finally died away, she used the rest of her strength to retreat out the way she had entered the hideout, out the driver's door, and under the truck. She had no energy left to run, and there were too many Gages standing guard around the mine even if she had. So underneath the truck, in a mixture of tire-trodden mud and snow, she half buried herself, hoping she would be able to disguise herself and survive until nightfall.

That's where Gath had amazingly found her after he detonated the vests in the mines. While the able-bodied prisoners fled for safety, Gath loaded as many injured as he could find into the one transport vehicle available: that same truck.

He noticed blood-stained snow from underneath the truck, and when he bent down to help the injured prisoner, found Deidra instead.

She was unconscious but breathing. He carefully laid her in the back with the others and tore out of there while chain-reaction explosions rocked the mine system behind him.

Ironically, he, Deidra, and his truckload arrived in Jasper not far behind Luther and me. We pirated the next train passing through. No one had dared try to stop us after our story and the evidence of the satellite prisoners with us.

Deidra's lashes shudder, and then she blinks. Her glazed, chocolate-brown eyes take a few moments before focusing on me.

"Hey there." I smile and reach for her hand. "You been sleeping any better?"

"Like a baby. The Healers have me on a strict diet and therapy schedule. I was able to take a few steps with crutches today."

"That's great." Unlike my clean gunshot wound to the leg, the bullet that hit hers had not only penetrated her thigh but torn a major tendon and chipped bone. Walking was a struggle, and if her leg didn't heal properly, she might always have a limp.

But I'm confident she'll fully recover. Deidra is made of tougher stuff than I am, and if I could learn how to run again, she can learn how to walk.

Deidra pushes her arms to her side to sit straighter. "What are you up to tonight? Want to play a game of Go Fish with an invalid?"

"Wish I could." I glance at my wristwatch. "But I just have time to say goodbye. I'm going to Cube 1776 with Gath and some other brothers. There are two strange vessels at the mouth of the Potomac, and we need to find out what they are."

Deidra bites her lower lip. "I wish I weren't so useless and could go with Gath too."

I lean closer to her side. "I told him I would tell you goodbye for him. He would have come himself if he didn't have to organize the team."

She gives me a lopsided grin. "Thanks for that."

"I promise I'll watch out for him." I stand and push the uncomfortable bucket toward her cot. It might make a better bed stand than seat.

"You watch out for each other," she says. "I want you both back here in one piece."

"Sure thing." I press a smile to my lips, but her words stir an unsettling chord. "I only wish someone were watching out for Luther."

"He hasn't returned?"

I shake my head. "No, and other than this train Gath has resurrected into service, the rest are nonoperational until this gale clears."

"Then he'll probably be on the first train he can get."

"I hope so." I reach down and give her a squeeze. "Pray for him—and us—if you think of it."

She frowns. "You're starting to sound like Gath. Do you really believe in all that God business?"

I open my mouth and try to form the words. The Portia from a few months ago would have said *of course not*. But I can't take credit for our miraculous escape and the success of our satellite revolt. God was there right when I needed him.

On the other hand, he had also allowed Dad to die, yet I still have my brother and new friends who are as close as family. I've felt peace, maybe his presence, in so many lonely places, but I can't try to explain that now.

"Yes." I let my hand rest on her shoulder for a moment. "I don't understand it all, but I do believe."

She rolls her eyes. "If it helps you sleep at night, good for you."

"Deidra…"

"All right, but I don't know what good my prayers will do." She shifts beneath her sheets and stares at her blanketed feet. "If there is a God, he wouldn't want anything to do with me after all I've done."

I don't have an answer for her, and I'm running short on time. "I wish I knew more, Deidra, but I don't think his love depends on us."

I hesitate, then reach inside my jacket. "I brought you this—found it in the archives. I thought that maybe some reading would help pass the time."

"A Bible?" She takes the small zippered book that's a little bigger than her hand.

"I just thought…"

"It's a nice enough thought." She drops the book on the bucket and then masks her frown with a laugh. She makes a shooing motion with her hands. "You'd better get going, girl. Don't keep my man waiting."

I swallow a lump in my throat and part the curtain to make my exit. "We'll be back soon. I hope."

CHAPTER 3

~ Luther ~

Friday, 6.26.2150
Chrysoprase

Holding his breath, Luther gently retracts his hand and lets his mother's wrinkled fingers rest on the silky sheets of her bed. His arm is numb from holding the same position, but he couldn't bear to leave her until she fell asleep.

His once steaming tea mug sits cold beside him. At least she had drunk most of hers. Next to the mug, a small, metal cowbell perches on the edge of the bed stand. She laughed when he placed it there, but he'd been serious: If she needed something, she was to ring it, and he'd come running.

Right now, though, she should sleep for several hours. What she needs more than anything is rest of body and mind.

But his father's sudden abandonment had sent her already weakened immune system into a tailspin. Bronchitis turned into pneumonia, and she didn't take care of herself. If he hadn't arrived when he had...

Luther pushes the thought aside. He is here and going to make sure she grows strong again. But how long will she need to recover? He can't stay forever.

He slips out of the room. Just beyond is the kitchen window that reveals the seeping darkness of another day done. At least the rain has stopped. He could use some fresh air.

Careful not to make a sound, he steps into the yard of his childhood home and closes the door. If only he could go back in time eleven years ago and stop the train wreck that derailed his family.

He treads the tall, wet grass toward the neighbor's house—the place Portia, her father Abram, and brother Darius once called home. It had seen plenty of residents since Gage Eliab had evicted them, but now, it sits empty and neglected.

Portia's swing dangles from one rope, a broken reminder of a past he can't repair. How he has tried! The one redeeming spark is Cotton herself.

His pet name for Portia brings a smile to his lips. Her whitish-blonde hair had reminded him of the soft cotton the harvesters picked. But time stained that too. He had barely recognized the dark-haired beauty whose features Lord Osborne had manipulated. But slowly, her roots were starting to show, and eventually, those ridiculous facial treatments would fade.

If only time could naturally restore his family. His brother Jotham's betrayal of Portia's brother had stolen so many years from Portia and him. Now, he's realizing what else Jotham had stolen.

All through his teens, Luther tried living up to his father's expectations. Burke Danforth set Jotham on a pedestal after his firstborn was drafted to the Crystal Globe. Of course, Jotham only received the slot because he had agreed to betray Darius to the CGA. But prestige was prestige, and his father had been consumed with building a family reputation of greatness.

Luther runs his fingers along the frayed swing rope. How misled his father was! Yet he is no one to judge him. He'd spend the better part of his young adult life trying to meet the man's expectations—but no matter what he accomplished, his father never held him in the same esteem he did Jotham.

Even after Luther had received his draft to the Crystal Globe the honest way, his father hadn't been satisfied. "You still have to earn that Dome seat, son," he had said.

Now, there wasn't a Dome, yet his dad refused to accept he had been wrong—they had all been wrong about what mattered.

If only he had beaten Jotham home! But he hadn't. Jotham had returned first and convinced his father to join him and Felix's team at Deadwood. The mercy was that his mom was too sick to travel, and they'd left her behind.

Luther grips the second rope, dangling apart from the swing, and snaps the brittle fibers. Jotham hadn't come home to visit his parents or even written since he left for the Crystal Globe. The reason he's interested in their father now must be a selfish one.

The answer Luther suspects sickens him. Burke Danforth is a gifted Maven—a researcher whose work in medicine has provided local Healers lifesaving, alternative remedies when the rationed cures run out. If his dad can make miracles from his knowledge of nature's resources, how might Felix twist his gift into something terrible?

Luther inserts the second rope into the swing seat and knots it in place. The seat hangs crookedly, but it's usable again.

Though he may never have a perfect relationship with his father, he can't sit back and let his brother destroy the chance of a good one. Somehow, he has to rescue him from Deadwood, a place Gath has described as an impenetrable fortress.

But there's always a way.

Luther tugs hard on both ropes and sits on the wooden seat. It's too low for his long legs to hang from, so he drags them across the grass.

To think his little Cotton used to sit here and wait for him! She's waiting for him now… but this time, she's hundreds of miles away.

He'll have to find a neighbor willing to watch his mom. He can't stay. The longer he waits, the more Cotton will worry—and the more time Jotham will have to deceive their father.

A soft, clattering ring interrupts his thoughts. Is that a dinner bell?

Luther jumps to his feet. No, that's the cow bell he gave his mom. He runs toward the door, swings it open, and ignores the fact it doesn't cleanly latch.

Adrienne Danforth lies on her side pinching the cow bell between her fingers. Her graying hair traces down her left shoulder. Even in her fifties, she's still a lovely lady. How could Dad have left her?

"What's wrong, Mom?" Luther reaches for the bell and clasps her hands. They feel clammy from breaking a fever.

"Oh, nothing." She smiles and squeezes back. "I just wanted to see if this cow bell actually worked."

He laughs in relief and replaces it on the stand. "I said I'd come running if you needed me. I keep my word."

Pride and sadness flicker across her face. "I know, Luther. I only wish…" She places her hand across her mouth to keep from saying more.

"Mom." He edges onto the bed and wraps his arms around her slender shoulders, but nothing he says can change the fact her husband walked out on her for their no-good son.

She presses a sad smile to her lips and leans against him. "Bring them back. Won't you?"

He swallows hard. *Them*? He wants to bring Dad home, but Jotham will never listen to him. And if Luther's honest with himself, he doesn't want back the brother whose shadow he's had to live beneath all his life.

But what can he say? "I'll try, Mom."

For a long time, he stays there, holding her frail frame until she gradually relaxes. Maybe she's fallen asleep again.

As he releases her onto her pillow, her eyes flicker again. "You need to be leaving soon."

"Yes, but I won't leave until you're stronger or someone else can watch out for you."

"I'll be fine. Ask Clair from next door to look in on me every day, but you've been gone from your friends long enough. They'll be worried about you. She'll be worried about you."

Warmth seeps into his face. "Yes, she will be."

Mom chuckles and blinks to keep her eyes awake. "You don't have to pretend, Luther. I know you've always loved the girl next door, even when she left for good. You never cared for any other girl the way you did for her."

The way I do for her. He wants to add, but he waits for his mom to finish.

She motions toward the antique dresser across from the bed. "Go to my bureau, please."

He winces as the pins and needles again prick his legs but ignores them as he strides to the furniture. "What do you need?"

She shakes her head. "No, this isn't for me. This is for you. Open the top right drawer. Beneath some old letters, do you see a ring box?"

Luther shuffles beneath the crinkled pages until his fingers brush a satiny box. "Yes, I found it."

"Open it."

The hinge threatens to snap, but he gingerly opens the top. Inside is a delicate golden band set with a blue sapphire. It was his grandmother's wedding band. Though she's been gone a dozen years, he remembers the ring on her withered finger as if she were alive yesterday. His grandmother had always been kind and loving toward him, though Jotham dominated his father's attention. But her visits from an adjoining cube had grown fewer due to her declining health, and his father had refused to let him skip school to "waste time on an invalid."

Luther turns the ring over in his palm. "You've kept her ring all these years?"

"Yes, I thought one of my boys might like to give it to his girl someday." Her words are quiet and soft but send his heart pounding.

The sapphire matches Portia's own blue eyes. Would she say yes to him if he asked her? Would the system agree to match them?

He suddenly smiles. What system? Why do they have a system in the first place? Does he really need an advanced algorithm to determine if he and Portia are right for each other? He'll have to talk to Darius and insist that when they revive a new form of government, the compatibility system goes.

He's known for a long time that Portia is the girl for him. He's wanted her by his side ever since they beat all those boys in that three-legged race as kids. He's wanted to protect her ever since her brother's trial when he felt so helpless. He's wanted to kiss her ever since he carried her half-frozen body to the dorm room on Greek night. He's wanted to wrap her in his arms ever since he placed her in a satellite train that almost separated them forever.

"Luther?" His mom's voice breaks into his memories.

He inserts the ring into its case and clasps it shut. "This is mine to give?"

"Yes, son." Her voice catches. "Now go find your girl and our boys. Maybe one day soon, we can all be happy here again together. I hear the Abernathy's old place next door is up for reassignment again. Maybe you can fix it up nice again, and…"

"Mom." Luther lowers his tone. "Don't put the cart before the horse."

She chuckles. "You're right. I just want that home to have some joy again."

He slips the ring case in his jacket pocket. This place hasn't felt like home since Portia and her dad left all those years ago. Can he really reclaim all the wasted years? And does she feel the same way he feels about her? They've been so busy trying to survive there hasn't been time for any personal conversation.

Can two people find time for love when every moment of living is consumed with crisis?

Luther leans down and kisses the top of her head. "Me too, Mom."

Kristen Hogrefe

CHAPTER 4
~Portia~

Friday, 6.26.2150
Crystal

I'd forgotten how painfully uncomfortable cargo cars can be. The stationmaster had done Gath no favors in giving him an old engine and two battered cars, last used to transport livestock. The wood floor not only scratches against my back but also smells like a stable.

Not that my companions care. Their contented snores keep the space sounding alive, even though at least two of them keep watch.

Why did I volunteer to come? I could be sleeping in my own comfy dorm bed and not reeking of cow manure.

I readjust my backpack doubling as a pillow and stuff my head against it. But the unsettling answer accuses me that I simply don't know how to deal with quiet and waiting any more. I'm so used to action that inaction is a worse sentence than a night spent in a rancid train.

But what if Luther returns before I do?

I toss onto my other side. So what? He deserves a taste of the bitter waiting and wondering.

But what if he's hurt? What if he needs my help? Now, I'm

traveling farther away from him.

I clench my teeth. Why can't I stop thinking about Luther? Why is worrying about him so miserable?

A man next to me grunts. "Will you stop hitting that bag?"

"Sorry." I mutter and roll over again. Apparently, snoring doesn't always mean sleeping.

A chuckle that sounds more like rumbling thunder resonates from the cargo door. Gath must be awake and standing guard as he's done on every train ride before.

Who am I kidding? I'm not going to sleep either. I snatch up my bag and pick my way around the sleeping bodies using my small flashlight. Some other guys grunt at the light, but they can deal with it.

I extinguish it when I reach Gath whose lanky frame stretches along the door.

"You should sleep," he says.

"Can't. Mind if I join you?"

"Sure." I can hear the grin in his voice. "Guess we two insomniacs can keep each other company."

"You don't sleep well at night either?" I whisper.

He sighs. "I haven't since we escaped. It will take some time for the memories to heal."

I know what he means. When I was working like a mule or running for my life, I didn't have time to think. Sleep was my only escape and a necessary part of surviving. Now, sleep offers anything but escape. It's where I relive the horrors of Warren.

I'd rather worry about Luther than remember them.

I lean against the door. "Will it get better?"

"Yes." His voice catches. "Prayer and meditating on Scripture are the two best cures I've found, but both still take time."

I rub my tired eyes. "I've called out to God a few times, but I have no idea where to start."

"Prayer is talking to God about anything." Gath's gentle tone falls like balm on my spirit. "Tell him your fears and nightmares. Ask him to rescue you from them."

"And what does meditating mean?"

"You spend time reading the Bible and memorize promises that help you focus on God's goodness and faithfulness."

"Promises?" I peer into the darkness, trying to read his expression, but there's no light. I can't even see my hand, and there's no point turning on the flashlight and annoying the men again.

There's a pause, and I wonder if Gath heard me.

Then softly, his voice takes on a reverent tone. "For God hath not given us the spirit of fear; but of power, and of love, and of a sound mind. 2 Timothy 1:7."

His words fill my tired soul with hope. There's so much fear in my mind for the future.

Gath's boots scrape across the floor. He scoots closer until his arm brushes against mine.

"Try to sleep, little sister. We've got at least another hour to go, and we won't have more than a few hours to rest at Red's hostel before we leave for the point before dawn."

I lean against him and try to quote the words until the letters blur and my eyelids grow heavy. Maybe because I spent all those nights in Warren with Gath at my side, his presence now makes me feel safe.

Or maybe there's something to those words.

Either way, I unashamedly press my head against his arm and give in to sleep.

"Glad you came." Red places steaming mugs of hot tea in front of us. The eight of us line the bench seating of the hostel owner's long wooden table, every one of us soaked to the core. As soon as our train had reached Cube 1776, another rain band unleashed its fury. Maybe my boots will dry out by morning, but I doubt it.

"Any more ship sightings?" Gath scoots a mug toward me. The brew tastes bitter but makes my shivers subside.

"Several," Red says. "The ship has since entered the mouth of the river and is slowly moving upstream. You'll likely intercept it well before you reach the point."

"Have you seen anyone on board?" I ask.

"Not with this weather." Red balances the now-empty metal tray in his leathery palm. I'd first met this bull-moose-sized man during my first tripping outing with my Greek. His coarse, brown hair runs trails to the nape of his neck and probably hasn't seen a barber in months.

As busy as he is running the hostel and manning one of Darius's Morse code lines, I'm not surprised.

"Rumors are sparking that everyone's dead on board, but that's nonsense," Red continues. "Someone has to be alive to steer it."

A chill creeps down my spine. "Do you think Felix is behind

it?"

"It's possible," Red says, "but it's not like any of the vessels the CGA has used before. It's different, almost like someone took a model sailing ship off a collector's counter and manufactured it real size." He scratches his head. "You'll have to see for yourself at daybreak."

I sip the steaming tea. "And what about the other boat?"

Red exchanges a questioning look with Gath. "What other boat?"

Gath tastes the brew and grimaces. "You said there was another dark vessel in the water, right?"

Red turns back to the kitchen. "It could've been a shadow."

"Then why did you bother telling me about it?" Gath asks.

Red hesitates. "It seemed important at the time. I thought..."

"You thought what?"

He frowns. "I thought it could have been one of Felix's subs, but now, I don't think it is."

"Subs?" I grip the mug tighter. "As in submarines? Felix has submarines?"

One of the other men murmurs. "If they have subs, we're sitting ducks. What's our defense?"

Gath holds up a hand. "Whoa, we don't even know if it is a sub. And right now, it's 0100 hours, and we're all wet and tired. Clean up and be ready to haul out of here by 0600."

"Breakfast is at 0530," Red adds. "Your two rooms are the first two at the top of the stairs. The smaller one is Portia's."

The six men shove off the bench and lumber up the stairs. I pretend to finish my tea.

Red winks at me. "Off to bed with you, too, little lady."

"Not really tired."

"Your eyes are bloodshot," Red argues.

I stare into my half-drunk tea, too embarrassed to tell him I'm afraid what death-bearing ships my tortured mind will distort into nightmares.

"It's been a long day," Gath soothes. "I know you're wired, but at least try to sleep."

Red shoots me a concerned look. "Wait, I have something that might help." He disappears into the kitchen and emerges moments later with another steaming mug.

I groan. "Red, I can't…"

"It's herbal." He slides it toward me. "Drink it, and you'll fall asleep like a baby."

I sniff it skeptically. It smells as bad as the last one. I close my eyes and take two solid gulps before gasping for breath.

"Drink it all," Red encourages. "Pinch your nose if you have to."

I would laugh if it didn't taste so foul. Once Red's satisfied that I've emptied the mug, he tugs me off the bench and shoos me toward the stairs. "Get some sleep. I'll make sure no one bothers you."

I mumble my thanks and start up the stairs like a child past her bedtime.

"She's changed, isn't she?" Red whispers behind me.

"We both are," Gath says. "Neither of us sleeps well at night."

"But you've come out of this before. Does she know there's a light at the end of the tunnel?"

"I think so," Gath replies, "but she's seen and experienced more horrors than a dozen soldiers will in a lifetime. She needs time to heal, and we don't have that luxury. Staying busy is the next best thing."

"I hope you were right to bring her." Red's voice deepens. "There's something I need to tell you." But his voice trails off, and I can't hear the rest of the sentence.

I push open the door to my small room. Inside is a twin bed and wood bed stand. On it, a candle in a holder rests next to a cup of water.

Red's simple thoughtfulness warms my heart. I strike a match to light the candle, and after closing the door, undress in its glow.

I hang my wet things over the foot board and slide under the thick quilt on the bed. I should blow out the flame and try to sleep.

But I don't. Instead, I watch its flickering dance until my eyes droop, and I enter the dark space where reality blurs and dreams descend.

A loud pounding noise jolts me awake before I can catch all the demon ships taunting my tired brain. Squinting at my wrist, I read the time on my watch: 0520 hours. I have ten minutes before breakfast.

None of my damp clothes are dry, but I don them anyway and carry my muddy boots downstairs. There's no point tracking dirt and making more work for our one-man host.

Gath appears from the kitchen, carrying a tray of metal bowls that faintly smell of cinnamon. It's probably poor-man's oatmeal or Red's tasteless grits, but after living at Warren, I never complain about food anymore.

Deep bags make Gath's bloodshot eyes look even more sunken.

I reach for the tray. "Didn't sleep well, huh?"

"I hope you did." There's a tightness in his tone that makes me do a double take. Is he angry?

"I got a few hours," I say and slide the bowls toward a few of the other guys who lumber onto the bench. "Is everything okay?"

"No." Gath tenses his jaw but doesn't explain. He disappears inside the kitchen, leaving me with a hard knot in my gut.

I stare at the grits. I want to eat them but won't be able to until Gath tells me what's bothering him. Shoving off the bench, I leave my untouched breakfast and round the corner to the kitchen door.

Strange, it's closed.

I twist the handle and help myself inside. Red stands with arms squared over his stained white apron facing Gath, whose back is toward me.

"When were you going to tell her?" Gath demands.

Red looks ready to snap. "Are we really going through this again? It's not my place."

"She deserves to know." Gath's voice sounds more like a growl. "We're a team. We shouldn't be keeping secrets from each other, especially not when…"

"Darius thought it was best and made us swear not to tell."

At my brother's name, the hair on my neck bristles. "Uh, hey, is everything all right?"

Gath steps aside and motions to Red. "Tell her."

"Tell me what?" My legs tremble. Why are they both so angry?

Red turns crimson. "It's not your business right now, Portia. You've got to understand. Not knowing some things is for your good."

My good? What is he talking about?

Gath steps toward me. "If you won't tell her, I will."

Red grits his teeth. "Not your place, man."

"She's going to find out soon enough."

I hug my arms around my chest. "Find out what?"

The kitchen door flings open. Gil, a thick, stocky member of our team, bursts inside. "It's here. Locals just spotted it."

"You mean the ship?" I ask.

Gil nods. "And there's another dark one in the river, too. Could be a sub."

Red yanks off his apron and brushes past Gath. "10-4. Let's move."

Kristen Hogrefe

CHAPTER 5

~ Portia ~

Saturday, 6.27.2150
Crystal, Cube 1776

The gray, pre-dawn hour blurs the line between water and sky, but there's no mistaking the ghostly white sail cutting through the fog that clings to the river's surface. The vessel slices a slow line through the glass-like water.

Our group huddles behind a rocky outcropping. "There's a sandbar off to the right ahead." Red points across the river. "I think they're going to run aground. One of the locals has a Jon boat along the bank we can use to cross."

"We should break into two teams," Gath says. "I'll take four with me to investigate the ship. The rest of you, stay here with weapons ready to provide cover. If the coast is clear, I'll fire three successive shots into the air and send two back to get the rest of you."

Gath rattles off the names of four men to join him. I want to go too but bite my tongue. Gath didn't choose me, and this is his mission. I understand enough about chain of command to know my place.

He must sense my disappointment, because he unslings the

rifle on his shoulder and hands it to me, along with two extra mags. "I want you to take this and go to the next group of boulders up ahead. They're right across from the sandbar. Stay with Red, Gil, and Harley and keep our backs safe."

I accept the bolt action and nod. "Yes, but I'm better close range with a handgun."

He presses his lips into a smile. "I've seen you and Luther at our range. You're a good long shot."

"Yes, sir." When Gath's in Gage mode, there's no point arguing.

Red tugs at my elbow as Gath and his team wade into the shallows and dislodge the boat. "Stay close. I don't like how quiet that vessel is. There's no sign of movement."

"But someone's steering it, right?" I check the rifle to make sure it's loaded. It is. As Gath says, the only good weapon is a loaded one.

Red doesn't answer but stays glued to my side. Part of me resents that he thinks I need a bodyguard. The other part warms to the fatherly protectiveness that so many of my brothers display toward me.

My heart squeezes. Since Dad's been gone, Red watches over me like a hawk. He had even trailed my train trips between Jasper and Crystal when I'd been working for Osborne to make sure I stayed safe.

Gil and Harley scope out the next set of boulders. Both are ex-Gages who seem to read the other's mind. They communicate with hand signals, and I wonder if they trained together.

The two men motion toward a rocky ledge just beyond them as daylight cuts through the fog. Red and I scramble up the steep incline and then steady our weapons in a seated position. I press my elbow into the crook of my knee and squint through the rifle's scope.

Sure enough, the ship hits the sandbar, and the current pushes it firmly into the shallow bank. I trace Gath and company's progress across the swollen river. They're rowing hard across the current and will overshoot the sandbar at this rate. But with that muscle, they'll cross safely and circle back.

The lens goes black. I blink and glance up from the scope. But the problem isn't with the scope. It's the object filling its view.

My throat constricts. "Red," I whisper. A black submarine—for it can't be anything else—has surfaced in the center of the river. Our team rowing in the boat doesn't notice that it surfaced behind them, because they're intent on reaching the ship.

Red's jaw tightens. "I see it."

The long, smooth exterior snakes through the water parallel with the ship that's now beached on the sandbar. The sub stays in the river's deep channel and remains motionless in the current.

I peer through the scope again. "It seems to be guarding the ship. Do you think—Could it be a trap from Felix?"

Red shakes his head. "I don't think so."

I switch to a prone position to get a steadier look. In my peripheral, Gil and Harley also assume sniper-like stances. "How can you be sure?"

But my question hangs unanswered in the air now thick with suspense. I slowly sweep the lens across the emerged outer hull.

"What do you call that top part that's taller than the rest of the sub?" I ask Red, though he probably doesn't know much more about submarines than I do.

"It's a conning tower." He replies without hesitation, but his voice is low, tense.

A hatch on the top opens, and I hold my breath. Someone's getting out.

"Hold your fire," Red barks at Gil and Harley. His harsh, urgent tone makes me jump. How does he know Felix isn't behind all this?

Then I see it. There are two initials carved into the top of the conning tower. Though crude, they're unmistakable.

FV.

Fraternitas Veritas.

My palms sweat, and I strain with all my might to make out the faces of the men who have emerged. There are two of them, but their backs are toward me.

One is nearly two-thirds larger than the second slender man. His wiry gray hair and shoulders thick like an ox send blood surging hot through my veins. Though I can't see his face, I'd know those hardened shoulders anywhere. And the scarred neck of the shorter man…

I drop the rifle, not caring that it clatters noisily on the rocky ledge. I slide toward the dangerously steep incline and shimmy down.

"Portia!" Red snatches for me but misses.

He shouts something else, but I can't hear for all the roaring in my ears.

Foxworth is the scarred man, and the first is my father

"Dad!" The raging river swallows my screech. I cup my hands over my mouth and then wave from the bank.

My boots splash in the frigid shallows. If the water weren't freezing, I'd probably dive in and drown myself trying to reach him. Sure, it wouldn't be a sane move, but when you've believed for months the lie that your father is dead, sanity doesn't fit well into the picture.

Strong hands grab my waist and pull me from the river.

I kick against Red, but he pulls me into his chest with a vice-like grip. I grit my teeth. "Let me go."

"I'm not letting you drown yourself." He drags me with him into the tree cover. "Not after I've kept you safe all this time."

"Kept me safe?" I try to shove away, but he holds me tighter. "Warren isn't my definition of daycare."

"I'm not talking about Warren." Though he keeps me close to his chest, he uses one hand to brush my tangled hair from my face. "But if I could have kept you out of that hellhole, I would have."

I take deep breaths, only to find my fury replaced by choking sobs. "You knew all along Dad's alive? Why didn't you tell me?"

He tugs me with him to the ground. Though he doesn't release me, he holds me more loosely on his lap like a father would a naughty child.

"Darius feared that if you knew your father was in charge of the Brotherhood's secret Pelagic Project, Eliab and Felix would torture you for information."

"Pelagic Project," I whisper. "Lord Osborne asked me about it, but I didn't know what it was."

"All the better," Red says. "From what I've heard about Osborne, he would have pried it from you with his own creative methods."

I shiver. Osborne had been a cruel master, but I had to work for him in order to help Darius.

Darius.

I stiffen in Red's arms. "Darius knew all along that Dad was fine but made me believe he was dead?"

Red hesitates. "He knew you'd go looking for him if you had any hope…"

"But he told me I'd never see him again." My voice croaks. "Did Dad want me to think that?"

Red pats my back and releases my waist. "He wanted you safe and told Darius not to let you worry. He knew he wouldn't be able to communicate with you while working on the project and asked me to look out for you."

My face warms. "Thanks for that." Red was just following orders. I have Darius to thank for all the nights I cried myself to sleep. I clench my fists, wanting to pound them into my brother's chest.

But I rise and brush myself off. "I have to see Dad."

Red jumps to his feet as if prepared to tackle me again. "You will, but we've got a job to do first. There's that ship…"

The crack of a bullet cuts his sentence short. Red jerks his head at me, and we push through the brush to the shoreline.

I blink in confusion. Gath's party had safely banked, and the men now wade in the water, hands gripping the boat's sides and their firearms.

Then I see why. Crouched in the bushes and circling ever closer is an army-sized mongrel pack.

I gasp. "There have to be at least twenty. I've never seen so many in one place."

One mutt lies dead in the sand, a warning the others don't seem to heed. They communicate with high-pitched yapping noises. Tattered hair spikes on their emaciated spines. Teeth flared, the mongrels hunch low and snarl at the five men in the shallows.

"I wonder if they smell death." Red's words make my skin crawl. "What is on that ship?"

The vessel has driven itself into the sandbar and now tilts about fifteen degrees on one side. It won't be going anywhere soon.

Dad and Fox remain exposed on the submarine tower. Their rifles glint in the morning sunlight. Foxworth's barrel flashes, and another shot echoes. They're firing on the pack to break it up.

I glance to the rock formation Red and I had abandoned. Though I can't see them, Gil and Harley must also be in position to cover our team.

I can, however, see Gath. With weapon ready, he leads the men out of the water and along the banks toward the ship. A few mutts dare to draw close, only to drop dead on the shore. Gath tosses a climbing rope with attached pick onto the ship's deck and tests his weight. Satisfied, he grips the rope and climbs it. Two others follow him while the rest stand guard on the shoreline with their weapons drawn.

I hold my breath as Gath disappears from view onto the deck. If I were higher, maybe I could see.

"I feel helpless," I mutter. "What's going on?"

"We should get back to our post where Gath asked us to stay." Red starts for the rocky outcropping again. "You coming?"

The last place I want to be is staying put on a sniper's perch when Dad's a few hundred meters away, but I've caused enough trouble for Red. I nod and follow while we retrace our steps, parting ways just long enough to reclaim my rifle.

CHAPTER 6

~ Gath ~

Saturday, 6.27.2150
Crystal, Cube 1776

"Cover me." Gath flicks his fingers at his two companions, motioning them to wait outside the entrance to the ship's bridge. With handgun drawn, he slinks inside the command room's door, which remains slightly ajar behind him.

But the cabin is empty. The control panel stations for the crew sit vacant.

Subtle movement at the tall captain's chair sends fresh adrenaline pumping. He follows the bony outline of two legs underneath the leather chair.

CGA! Identify yourself! The words nearly slip from his throat, but he's not CGA anymore.

"Brotherhood militia!" He barks instead. "Hands up and identify yourself."

There's no response.

He clears his throat and tries again. "Hands where I can see them!"

One of the bony feet twitches, and the chair squeaks as it slowly swivels. Blood rushes from Gath's face as the man's gaunt frame and vomit-stained uniform appear.

The man sagging in the seat resembles a skeleton more than a sailor. Sunken eyes stare out from a flushed face. Sweat saturates the man's soiled shirt. Though the cabin is comfortably cool, the place reeks.

What's wrong with him? And what would cause that stench?

Behind him, boots click with almost imperceptible stealth. "Hold your position!" Gath calls over his shoulder. He doesn't want his companions anywhere near this man. There's no need to expose more of them to this strain.

The man rolls half-conscious blue eyes at him. "You here to kill me?" His voice rasps.

Gath lowers his weapon. "No, man, I'm just here to see what brings this ship to these waters."

It's impossible to tell how old the man is. Perhaps he's in his mid-thirties, but how can one still in his prime smell like death?

The man's voice shudders with each breath. "He sent us here. Said there was food."

"He?" Gath props the outside door open with his foot. Maybe with fresh air and distance, he can avoid whatever death sentence this man is under.

"Viceroy Plume." The man closes his eyes. "He told us the ASU had food, and we'd been selected for a special exploratory mission. We thought we'd been given a chance at life."

He coughs, a sickening wheeze that rattles his lungs. "Three days after sailing, one of the viceroy's escorts came down with the flu, but we'd come too far to turn back. Even if we had, they wouldn't have let us in port. People fear the plague more than starving."

"Starving?" Gath repeats. "Where are you from?"

"Rosh Province of Wales." He pauses for a labored breath. "Though it doesn't much matter. Famine is everywhere."

Famine. Plague. Does the outside world need more help than they do? Is that why the Rosh League won't let go of a rebellious commonwealth like the ASU?

Gath edges into the doorway. "What's your name? And how can we help?"

The man wheezes. "Call me Deadman. That's what I am."

"Is there no cure?" Gath holds his breath. Is the disease airborne? Has he already been exposed?

"Probably some Rosh physician has a vaccine, but there's none of that for people like us." He squints open his glazed eyes. "If you could leave buckets of clean water and any food you have on the deck each day, those of us strong enough will care for the dying until we die ourselves."

Those of us strong enough. Is this man one of the healthier ones?

"How many of you are left?" Gath inhales the fresh breeze that wafts through the doorway and hopes it might dilute the contaminated cabin.

"Just eight of the thirty-five. They're below deck. I'm the only crew left." He hazards another breath, then narrows his eyes. "Will you help us, or let us rot?"

"We'll do what we can." But how much can they really help the plagued survivors? "Hold tight. I'll come back."

Closing the door to the bridge, Gath takes the stairs to the deck by twos and gulps down clean air. His two companions meet him halfway while below them on the shoreline, another man discharges a fresh round to keep the mongrels at bay.

"What's going on?" the first asks. "It's like those beasts know there's carrion on board."

"They know all right." Gath says. "How does that saying go? Where there is a dead body, there the vultures will gather."[i]

"You mean they're all dead?" The second scans the deck. "It really is a ghost ship then."

Gath shakes his head. "They're not all dead—yet. There's some kind of virus on board. I don't know if we can help them or not, but we should try."

"What kind of virus?" The men step backward toward the rope.

"It's a flu." Gath starts to wipe sweat off his brow but stops. He shouldn't touch his face or anywhere near his eyes until he's washed every last inch of himself.

"We need a Healer's advice," Gath says, "and the three of us need to evacuate and quarantine ourselves."

One starts to protest, but the other nods in agreement. "Right. We should send the two men below to warn Red's team to stay away. They can come back for us later."

The second man shouts the order to the men on the beach, and Gath discharges six rounds into the air.

Red will know what he means. Get the hell out of dodge.

His only worry is that Red runs toward danger, not away from it, and Portia is too pig-headed to know the difference.

The second man returns wearing a grim expression. "Gath, look port side. We've got another problem."

The three rush to the rail. There, in the river's channel, the sun glints off the metallic shell of a submarine.

A burst of gunfire reverberates across the river. I drop to prone and shove the stock firmly into my right shoulder.

Red nudges my leg. "Get up. That was the signal."

"What?" I jerk my neck to squint at him.

"Three shots?" He says. "Gath said that was our signal to join them."

I blink. "I heard more than three."

He bites his lip and shakes his head. "That's our cue. Come on."

I jump to my feet and peer at the ship where Gath's dark form is barely visible on deck. The two men on shore start for the Jon boat, careful to keep their backs to the water and their guns ready to shoot the mongrels lingering in the bushes.

The four of us on the ledge return to the shoreline where I pace while waiting for the rowboat. Dad and Fox have disappeared from the submarine tower, and I can't see onto the ship anymore. Red looks about ready to put me on a leash, but before the dingy fully beaches, I jump into the water and wade toward it.

"Can we stop at the submarine first?" I call to the sweat-drenched men rowing toward me.

One scrunches his brows. "Wait. Aren't you supposed to go back?"

"Go back where?" I twist in time to avoid Red who's waded

into the water behind me.

"Portia, get on shore." His eyes flash with a warning, much the way my father's do when he expects to be obeyed.

But Red is not my father, and I'm no longer a child.

I step deeper into the river and glare at him. "That wasn't the signal, was it?"

"It was the signal but not the one you wanted to hear." He holds out his hand. "Now come on. Gil's taking you to the hostel. Harley and I need to join the others."

I pull away until the water nearly reaches my chest. "I'm part of the team, and my father's out there. I'm not retreating like a coward."

"Gath's orders." Red all but growls at me. "Returning to base isn't cowardly when it's a command."

Despite the icy water, my blood steams. Why did Gath let me come if he planned to treat me like a baby? He of all people should know I can handle ugly.

Has he been hiding the truth about my father too?

I make a split-second calculation. The current is strong, but if I can swim with it toward the submarine…

"Portia!" Red lunges at me too late.

I suck a deep breath and dive past the Jon boat. One of the men tries to stop me with his oar, but the current snatches me past him.

I underestimated its strength. Though I'm a decent swimmer, I can't swim into it as fast as it pulls me downstream.

Sputtering, I spin my arms harder in the water. Overshooting the sub means getting swept away. If I don't drown, rabid mongrels will devour what's left of me if I reach the edge of the sandbar.

The charcoal metal machine blurs in my vision. It grows larger as I near, but it's still too far.

I'm not going to make it.

My arms feel like rocks, and my chest burns, but I keep kicking.

There's a dull shouting, or maybe it's the river drowning out my senses. The current takes on arms and legs of its own, lurching beside me, tugging me down into the dark depths.

I'm sorry, Dad. I swallow mouthfuls of water that choke my lungs and stretch icy claws into my darkening consciousness.

I only wanted to see you once more…

~ Gath ~

Gath has hauled up several buckets of fresh water for the survivors on board when Dirk lets out a string of curses. "What's the fool doing?"

Gath jerks his attention to the river, and his heart lunges to his throat. "No, Portia!" He shouts, but by now, she can't hear him or the company screaming at her from the other side.

What possessed her? But that doesn't matter. He's got to get her, except that jumping from the deck will break his legs in the shallow sand—or worse. Gath darts to the other side and grimaces. Since his companions left, the mongrels have returned in droves. Some paw and attempt to jump up the steep sides of the ship, only to slide back down. Getting past them will take too long.

He has no choice. Gath unfurls the knotted rope from the bucket and lashes it around his waist. Better to jump to his death than stand around and watch the girl he loves like his own blood drown.

"Don't do it, man!" Dirk shoves a hand in his face.

"Stand down."

"It's suicide!"

He's about to punch Dirk in the face when Eddie shouts, "Look!"

Gath sidesteps Dirk and leans over the rail. A hatch on the submarine tower gapes open, revealing two men. The first secures one end of a rope to a tie-off point while the second hulk of a man dives with the other end into the water.

There's one person who rivals his own giant-size build. The Brotherhood's most famous Tooler pummels the river and reclaims the daughter that belongs to him.

"Abram Abernathy," Gath breathes. "Thank God."

CHAPTER 7

~ Portia ~

Saturday, 6.27.2150
Crystal, Cube 1776

I turn to my side and choke up what's left of breakfast and what feels like a gallon of water. Strong hands hold my shoulders until there's nothing left to hurl. Sputtering for air, I collapse again onto the ground that rolls like my angry insides.

Hands squeeze my skin. "Take it easy, sweetheart."

The bass voice makes my heart hammer. "Dad?"

He chuckles softly, and his lips brush my hair. "I'm here."

I reach up and encircle my arms around his neck. "I thought…"

"You thought crazy, that's what." He pulls me into his chest. "The sane daughter I knew would never have jumped into that river."

"They told me you were dead."

"And you believed them?"

I cough. "What else was I supposed to do? Darius and Foxworth both said you died in the fire."

He blinks at that and swings his neck. "Hey, Fox?"

Boots patter along the ground—only, it's not ground. It's

metal. It's a sub.

I slowly sit up as the blurry form takes shape. Fox pauses in front of us, hands still holding the rope that pulled Dad and me to safety.

"Sir? Is she all right?"

Dad rises and pats his shoulder. "Thanks to your fast thinking, she is. But what's this she tells me about a rumor I'm dead?"

Fox coils the rope between his hand and elbow. "Darius's orders, sir. With you gone, I did what he asked me."

"He asked you to tell Portia I was dead?" Dad's voice rises with the question.

"He said it was for her safety."

"Safety?" Dad growls. "The girl's mad enough to drown herself. What's been going on while I've been gone?"

"With all respect, sir, we have other problems right now." Fox deflects the question and motions to the beached ship. Three men wave frantically over the railing and call out to us, but my ears are too clogged to understand. And now that the adrenaline rush is over, my teeth chatter uncontrollably.

Dad scoops me in his arms and reaches the hatch. "Find out what's going on. I'll join you in five."

He carries me down a narrow stairwell to a world that doesn't seem to belong with my own. We're in a command room with panels, buttons, and screens. Manning them are sailors wearing headsets.

Their demeanors remind me of the blank faces of Warren prisoners. They're hard and emotionless. No doubt they have pasts they'd rather keep to themselves.

One man, half dad's size but solid like stone, stands. Dad steps toward him, and to my chagrin, lowers me into his arms.

"Get her out of these wet things and into something dry." He passes me off like a doll. "Remain stationary. There's a situation on the ship, so have the crew stand by."

"Yes, sir." He carries me stiffly through a hallway to what I assume are crew quarters. The low ceilings and cramped spaces remind me of Dad's tunnel system. If a man his size can feel at home here, I can too.

The stranger opens a door, revealing a small room with a twin bed and a metal chair. He places me on it and strips off my jacket.

"I can—do it." I protest through chattering teeth. No stranger is going to undress me.

"Okay." He yanks a blanket off the bed and hands it to me. "I'll be back in two minutes with something hot. You'd better be in that blanket." He mutters something. "See if I can find a uniform that might fit."

I peel off my layers with trembling fingers but manage to modestly wrap myself in the blanket before he returns. Why would Dad leave me with a complete stranger? He must trust him.

The man returns with a steaming mug of tea and a neatly folded uniform. "Drink this and put these on. They're going to be big, but I added a few extra holes in the belt."

"Thanks." I grimace at the bitter brew. "What's your name?"

"You can call me Cob."

"Thanks, Cob."

He grunts, steps out of the small quarters, and closes the door behind him with no invitation for me to follow.

But the door isn't locked, which is all the invitation I need.

I slip into the uniform, which fits like oversized pajamas, but the belt holds the baggy pants in place. With the blanket still wrapped around my shoulders and gripping my unfinished tea, I unlatch the door.

As if I've crossed a forbidden barrier, the submarine shifts, and I stagger for balance. The tea splatters, but the blanket catches most of it.

The lights in the empty hallway fade to a dull red and illuminate the path to the control room. After I bundle the stained blanket around the now-empty mug, I toss it inside the room before retracing Cob's steps.

Voices from ahead echo in the hallway.

"... We'll load what supplies Red can spare and bring them back," Dad says.

"But who will deliver them—given the circumstances?" The man's tone is low, but I think it's Cob.

There's a heavy pause. "Gath volunteered."

"Guess that makes sense since he's already been exposed. We'll have to quarantine all three anyway."

Gath? Exposed to what?

I step over a joint in the floor and push aside the uneasiness in my stomach. "Dad?"

He glances over Cob's head and beams broadly at me. "There's my girl." Dad strides to my side and wraps an arm around my shoulders.

"Boys, this is my daughter Portia."

Heads turn from their screens and nod silent hellos. I smile but something about them sends a pang through my heart. I see why Dad calls them boys. Most look no older than Darius or me.

Then, I understand. Their eyes hold the same heavy history as my own. Are they former satellite prisoners?

"What's going on?" I whisper.

"We're moving upriver to get as close to the cube as possible," Dad says. "A lot has happened since you tried to drown yourself."

I pull back. "I wasn't trying to drown myself. I was trying to get to you, and everyone seemed determined to stop me."

Dad's eyes settle on Fox, who's busily working at one of the stations. "I'm sorry, sweetheart, but we'll have to talk about that later."

I gulp, wishing my family didn't always come second to survival. "What did I hear you saying about Gath?"

Dad doesn't answer my question but turns to Cob. "What's our ETA?"

"Five minutes, Skipper."

"I'll be back in four." He tugs me toward the hallway again and down the corridor.

"You built this, didn't you?" I ask.

He gives me a proud smile. "I did. Avalon's solid."

I gasp. It's been such a long time since Dad's spoken her name. "Avalon? You named the ship after..."

"After your mother? Yes, I did. It makes my family feel close, even when we aren't."

His smile fades. "We found the broken sub at an old port by accident, and Darius challenged me to rebuild it. Said we'd need a mobile ops station and weapons defense to have a prayer of fighting Felix and his Rosh League backing. I spent the last several months on the project, partly as a way to keep my mind off what might be happening to you."

Dad pauses. "I nearly went mad when Darius said no one

knew where they'd sent you. But he promised to find you and reminded me you're a fighter—that we all had to be to get through this."

He leads me down an adjoining hallway to a somewhat larger room, perhaps a mess hall. Dad pulls out a chair for me and then sinks in one himself.

"Did Darius tell you when he found me?" I ask.

"Yes, but he didn't tell me everything." The hard lines in his forehead deepen. "And apparently, he held out on you, too."

"That's one way to put it." I mutter.

Dad reaches across the table to cup my small hands in his. "I'm sorry, sweetheart. I wish I'd done as sound a job building my family as this boat."

Hadn't Dad done his best? I don't know what else he could have done with all the cards he'd been dealt.

"Not your fault." Darius was another story. I squeeze his hand. "Now what's going on with Gath?"

Dad sighs and closes his eyes. "He and a few others investigated the ship."

"Yes, I know," I say. "He told Red and me to lag behind with a few others to cover them. That's where I was when we spotted your sub—and I saw you."

"And then you went A-wall?" Dad squints at me.

I stiffen. "Red wouldn't let me go to you, but never mind that now. What did Gath find?"

His shoulders slump as if another weight now burdens them. "The ship left a Rosh League Province in search of food, to escape a famine. A few days into the voyage, a crew member succumbed to the flu. There are only eight survivors, for now."

My head swirls. Famine? Flu? What does that mean?

I force myself to focus on facts. "How did the ship find us here?"

"The man Gath spoke with said their viceroy gave them our coordinates."

His words sink in as a sickening feeling grips my stomach. Could this viceroy be the same one Alexis had mentioned? "Did that—viceroy—know one of the crew was sick?"

"Gath doesn't know, but it certainly looks suspicious." Dad checks his watch. Our four minutes are almost up.

"So right now, we've got a few problems," he says. "First, we have to keep the ship quarantined. Gath's promised to give them supplies to try to save any who are strong enough to fight the virus. That's where we come in—helping deliver what supplies Red can spare and temporarily guarding the ship to keep curious cube dwellers from exposure."

Exposure. I shiver as its ramifications sink in. "Gath's been exposed, hasn't he?"

Dad slowly nods. "That's our second problem. He and his two companions may have been. Gath said that once he delivers the supplies, we have to quarantine them too."

Oh, Gath. Why do you have to be so selfless?

"Can't we do something to help them?" I whisper. "Gath is family." And what will Deidra say? This could break her heart.

Dad stands. "He plans to camp out in the library ruins for a week with the other two."

Those library ruins had been the place where I first saw Gath's heart behind his hardened Gage shell. He'd rescued me from a Trader and helped keep Luther alive until Red could tend his injuries. Did this man never stop giving, and why can't I be more like that?

"We'll send them off with all the supplies they'll need," Dad continues, "but honestly, it's a waiting game. When we get to the hostel, I want you to pack for them while I gather what I can for the ship survivors."

I push back my own chair, but my legs feel wobbly. "Is this what Gath's signal meant and why Red tried to keep me from crossing?"

Dad brushes my cheek with his hand. "Yes, sweetheart. Sometimes, a refusal is protection in disguise."

When Red and the others from our team reach the hostel, I've already spread half the contents of his pantry and medicine cabinet across his wooden dining table in my efforts to organize supplies. Red's glare burns the back of my neck but probably has less to do with me raiding his stuff and more with my lack of listening skills.

I try to ignore him while he instructs Gil and Harley to take a stack of buckets to a nearby spring and fill them with fresh water for the ship survivors.

They've no sooner disappeared than he marches toward me and grabs my arm. "You pull a stunt like that again, and I'll…"

I try unsuccessfully to twist out of his grip. "Listen, I…."

"No, you listen." He spins me to face him. "You nearly got yourself killed. What would I have told your father then?"

I yank away. "That his crazy daughter loved him, despite

everyone keeping them apart."

Red folds his arms. "It's not like that. You don't understand how cruel some men can be."

"Oh, don't I?" I stuff canned beans into one of the sacks to give my frustration somewhere to go. "Eliab and Osborne gave me a pretty good idea, and don't forget Felix is still at large."

Red runs fingers through his wiry hair and shakes his head. "You don't get it, do you? You'll always be your dad's baby girl and Darius's little sister. Kids like you make me thankful I never reproduced. I'd lose my mind trying to keep you safe."

"Well, then, consider yourself relieved of duty," I snap. "Dad's back, and besides, I can take care of myself."

I bite my tongue but not before the words slip out. There's a sadness in Red's eyes that suggests worry is a kinder companion than the lonely life he's endured.

"I'm sorry." I soften my tone and stretch a hand out toward him. "I'm sorry I've been so much trouble. Let's be friends?"

A grin tugs at his hardened lips. "Shoot, kid, just cause you're crazy doesn't mean I don't love you." He squeezes my hand and bear hugs me.

I laugh. "Okay, glad that score is settled. Now, I hope you don't mind that I've ransacked your place, but Dad said I need to get supplies ready for Gath."

"I'm glad you got a head start." He noses through the one pack I've already finished and nods his approval.

There's a faint click, then another, and Red's head shoots up. "Be right back," he says.

"Okay." I recognize the signal. Darius routed Morse lines throughout the squares to communicate among our Brotherhood's secret members. I can only imagine the time and ingenuity that task must have taken.

How can Darius be so brilliant mechanically and so dense relationally?

When Red returns, I've just finished with the last of the sacks. His frown makes my heart sink. "What's wrong now?"

"You have to go."

"Go where?" I sling one of the sacks over my shoulder and move it toward the door.

"Darius wants you at headquarters, said something about a Translation with a foreign ally. Apparently, Felix is mobilizing an assault, too, but he didn't say what or how. There's a train you can catch at first light."

I set down the sack with a sigh. "We have to get these supplies to Gath before he leaves for the ruins."

"Let your dad and me worry about the supplies." Red places a hand on my shoulder. "You nearly drowned yourself this morning. You need rest."

My lip trembles. Leaving Dad is bad enough, but abandoning Gath without saying goodbye makes me feel like a coward all over again. I'd left him behind at Warren once, and now, I have no choice but to desert him once more. "Did you tell Darius about Gath?"

"I told him you'd explain about Gath and that I'm sending you, Gil, and Harley on the morning train."

Gath would want me to go. He always wants the best for everyone but himself.

The heaviness on my heart grows as I mount the stairs to my room half an hour later with another mug of Red's awful tea, which he made me vow to drink. Maybe it will help me sleep.

I'll need all the fortitude I can muster to confront Darius tomorrow about his deception regarding Dad. And then I'll need some serious grace to shelve my personal angst and help with whatever new problems threaten our land.

Kristen Hogrefe

CHAPTER 8
~ Portia ~

Sunday, 6.28.2150
Crystal

I hug my knees to my chest and huddle low against the rail for protection from the wind. Instead of the usual enclosed train car, ours is an open platform with plywood fencing to transport cows or sheep. The open car exposes us to the elements, but at least it's not raining.

The benefit is that the fresh air masks the animal scents. The problem is that Gil, Harley, and I are sitting ducks, ready for any hunter to pick off at his convenience.

"Hate this," Gil mutters and slides lower along a fence corner. "If Felix and his CGA loyalists are on the offense like Red said, we're easy targets."

I swat at a fly buzzing around my head. "Guess we'd better hope they have better targets than a lone train."

Harley grunts. "Trains would be my first target. What better way to cripple us than destroy what little infrastructure we have?"

"Maybe not," I say. "I'd wager Felix wants to reclaim control of the population. Destroying the rail lines won't help his cause if he wants to move his Gages in place again."

"Then what do you think he's up to?" Gil pulls out his canteen and swigs.

"No idea." But what I know about Felix makes one thing certain: it won't be for any of our good.

Without warning, Gil spews the water from his mouth and chokes. "What in the world…?" He yanks his handgun from his belt and falls into prone, pressing the barrel between the fence slats.

I duck instinctively and crane my head to see what's spooked him.

"There!" Harley crouches and points to my left.

In the distance, an object the size of a raven buzzes toward us. But no bird glints like metal and flies in such a targeted path.

"It's headed for us," I whisper.

That's all the invitation Gil needs to shoot. He pegs the object, which explodes upon contact.

He shakes his head. "It's like shooting clay pigeons, only those don't burst into flames."

The burning object disappears into the fleeting pasture. Could that contraption be part of Felix's offensive? Whatever the case, the train station can't get here fast enough.

"Uh-oh." Gil pulls spare mags from his pack and slams a fresh one in the butt of his weapon. "Incoming at two o'clock."

What looks like a gray cloud in the distance grows closer, revealing dozens of the flying projectiles hovering together.

Harley copies Gil's example and then shucks his rifle. "First one must have been a scout."

"But what are they?" Panic boils over inside me. Our train chugs forward but not fast enough to keep the mechanized flock from catching up with us.

"Don't know, but there's nowhere to hide," Gil says. "Guess we're about to find out how good a shot you really are."

I ready my handgun's own spare magazines and shuffle to a prone position by the fence slats. My heartbeat pounds in my ears. Unlike the time Orbit trained me at the Excivis, I have no earplugs, but hearing protection will have to take second place to survival.

I close my eyes and focus on my breathing until its rhythm follows the steady and almost imperceptible rise and fall of my sights. If only I had Gath's rifle now! It would be more accurate long distance than my handgun.

"Ready!" Gil calls.

Orbit's words from my training at the Excivis echo in my memory. "Front sight press." Those three simple words are more vital than ever.

"Focus on the sights, not your target," he had said. "If you look beyond the sights, you'll miss. If you let the target blur between the sights, you'll nail it."

I take one more deep breath and choose one of the projectiles. Training my eye on the front sight of my handgun, I follow the object for a few moments to adjust to its steady forward speed and then squeeze the trigger.

The object explodes. Gil whoops beside me and fires at a second.

"It's like shooting flying squirrels!" Harley hollers before taking his own aim.

As the rest of the pack approaches, there's too much gunfire for any conversation. If only I could block out the incessant blasts that ring in my ears and tempt me to flinch.

I reach for another magazine but find it empty. Lowering my handgun, I snatch at all the empty mags. "I'm out!" I cry.

"Here!" Gil snatches at his sack and tosses me a bag. "Try these reloads."

I finger a round, almost double the size of my 9-mil. It might be a 45 load. No wonder we're all going deaf.

"Wrong caliber," I shout. "But I'll reload some of yours." I bear crawl to his growing pile of discarded magazines and use my thumb to pinch in fresh loads.

Harley curses as his own supply runs out. "There's no end to these things."

I pant in frustration and chuck a new magazine into Gil's outstretched hand. Though smaller, the swarm still persists as if a silent force draws it toward us. Between Gil's blasts, I detect a humming sound, probably the result of whatever mechanical wizardry makes the devices tick.

Gil wipes sweat from his forehead and aims again. "We don't have enough ammo to stop them."

"Blasted drones." Harley mutters.

"Drones?" I repeat the strange word.

"Yeah, I'd heard we—the CGA—developed flying probes, but I've never seen one up close."

Drones. Probes. Whatever they are, they can't be good.

One pulls away from the swarm and heads straight toward my stretch of fence.

"Gil!" I shriek, but he's too busy shooting down a different one. I stiffen as the tube-like drone hovers above me.

Its design lacks the detail my imagination had filled in. There are no beady eyes or razer teeth, just a stubby, oblong casing and a knobby round compartment underneath.

After hovering above me for a moment, the drone beeps rapidly in succession, and releases something from its underside. The metal framework unhinges itself, and a round object falls toward me.

I roll away, bracing myself for a blast or discharge.

But nothing happens. The round object bounces across the car's floor until it catches in one of the fence grooves.

Gil's stopped shooting, and in the eerie-like aftermath of the bullet-storm, two other identical objects ping across the empty car floor while their carriers buzz back to the drone pack. The hovering cloud gradually grows smaller until it disappears from sight.

The three of us exchange glances. That's it?

Gil shakes his head. "They must be heat-sensing, or why else would they converge on us and then leave?"

I crawl to the fence where the object caught. It appears to be some kind of gray plastic. The egg-shaped housing consists of two halves threaded together.

"Don't touch it," Harley calls to me.

"But if I don't touch it, how will we know what it is?"

He shakes his head. "Probably a trick."

"Maybe a time bomb," Gil adds.

"Or a message," I argue.

They shrug at me but pull farther away. Apparently, if I'm going to blow myself up, they'd rather not.

I suck a deep breath and grasp it. The plastic housing is warm but not scalding. I twist the two halves apart, and a folded note flutters out.

Snatching it before the wind carries it away, I unfold it and read.

Do not support Rogues. They will not save you when famine strikes. The ASU will welcome you back when you turn in these traitors. Refuse, and risk the Firstborn strain.

I scrunch my brows. "What in the world?"

"What's it say?" Gil asks.

I read it out loud while Harley unscrews a second. "This one says the same thing." He mutters. "What crazy man writes riddles like that?"

My gut twists. If only it were a riddle. If Felix is behind this, he no doubt means what he says. The word *strain* hits close to home in light of the flu on board that death ship.

Gil reaches for the third and unscrews the halves. He frowns. "This one's different but doesn't make any sense."

Harley scans the horizon as if suspicious the drones will return. "Go on."

Gil reads, "Orbit to Sage: Pharaoh provoked ten plagues. We'll defeat you with two. Find a Red Sea or brace yourself for Firstborn."

Orbit to Sage. The words pound in my ears. It's a message for me.

Harvey's face contorts in an angry scowl. "Give me that." Gil offers it, and he snatches it away. "Riddles. Worthless riddles." He rips it in half.

"No, wait!" I lunge toward him before he can tear it further.

"Don't tell me you think it makes sense."

I pry the two pieces from his fingers and look away before he can read the truth in my eyes. "Darius will want to see this."

He snorts. "Won't make any difference. He can't keep the

citizens safe from what's coming our way."

"And what do you think is coming our way?" I demand and try to piece together the shredded edges.

"Nothing good." Harley sulks into a corner while I tuck the messages into my bag. Exhausted, I slide onto the floor, close my eyes, and replay the words over again.

Pharaoh—Wasn't he the ruler of Egypt? My fellow candidate Jael had been distracted trying to find information in the archives on that place when she should have been helping me find the United States and Declaration of Independence.

Why had she been so curious about it? And what does she know that can help decipher Orbit's message? Is the Red Sea a literal place or something else?

More troubling than the message itself is that he dared to send it. After Orbit had shot Eliab, our employer Lord Osborne ordered him back to Felix to take Eliab's place as Commanding Gage. I can only guess he was successful and now works for Felix from Deadwood.

So why dare this message? Does he even know Osborne is dead, and he has no employer?

If so, which side will Orbit choose? This message gives me hope he'll help the Brotherhood.

No, Orbit is a mercenary, a work for hire. He has no loyalties but to his former boss and his own welfare. Still, we had worked together. Maybe he wants to give me fair warning we're about to enter a war we have no prayer of winning.

But what choice do we have? We'll fight or hope Jael can find us a Red Sea.

When the train pulls into the Crystal station, the place buzzes with people. Had it just been two days ago when Gath bribed the station master into letting one train take us to Cube 1776?

Now, a few trains idle on the tracks, their steaming engines evidence of change, restlessness, and yes, fear. The gale might be over, but a bigger storm is brewing from the Black Tundra.

Once the train stops, Gil, Harley, and I jump to the platform. A few onlookers stare at our magazine belts and bulky ruck sacks, but most ignore us. They're too busy trying to get where they want to go.

When we reach the university's deserted square, I part ways with my companions. They need to report in to the station—what used to be CGA headquarters, a place that now serves as the living quarters for some of our own militia.

I refuse to set foot in the place. Too many horrible things happened there, like my first interrogation with Eliab and later my "corrective" treatment. I'd rather see the place abandoned, but Darius insists it's a viable training center and safe house.

But I'm becoming more convinced that no cement walls can keep anyone safe from whatever warfare Felix has coming.

I stop by my own dorm room to ditch my sack and take a quick shower. Then, I tuck the two drone messages into the pockets of some clean cargo pants and slip into my brown jacket. It still smells of gunpowder from the morning's drone showdown.

As I head toward the library, my stomach rumbles. It's been a while since breakfast, but food will have to wait until I find Darius.

But no one's in the library, and the portal proves empty. I scribble a message on the dry erase board in case Darius comes, but I guess he must be at the old CGA fortress.

He knows how much I hate that place, so he can find me here.

Closing the portal door, my gaze lingers on the darkened archives. Though my stomach demands a visit to the mess hall, the messages in my pocket burn. I flip on the epileptic overhead lamps and start down the long, center aisle.

The texts on Egypt tempt me, but I bypass them for the section on the United States of America. That's where I'd seen another copy of the Bible. I don't want to ask Deidra to give back the last one I'd found. I just hope she's been reading it.

I spot the large black book on an upper shelf but can't quite reach. Placing one foot on a second shelf, I hold my breath to keep from choking on the layers of dust and hope the rusty metal frame will hold.

Something creaks in the distance, and the echo clatters my way. Perhaps Darius has come looking for me. Well, he can wait one more minute.

Yet an involuntary shiver makes me freeze for several moments. Had it been on this very aisle where Felix had tried to turn me over to the Trader? The man's dark form had been waiting in the shadows like a grim reaper to claim me.

And then I had stabbed Felix with my dad's karambit and run. I'd lost that precious gift from my father in the process, and Gage Eliab had produced it at my trial. What had become of it?

"Focus, Portia," I mutter and lift my chin toward the leather-bound book, still out of reach.

With one foot firmly leveraged into the frame of the second shelf, I shove off the ground with my other foot and swing it onto the third shelf and then the fourth. With my free hand, I reach for the book.

Footsteps behind me send the blood pounding in my ears. I

grasp the book and jerk my head around.

A tall man in a gray trench coat appears in my peripheral, the way the Trader did months ago.

With a gasp, I drop the book and lose my footing—and swing from the shelf with my feet dangling.

CHAPTER 9

~ Portia ~

Sunday, 6.28.2150
Crystal

"Cotton!" Luther rushes forward and reaches for my waist, then gently lowers me to the floor. "What on earth are you doing?"

I blush and bend to retrieve the book on the floor. "I was trying to get this."

He steps closer and circles his arms around me. "You could've asked someone to get it for you."

My cheeks grow hotter. "There wasn't anyone to ask."

He kisses my hair. "I'm sorry I've been gone so long."

I look into his dark eyes. He has no idea how long his absence felt, how much has happened since he left. But there will be time for that later. At least, I hope so.

"Did you find your parents?"

Luther sighs and releases one hand to brush the long bangs from my face. "Yes and no. Mom was home but so sick I thought I wouldn't be able to..." He chokes off the words. "She's better now, though still weak."

"I'm sorry," I whisper.

He lowers his gaze. "Dad left her. Jotham convinced him to

join Felix's forces in Deadwood."

I frown. "What for? I thought Jotham didn't care about your parents."

"He doesn't. That's what has me worried."

"I don't understand."

More boots clatter on the metal stairwell, and Luther tugs me down the aisle. "I'll have to explain later. Darius sent me to find you so we can meet. Gil and Harley briefed us on what happened. There's more brewing than my family's problems."

"Yours and mine," I mutter as we return to the central aisle leading toward the portal door.

"Huh?"

"Dad's alive, and all this time, Darius made me believe he was dead."

Luther's eyes widen. "What? He's really okay after that explosion?"

"Yes, I saw him this morning—nearly drowned in the process."

He stops short. "You nearly drowned? You've got to be kidding."

"Wish I were." We reach the portal door. I shift the Bible under my arm and grasp the handle but don't turn it. "You might need to restrain me, because I want to punch my brother right now. It's not funny that half the Brotherhood knew my dad was fine, and he told them all to lie to me."

Luther slips his hand over mine. "He must have had a reason."

I snort. "You sound like Red. Apparently, no one thinks I can handle myself under pressure."

"That's not true." Luther turns me toward him. "We just don't want you to have to deal with it."

"Too late for that."

He squeezes my hand. "But I can keep you from feeling any more of it."

If only that were true. I huff. "You still might need to restrain me."

He winks. "With pleasure."

Swatting him away, I twist the handle and enter the small space where yesterday, Gath had joined us. The idea of him spending the next week in the musty library ruins, wondering if he'll succumb to a fatal flu, wrenches my heart.

Darius and Alexis sit across from each other, each with arms crossed and faces flushed.

"You set up a meeting with them without consulting me?" Darius demands. "I was the one who got that connection working, so you could have at least…"

"You were busy, and I wasn't about to miss the chance to connect while Orvieto's temperamental Translator was in signal," Alexis cuts him off.

Luther lowers his head close to mine. "What's going on?"

I tap the door closed with my foot and whisper back. "Alexis thinks an international ally can help us and wants to talk with a group called the Orvieto Confederation. Have you heard of them?"

Luther frowns in thought. "Orvieto? I don't think I have, but then, I was only an intern with Eliab."

Goosebumps creep up my arms at the reminder. Though Eliab is dead now, he had dogged my family for so long, and Luther had to conceal his true allegiance to the Brotherhood while working for him. But then, we both had worked for intolerable men. Osborne had been an equally cruel taskmaster. I wonder if an alliance with Orvieto will prove suffocating. Maybe that's what my brother fears.

Darius shoves off his chair with restless impatience and greets Luther and me with a terse nod. "Glad you finally got here."

I bristle. "Barely is more like it, thanks to a death ship, a surprise submarine, and heat-sensing drones."

Darius retreats behind the podium as if to barricade himself from my oncoming barrage. Oh, but he deserves it.

Lucky for him, Luther places a warm hand on my shoulder, a reminder that losing my cool won't help us. "Why don't you start at the beginning and tell us what happened?"

Alexis's face puckers in concern, and she pats the seat beside her. I don't want to sit, but Luther nudges me toward her. With a sigh, I fall into the plush chair and let the Bible rest on my lap. Darius studies it with a questioning eye but motions for me to begin.

"I shouldn't have let you go," he mutters after I finish.

I grip the arms of my chair. "No, you shouldn't have told me Dad was dead."

"But what can we do for Gath?" Luther asks. "Has anyone told Deidra?"

I wince and curl my legs underneath me. Here I am, wanting to fight with my brother, when our friend's life is in danger. At least Luther can help me focus on what matters more.

I lower my eyes. "I haven't had time to tell her. I'm not sure what to tell her."

"Maybe it would be better not to," Darius says. "Say he's needed in Cube 1776 for a mission and leave it at that. No need to make her worry if she doesn't need to."

I glare at my brother. "Even if the truth hurts, it's better than a lie."

"Lies can protect us," he retorts.

I jerk my knee to my chest, sending the book from my lap into the groove between Luther's and my seat. Hadn't my father told me that same thing?

But there's a difference between safety and freedom.

Luther rests a hand on my knee. "We should talk with Lydia. She's a Healer's daughter and a Healer in her own right. She might have an idea of how we can help Gath."

I nod. "Speaking of Lydia, where is she? I thought she'd be here."

Darius shifts behind the podium. "I have her working on a project for me, based on the intel I wanted to talk to you about. I think there's a connection between Orbit's warning message to you from that drone and information we've intercepted."

"Go on," Luther says.

"Those drones are delivering the same message—the one from that first drone you told us about—all over the squares. We've got a grass roots effort in place to warn people against Felix's fear tactics, but we suspect there's a ring of truth to them."

Darius taps on the keyboard behind the podium, and the Translation screen turns a hazy blue. After a few clicks, Darius projects his screen onto the main one.

A chemical strand, something from my undergraduate biology class, appears along with markings I don't understand.

Darius retrieves a laser pointer from the podium and encircles the image. "This is what Felix calls the Firstborn strain."

My throat constricts. "Those are the same words from Orbit's message. Is that—is that what's on the ship?"

"Don't know," Darius says, "but the thought has crossed my mind. Still, this strain doesn't seem as potent. From what intel we've gathered, someone with Firstborn will be dead within 24 hours."

I shudder. "That's awful."

"Even more awful are the test subject images from Baytown satellite."

I close my eyes and rub my temples. "I don't want to see."

"I'm not going to show you," Darius says. "The point is Felix doesn't plan to play around. But we don't know when or where he's going to strike."

"If Felix infects ASU citizens, isn't he jeopardizing the safety of his team and any who plan to return here?" Luther asks.

"I asked the same question, but turns out, the virus isn't communicable from person to person. It's an aerosol that's absorbed into the skin, and once the person is dead, the virus has run its lifespan and dies."

I stare at the spiral on the screen. Felix killing his mother seems almost merciful compared to his plans to use this virus on innocent citizens.

"Wait, if that's the case, Gath doesn't have to stay in quarantine," I say with a hopeful smile.

"But we don't know if we're dealing with Firstborn or a different flu altogether." My brother shakes his head. "We have to play it safe."

Alexis, who had been sitting quietly, straightens in her seat. "This is all the more reason to keep our appointment with Orvieto, which starts in half an hour."

Darius's face flushes. "About that…"

Alexis holds up a hand. "We won't know if they can help us unless we talk with them."

"People on the other side of the world can't do a thing about what's going on here." Darius waves his hands in frustration.

"But they might want to try," Alexis says. "If that side of the world is dealing with a global famine, we might be able to provide them food in exchange for their muscle."

"Assuming they have muscle, as you call it," Darius says. "I still don't see how they can do anything to help us fight against Felix."

Alexis taps on her watch. "We'll find out in less than thirty minutes."

Darius starts to say something, but Luther interrupts. "It can't hurt to talk to them, but we need to come across as unified leaders, not quarreling rebels."

Darius nods slowly. "What do you suggest?"

Luther removes his hand from my knee and leans forward. "First, we need to agree on our titles and roles. This confederation—Orvieto—will want to know who we are and why we have the authority to talk with them."

I wrinkle my nose. "What do you mean by titles?"

"Like, the Friend," Luther explains. "Other countries use different terms like president, dictator, commander-in-chief, or prime minister."

"But the Dome and CGA controlled elections," I say. "I don't think citizens would know how to vote, and we certainly don't have time for an election."

"That's right," Luther says. "All of us just need to have the same story. The ASU is in a state of emergency. We've overturned the established government because of its atrocities against civilians and have formed an interim government."

I glance from Luther to Darius to Alexis. We hardly look like an interim government. We're more like a rag-tag group of survivors.

Alexis's eyes light up. "You're exactly right, Luther. If we want Orvieto to take us seriously, we need some structure." Her body language grows rigid, but she clears her throat and looks Darius squarely in the eye. "Abernathy, I may not agree with you half the time, but you're the Brotherhood's leader and logical one for this group."

Darius looks about ready to growl but swallows hard. "Thank you, Alexis. We don't agree, but I appreciate your honesty and experience as a Dome representative." He hesitates. "Will you serve as diplomat? That will make the most sense since you've already contacted Orvieto." Though his tone still holds disapproval, there's a hint of respect. Maybe those two will find a way to work together.

"I would be honored," Alexis says, "but how should I introduce you?"

"Introduce me?" Darius asks.

She motions in the air. "I mean, your title."

Darius rubs his jaw. "I don't really care—just don't call me the Friend. The Caesuras have ruined that title."

"How about president?" I suggest. "That's what the previous civilization called its leaders."

My brother shrugs. "Sure, that works for me. But what about

you two? I want your input about this Orvieto matter."

The edge returns to his tone. More than likely, he wants us to help him outvote Alexis against it. But that's not how a balance of power works.

"Back in the United States, there were three branches of government," I say. "I learned this in my Revisionary theory course. There was the executive branch of the president, the judicial branch, and the legislative branch. The judicial branch was similar to our Court Citizens, and the legislative branch—well, I guess that would be like our Revisionaries."

The word catches in my throat. I had worked hard to be a Revisionary and fallen short. But then, some dreams are never meant to be anything but reshaped.

Darius drums his fingers on the podium. "Luther can be the judicial, and you can be the legislative."

Luther grunts. "Judicial? Call me your Chief Court Citizen or something like that. I like our terms better."

He nudges me in the side. "And this one here can be our Doctor Revisionary."

I pull away and shake my head. "No, I'm not worthy of that title. I wouldn't have been picked for a Dome seat even if I hadn't gotten arrested and sent to a satellite. Felix's scores were better than mine, and Jael's probably were, too."

Darius dismisses me with a wave of his hand. "Felix probably cheated, and Jael's not here, so like it or not, you're it, Doc."

I chew my lip, knowing I've been outvoted, as Alexis talks Darius through the steps for starting the scheduled Translation.

Doctor Revisionary. It's just a title anyway. Anyone can claim a title, but I hate feeling like a fraud. Even with all my training, I know so little about what makes a good Codex—or Constitution like the Founders called theirs.

Is this how they felt? Inadequate but brazenly brave?

The translucent blue light expands from the screen and along the floor's edges. Luther tenses beside me, but then, this probably is his first Translation. For me, it's like going back in time to memories and meetings I'd like to forget.

"Here goes," Alexis says. "I hope this works."

Darius's rigid posture suggests he hopes it won't.

When the blue haze fades, a panel of five people sit facing us. Luther nearly jumps out of his seat at how lifelike the representation is.

The five individuals—three men and two women—dress in deep navy suits, which makes their tanned olive skin appear even darker. We stare at each other for several moments before Alexis makes introductions.

Afterward, the lady in the center chair taps a mic in front of her. I don't understand why she would need to do so. We can hear her fine, unless it's for others on her end to listen in.

"Thank you, Diplomat Alexis. My name is Abra Bianchi, acting chairwoman of the Orvieto Confederation." Her thickly-accented voice nevertheless articulates perfect English. She appears as perfectly manicured as Juliana Caesura once did, except Abra is a more exotic version with bobbed black velvet hair and purple-rimmed glasses that seem almost too big for her face.

The chairwoman continues, "I assume these introductions mean you are the Rogues responsible for the temporary overthrow of the Rosh League's leadership."

Alexis takes a deep breath, as if considering her next

statement, but the time costs her the opportunity. Darius pounces on the chairwoman's accusation. "Despite your fickle Translation connection, you've heard about our situation here?" His tone lacks all diplomacy. "The bottom line is: Do you want our help, and do we want yours?"

Bianchi offers a tight-lipped smile. "I respect your candor, Mr. President, but without our help, your victory will be short-lived."

Kristen Hogrefe

CHAPTER 10

~ Portia ~

Sunday, 6.28.2150
Crystal

I hold my breath, half expecting my brother's temper to flare. Instead, he tightens his jaw and gives Alexis a terse nod. Perhaps he doesn't trust himself or needs time to determine if her threat is legitimate.

Alexis clears her throat. "Perhaps some clarification would be helpful. First, is it true that your continent is reeling from famine?"

Bianchi's lips tremble slightly. "We are managing, but yes, many are starving."

"We're sorry to hear that," Alexis says. "On our side of the world, we're having regular harvests. Perhaps there is something we can do to help."

The chairwoman's lips part in a proud smile. "Perhaps we can help each other. As you may or may not know, the Orvieto Confederation is a small group of countries that's banded together to oppose the Rosh League's domination of Euro-Asia's people groups. The Rosh League has capitalized on suffering, beginning even before the trans-continental disasters of the last century."

She must be referring to what we've called the Apocalypse. I suppose *trans-continental disasters* does sound more sophisticated.

"How have you managed to evade their domination?" Alexis asks. "If they are as powerful as you say…"

"The greater their reach, the harder their ability to maintain order." Bianchi folds her hands in front of her. "Don't flatter yourself in being the only unruly province they have to supervise. However, your situation is a little different, because I've heard they kept you in the dark all these years after an electro-magnetic attack. Ignorance is a powerful tool."

"It is indeed," Alexis says, "though I'm curious how you even know about our existence."

"America couldn't have just disappeared. There had to be something left of the greatest country on earth."

Alexis seems at a loss for words. As a Tooler, she's probably clueless about the past civilization's rich history. I'm nothing but a novice myself.

"Don't think the Rosh League is the only one with advanced technology," Bianchi continues. "We've done our share of spying, but until now, there was no reason to interfere."

"Interfere?" The word jumps from my throat before I can catch it. Groaning, I realize I'm like my brother in more ways than one.

But when your foot is in your mouth, you might as well swallow it. "You've known all along that the ASU has lied to and mistreated its citizens, and you stood by and did nothing?"

Bianchi glances at her notes, though she doesn't seem rattled by my outburst. "Doctor—Revisionary," she begins, "you assume that because we've managed to stay out of the Rosh League's grasp that we are some great nation. We are great in terms of history and the sheer fact we've survived when so many others have fallen.

"However, our security lies in our strategic location. We're a peninsula, and our scientists have developed hydro-shields. Our only land front is to our north, and we've taken great pains to ensure that for several hundred kilometers, our neighbors remain free. If the Rosh League's forces ever break through, they will have to crush those allies before reaching us, and to our credit, we've prevented that from happening."

"Scientists," I mutter to Luther. "Do you think they're like our Mavens?"

A shadow crosses Luther's face. "Yes, I'd guess so. But this hydro-shield stuff is beyond me."

"If you just care about preservation, then what can you do to help us?" Darius demands, his voice tight.

The screen glitches but resolves itself. Maybe Bianchi missed my brother's sarcasm. She politely bobs her head. "We are not proud to admit we've known of your abuses and done nothing to stop them, but it would take another world power like the former United States to combat all the atrocities committed by the Rosh League."

I force a conceding smile. She has a point.

"But the present is the best place to begin if we are to remedy the future." Bianchi sweeps her hand to acknowledge the others sitting on the panel with her. "We five represent the five countries that formed the Orvieto Confederation: Italy, Switzerland, Austria, Slovenia, and Corsica. Separately, we are countries isolated by language and culture, having only proximity in common. Jointly, though, we represent the last nations holding out against the Rosh

League, to our knowledge. And we have our own defensive arsenal we can deploy for your aid if we agree to work together."

The others at the table nod in agreement.

Arsenal? What does that mean? But another question cuts in line. "If you five all speak different languages, then why did you decide to make English your baseline language?"

Bianchi smiles. "We formed our confederation right before the trans-continental disaster took place. At that time, the United States—and other countries like England—assured us of their full support."

"So the confederation was supposed to be much bigger?"

"That's right."

"Then why…?"

"Why didn't we change the language?" Bianchi finishes my sentence with a sigh. Another glitch attacks the Translation but relents before I miss her answer.

"Let me back up a bit," she begins. "Orvieto is a small, mountain-top town in Italy. There's nothing more impressive about it than any of our other incredible cities, but according to history, our Filippo Mazzei corresponded with America's Thomas Jefferson right around the time of the Declaration of Independence."

Jefferson. Now there's a name I know.

"Based on historical accounts and letters between the two, it's believed that Mazzei actually suggested some of the ideas, if not the wording, of key lines in the Declaration itself," she says. "For that reason, Orvieto began a tradition in the year 2013 to celebrate the Italian contribution to the American ideal."

A sad smile crosses her face. "Orvieto Forever, we called it.

But apparently, nothing is forever."

"Still, we celebrate it." The man to her right stares intently at us. "We celebrate what was and what may yet be again."

At that moment, the screen goes blank. "What happened?" Luther asks.

Darius checks his control panel. "Everything is fine on our end. They must have a bad connection."

Alexis paces in front of the screen. "But surely if their Mavens—scientists—are as advanced as they say, they shouldn't have any issues."

Darius gives her a hard look. "Maybe they're bluffing. Maybe they're the ones who need our help. Maybe they're wasting our time."

"We're the ones who contacted them," she argues.

"You're the one who contacted them," he corrects.

The screen blips on again, and an unfocused image breaks through. The panel members now appear pixelated, though still present.

Alexis steps forward eagerly. "Can you hear us?"

"We never stopped hearing you," Bianchi says with a terse smile.

Darius colors and pulls back.

Bianchi clears her throat. "Our Translation equipment is fine. The problem is that we don't have a secure connection, and the Rosh League's hacking algorithms are more advanced than you can even begin to imagine."

"Then how do you communicate confidentially with your member nations?" Alexis asks.

"We created a modem with so many layers of password

protection and cloaking that they haven't been able to detect it," Bianchi explains. "The trick is that both sides of the Translation have to have one present for the connection to work."

"I can make anything," Darius says. "Just tell me what to do."

The panel members murmur and shake their heads. "This connection isn't secure," Bianchi says. "We can't take that risk. You don't understand what the Rosh League would give to get their hands on this modem."

She pauses and offers a wry smile. "You're welcome to come pick up a copy if you think our alliance is worth the waste of your time."

I wince and wonder if Darius will accept the personal jibe. He does rather deserve it.

"The Orvieto Forever celebration begins…"

Before the chairman can finish, there's a crackling sound, then silence. The pixelated hologram vanishes.

Alexis sighs. "I think we lost them for good this time."

Darius types furiously at the keyboard. The Translation ends, and the interface shuts down with a fading humming. He grunts. "I don't plan to let them eavesdrop on any more conversations."

Luther stands and walks toward a dry erase board next to the Translation screen. He uncaps a marker and starts drawing circles.

"What's that, Luther?" Darius asks.

"I'm laying out the pros and cons." He scribbles something in a circle and moves on to the next.

I smile as the others look on in silence. It's hard not to like a guy who knows how to organize his ideas.

Luther caps the pen and taps on the board. Then, he takes us from circle to circle, summarizing the conversation we just had.

"From what I can tell, we need them as much as or more than they need us."

Darius crosses his arms. "Who's to say they don't plan to exploit us like the Rosh League did?"

"That's a risk," Luther agrees.

"But if they celebrate each year the principles from the Declaration of Independence, I don't think they will," I pipe up.

"The bigger question is how we get that modem." Alexis runs her fingers through her bobbed hair. "We don't have the means to cross the ocean, let alone navigate to Orvieto."

"Orvieto?" I repeat.

"Yes, that's where they hold that celebration, and the only location they mentioned in specifics. I think it's safe to assume they would want us to meet them there."

"But we don't know when," Luther says.

"I think we do," I counter. "The Declaration of Independence was adopted on July 4, the day Americans celebrated as Independence Day."

Alexis gasps. "That's next week."

"It doesn't matter," Darius adds quickly. "Getting there is impossible, so let's stop wasting time and talk about a more practical plan of action."

I jump to my feet. "It's not impossible, and you know it."

Darius rubs his jaw as if I'd punched him. "Drop it, sis. That's not an option."

Alexis and Luther exchange confused looks.

"Why not?" I demand. "Dad was missing for months. Don't tell me that submarine isn't state of the art. I bet he could get us there and back in less than two weeks."

"Us?" Luther drops the marker and stares at me. "You wouldn't be going."

Darius glares at me. "No one will be going. That submarine and its counterparts are our secret coastal defense and intel. We can't risk years of planning and months of execution on a whim."

"Counterparts." I pounce on the word. "That means we have more than one sub?"

"They're not fully operational yet," Darius hisses. "And if you breathe one word about the Pelagic Project outside this room, you'll be putting good lives in danger. That's why I didn't tell you in the first place."

"Because you don't trust me."

"Because you didn't need to know."

My face feels the temperature of a brick oven. What has happened to us? How can the brother I adored make me this angry?

"I think we should talk to Dad and see what he thinks."

"This isn't personal, Portia, but Dad knows his place in the mission right now. You need to figure out yours." Darius's sharp tone sends hot tears brimming in the corners of my eyes.

I blink them away. "Fine, if you don't need me here, I dare you to send me to Orvieto with Dad. Like it or not, we need allies— Luther proved that. But don't worry. If I never return, it won't be any sweat off your back."

My brother's hard shell cracks, and his eyes flicker. "Portia…"

I hold up a hand and push past Luther who tries to intercept me at the door. "If you need me… Never mind. I doubt you will."

I shove open the portal door and race up the stairs to the exit.

Deidra stares at me with wide eyes and twists her bedsheet in her hands. I finally finish the story and smack the uncomfortable up-side-down bucket of a seat with my palm.

Hitting the darn thing only hurts my hand but helps release some of my pent-up tension.

"You need to go for a run, girl," Deidra says. "You're about to boil over."

I haven't run as much as I should since returning to Crystal. There are too many memories from that track, but today, there are enough other problems to distract me from them.

I rub my sore hand. "You're right."

"If I could, I'd join you." She massages her thigh. "Crutches look deceptively easy, but I'm determined to conquer them."

Her indomitable spirit challenges my own. "You will soon."

She shakes her head. "No, I will now. You go running, and I'm going to practice some more. I have to get out of this ward and get to Gath."

"But you can't. He's quarantined."

She nearly growls at me. "*Can't* doesn't belong in my dictionary, and it doesn't belong in yours. I'd rather that strain kill us both than never see him again."

I gulp. I don't want to lose both of them.

Deidra grabs my hand. "Listen, don't worry about us. I promise to talk to Lydia first and take with me any herbal remedies she can spare. If Gath can sweet talk the conductor into giving him a train, you'd better believe I can too."

"But you're…"

"On crutches?" She snorts. "Trust me. After a little more practice, I'll probably outrun you with two good legs. Besides, Gath and I have survived worse. You've got to convince Darius to let you go to Orvieto. And if you can't convince him, find a way to go anyway. We could take the same train back to Cube 1776."

"Like I could steal a sub," I mutter and pull my hand free.

"You could fake orders," Deidra counters. "Your dad's the skipper, right? I'm sure he'd believe you. You could be halfway to Orvieto before Darius even knows where you are."

I rub my temples. "You're insane. When Darius found out, he would kill me."

"You're his sister. He wouldn't kill you."

"But I could kiss goodbye any hope of ever having a good relationship with him again." I groan. "My family is such a mess."

"The world's a mess, Portia," Deidra says. "Sometimes, it has to get messier before it gets better."

"But we all agreed Darius is the president. He's the guy we're all supposed to listen to."

Deidra snorts. "What's a title if he doesn't act worthy of it?"

I shake my head. "Listen to you, the girl who took orders from Osborne for a decade."

Her eyes narrow to slits. "I was a fool, willing to throw away my future for revenge. That was a personal mistake. We're talking about the future of our country."

"But what if I'm wrong?" I kick back the bucket. "What if the Orvieto Confederation can't help us, and my stubborn mistake costs us the Avalon and safety of her crew?"

"Then you take ownership, pick up the pieces, and try

something else. Taking risks is what heroes do."

"I'm not a hero."

She cocks her head and grins. "No, girl, you're a heroine."

Kristen Hogrefe

CHAPTER 11

~ Luther ~

Sunday, 6.28.2150
Crystal

Luther nods as Alexis excuses herself and watches in silence until she disappears out the same door Portia left moments earlier. It swings closed behind her with an accusing click.

Darius exhales the minute she's gone. "Women."

Luther arches an eyebrow. "Yeah? They don't tend to appreciate when we keep secrets from them."

"It was for her own good." Darius mutters. "She doesn't know how to keep jobs from getting personal."

Could Darius really be this dense? Luther has known the man from boyhood, but surely his hardened life can't have numbed him to the fact Portia is starving for family, love, and belonging.

"Can you blame her?" Luther asks. "She's already lost most of her family."

Darius shoots him a warning look. "I know what she's been through. I've been through it myself, but going soft won't solve any problems. I have to do what's best for the ASU, not what's comfortable for my sister."

Luther bites his lip. For all his genius, Darius doesn't

understand girls. They need to love and be loved, and the fastest way to kill love is with lies. After the hell Portia has been through, she could use more than Darius's table scraps.

If only she'd let him close enough to help.

Luther studies the blank screen before them. "You won't consider sending your dad to Orvieto?"

"No, we don't have the time or resources to spend on false hope."

Luther shifts his focus to his friend. "Isn't our Brotherhood built on slim odds?"

Darius groans. "Come on, man, don't give me that. You know I'm doing the best I can to hold this place together. What I can use is your help on another matter." He reaches to switch off the lights, leaving just the exit lights glowing overhead.

Maybe if Darius let go of some control, their members would rise to the challenge. Though Luther doesn't want Portia any farther than a stone's throw away, there might be some merit to this Orvieto opportunity. He'd have to wait for Darius to cool down before trying a different approach.

"What's on your mind?" Luther starts for the exit, but Darius motions toward the door on the other end of the portal. He pauses mid-step. "Where does that go?"

"This door leads into the below-ground levels the Crystal Globe didn't want its candidates knowing about." Darius pops open the door and pauses for a moment on the other side. "Coming?"

The skin on Luther's neck tingles. Is this the place Portia once told him about when her weasel of an adviser took her to meet the dean? But what could possibly be dangerous about a few below-ground offices?

Luther catches the door and follows Darius down the emergency-lit halls. "Where are we going?"

"Seven stories down."

They reach an elevator, and Luther stops, but Darius strides past it. "Uh, elevator?" Luther calls after him.

Darius waves him onward. "No good. We may temporarily have electricity, but I don't trust Felix—and no one would think to search for us in a locked elevator in this deserted place."

"Right." Luther strides past it and follows Darius into a dimly-lit stairwell. Their steps reverberate on the metal stairs until he's lost count how many stories down they've come.

Darius shoves a door open and enters a walkway that smells like chemicals. Toward the end of the hallway, bright light from an open doorway filters into the murky corridor.

Who else could be down here? Luther feels for the Glock 17 on his hip, but Darius shakes his head. "No, man, you won't need that. Leave it holstered, or you're likely to scare her half out of her wits. She claims the place makes her claustrophobic as it is."

"She?" Luther crosses his arms. "What's going on here?"

A half-smile jerks at Darius's lips. "I'm about to show you, but you have to keep this under wraps. You'll understand why in a minute."

Luther frowns, but Darius doesn't give him time to answer. The man expects him to accept his word without question, like a president. Or a dictator?

Darius taps on the open door to make their presence known. There's a girlish squeak from inside and something glass drops.

"You have to stop doing that!" The woman shrieks.

Lydia?

Luther trails Darius through the doorway but stops short. Rows of metal tables with strange instruments and sinks line the room. Along the walls are vials, various microscopes, chemicals, and who knows what else. A large dry-erase board, plastered with equations, covers almost the entire length of one wall. There's no mistaking the place is a lab. But why is it all the way down here?

"What is all this?" Luther asks and inspects a petri dish on one of the tables.

"Don't touch anything," Lydia says. She's wearing a white lab coat and gloves. Except for a wayward strand of brown hair, the rest of her long hair sits atop her head in a tight knot. She looks nothing like the Court Citizen candidate who had shared so many classes with him.

She softens her tone with a smile. "The Mavens left for the night, and I told them I'd clean up but not touch anything." She wipes around another cluster of petri dishes with meticulous attention not to move them.

"Mavens?" Luther turns to Darius. "You've got a bunch of scientists playing around down here? What for?"

"Lydia is overseeing a special project for me." Darius steps behind her and peers over her shoulder. "Any progress today?"

Luther cocks an eyebrow. He's never seen Darius get close to any woman, and here he is practically breathing down Lydia's neck.

"We'll have a new report ready tomorrow, but I think we're getting closer."

Do they expect him to read their minds? "Closer to what?"

Darius tugs a laser pointer from Lydia's front pocket and

directs his attention to the white board. "Closer to cracking the coded formula we intercepted."

He pauses. "Let me back up. Do you remember Portia telling us about the message she thinks Orbit sent her? And then, I showed you a visual of intel on the Firstborn strain we intercepted?"

Luther nods. "Right, we were talking about that before the Orvieto Translation."

Lydia jerks her head. "Oh, how did that go? I'm sorry I missed that."

Darius holds up a hand. "I'll fill you in on the Orvieto-waste-of-time in a minute. But first, I need Luther to understand our mission here. I think he'll appreciate we're taking real action to beat Felix to his punchline."

Luther's head feels like someone is pounding nails. Will this day never end? "What do you mean?"

"The intel we intercepted was a direct transmission from the Rosh League to Deadwood," Darius explains, "meaning that we received the virus DNA at the same time Felix did."

"So?"

"So, if our Mavens can move faster than his—and I think they can, given the facilities here at the Crystal Globe—we can launch their own virus against them before they can use it on the people."

Darius's words take a moment to sink in. "Wait, you're suggesting we deploy this lethal virus on Deadwood?"

Bile rises in his throat. Darius doesn't know Luther's own brother and father are somewhere in that frozen tundra fortress.

"Why not?" Darius studies him with the unforgiving glare of a soldier. "This is war, Luther. I thought you, of all people, would understand."

"I get it." Luther mutters. "But surely this is a last resort? Or do you have the virus ready to launch?"

Darius snorts. "Not yet, but Lydia thinks we're close."

Luther glances to Lydia. "I still don't understand how you're mixed up in all this."

"I'm a Healer's daughter, remember?" She sighs. "I understand enough science to oversee the Mavens and not enough to do any of the real work. Darius said he wanted someone he could trust on the project, and unfortunately, that's me."

Luther spins to study the cryptic formulas and equations spelled out on the board. He has to choose his words carefully, or he'll lose Darius's trust. "I agree it's smart for you to crack the virus's code, but don't you think using it should be a last option? You said yourself the havoc it wreaks is horrendous. The thought of using it on our enemies seems almost inhumane."

"This is war, Luther."

"I know." He waves his hand impatiently. "But surely we should exhaust all our options first—or at least pretend to use them as decoys to buy our Mavens the time they need."

Darius folds his arms. "I'm listening."

"How long would it take to send Abram to Orvieto? I've heard subs can move fast."

Darius sputters, but Luther rushes on. "Seriously, you're never going to have peace from Alexis or Portia until you attempt to form international allies. And even if you succeed in obliterating Deadwood, what's to keep the Rosh League from hurling all its wrath on us? Some international muscle couldn't hurt—and it would give you the time you need to finish this program without Alexis breathing down your neck."

His friend forces a frustrated sigh. "Dad could be there and back in about ten days, but his absence would create a vulnerable spot. And we don't know when Felix will attack."

"What if we create a second decoy—something else to distract him?"

Darius bites his lip. "Do you have something in mind?"

Luther sucks a deep breath. This might be his chance to rescue his dad and buy them all some time. "Send me to Deadwood. Contact Felix, requesting a diplomatic meeting. Suggest we can talk out a truce and spare the citizens further injury."

"Absolutely not." Darius sets his jaw. "First, we both know Felix would never agree to a truce when he appears to have the upper hand. Second, we have nothing to bargain with."

"We have food," Luther disagrees. "We could offer part of our harvest in exchange for self-rule. I think the practice is similar to an excise tax some colonies had to pay in tribute."

"It would never work."

"It doesn't have to work, and naturally, Felix won't agree. But it will buy us time."

"I'm not sending you to Deadwood. If you want to plan some diplomatic sweet talk with Alexis and then translate with Felix, fine. But I'm not losing a good man to a fool's mission."

Luther's window of opportunity is closing fast. "An in-person meeting would suggest we're serious. A Translation seems almost cowardly, given our situation."

"The answer is no." Darius turns to Lydia. "Are you about finished? You can call it a night and leave with us."

"Yes, thanks." She yanks off her gloves and tosses them in a disposal canister. "This place creeps me out when all the workers have left."

Darius slips a hand around Lydia's waist and then kills the lights. His friend isn't wasting any time sending a clear message about his romantic intentions. But Darius needs to keep his head in the game.

Luther clears his throat from behind the two. "If you won't send me to Deadwood, will you send me to Orvieto with Abram?"

He winces at the frustration in his own voice. Maybe if he weren't so tired, he could reign in his emotions better.

They reach the stairwell and begin their ascent. After a long pause, Darius heaves a sigh. "I'll have the orders ready for Abram in the morning, and I want you to personally deliver them."

Wait, is Darius actually agreeing with his Orvieto plan?

"And don't say a word to Alexis or Portia," Darius adds. "It would be better for them not to know about the mission until it's over."

Luther frowns. "But Alexis is our diplomat."

"Diplomat, maybe, but I can't trust her to make judgment calls, and she makes too many assumptions. Abram will simply do the job, get the modem, and return with it so we can proceed from there."

"And Portia is my…"

Darius smirks. "You left her for how long to visit your parents? Surely you two can survive without seeing each other for a few days."

"Okay."

Darius falls behind while Lydia seems to climb the stairs as if her life depends on it. The poor thing really doesn't like confined spaces.

"Luther?" Darius's voice hovers above a whisper.

"Yes?"

"Not a word of this to anyone. I need someone I can depend on, and right now, that's Lydia and you."

Luther's chest tightens. "Portia would do anything for you."

Darius snorts. "I love my sister, but I'm not very high on her favorite-person list. I don't know if she'll forgive me for not telling her about Dad, and until she cools down, I can't involve her. You know how emotions mess with your head."

Luther nods upward to where Lydia is still climbing. "Yeah, so should you."

Darius elbows him in the ribs. "Hey, you're the one who's so distracted by my sister you're not listening half the time."

Luther blocks a second jibe. "That's different. I've been distracted by your sister since forever. You're the one in uncharted territory."

Even in the dull lighting, he can see Darius's broad grin. "Yeah, in over my head is more like it. But the pursuit is worth going under."

Lydia's pounding feet above them stop. "Would you two quit mumbling? It echoes something creepy. Goodness, I can't stand this place." Her feet resume their marching double time.

Darius chokes down a laugh and takes the steps by two to catch up with her.

Luther picks up his own pace but keeps some distance between them. The weight of their world rests on the shoulders of a few twenty and thirty somethings who should be spending their youth on love and living, not fighting for their lives.

But happy endings are only promised in fairy tales. Still, he's got one chance to forge a life with Cotton, if she'll have him. Surely love can make a way in a wasteland-world.

CHAPTER 12

~ Portia ~

Sunday, 6.28.2150
Crystal

Can I really be this out of practice? After mile two, my breath comes ragged, and sheer willpower alone keeps my feet moving.

There are too many problems, and I haven't had a good night's sleep in forever. Maybe that's why my legs feel like lead.

"I can't do this anymore." I choke on the bitter words. Gasping, I rest my hands on my thighs. If running is eighty percent mental, then I admitted failure with that death word *can't*.

No one said running would be easy. No one said life would be easy.

"You look kind of beat, baby." Luther's voice makes me jump. I whirl to find him standing feet away.

Baby? What happened to *Cotton*? Yet the endearment sends my already increased heart rate even higher.

He reaches my side and wraps an arm around my waist.

I pull away. "I'm gross."

"I don't care."

There's mystery and passion in his dark eyes. I drop my gaze. "What's that in your hand?"

"Oh, this?" Luther lifts the object toward me. "I found it in the portal on my way out. You must have dropped it."

It's the Bible I'd pulled off the shelf. I wipe sweaty palms on my pants and accept it from him. "Thanks for bringing it."

Luther fidgets and finally tucks his thumbs in his pockets. Why does he seem at a loss to know what to do with his hands? "Why did you want it so badly?" He asks at last.

I run a finger along the worn leather spine. "I thought it might hold answers. Orbit's message said to 'find a Red Sea' and also talked about Pharaoh."

"Then why didn't you find a text on Egypt?"

I shiver in the cool evening air. "Walk with me to my apartment?" I'm done running, so I might as well clean up instead of catch cold from being wet.

Luther grins. "Cold, are you? I can warm you up." He reaches for my waist again.

I roll my eyes but don't push him away as we start for the dorm. If he wants to hug a sweaty girl, that's his problem. "Do you remember what I told you about Gath's story?"

"Which part?" He smiles down at me.

"The part about the prisoner Christopher."

"Right, he's the kid who broke Gath's hard shell by forgiving him even through the torture."

"Yes, Gath credits Christopher for leading him to Jesus Christ," I explain. "Anyway, Gath told me that the Bible holds all the answers to life, and so I thought if the Red Sea is important, the Bible might say something about it."

Luther chuckles. "The Red Sea is probably on some old-world atlas. I'm sure you don't need the Bible to find it."

"But I think Orbit saw me reading the Bible in Osborne's library," I insist. "It could be a clue he knows I can find."

"Could be." Luther pauses. "What do you think of Gath's story? I mean, about all that religious stuff?"

"I think it must be true. What else could explain such a radical change in Gath? He says he was as cruel or worse than Eliab." An involuntary shiver races up my spine. Though he's dead, Eliab still haunts my dreams sometimes.

Luther seems to notice and pulls me closer. "I don't know. Guess I need to look into his story some more. Maybe you can lend me that book when you're done with it?"

"Of course." Having someone to read it with might help me make better sense of it.

When we reach the dormitory, Luther steps ahead to get the door. The halls are silent but for the pattering of our feet. He stops at his room, right next to mine, but doesn't open the door. "I know you probably want a shower, but we need to talk soon."

I fumble for my key. "About what?"

He gives me a lop-sided grin while fidgeting with his own key. "For starters, you need to get that meeting with Darius off your chest and let me in on any crazy ideas you're stewing on."

It's my turn to laugh. How can this man read me so well?

But my laugh catches in my throat as his voice drops two octaves. "And then, we need to talk about us."

I jam my key in the lock, but keys don't fit when they're backwards. Blushing from my roots, I stare hopelessly into his dark eyes. Why am I being ridiculous? I've known Luther since childhood, but ever since that first kiss, nothing has been the same.

He gently takes the key from my hand and inserts it into the lock. With a twist, he opens my door. "Get cleaned up, baby, and knock on my door when you're ready."

My heart thuds in my chest. Ready? Ready for what?

"Okay," I mumble and close the door behind me. I take an extra cold shower to get my head back in the game.

But can I even reason with a run-away heart? I have to try. A world like mine requires eyes wide open.

Still shivering, I blow dry my hair. Blonde roots form a stark contrast to the black dyed tresses. Talk about uneven.

I press fingers against my cheeks, wondering how long Patrick's implants will take to fade. What had he said, six months? I never thought I'd miss my baby face, but I hate my enhanced facial features. Or maybe I just hate anything fake.

"You're such a hypocrite, Portia." I scold my reflection in the mirror. I've lied to Luther too many times in the past. If I can't be honest with him, what's the point of a relationship?

I comb my layers into place and don a clean pair of sweatpants and an over-sized sweatshirt that a former candidate left behind. A dumpy look seems like a smart safeguard tonight.

Luther answers the door with damp hair and a jagged grin. My insides flip. No fair. I'm dressed for comfort, and his fitted black shirt and military-cut pants suggest something completely different.

I stuff my free hand in my bulky front pocket and nibble my bottom lip. "Uh, you wanted to talk?"

He doesn't invite me inside, and maybe that's a good thing. Instead, he steps into the hallway beside me and shuts his door. "Yeah, walk with me."

I frown at my sweats. "I'm not dressed for outdoors, and

frankly, I'm too tired for a walk. Maybe we should do this another time."

He takes my hand and tugs me down the hall. "There may not be another time for a while. I'm going to Cube 1776 tomorrow."

My eyes widen. He's going? Does he somehow know Deidra's and my plans?

He laughs and shakes his head. "Let me guess. You've got some crazy idea to go there yourself?"

"How did you…?"

"Because I know you, Cotton. When you're angry, you do impulsive things."

I jerk my hand away. "Do not."

He snatches it back. "Do too."

I hate that he's right, though I think Deidra has me beat. Her idea for me to fake orders seems like overstepping good sense, but I had agreed to help her travel to Cube 1776.

We reach the end of the hallway past the stairs and find a small candidate lounge, complete with couch, chairs and a wraparound window viewing the deserted courtyard. Could it be that less than a month ago, this place buzzed with life and activity? Now, there's an eerie stillness as if nature is holding its breath before a storm.

Luther drops down on the couch and pulls me next to him. "You might as well tell me what's going on in that head of yours. You know I've got your back."

I rub my temples which pound from lack of sleep. "I know, Luther. I was planning to tell you."

His warm eyes silently encourage me to go on.

"I told Deidra about Gath, and she wants me to take her to him—or at least help her get there."

The warmth vanishes, replaced by a warning look. "Gath is like a brother to me, and I know he wouldn't want you girls taking that risk."

"Maybe not," I retort, "but what do you think he would do if we were in his place?"

Luther opens his mouth to speak but swallows the words with a sigh. "That's different. We'd take care of you."

"And Deidra wants to take care of Gath. What's different about that?"

He stretches an arm around my shoulder. "It's our job to protect you, and right now, we can't do that if you keep running toward danger."

Part of me feels special, but he's still missing the point. "I don't remember putting out a help-wanted ad for a bodyguard." I poke him in the ribs.

He draws me to his chest and squeezes. "Oh well. I'm not letting go."

My pulse races at his closeness. "But I still need to breathe."

Luther relaxes his embrace, and I can see his face. There's a sudden change in mood, but I don't know why. Perhaps it's because the twilight has faded to black night. Perhaps it's because a new day will begin in a few hours, and neither of us knows what it will bring.

"I have something I want to ask you, Portia." Luther shifts to one side and reaches in his pocket.

I stop breathing. He only calls me Portia when he has something important to say, and what can he possibly have in his pocket?

And then it happens. He slides onto his knees next to the couch and takes my left hand.

My vision blurs as tears threaten to break free.

"Baby, you should keep breathing." He squeezes my hand and chuckles.

"But I'm…" My brain doesn't have a coherent thought. "I'm wearing sweatpants, an ugly sweatshirt, and not even mascara."

He laughs. "I don't care. You're always beautiful to me. Besides, I don't know when I'll get you all to myself again, so please, let me get through this?"

Is he really doing this? Now?

"Portia, I don't know when I started loving you. Maybe it was during one of our crazy three-legged races as kids or that night on the train when you nearly tasered me. I just know when I put you on that satellite train, a piece of me died and didn't come back to life until I found you at Alexis's house."

He gulps for air. Maybe I'm not the only one having a hard time breathing.

"We're in danger every day, and I can't promise what tomorrow will hold, but I don't want you going through this crazy life alone and wondering what my intentions are. Our world might never return to what we once called normal, but that doesn't mean we can't plan a life together."

Luther opens his palm to reveal a delicate sapphire ring. "This was my grandmother's, and I don't want any girl but you to wear it. I understand if you need time, and we can wait as long as you need. But I have to tell you what you mean to me."

He takes a deep breath and exhales. His dark eyes hold such hope and intensity. "Portia Abernathy, I love you. Will you marry me some day?"

My heart flip flops like a fish out of water. Salty tears trickle down my face

How long have I loved him? I've kept myself guarded for so long that I don't even know. Maybe I knew when he pushed me to run and train beyond my limits. He never gave up on me! Or maybe I knew that day when we both nearly lost our lives to the Trader attack in the library ruins, the same ruins where Gath now waits to learn his fate. Is it wrong to hope for happiness when other people I love don't know if they'll survive tomorrow?

Poor Luther will turn blue if I don't answer soon. I push aside all other thoughts and focus on the man who's offering me his love.

With a shy smile, I slide to the floor next to him. He doesn't seem to mind my salty kiss. "Yes, Luther." I brush his dark hair from his forehead and stare deep into his eyes, wide with joy and warm with passion.

His grin sends my head into a tailspin. He slips the ring onto my finger and wraps me in a dizzying embrace.

I gasp for breath and laugh. "Kiss me like that again, and you'll have to resuscitate me."

He traces a finger on my lips. "Mouth to mouth? I can handle that."

I laugh. "I can see that." Leaning into his strong arms, I caress his face. "But Luther? Since Dad's alive, you should talk to him, too, though I can't imagine him saying no. And I will need some time."

He rests his head against my own. "I'll ask him, and we'll wait until you're ready. Just don't wait for the world to be ready, because it never may be."

"I know," I whisper.

He tugs me closer, then scoops me into his arms.

"Where are we going?" I ask.

Luther retraces our steps down the hall. "You're going to bed. I know you're tired."

"What about tomorrow?" I yawn.

"Since I know you and Deidra will go anyway, you're coming with me. I'll make arrangements tonight and brief you in the morning."

I peck his cheek. "You're the best."

"Please promise to be good? I don't want anything happening to my fiancé." The care lines in his face seem to deepen. Am I responsible for those being there in the first place?

"I'll try." We reach our rooms, and he sets me down with a respectful kiss on the forehead.

"That's it?" I tease.

He chuckles, but his voice grows husky. "You need to go to bed, not take a cold shower."

If he only knew I'd already taken one.

"Right." I blush like a school girl. "Good night, Luther."

Kristen Hogrefe

CHAPTER 13
~ Luther ~

Monday, 6.29.2150
Crystal, Cube 1776

"Wake up, baby." Luther strokes Portia's tousled head, leaned against his shoulder. It feels good to have her by his side, his fiancé by his side.

She murmurs and rubs her eyes. "Are we there already?"

"Yeah, the train is slowing. We're here." He lets her slide off his shoulder so he can check the cracks in the train car that serve as peepholes. The horizon looks quiet, almost too quiet.

At least there are none of those drones Portia encountered on her last trip, but he'd made sure they had an enclosed cargo car for transport, just in case.

Careful not to trip over Deidra and her crutches, he picks his way toward the heavy door and yanks against it, giving him enough room to stand in the gap. The late morning sky hangs low with overcast clouds, threatening rain.

The cracked wood of the old platform blurs at his feet. He doesn't expect Red or anyone else to greet them, given the circumstances, but still, he'd prefer a larger group, especially with Deidra on crutches.

"Time to go, girls." Luther swings Portia's backpack and his own across one shoulder and his rifle across the other. She grabs the second rifle, along with the supply pack Lydia helped Deidra pack for Gath. It's almost half her size. His girl is a tough little thing.

And she's fiercely stubborn. He had to make her swear she would stay with Red when he takes Deidra to the ruins. After all, there's no point exposing all of them to this freak strain. She had agreed, though reluctantly.

He still has to find a way to tell her about Darius's assignment, what her brother had dubbed Operation Orvieto. Though Darius may not want him to tell her, Luther is done with deception. He plans to marry this girl, and he can't be keeping secrets from her.

But will she forgive him for leaving her behind and taking her father? Abram has to go—he's the sub's captain—but so far, he hasn't had the heart to tell his sleepy girl he has to leave her again soon. He'll have to find a way before this day ends.

"Is everything okay?" Portia jumps out the train behind him. She's pulled her shoulder-length skunk-blonde hair into a pony tail. Osborne's black dye is growing out, and her whitish blonde roots are reclaiming ground. It's a comical style, but she somehow makes it look cute.

He gives her pony tail a playful flip. "Yeah, I'll just be glad once we get to Red's place."

Behind them, Deidra digs her crutches into the dirt with a determined grunt. "Don't worry. I'm not going to slow you down."

"You're like a crazy biped on those things." Portia laughs. "I can tell you've been practicing."

Luther offers a smile he hopes looks more confident than he

feels. "Impressive, but the ruins are a long hike on foot." How can he warn her that attempting it on crutches will take twice as long? Does he have the time to take Deidra and still leave for Orvieto on Darius's timetable?

They walk on in silence. At least they respect that danger can lurk unseen. If only they could understand that keeping girls like them safe makes guys like him and Gath lose sleep at night.

With a sigh of relief, Luther pops open the door to Red's hostel so Deidra can crutch through. Portia seems content to wait behind her until she sees someone inside.

Her eyes light up, and she darts around Deidra, nearly toppling her over. "Dad!"

Luther flexes his shoulders where the straps dig in, but their discomfort is none like the one building in his chest. In theory, asking Abram for his blessing shouldn't worry him.

But he hadn't planned to see him at Red's, and there's something about the man that's much more intimidating in person.

Deidra catches her balance and clears the doorway. Her tight lips and pale face betray the fatigue she pretends isn't there. She collapses onto a chair and rubs her arms.

She's not kidding anyone. There's no way she'll have enough energy for the ruins today, and he'll have to convince her to be reasonable.

His focus shifts to the tangled hug Portia is giving her dad. "Didn't expect to see my baby girl back this soon." The giant of a man ruffles her hair and tugs her close.

Luther's chest tightens. Portia will always be her dad's baby girl. Will Abram agree to trust her to him?

As if reading his thoughts, Abram glances to him. "Come on

in, son. Do I have you to thank for keeping an eye on my daughter?"

Red appears behind him, carrying a pot of coffee. The hostel owner motions toward the table. "Watching out for your girl isn't a one-man job, Abram. She could use a whole army."

Portia crosses her arms. "Now that's not fair."

He sets down the coffee and holds up his hands, but there's a glimmer in his eye. "Your dad's here now, kid. I wipe my hands of you."

"Now, Red…" Portia trails him to the kitchen, arguing the whole way. Red must still be sore she nearly got herself killed on his watch, but Luther doesn't doubt she'll break down his barriers. Red has always had a soft spot for Portia.

Luther grunts. At least she's wearing his ring now. Or is she? He hadn't noticed it when they left the train, but he had been focused on making sure they didn't have any unwanted company.

He has to get his head back in the game. "It's good to see you, Abram. This is Deidra, Gath's…"

"Girlfriend," Deidra finishes.

Abram blinks but recovers quickly. "Gath has always been a private person, so I guess I shouldn't be surprised he never told me about his girl. It's nice to meet you. I'm Portia's dad, but you can call me Abram."

Deidra smiles and crutches toward the table. "Don't worry about it. Gath and I both thought the other was dead for years. I don't aim to lose him again."

Red and Portia reappear carrying steaming bowls of baked beans. "Glad to see we arrived in time for lunch." She smirks at Red. Two minutes in the kitchen apparently broke his defenses.

The hair on Luther's neck prickles. Jealousy isn't a natural feeling for him. Surely, he's being too sensitive.

"Perfect." Red winks. "Guess who gets KP duty."

Portia laughs but stops short. "What is it, Luther?"

He drops his gaze and slides onto the bench seat next to her. "Nothing, Cotton. Let's eat."

She slips her hand into his as Abram helps Deidra with her crutches. Luther squeezes back and feels her smooth fingers. No ring.

He leans down to whisper. "Is everything all right? What happened to your ring?"

She blushes and cuts her eyes toward her dad who's watching with a smirk on his face. But Luther doesn't care if he sees. The man has to know he's always loved his daughter.

Portia edges closer. "I tied it onto a cord around my neck. It's the closest thing to my heart, which belongs to you." She lowers her voice more. "I thought you might want to talk to Dad first before he sees what you've done." With that, she pecks his cheek and scoops a spoonful of beans into his bowl.

"Have you heard from Gath since he and the others left?" Deidra asks.

Red exchanges a look with Abram. "There's no Morse lines that way, so unfortunately, we haven't. But we sent enough supplies with them to last the week. And if anyone knows how to survive, it's Gath."

Deidra shifts in her seat and gives Red a glare that would make most grown men cringe. "He shouldn't have to worry about surviving right now. He's not on a satellite anymore."

Luther swallows his beans to keep from choking, while Red

clears his throat. "With all due respect, ma'am, the flu on that ship would kill hundreds, if not thousands, if it spread. There were only eight survivors on the ship we quarantined when Gath first boarded her. Now, there are two—and that's with the good food and herbal medicines we've been providing."

Beside him, Portia stirs her spoon in the bowl. Has she even taken a bite yet? "Do you think those two will survive?" Her lip quivers.

"We hope so," Abram says, "but the men seem to have given up, which isn't a good sign. The leader—the one Gath found first—told us to call him Deadman. I'm afraid they might both die before we can learn more about them."

Deidra's face flares, and she snatches one of her crutches where she had leaned it against the wall. "I didn't come here to talk about a hopeless cause. I came here to help Gath, nurse him if he needs it, and die with him if it comes to that."

Red and Abram seem frozen to their seats, unsure of how to handle this fireball of a woman they just met. Luther stands and strides toward her. "Deidra, I promised I would take you to him, and I will. But sit down. We don't have time for me to make a round trip with you today. And you can't go on your own. You can barely walk."

"Can't you spend the night there and return in the morning?" she challenges.

He takes a deep breath and returns the crutch to the wall. "Deidra, I love Gath like a brother, but I have other work to do. I can't do it if I expose myself to this virus. I'd have to remain in quarantine, too. Tomorrow, I will take you as far as the outskirts of the ruins, but you'll have to find Gath on your own from there.

I'll wait to leave until you signal me that you've found him."

Red passes Abram the waning bowl of beans. "He said that if we needed to find him that he would camp out in the first library building, the one you and Portia explored together."

Luther would never forget the place where the Trader had attacked him and Portia, though thankfully, she had been unharmed. If only he could say the same for himself. Gath had to carry him out and most of the way back to the hostel. He owed that man so much.

Deidra taps her fingers impatiently on the table. "But surely we don't have to wait until tomorrow…"

Beside him, Portia bristles. "Deidra, you've never crossed that territory. It's a breeding ground for starved mongrels, cut-throat traders, and the dregs of humanity. Luther returning alone at night is out of the question."

Deidra huffs and grabs her spoon. "Fine. We leave in the morning. But what other business is so important that you have to return right away?"

Luther glances at Abram and hesitates for a moment. He'd rather wait to talk to him in private about Darius's errand, but with the preparations to make for the journey, they'll need all the time they can get.

He pulls the folded orders from his jacket pocket and hands them to Abram. "Darius has a mission for the two of us, and it's time-sensitive."

Portia drops her spoon. "What are you talking about?" Her blue eyes accuse him for not telling her sooner.

"Cotton, I just received them myself." He places a hand on her arm. "I wasn't keeping secrets."

She frowns. "But where are you going?"

"A place called Orvieto, it seems." Abram's brows furrow as he reads his son's message. "It's in the Mediterranean? What's this all about?"

Portia's face lights up. "So Darius did change his mind about allies! But why is he sending you and not Alexis or me?"

Red shakes his spoon at her. "No one in his right mind would let you out of his sight."

Deidra points at Red. "Oh yeah? Well, from the way I see things, you all let her out of your sight for four months, and she survived."

Luther holds up a hand. "Let's back up. Darius didn't agree to form an alliance with Orvieto, and he didn't ask me to negotiate anything. He's just asking for Abram and me to get their modem so that we can communicate."

Portia crosses her arms. "But why you? I could go with Dad, and you could stay here, take Deidra to Gath, and then do all the other important things Darius doesn't tell the rest of us about."

That spark in her eye sends his pulse racing. His fiancé traveling across the Atlantic is the last thing he wants.

He reaches for her hand, but she pulls away. "Baby, it's too dangerous." Surely, she has to understand that.

Deidra scoffs. "You men. Too dangerous? She lived in Warren for three months and served as Osborne's runner after that. I'm not sure how a submarine pleasure cruise can possibly be more dangerous."

Abram arches an eyebrow at Deidra and rubs his bristled chin. "International waters are dangerous. We never know who we'll meet and how friendly they'll be. There's no guarantee we'll come back."

Portia jumps to her feet and shoves the bench away. "Then you're not leaving me behind. I lost you once, and I'm not losing you again."

"Cotton…" Luther reaches for her. Doesn't she get that he feels the same way about her?

She bites her lip and glances at him with a look that could make a stone bleed. "Excuse me." She darts toward the stairs.

With a groan, he rises to follow her, but Abram mirrors his move. "Let her go, Luther."

His chest tightens. Let her go as in up the stairs, or let her go as in to Orvieto?

"She's right," Abram continues. "Darius did her wrong in not telling her about me, and she can do as fine a job as you in collecting the equipment Darius wants. She seems to know as much about Orvieto as you do anyway."

No, this can't be happening. Luther takes a deep breath to steady his soaring pulse. "But, sir, Darius wants me to go."

"Darius may be the leader of our Brotherhood, and though I take orders from him, same as you, I'm still his dad. If I go on this trip, I take my girl with me. Besides, Portia's right. You're needed here."

His reply chokes in his throat. He can't lose Cotton again. He just got her back.

Luther swallows hard. "But, sir…"

Abram crosses his arms. "Luther, I know you love her. And I'll bring her back. But you've got to let her go."

He'll bring her back. But a moment ago, Abram said there was no guarantee any of them would return.

And hadn't Darius made a similar promise when Portia landed in that forsaken mining camp? Instead, she had rotted for three months before they could convince a black-market thug to smuggle her out. And then Osborne placed those awful conditions on her.

But Abram is her father. Surely, he can trust the man.

Luther slowly nods. "All right. She goes."

But somehow, the concession feels like the worst decision of his life.

CHAPTER 14
~ Portia ~

Monday, 6.29.2150
Crystal, Cube 1776

I stare at the splotchy stain on the ceiling as I have for most of the night and finger the ring on my neck. Who am I supposed to be? Dad's little girl or Luther's fiancé?

Why can't I be both, and why can't life be less complicated?

I roll to my side and squeeze my eyes shut. I did a rotten job in both roles yesterday. Luther had insisted on going to the submarine with Dad, Red, and me. We'd spent most of the afternoon loading supplies, and then the rest of the evening packing the sack Luther would carry for Deidra's trip to the ruins. All the activity helped check my busy, frustrating thoughts. Why should Darius confide in Luther and not me?

My brother will be angry enough when he finds out I'm going in Luther's stead, but he'll have to answer to Dad. That is, assuming we both return.

Poor Luther. No wonder he stares at me with such anxious eyes.

I fling off the blanket and shove my arms in my jacket. What's the point of sleeping? Dawn can only be an hour away, and all of us part ways after breakfast.

Beside me, Deidra's deep breathing cautions me to be quiet. I'm both amazed and envious she can sleep anytime, anywhere.

I reach for the door handle but hesitate as a dozen boots scrape the hallway floor. Red still has a hostel to run.

Muffled voices mutter outside my door, and a deep voice retorts. I grip the handle harder. Luther?

Cracking open the door, I squint into the dark and find his dark silhouette leaned up against the frame. "What are you doing here?" I whisper.

He jumps to his feet and searches my face with bloodshot eyes. "What am I doing here? This hostel is full of too many bad memories and too many men I don't know."

Right, the last time we'd been here together was as part of Gath's group of candidates. We'd been hunted by a Trader who had almost given Luther a concussion.

I close the door and slip my hand into his. "Let's not waste this moment on the past."

He squeezes back and tugs me with him to the floor. "All the workers are downstairs, so right here's the quietest spot we'll find."

A hardwood floor in a hallway isn't my definition of private, but I don't argue. I press my head against his shoulder and wrap my arm around his. "I'm sorry things haven't worked out the way you wanted, but I will come back. The trip will be so short that you won't have time to miss me."

He grunts. "I doubt that but thanks for the optimism."

"Did you talk to Dad?"

Luther rests his head on mine. "Yeah."

I wait for him to continue. Had Dad given him a hard time?

"He gave me his blessing but..." Luther's voice sinks. "He said now is not the time to think about starting a life together. He wants us to wait until things settle down and you get a little older."

I bristle. "Settle down? We don't have any idea when or if our lives will return to normal. And as far as age, I'm twenty and an old one at that. I've seen more in my twenty years than some people from my dad's generation saw in a lifetime."

"He just wants us to wait and be sure we're ready." There's a hesitation in Luther's voice. Is he having second thoughts about asking me?

"You don't think..." I try to focus my thoughts. "You think maybe I'm not..."

"Oh, Cotton, you're the only girl for me." Luther brushes his lips on my forehead.

I nuzzle deeper into his chest, feeling the weight of sleep that refused to come all night. "I'm glad that's settled." My whisper ends with a long yawn.

Sometimes, quiet company speaks the loudest.

"Oh, my!" Deidra nearly trips over us, waking us both an hour later.

"What on earth..." She slams her crutch against the floor, missing us by inches. "I wondered where you went."

"Couldn't sleep." I accept Luther's hand as he pulls me to my feet.

Deidra shrugs her pack to adjust it on her back and nods toward the stairs. "See you at breakfast."

Downstairs, a door slams against the frame, and wood splinters. Luther gives me a worried look and bolts down the steps, with Deidra crutching close behind.

After retrieving my pack from the room, I take the stairs by two to join them. The shouting downstairs makes my blood rush hot. Who is causing all the ruckus?

I glimpse a patch of cropped black hair, but Red's towering form blocks the man from view. Red raises his voice and points at the gouge in the wall where the door slammed.

"Sorry, man, but it's urgent. Luther needs to come with me." The man's voice scratches against a dry throat.

"Harley?" I call from the base of the stairs. The ex-Gage who fought with me on that drone-infested train ride jerks his head my way.

"What are you doing here?" We blurt the question in unison.

A shadow crosses his eyes as he glances from Red, to Luther, to me. "I thought you were in Crystal? Darius said he sent Luther…"

"Long story," Luther cuts him off and steps next to me.

"Doesn't matter," Harley mumbles. "Darius will want you both back pronto."

"What are you saying?" Luther demands. "I've got work to do."

Harley crosses his arms. "Orvieto is off. Crystal just took a severe hit from a drone swarm."

"Drone swarm?" I repeat. "You mean like the heat-tracking ones that dropped those messages?"

Harley's face contorts to an angry glower. "Yes, same concept, only these didn't drop messages."

My breath catches in my throat.

"Think fire bombs," Harley finishes. "At least half of the

Crystal Globe University is smoldering right now, including the dormitories, hospital, and library."

"No!" Deidra pales. "All those patients…"

I squeeze her shoulder. She could have been a casualty herself if she hadn't stubbornly insisted on finding Gath.

And what of the library? I can just hope the damage didn't reach the archives and portal room. It's our link to the outside world, whose help we desperately need, whether Darius thinks so or not.

"We got out as many patients and Healers as we could," Harley says, "but we've got to organize a defensive before the next round strikes, which could be any moment. And if they hit the tracks, we're stranded."

Deidra squeezes me and lifts her chin toward Luther. "You need to go. I'll get to Gath on my own."

Luther shakes his head. "You don't know the way. It's too dangerous."

"I'll take her." Red yanks off his splotchy apron.

"No, Red." Luther's voice turns steely. "I promised."

Red jabs a finger into Luther's chest. "Listen, Darius asked for you, so that means he needs you. Truth is, he needs Gath, too."

Deidra nods. "Gath knows how to run a defense and offense at the same time. But we've got to make sure he stays alive first."

"We'll work out a system so you and Gath can communicate with me," Red says. "Giving him something to work toward will keep his mind in the game and also keep his spirits up."

Red gives Deidra a small smile. "I'm sure having you there will take care of the rest."

Luther slaps Red's shoulder. "Thanks, man. I owe you. If

there's anything I can do to help from Crystal, send a wire."

Harley clears his throat and turns to Luther. "I hate to rush goodbyes, but we need to head back as soon as I shovel some of that breakfast in my stomach."

Red motions toward the kitchen. "Help me finish, and you can have first dibs."

No sooner does Harley disappear with Red than someone else gives the front door handle a hard yank. Dad strides inside, his face half hidden by a gray wool beanie cap and another day's growth of beard.

He gives Luther a terse smile and focuses on me. "You ready, sweetheart?"

My mouth pops open, but no words come out. Can I still go with him? But then, Harley will know I've ignored Darius's wishes. If my brother doesn't want Luther going to Orvieto, he certainly won't want me going.

"She's ready." Luther's words knock the wind from my chest. I gape at him. He still wants me to go?

"But you have to hurry. Darius has technically called off the Orvieto mission, because Felix has launched his first attack against Crystal." He lowers his voice and motions toward the kitchen. "His messenger is with Red now. I'll stall and then say you already left."

"You think we should still go?" I whisper.

"More than ever." Luther pulls me to his side. The action contradicts his words but makes clear how he feels. "Darius is stuck in reactive mode. If there's a chance we can get outside help, we need it."

I glance at Dad, wondering whose side he'll take. He frowns. "This is tricky business. Darius can still communicate with the

Avalon. He'll just tell us to turn around. Besides, if Felix has woken up, you're going to need my submarine's help to monitor coastal defense."

"It's your call, sir, but I think Orvieto is still more important. And I have a plan that might keep Felix distracted till you return."

Goosebumps crawl up my arm. How could Luther draw Felix's attention without putting himself in the line of fire?

"It's my son who has me more worried," Abram says. "Agree with him or not, he's our leader."

"I agree," Luther says, "but he sent me to do this mission. I'm delegating it to you and Portia. We always knew Felix would strike, but there's more urgency for this mission now than before."

Abram rubs his jaw. "Okay, we'll leave. But if Darius tells us to come home, I'm turning around."

"Deal." Luther turns his eyes on me, and for a moment, I forget about the others in the room. "I know you can do this. Just take care of yourself, Cotton, and promise to come back. Otherwise, I'll hate myself for sending you."

I kiss him full on the mouth. I don't care Dad's watching. "I will."

Luther releases me, and I give Deidra a quick hug while Dad shakes Luther's hand. Then, he spreads a long arm around my shoulder. "Let's go, sweetheart. We've got a sub to catch."

"Dad?" I follow him down a narrow ladder leading inside the submarine and notice all the details as if for the first time.

But then, I wasn't exactly paying attention the last time I entered Avalon.

"Yes?" He maneuvers through the compact spaces with surprising agility. Since he apparently redesigned the gutted interior, he could probably make his way around blindfolded.

"How long will it take to cross the ocean?"

"Depends on several factors," Dad said. "But my estimate is four-to-five days."

We continue to climb down the metal ladder which he calls part of the bridge access and land in the communications room. I recognize none of the men there.

"Operation Orvieto is a go," Dad nods to one man. "Prepare for departure." He turns to me. "I'm going to show you my cabin, where you'll be staying."

"What about you?" I ask, following him through the maze-like halls.

He grins. "There are plenty of bunks with the crew."

Dad pops open the door to the same small room where Cob placed me before. I had assumed it was one of many, not the captain's quarters.

"How many crew are there anyway?" I set down my pack and take in the small room, complete with twin bed, chair, and a small stand.

Dad rubs his jaw. "There's fifty of us, and most are satellite survivors. If they don't seem especially friendly, cut them some slack."

"I can appreciate that," I say. "But fifty? Where are they all hiding?"

The rumble that emerges from my dad's throat makes me

blush at my ignorance. "It's okay, sweetheart. I'll get you a tour at some point, and you'll see how many parts and roles there are. And consider, someone always has to be on shift. But now, I need to go to the control room."

"Can I come with you?" The prospect of being left alone in this cramped room makes me cringe.

He shakes his head. "Stay here until we're submerged and on our way. You don't have sea legs, and depending on the wave action, it's a bumpy ride at the surface."

I fall onto the creaky bed. "Yes, sir."

Dad laughs. "Don't worry. Once we're underway, Avalon is as stable as a house." He crouches to exit the door and closes it behind him.

I fold the flat pillow in half to prop up my head and rummage in my pack for the only book I have—the Bible from the archives. Might as well try to make something useful of this confinement.

Flipping to the index, I search for the word "plague" and hope to find the one that relates to Pharaoh. I don't have to look far. The second book called Exodus recounts a showdown between a man named Moses and Pharaoh, the king of Egypt. I skim the chapters and then go back slowly, trying to figure out the plot.

So that's it. Moses was from a country called Israel and God's messenger to Pharaoh, who had enslaved his people. Moses told Pharaoh to let the people go, and Pharaoh stubbornly refused.

And that's when the plagues started. I snatch a notepad on the stand and start a list as I read through the crazy story.

1. Water changed to blood
2. Frog invasion

3. Gnat infestation

4. Flies everywhere

5. Livestock dying

6. Boils on the people

7. Hail storm

8. Locust swarms

9. Darkness over the land

10. Death of the firstborn

My eyes stop on that last word. It's the name of the strain Felix is threatening to use against us.

But the firstborn deaths were the last plague. The drone message had said Felix would defeat the ASU with only two. If these exploding drone bombs are the first, then is this deadly virus next?

My stomach tightens as the room sways, and I clutch the Bible tighter. What Red Sea can save us from Felix's schemes?

I scan ahead as the story continues to unfold. Pharaoh finally relented and let Israel go, only to change his mind and pursue after them. The Israelites panicked, because they appeared trapped between the Egyptian army and the Red Sea.

Then their leader Moses said something that sends chills up my spine. *Fear ye not, stand still, and see the salvation of the Lord.*[ii]

What salvation indeed! God parted the Red Sea so that Israel walked through on dry ground, and when Pharaoh's army attempted to follow, the waters returned and covered them.

Is this trip across the Atlantic our Red Sea crossing? Will God provide the help we need through the Orvieto Confederation?

The submarine shifts, and I grip the side of the bed. I can only hope we'll get to Orvieto and back in one piece before Felix destroys what's left of our country.

Kristen Hogrefe

CHAPTER 15

~ Luther ~

Monday, 6.29.2150
Crystal

Luther mentally measures the gnarly crack that runs the length of the portal wall. If it were any wider, he might worry about the room's integrity.

But right now, cracked walls and the ruins of the library's main floors seem trivial compared to the expression Darius wears.

"Call them back!" He sputters at last. "I can't believe you sent my sister and Dad after I told you to return."

Luther takes another breath to control his rising heart rate. "I thought we had agreed Orvieto was important? Now more than ever, we need allies."

Darius glares at him. "We need a defense, and you just sent our only operational submarine across the Atlantic."

"They'll be back soon enough." Luther keeps his voice level. "And meanwhile, I have a plan for buying us some time."

Though his face remains red, Darius doesn't respond. Good. Maybe he's finally listening.

Luther picks a marker off the podium and scrawls a simple map on the dry erase board. His train tracks look more like fence posts, but they convey the idea and help him focus on something other than Darius's deepening scowl. "Contact Felix and request a ceasefire for a diplomatic meeting. I'll take the train as far north as I can and request an escort to Deadwood."

"Out of the question." Darius grabs his own marker and crosses an X through the train track. "If you go to Deadwood, you'll never come back, and I can't afford to lose a good man on a pointless errand. We've already talked about this."

"But I worked with Felix, remember?" Luther presses. "He'll expect us to contact him after his fire bombs. A logical request would be to try diplomacy, and the rules of war require—"

"There are no rules in war." Darius cuts him off. "Felix won't play fair, and you'll waltz right into his hands."

Luther ignores him. "My brother is there, too, and perhaps even an adviser to Felix. Maybe I can reason with Jotham."

Darius scratches the name Jotham on the board and then draws a slash through it. "You can't reason with a man like him. Or have you forgotten he betrayed me—his best friend—for a chance at the Dome?"

"Blood is thicker than water," Luther mutters. "My brother may be a scoundrel, but he's still my brother."

"I wish I could believe you, but war divides families."

"Look, we need time." Luther taps the hard end of the marker on the board for emphasis. "I understand you can't protect me, but I still need to go. Even if Abram and Portia weren't on their way to Orvieto, you need time to regroup what men we have and plan an offensive. And since I haven't heard any updates about your Firstborn program, I'm guessing Lydia still needs time, too. Unless you have a better plan, my visit to Deadwood makes the most sense."

Luther scrawls a stick-figure sub in the Atlantic and writes the words *Orvieto* and *allies* on the other side of the board.

Darius sighs. "You're right about one thing: We do need time. But we're very close to developing the strain."

Luther draws and circles two more words: *Firstborn* and *offense*. "Then my trip to Deadwood helps us on three fronts: the Orvieto one, the virus program, and the obvious military one."

Darius caps his marker and drops it on the ledge. "Okay, but I need you to write a letter first."

"A letter?" Luther frowns.

"A letter to my sister," Darius says. "If you don't come back, she's got to know this was your hair-brained idea and not mine. The last thing I need is to give her another reason to hate me."

Luther grips the marker in his hand. "I'll come back."

"That's what everyone says."

Someone bangs on the door, and Darius spins toward it. Luther pulls out his 9 mm handgun and motions to Darius that he'll cover him. Few people know about the portal, so chances are the visitor is one of their team.

But they can't afford to assume anything.

Darius cracks open the door and then relaxes, pulling it wider. "Harley. What's going on?"

"There's another drone swarm." The ex-Gage pants out the words. "It will be here in ten minutes max."

Darius swears. "Shoot them down. We can't let them strike here again."

"Already on it, sir. But there are so many…"

"I'll come with you." Darius turns to Luther. "Contact the

Deadwood Translator and get Felix on the line. Ask for a ceasefire. We need time."

Luther nods, and Darius races after Harley up the stairwell. Luther doesn't bother to shut the door but runs toward the interface, switching it on. But can he reach Felix in time to call off this strike? And will Felix even listen to him?

Bluffing to Darius to get to Deadwood is one thing. Getting Felix to buy into the plan is another.

"Come on," he mutters as the Translator warms up. He's never actually programmed one of these, but he's watched enough people operate one. Surely, it can't be hard.

At least the authorization and access codes pre-populate. Next, he enters the eight-digit date code for today and glances at his watch to confirm the exact time. The last thing he needs is to accidentally perform a Simulation back in time instead of a real-time Translation.

Then, he scans the map grid for corresponding receivers in the Black Tundra.

Oh, no. There are two. And both have cloaked identifiers. One must be the Deadwood fortress, and the other might be the Gage training headquarters.

He doesn't know the geography of the northern wasteland. However, his gut suggests Deadwood will be closer to the coast to accept international vessels.

Hesitating a moment, he selects the coastal receiver and holds his breath. Perhaps no one will answer.

The Translator hums while attempting the connection, and the screen turns from dull gray to an opaque blue.

A man's silhouette slowly comes into focus. Luther

straightens. Where will he even begin?

The fuzzy form takes on dimensions. Of all the man's features, his narrow shoulders, clear-cut jaw, and taunting black eyes imprint the most in his mind.

Maybe because they belonged to the only man who could get away with bullying him in his boyhood. And though Luther is now twice his size, the man still seems to hold leverage over him.

"Hello, brother. Somehow, I thought it might be you." Jotham's voice rakes with sarcasm.

Luther tightens his jaw. No, surely there's someone else he can reason with other than his older brother. Jotham will never…

"Is your wanna-be band of rebels having a rough day?" His lips curl into a sneer. "Don't worry. We're sending some fanfare to help spice up the place."

"Call off the drones." Luther drops his voice an octave. "I want a conference with Felix."

Jotham chokes on his laughter. "You want a conference? Little brother, haven't you learned that you don't get to call the shots unless you're winning the round?"

Luther counts to ten in his head. He has to get an audience with Felix. "I get that you're the lucky underling assigned to monitor the Deadwood Translator, but I bet that means you're supposed to report Translations, not hold conference with the callers. I'll wait to say anything more until you do your job and put Felix on the session."

He pauses and mimics Jotham's condescending smile, the one his brother had mastered in his teenage years. "Remember, I worked with Felix. He'll be interested in what I have to say."

Jotham narrows his eyes. "You can tell me anything you plan

to tell him. I'll decide if it's worth Felix's time and attention."

Luther crosses his arms and holds his breath. Will his bluff work?

"We're done here," Jotham says.

For a moment, panic rises in Luther's throat. He has to raise the stakes and buy more time. He has to get through to Felix.

No, he has to hold his ground. He has to play like Jotham.

Luther stares hard at his brother and relaxes his arms. "Perfect. If Felix won't talk to me, I won't help him get what he wants."

A flicker of hesitation crosses Jotham's face. "And what is that, little brother?"

"Just give him my message." Luther disconnects the session, and the screen fades back to gray.

He swipes beads of perspiration off his forehead. Talking with Jotham is more stressful than asking Portia's father for permission to marry her. And that man knows how to interrogate.

Luther's thoughts drift Portia's direction, but he reigns them in. Now isn't time to daydream. She has a job to do, and so does he.

Will his brother deliver the message? Will Felix do what he asked?

He stares at the Translator. Any moment, the invitation to Translate could come through from Deadwood.

But how long can he play the bluff? He has no idea how to get Felix what he wants, but he has to make the Friend think he does. He has to make him believe the Brotherhood is willing to cooperate on certain terms.

Darius would be furious if he knew what he was considering, but diplomacy has saved countries before.

Can it save the ASU now?

The screen hums. That must be Felix.

Now is his chance to find out.

The train station comes into view, and Luther stuffs a clammy hand into his coat pocket while Darius sidesteps another mud puddle. The early afternoon sky looks more like evening with its dreary rainclouds, which have momentarily relented.

"Here's the letter you asked for." He hands it to Darius, who had insisted on seeing him off.

"I hope you know what you're doing." Darius takes the envelope and stuffs it into his own coat. "And I hope I'm not making a terrible mistake in letting you go."

"It's my choice." Luther glances sideways at him. Even so, he can't shake the uneasiness that weighs down his spirit like a load of bricks.

As they reach the Crystal platform, he sets down his pack in front of the stationmaster's booth. "That cargo train ready to head north?" he asks.

The man stamps his ticket. "It's leaving in half an hour, just like I told your friend earlier. I'm afraid that it can only take you to the Jacinth outpost. No trains dare venture into Amethyst with the way things are these days."

Luther nods. Jacinth is the square to the south of Amethyst, the northernmost one where only fur traders and trappers work. The Black Tundra covers all the surrounding terrain, too frigid for citizens to live. That's why the CGA had chosen it for its Wasp training center. Only the cruelest can survive that climate.

It also made a perfect location for the Deadwood fortress, a secretive compound whose purpose had been hearsay. Some said it was a laboratory. Others said it was an impenetrable retreat.

Either way, Luther is about to find out.

He offers his thanks to the stationmaster and turns to Darius. His friend looks more like a kid caught with his hand in the candy jar than the confident leader the ASU needs.

"Thanks for buying us some time," Darius mutters. "I owe you."

"You owe me nothing." Luther shrugs his pack on.

"You convinced Felix to call back those drones. There's no way we could have shot the whole swarm down in time."

"I bluffed, but I'm glad it worked." Luther extends a hand to his childhood friend. "Listen, if for some reason I don't come back..."

"Hey now, none of that talk!" Darius slaps him on the shoulder.

Luther snorts. "I know, but in all seriousness, anything can happen. Just make sure Portia gets that letter, either way. If everything goes well, though, I'll be back before she has a chance to miss me."

"I like the sound of that plan." Darius grins. "See you soon, brother."

The word twists his gut. In many ways, Darius has been the brother he'd always wanted, the brother he wished Jotham could be.

But he's a fool to think Jotham will ever change. No, this

mission isn't about Jotham. It's about stalling for time and hopefully, rescuing Dad.

Although Dad's always favored his older brother, his father is a good man. Whatever twisted logic Jotham used to convince him to leave Mom and join Felix, Luther has to find a way to undo it.

He swings himself through an open cargo car and waves at Darius. His friend waves back. He should feel guilty for deceiving Darius about his true motivation to travel to Deadwood, but he doesn't.

After all, he's helping the Brotherhood at the same time. If he can rescue his dad, one of the ASU's most gifted Mavens, Lydia might get the extra help they need to finish their work on that strain.

It's a win-win all around. That is, as long as he succeeds.

Kristen Hogrefe

CHAPTER 16
~ Portia ~

Monday, 6.29.2150
Atlantic Ocean

The rolling sensation has stopped, maybe it had a long time ago, but my stomach only now registers stability. I swing a cautious leg over the side of the bed and hope Dad's right that most of the trip will feel as solid as dry ground.

Someone raps on the door. There's something impatient about it that doesn't fit Dad's character.

I press a cautious foot to the floor. "Come in."

The door swings open, and a thick, swarthy man fills most of the doorway. He ducks his head inside. He's wearing a beanie cap, but his sun-bleached hair pokes out from underneath.

"Rig!" I jump to my feet. The last time I had seen him was the day I broke him out of Warren.

The former pipeliner's grin spreads, revealing crooked teeth. "Well, look who it is! Hey, Waspy, I hear you don't have any sea legs."

I grimace. "Ugh, don't call me that. I hated having to impersonate a Wasp."

He snorts. "You made your bed with one. I thought you might

like the title."

I frown, annoyed he thinks my relationship with Gath was something more than a friend. But Rig had hated Gath then and only grudgingly gave up his vendetta. Surely Darius helped set the record straight that Gath had changed?

I shove those thoughts aside. "What are you doing here?"

"It takes a lot of men to operate one of these girls." He pats the wall. "I helped build them for the CGA in Baytown. I was on assignment for Osborne when I heard you all pulled off the Warren stunt. I dropped his dirty work and ran to see how I could help. When I overheard another fella saying Abe needed crew for a classified submarine project, I volunteered. And since he knew me from Baytown, he agreed to let me on board."

Abe. It still sounds strange to hear my brother referred to by his assumed satellite name.

There's an awkward silence. Why is he here? Had Dad sent him? I clear my throat. "Well, it's good you know what you're doing. I don't know anything about subs."

He smirks. "So I hear. You ready for a tour, Legs?"

I kink an eyebrow at him. "Seriously? Don't call me that."

Rig rubs his stubbled chin and grins. "Sheesh, you're sensitive. What do I call you then?"

I tilt my chin, "Portia—It's my real name." After using more aliases than I can remember during the last few months, I'm more than ready to just be me.

"Portia?" he repeats. "How do you even spell that?"

I roll my eyes. "P-O-R-T-I-A."

"Huh, I like Legs better."

"Oh yeah?" I cross my arms. "How do you think Abram would

like you calling his daughter Legs?"

His eyes widen. "Wait, you're Abernathy's girl?"

I smirk. "Yeah, did Dad leave off that part?"

Rig lets out a low whistle. "He just told me to let you out of his cabin, to tell you that you're free to walk about now. I guessed he must have found himself a girl, so I planned to make a good impression... a guy needs something pretty to look at. Anyway, he was busy working in the comm center, so I volunteered."

"Very chivalrous of you." I make a mock bow. "But yes, I'm his daughter. You can call me Portia from here on out."

"Portia," he mumbles. "Well, since you're here, and I'm here, let's make the best of it. C'mon. I'll show you around."

I follow him out the door to the right and recognize the communications room Dad led me through when I first came on board.

He's leaning over one of the crew's shoulders and smiles at me when we enter. "Doing okay, sweetheart?"

"Fine," I say. "Rig here has volunteered to show me the ropes, if that's okay with you."

Dad gives Rig a hard stare. "Do you have time for that before your shift?"

Rig straightens. "Yes, sir. I'll show her the galley, bathrooms, and medical berth. Shouldn't take long."

"Sounds good," Dad says. "But add one final stop. Show her the maintenance workshop, too—or what used to be the maintenance workshop."

Rig nods. "I can show her that first if you'd like since it's around the corner."

Dad shakes his head. "No, save it for last." He turns to wink at me. "I think you'll like what I've done with the space."

My curiosity peaks. "I'm sure I will."

Rig leads the way from the comm room to what he calls the ladder, a narrow set of stairs running to the deck below. "This way to the galley, sweetheart."

I stop in my tracks. "Only my dad gets to call me sweetheart."

The no-nonsense mask he donned for my father has completely disappeared. "Only your dad, huh? I figured for sure Legs would have a boyfriend. What about…"

"First, don't call me Legs again," I cut him off. "Second, Gath and I are best friends, nothing more. And third, I do have a fiancé, and he can call me whatever he wants. But you're not him, so it's still Portia. Are we clear? I'd like for us to be friends, but I'm pretty sure I can manage a self-guided tour and then let the captain know all the names you've been calling me."

Rig's face flushes. "Yes, ma'am. Truce?" He holds out a hand.

I give it a hard shake. "Truce. Now lead on."

He introduces me to the chef in the galley and then takes me to the mess hall where several crew members play cards or watch a screen on the wall. It's smaller than the Simulation and Translation screens I'm used to seeing, but it appears to be the same concept.

Only, there's a moving picture on it, like nothing I've ever seen. A muscular man in a crazy outfit fights what I can only guess to be some kind of alien army. If this is a Simulation to some place in the past…

Rig laughs at my expression. "What? You've never seen a television before?"

"No, what is it? And what's going on? Who are those

people—or things?"

"It's playing a movie, what people used to watch for entertainment in the old days."

"Entertainment?" I gasp. "But they're killing each other."

He laughs. "It's all fake. These superhero stories are always about crazy people saving the world from monsters or aliens. Don't worry. The good guys win—most of the time."

I wince as the violent scene continues. "I don't understand."

"Me neither, but they sure are fun to watch—better than arm wrestling or boxing matches anyway." Rig waves at another member and then turns his attention back to me. "I stumbled upon the cases when I was refurbishing the sub. It took me a while to figure out what they were for, but when I did, I was stoked. I've got all the guys hooked."

I give Rig a skeptical look but don't say anything else. There are some parts to the past civilization I don't understand. I just can't picture George Washington watching something like that. Maybe this technology came after his time.

"The head is this way." Rig pauses in the hallway outside the door. "Now, listen, I know you're the captain's daughter, so maybe you get some special privileges, but here's how bathrooms work on a sub. Showers are 3-5 minutes max, because we've got to cycle out the dirty water for clean."

"Not a problem," I say. "We've both lived on satellites, Rig. I think I can manage."

He smirks. "Ha, that's right. You did kind of smell when I first met you."

I snort. "Speak for yourself."

Rig holds up a hand and motions beyond us. "Crew bunks are

through that hallway, but I'm pretty sure your fiancé would appreciate you staying out of there."

"Definitely." I remember the ring on my necklace. Luther didn't like the idea of me coming in the first place. I wonder if he realized I'd be the only female on board?

"There's a bunch more to the sub, but I doubt you care to see things like waste management equipment and the engine room. And if you do, your dad can show you later."

We retrace our steps up the ladder and past the comm room. Dad's no longer there, but I remember his words about the maintenance workshop and quicken my steps. What surprise does he have for me?

Rig pauses before a doorway. "I haven't been to the maintenance room for a while, so I don't know…"

I rush past him and stop in my tracks. Dad has transformed the small space into a Translation room. On the wall is a wide screen, much bigger than the one in the mess deck, with the operation interface housed below it at a small table. A love seat faces the screen, and there's a small bookcase by the wall.

"Woah." Rig steps behind me.

"My dad's incredible," I whisper.

He slaps my back and hoots. "This. Is. Awesome!"

I frown at him. "Why are you all excited? Have you ever seen a Translator…?"

"Wait till I tell the guys we can watch superhero stories on the big screen!" He makes a *yessss* sound until I shake a finger in his face.

"Rig, this is not for your moving stories. This is for communication purposes only."

His smile fades. "Huh?"

"It's a Translator. We use it to communicate with people in different time dimensions."

Rig steps closer and inspects the equipment. "Bummer, there's no player."

"I told you." I sigh. "It's not for your stories."

He grunts. "Well, that's a waste."

I shake my head. "Rig, think of it as an extension of your comm center. It just serves a different purpose."

He scratches his head. "Okay, whatever you say. Listen, I need to catch some sleep before my shift. I'll see you around."

"Thanks for the tour." I try to contain my excitement until he disappears down the hallway. Then, I rush to the controls and flip on the equipment, which hums to life.

Maybe this journey won't feel endless after all. I can talk to Luther and let him know...

"I see you found my surprise." Dad chuckles behind me.

"It's perfect!" I spin around and hug his neck. "Luther is going to be so surprised."

Dad smiles softly. "I'm afraid you can't use it for a Translation, sweetheart. We can't get a signal while we're submerged, and we can't risk sending one when we aren't. It could give away our position and jeopardize the mission."

My enthusiasm wanes. "Oh, that makes sense. Guess I wasn't thinking."

He squeezes my shoulder. "Still, from my testing, you can use it as a Simulator, because all those dates are already programmed into the software."

I perk up at that thought. "Really? That would be wonderful.

There's so much I'd like to know about the past."

"Then help yourself." Dad pats my hair. "I'm busy for the next few hours, but I thought we could grab some food together afterward. How about I stop by for you at 0200?"

"Sounds great, Dad." I grin. "You know where to find me."

If I don't make my choice soon, Dad will be back before I have time to finish a Simulation. But there are too many dates, and I'm scared I'll pick one where someone else dies.

I'm really tired of death.

An inspiration finally strikes. Alexis had said Orvieto started celebrating Italy's influence in American independence in 2013. What had she called it... Orvieto Forever?

I scroll to the year 2013 and then plug in the date of America's independence, July 4. Yes, there's a record for me to view.

Palms sweating, I randomly select a time in the evening and submit my request. Surely nothing morbid can happen at a celebration—at least nothing like watching soldiers die.

The translucent blue haze blurs the room and pulls me into the pixelated past.

For a moment, I panic. Bodies press against me from all sides, but they're not shoving. They're just squeezing tighter, straining forward.

None of the people notice me, for their gazes fixate on something ahead. But I can't see through the crowd, because I'm short.

Night cloaks the landscape, but there's a strange blue hue. Is it an after effect of the Simulation?

I tilt my head skyward and gasp. No, this colored illumination isn't part of the Simulation. Standing like a mountain before me is a large building I've only seen in pictures—what was this structure called? A cathedral? Yes, that's it.

The ornate architecture demands the respect of time, but what's more astounding than the lighting that accentuates every detail is the symphony of sound that projects outward from it.

The music's haunting melody stirs my soul, and then a soloist joins in a language I don't understand. The tenor's emotion and sheer range send tingles up my spine. I have to see for myself.

But tiptoeing does no good. I suck a determined breath and begin squeezing toward the front. People with olive-toned skin and eyes darker than Luther's cast reproachful glances my way, but no one tries to stop me.

After what feels like an hour, I break through to the front of the crowd and find myself at the edge of the platform or stage. There, a stone's throw away stands a slender man in a black tux. His eyes appear to be closed, but he's singing—and oh, what a song! His voice leaves me with a soaring sensation. If only I could understand the words, but perhaps I don't need to.

Behind him, an orchestra with more members than I can count create the spine-tingling accompaniment. Women with graceful arms bend with their bows over cellos, while others tip violins beneath their chins.

I've only read about such instruments. To hear them working together brings tears to my eyes.

As if in a spell, I sway as the magical music unfolds. When

one song ends, another man joins the soloist on the stage. He's a man with Gath's dark coloring, and he seems to take his cues from the man in the tux.

With a start, I realize they're singing in English. The simple melody pairs with words so rich my heart squeezes inside my chest.

Amazing grace, how sweet the sound that saved a wretch like me,

I once was lost but now am found, was blind but now I see.

I hug myself as tears charge past my lashes, and I don't fight them. *I once was lost... a wretch like me.* This is Gath's story.

This is my story. The singers continue verse by verse. I never want the song to end.

Through many dangers toils and snares I have already come.

Tis grace has brought me safe thus far, and grace will lead me home.

Home. Can the grace of Jesus really lead me to a place of rest? Can I really hope for a home some day?

The scene fades. I try to hold onto it, but too soon, it vanishes. I'm left sitting on the love seat, staring at the now-blank screen.

Goosebumps crawl up and down my arms. I want to go back. I want to see more of Orvieto. I want that kind of majestic celebration in my own land to honor liberty and justice for all.

But I can't stay in a Simulation, though I'm tempted to revisit the scene because I loved it so much.

A rap sounds on the door behind me. "You ready, sweetheart?" Dad pokes his head inside the room.

His face puckers in a frown. "Have you been crying?"

I wipe my hands across my cheeks and smile through the tear

stains. "Yes, but it was a good cry. I can't wait to go to Orvieto."

Dad grins. "You'll get your wish soon. If my estimates are right, we should get there July third."

"Yes!!" I clap my hands.

Dad laughs and waves me out of the room. "Come on, crazy head, let's get some food."

I hook my arm into his, but my thoughts are still in Orvieto. In a few short days, I might get to witness the Orvieto Forever celebration for real.

Kristen Hogrefe

CHAPTER 17
~ Luther ~

Monday, 6.29.2150
Jacinth

Luther cinches his hood so that it's tight around his ears and then braces for the biting arctic blast. He won't have to worry about torrential downpours, only blizzards and subzero temperatures once he reaches Deadwood.

Assuming he reaches Deadwood.

Leveraging his weight, he slides the cargo door open as the train slows to a nervous stop. Peering into the blackness, he catches a glimpse of two blinding headlights, no doubt belonging to some off-road vehicle equipped to handle snow and ice. That must be Felix's promised escort. At least he's keeping his side of the agreement this far.

Swinging on his pack, Luther jumps down next to the track. Shin-deep snow sucks at his boots, but he trudges through it toward the idling vehicle.

The piercing head beams catch the steam from the engine, creating a blinding spectrum of light. The passenger door opens, and a guard carrying an automatic rifle motions him forward. The man pops the back-passenger door open and nods for Luther to climb inside.

If Portia were here, he'd have to lift her, because the wheels are nearly as tall as she is.

Luther brushes the thought aside and complies with the guard's nonverbal instructions. Right now, he's glad Portia is nowhere near this god-forsaken place.

The guard slams the door behind him, and the vehicle lurches forward. There's a plexiglass divider between the front and back seats, so he can't communicate with the men up front.

Or, if they can speak to him, his escorts choose to stay tight-lipped, making his part of the vehicle feel like a cage.

Through the snow-dusted windows, he catches the first view of an illuminated sphere in the distance. Could that be the Deadwood fortress? The orb grows larger and gradually takes on dimensions. A fraction of the structure appears above ground. It's as if the fortress has sunken in the snow with only observation towers, flood lamps, and wire fencing that spike through the ground's frozen flesh.

But Luther knows better. From what he's heard, the fortress was carved into the solid rock ground, and most of it exists beneath the surface. It's complete with its own port that allows submarines to dock.

The panorama scene shrinks until the vehicle seems about to run into a wall. Then as if out of nowhere, a giant door parts in the white side wall, providing room for the vehicle to enter.

It immediately closes behind them. Now, man-made lighting with a yellowish hue provides visibility, but his window fogs at the change in temperature. He'll have his chance soon to get a better look at this garage.

The front passenger door opens. That must be his cue. He yanks on the door, but the handle snaps in his hand. Locked.

Luther sucks down a breath. *Don't panic. They will let you out.* But his pulse climbs with each passing second.

Finally, someone jerks the door open. The same escort greets him with a blank expression.

That's fine with him. He has no desire to get friendly with the guy who locked him in the monstrous truck's backseat. Besides, there's no use in small talk about the weather when you live in a place as desolate as Deadwood.

The guard swerves his eyes down the center aisle. "Follow me."

The "garage" is large enough to house all of CGA headquarters. Luther tries not to stare at the off-road vehicles stored in the hanger. If Felix is trying to impress him with resources, he's off to a stellar start.

At the aisle's end is a solid metal door. The escort places his thumb onto a scanner, and a green light blips above it. The door parts in the middle, and they enter a sterile white hallway.

Getting lost in this place will be easy. Finding his way out might be impossible.

Luther ignores the tightness in his chest and tries to shrug off the indifference of the men and women who stride past him. They wear identical gray uniforms, consisting of long pants and a zippered jacket. His black coat and hunter green pants stick out like a wild bull in a pony show.

Sweat beads on his neck, and he pulls off his hood. This place is temperature regulated. How can Felix manage that feat? He must have his own power grid.

His escort repeats the thumb scanning procedure at another door. He enters next to the escort, but the room is a dead end, not another hallway. It appears to be a small lounge complete with a sofa and few plush leather chairs and a dry bar on the end.

"Is this…" Luther turns to the armed guard, but the man crosses the door threshold and presses a button on the wall. The door snaps shut, leaving Luther staring at the solid metal sheet.

Real friendly, these people.

Luther helps himself to a glass of water and examines the room. There are no windows, only a mounted screen on the far side of the room by the sofa. As if motion activated, it blips on when he approaches it.

A live feed of Felix begins streaming—at least, he assumes it's live, because Felix's cheeky face is extremely close to the lens, and the visual keeps bouncing as if he's walking. He must be holding up some kind of small video camera to his face.

"Luther! Welcome." He flashes his immaculate white teeth and taps something in his ear. "Make yourself cozy. I can't meet with you until tomorrow morning, but I've arranged a tour of our facilities. I think you'll find it fascinating."

Felix pauses to acknowledge someone's question and then focuses on the lens. "Listen, I have to run. Enjoy yourself, and we'll chat soon."

Enjoy yourself? Felix always did have a strange taste in words. The screen blips off, and Luther steps back.

He's part annoyed Felix invited him to come today and won't see him until tomorrow. And he's part relieved. Stalling buys him more time to make his speech more persuasive and buys Darius more time to prepare for the next attack, assuming his diplomatic mission fails.

He has no doubt that it will. Their leverage against Felix is small, nearly non-existent, but he's going to milk his diplomatic training for all its worth.

The door snaps open again, and Jotham crosses the threshold, followed by two escorts. "Hello, little brother. It's about time you came to the right side of this scuffle."

Jotham's dark purple suit reflects his former Dome status, which seems ironic, since all representatives either went into hiding or fled with Felix. Either way, they wield no power unless Felix restores the Dome's authority.

But that's just like Jotham: He will cling to the appearance of importance even when he has none.

"Good to see you." Luther forces the words and strides toward him. Though his older brother shares his dark hair and eyes, any resemblance stops there. Jotham takes after Mom's modest build, while he favors Dad's side with his thick chest, broad shoulders, and height. He's at least a head taller than Jotham—has been for years.

So how can his brother still make him feel small?

Jotham mocks a yawn and then offers a condescending grin. "Mr. Caesura can't meet with you today, but he's given me permission to give you a tour."

"Okay." The less Luther says, the less he can fuel Jotham's superiority complex.

Jotham tilts his nose and motions to the escort to lead the way. "I thought we'd start with the cafeteria first. Thought you might be hungry."

While mock civility is easier to stomach than a cold shoulder,

Luther cuts to the point. "Thanks, but how's Dad?"

Jotham stiffens. "We'll save a visit to the lab for last as there are some current projects Mr. Caesura thinks will interest you. But first, let's get you a sandwich. There's something about the cold that makes a man hungry."

"Fine." Luther bites his tongue to suppress what he really wants to say. A shouting match with Jotham won't accomplish anything, except getting him locked in a room with no answers about Dad.

The cafeteria rivals the size of the one at the Crystal Globe University and boasts new conveniences he didn't even know existed. Jotham's chest puffs to twice its normal size as he explains contraptions called waffle makers, espresso machines, and ice cream coolers.

Luther lifts the cooler's lid and lets go as soon as the chilly air smacks his hand. Who could possibly crave ice cream when the weather here is so cold? Now the hot chocolate machine is a different story.

Yet as the hot, creamy liquid coats his throat, he fights a gag reflex. People back home don't have enough fuel for their stoves. How can people here not recognize the black and white paradox of their lives?

Perhaps they get comfortable and forget that real people are living and dying just hours south of them.

The hallways break off and resume in gradual circular patterns. It's as if Deadwood were arranged like a giant atom, subdivided into small particles.

"This is our Tooler division, organized into domestic and military." Jotham steps inside a factory-size space that stretches into several stories of equipment, work stations, welding centers, and about any mechanical wizardry he can imagine.

The sheer mass makes Luther's throat go dry. Abram works miracles with what little resources Darius provides him, but this facility outmatches their Tooling team in volume and resources.

Is that why Felix wants him to see all this? Does he want him to report on what an utter lost cause they're fighting?

"Impressive," Luther mutters and steps into the hallway.

Jotham frowns as if he had planned for a more exhaustive tour of the factory space. "It's mind-blowing, isn't it? I'm sure you've never seen anything like it. I hadn't until I came here."

Luther nods but doesn't comment. The last thing Jotham needs is encouragement to gloat. "Are we almost to the lab?"

His brother's grin turns devilish. "Right this way, little brother. Just one word of caution: Don't be alarmed by Dad. He's not quite himself these days."

Luther clenches his fists inside his jacket. What does Jotham mean? What has he done to Dad?

Jotham presses his thumb onto a scanner, and two glass sliding doors part, revealing a large room with a maze-like assembly of lab tables. At different stations, workers in white coats hover over samples, peer into microscopes, and otherwise completely ignore their entrance. An elevated platform and enclosed room tower above the space.

Luther scans the capped heads of the lab technicians. Despite their uniforms, surely he can spot Dad.

There, that's him—the one in the corner, huddled over a small cage. Though not nearly as large as Portia's dad, his own father stands above the average man. But now, he seems withered, shrunken.

His pulse quickens. "Dad?"

The man cocks his head for a moment. Then, he shrugs his shoulders and peers more intently into the cage.

Luther holds his breath as his dad picks up a syringe and then grasps something inside the cage. There's a mouse squeak, and then Dad's shoulders relax. He mumbles something to himself, scribbles a note, and then stretches his back.

Jotham taps Dad's shoulder. "Sorry to interrupt, Burke, but someone wants to say hello."

Anger pulses through his veins. Why does Jotham refer to their dad so impersonally? He inhales a deep breath and tries to ignore his brother. "Hi, Dad. It's good to see you."

Dad's tired hazel eyes shift toward him but don't focus. "Hello? Can I help you?"

"Dad?" Luther steps closer and grasps his arm. "It's me, Luther, your son."

For a moment, the glazed expression lifts. Dad clasps his hand with a hard squeeze. "Luther, my boy! What are you doing here?"

He searches his father's face. It looks worn, withdrawn. Somehow, he has to convince his father to return with him. "I'm here to negotiate a ceasefire with the Friend."

Jotham snorts. "That's Mom's favorite son talking. Luther, you've always been the dreamer, but you need to come to your senses. You're in no position to negotiate, but you're in a good spot for begging."

Dad's face tightens. "Adrienne," he whispers. "How is she?"

Luther turns his back to Jotham, blocking him from Dad's sight. "Mom's been real sick. She'd get better a lot faster if you were home."

Dad flinches and closes his eyes. "If only I…" His hand goes to his throat where the high-collared uniform tightly hugs his skin.

But it can't conceal the bulge underneath the collar. What on earth…

"That's out of the question." Jotham barges between them. "Burke is on a special project and can't be disturbed. We've wasted enough of his time."

Luther crosses his arms. "What's really going on here? And what's beneath that uniform?"

Jotham ignores his question and presses a firm hand on Dad's shoulder. "You've got work to do." Dad falls onto his stool and glues his gaze on the cage where a mouse lunges madly into the glass.

"He's got work to do?" Luther repeats angrily. "He's also got a wife."

Jotham glares at him. "We're leaving now."

"Not yet." Luther cuts between Jotham and Dad and yanks back his dad's collar. The fabric tears, and Dad grasps at his throat, gagging in surprise.

"What are you doing?" Jotham roars.

Luther points a shaky finger. With the fabric collar removed, he can now clearly see the shiny black metallic ring around Dad's neck. "What is that?"

"I—" Dad stammers. "We all get them?"

"Everybody gets them?" Luther stalks closer to Jotham.

"You're out of line!" Jotham taps on his wrist watch, which lights up to reveal a small screen. Maybe it's the same type of technology Felix was using earlier.

If he's calling back-up, Luther doesn't have much time. In one swift motion, he lunges for Jotham, wraps him in a neck lock, and yanks down his own collar—revealing a skinny neck devoid of any collar.

Jotham sputters, and Luther releases him. "See, Dad?" He points at Jotham who is feverishly trying to repair his uniform. "Someone's not telling the truth here, because big brother doesn't have a collar."

"Guards!" Jotham screeches into his watch-like device.

Luther leans closer to Dad. "Whatever they're doing to you, don't forget who you are and that we love you. Don't forget Mom."

Tears prick his father's confused, puffy eyes. "Tell Adrienne I'm sorry, but I can't…"

The glass doors part, and several armed escorts enter. Luther squares his shoulders and hopes the defiance he feels doesn't flame in his eyes.

"You paged, Mr. Danforth?" One guard asks Jotham.

Jotham fidgets with his destroyed neckline and glares at Luther. "This—this visitor…"

Luther laughs and slaps his brother's shoulder. Maybe if he plays the right part, he can bluff out of this. "My brother here—well, I guess I'm used to him rough housing with me. I forgot my place. It won't happen again."

The guard glances to Jotham. "This man is your brother?"

"Little brother, actually." Luther winks at Jotham who turns several shades redder. "He was just taking me on a tour before I meet with the Friend about a diplomatic errand."

His casual tone and relaxed body language do the trick. The escort's own guard goes down. He turns to Jotham. "What did you call us here for?"

Jotham narrows his eyes at Luther and then clears his throat. "Show our guest to his quarters. I can't continue the tour at this time."

"Very well, sir." The escort motions to Luther. "This way."

"I look forward to catching up more later, bro." Luther nods at Jotham and risks one last glance at Dad.

But Dad stares wide-eyed at the cage, and Luther follows his gaze. There's no movement any longer. The mouse lies rigid at the base of the cage. Its once white and shiny coat has turned a deadened gray, and its eyes bulge, red and lifeless.

Kristen Hogrefe

CHAPTER 18
~ Luther ~

Tuesday, 6.30.2150
Deadwood

Luther folds his hands and stares across the mahogany table at Felix. He's not convinced his former classmate is actually there. Every now and then, the light from the chandelier seems to glint off glass.

Or, maybe Felix really is there but remains concealed behind a transparent glass divider? That seems a bit paranoid, even for Felix. Surely Jotham hadn't convinced the new Friend that Luther was actually a threat.

Still, his brother had ordered him locked in his quarters for twelve hours. If only he had been able to sleep. But that ring around Dad's neck and the dark circles under his eyes tell him something is terribly wrong.

Felix leans forward. "I'm surprised Darius actually let you come. But tell me. How are all my old friends in Crystal?"

Luther takes a breath. He has to choose his approach carefully. He can't let Felix know how bad things are and how desperate the citizens are becoming.

"They would be better if you stopped plaguing the people," he says at last.

Felix rubs his jaw and smirks. "You don't like my pun?"

"Puns are supposed to be funny."

"You're so stiff, Luther." Felix spins in his chair. "I thought you, with all your cleverness, would have appreciated my plague analogy."

Luther crosses his arms and then quickly uncrosses them. He has to keep his body language open if he has a chance of negotiating with this playboy turned politician. "I didn't have to. Portia did."

Felix grabs the table and leans forward. There's a greedy glint in his eyes. "Oh, did she now? I'm not surprised. But how is my old study partner?"

Luther instantly regrets mentioning Portia's name. "She's fine."

Felix makes a popping sound with his lips and stares into space. "Let me see now. The last time I saw Frosty—well, I didn't realize it was her. Gage Colson later told me the story of how she had impersonated a catering maid and was part of the bait to lure in Gage Eliab. The little vixen."

Luther's jaw tightens. "Gage Eliab's death was unfortunate, and that madman Osborne was the one to blame for it—not Portia."

"You always make her out to be so pure." Felix rolls his eyes. "But she's no angel. I've got the scar across my gut to prove it."

Luther winces. Felix would bring that up. "I didn't come here to argue about Portia."

Felix arches an eyebrow. "Who's arguing? I pleasantly inquired about her health, and you're getting all testy." He taps his fingers on the table, and then a dangerous spark glints in his eye.

"Or have I struck a chord? Don't tell me. You and Portia are… an item?"

Heat surges through him, and Luther breaks eye contact. He can't focus on negotiating, not with Felix in a mood like this. And he has to get the topic off Portia before Felix develops a fixation on her as he did when the two were classmates.

Luther exhales and folds his hands again. "Darius asked me to come to see if we can find common ground to move forward peaceably."

Felix pushes back from the table and doubles over laughing.

Has the man completely lost his senses? For someone who scored top ranks in his class, he's acting more like a spoiled lunatic than a ruling Friend.

Felix catches his breath and slides to the table. "You can cut the diplomacy. We both know you're here because you're desperate. My guess is you're trying to buy time, though for what, I'm not sure. Care to share?"

Luther narrows his eyes. "Let's see if we can agree on one thing: Do we both care about the people of the ASU?"

The Friend shrugs. "Lives are cheap. People have their place and purpose, but sometimes, you have to sacrifice them for a greater cause."

"And what cause is that?" Luther demands.

Felix frowns. "Most of the world is reeling from a global famine, which so far, hasn't touched our continent. The ASU must provide the resources the Rosh League needs to help its citizens weather the crisis. And that's why I'm here: to get those resources back. It's up to your Brotherhood how much the people will suffer in the process. If you surrender nice and easy, fewer people get hurt."

Luther scoffs. "So that's it. We're still nothing more than a resource to Rosh? You all don't care a lick about the citizens. You just want their blood, toil, and soil."

"We can't all be visionaries." Felix smiles. "But if you convince Darius to cooperate without his puny resistance fighters spilling blood the whole way, everyone benefits."

"You benefit," Luther shoots back. "The people will be nothing more than possessions of the state."

Felix folds his arms. "Freedom is a luxury no one can afford these days. Would you rather be free, or would you rather be alive?"

"I'd rather be both."

Felix rubs his hands and smirks at him. "The only way you can have your cake and eat it is if you actually bring something to the table. And right now, you haven't shown you have even one bartering piece."

Luther leans in his seat and tries to count to ten to steady his pounding heart. Does he dare bluff? But if he doesn't, Felix will discount any suggestion for a ceasefire.

"I was hoping you and I could come to some kind of agreement that would benefit us both." Luther pauses. "But if not, the Brotherhood will seek allies elsewhere."

There, he'd said it. The effect on Felix is electric. The Friend tenses and once more leans forward. "Allies? You think there's one corner of this planet that will come to your aid?" But the tightness in his jaw suggests he doubts his own words. Does he guess Orvieto sympathizes with their cause?

Felix's eyes flicker with dangerous perception. "Don't tell me your little Pelagic Project stayed afloat and now you're going courting." He laughs at his joke. "But it's a waste of time. There's no one interested in helping you."

Luther opens his mouth but thinks better of saying more. His bluff is out, and only time will tell whether Felix believes him or not.

Either way, he's said all he came to say, and if nothing else, has given Darius another day before the drones return.

Felix stands on the other end of the table. "You have two choices. Surrender peacefully, and I'll do my best to get you personally pardoned. Your friends, however, I can't guarantee."

He's referring to Darius and Portia. Surely, he can't think that he would betray them to save his own skin? But then again, he is talking to the man who poisoned his mother for his own promotion.

"… unless I get permission for my experiment." Felix's eyes glint. "Those rebel Abernathy's are brilliant and would make perfect demonstrations."

Chills race up Luther's spine. "What are you talking about?"

Felix waves a hand. "Never mind that now. Your other choice is to prolong the inevitable. You've already gotten a taste of our capabilities. And those were the pre-show."

"Pre-show?" Luther stands and slaps his hands on the table. "People are dead."

"But I hear there was a survivor from the ship." Felix studies his nails as if bored. "Once we make some final modifications to the strain, that mistake won't happen again."

We. Does he mean Luther's father?

Luther tries to control the rage that makes his hands tremble. "Thank you for your hospitality. I'll be sure to deliver your message to Darius."

"And give my love to Portia." His gray eyes flash maliciously. "No thanks to her, I've never felt better."

Luther gives him a terse nod as an escort appears from behind him. He can only hope Felix doesn't give the order for someone to stab him in the back.

He doesn't think he will. After all, he's just the messenger, and Felix no doubt wants him to share everything he saw and heard to make clear the lostness of the Brotherhood's cause.

Still, as the escort weaves his way through the maze-like halls, Luther can't shake a sense of heaviness. Leaving now means abandoning his father. He's no closer to rescuing him than he was when he first arrived. But attempting to break him out of the lab is lunacy. Besides, he has no idea what that ring on his neck does, though its resemblance to the one Gage Eliab tried to test on Portia makes his gut twist.

Portia had compared it to the chair, and he knows too well what effect that has on prisoners. She had lost her personality for an entire month.

Is that what Jotham plans to do? Wipe their father's personality? But why?

His father is one of the ASU's most brilliant Mavens. If he has no conscience, he won't complain about any unethical experiments he's asked to do.

Bile burns in his throat. *Oh, Dad. Somehow, I'll get you out.*

They enter the giant hanger, and an arctic blast whips his face. The climate-controlled fortress forms a stark contrast to exterior conditions. The escort motions for him to climb into another all-terrain vehicle. At least it provides shelter from the cold clawing at his skin.

Slowly, Deadwood grows smaller until it's but a speck on the terrain behind them. Luther turns away from his window and stares at his hands. His only consolation is that if Felix decides to wipe out Crystal in the next few days, Portia won't be there for the destruction. For now, she's safely out of his reach.

And that's a good thing, because Felix shows every sign of someone bent on revenge.

Kristen Hogrefe

CHAPTER 19

~ Portia ~

Friday, 7.3.2150
Port of Civitavecchia

"Wake up." Dad's urgent whisper startles me. I shimmy upright from under my bed covers.

He turns on the overhead light, and I squint at its brightness. "What's wrong?"

"Nothing's wrong." He returns to the door, and a smile tugs at his bearded lips. "We're here. Get dressed and meet me in the galley. We're leaving in thirty minutes."

Adrenaline shoots through me, and I spring to my feet, though the clock reads 0300 hours. Who knows what that really means. Dad had explained how time zones work, but the concept still doesn't make sense in my head. Sure, I understand the earth's rotation around the sun is different depending on where I am on the planet, but exactly how many hours ahead I am from ASU time, I have no idea.

I stuff my legs into heavy black pants and pull a long-sleeved gray shirt over my head. It's a little big, but it was the smallest one Rig found in the clothing barrel someone had stashed on board. Apparently, Dad told him to find me something nicer than the

Gage uniform I'd been wearing.

I'm glad he did. If I meet Orvieto's chairwoman today, I should look presentable. But ever since Warren, my appearance has been one of the last things on my mind.

Perhaps the reason is that I no longer have to stress about disguises—no plastic glasses, recent hair dye jobs, or follow-up dermal treatments. I'm not a catering maid, a Wasp impersonator, or Osborne's kitchen girl any more. I'm myself. I guess I should try to pay some attention and put my best face forward.

I shrug into my jacket on the way to the galley and collide with Rig in the corridor.

"Watch where you're going, Legs," he mutters. I've given up scolding him about the nickname, but if Dad catches him calling me that, he deserves what he gets.

I press myself against the wall so he can pass. "Aren't you in a charming mood."

He glares at me through swollen eyes. "Got four hours of sleep, kid. Don't talk till after the hard stuff."

I shake my head and trail him to the galley. By hard stuff, he means black coffee. Dad won't allow the crew to drink alcohol on the ship, even off hours.

No one protests, at least not openly, because the chef more than makes up for beer with his food, a truly marvelous combination of white and red meat, carbs, and vegetables. None of us has eaten this well for who knows how long.

Red spared no expense in helping us. If Luther would let me, I'd give the hostel owner a big hug on our return. But Luther has always been suspicious of Red, which is nonsense.

I touch the ring beneath my shirt. I don't want to make Luther jealous, so a smile and thank you will have to do for Red.

Only four of us gather at the center galley table—Dad, Rig, Cob, and me. The chief of the boat offers no smile in greeting, but his demeanor from day one has been rough and no-nonsense.

Not that I judge him. No doubt he has his own sad stories to tell.

"Eat up." Dad nods at the steaming eggs and sausage. "We're taking some dry goods ashore, but there's no telling when we'll have another real meal."

"I thought you said these people invited you to come." Rig tears his sausage in half with his fingers. The man has no manners.

"They did," I say, "but they don't know we're taking them up on their offer. The connection broke before we could say either way."

He grunts, then licks his fingers. "Let's hope they haven't changed their mind."

I stab my sausage with my fork and nibble on the end. Although my stomach handles rich flavors better now, I still struggle to take big bites. Before, I couldn't stomach the fact that Gath had been starving at Warren while I roamed free.

Now, I still have a hard time swallowing. There's no way for me to know if he's contracted the strain or if he's doing fine.

I reach for my glass of water and gulp the sausage down. Maybe I'll stick to eggs.

"Where's everyone else?" I glance around the nearly-empty dining area.

"What do you mean?" Dad asks. "It's just us three going— You, Rig, and me. Cob's in charge of Avalon while I'm gone."

I frown. "Just the three of us?"

"Yes, a bigger group would slow us down." Dad talks between spoonfuls of oatmeal.

"But I thought you said we were here."

"We reached the coast," Dad explains, "but Orvieto is inland. We've got to hike or catch a ride on whatever transportation they use over here. Either way, we'll move faster as a small group."

"Don't worry, Le—" Rig catches himself and buries his gaze in his plate. Dad gives him a curious look but says nothing.

I smirk at Rig's discomfort. *Go ahead. Call me Legs in front of Dad and see who returns to this submarine in one piece.*

"I'm carrying." Rig talks with his mouth full and pats his side.

"Good to know we've got a hero," I mumble.

Dad crosses his arms. "I picked Rig to come, because I thought you two got along. Did I miss something?"

I want to say yes, that he's missed the entire backstory of how Rig tried to pulverize Gath and play me. But our days at Warren are in the past. Rig and I have a strange, silent agreement to be friends. It's weird, but it works.

Rig cuts his eyes at me and then to Dad. "No, sir."

"Portia?"

"No, sir." I push away my half-eaten plate. I hate being wasteful, but if I eat anymore, I'll feel sick. "I'm ready to leave when you are."

Dad rises and stacks his plate on mine. He nods at Rig. "Meet us in the control room in five."

"Yes, sir." Rig shovels the rest of his food into his mouth as if his life depends on it. At least he hasn't lost his appetite.

Dad hooks his hand inside my arm and leads me down the corridor. He leans down and whispers. "I have something for you."

My pulse quickens. "Really?"

He flashes a secretive grin. "Come on. Let's go to the maintenance room."

His last surprise was the Simulator that's kept me occupied for the last few days. What could top that?

We breeze through the hallways without saying a word. That's one unspoken rule of submarines I've learned. Since crew members work in shifts, someone is always sleeping. We use inside voices and never slam doors.

The dark maintenance room greets us, and I slide my hand along the wall to find the light switch. The room appears unchanged.

I turn to Dad with the silent question in my eyes, and as I do, he pulls a small sheath from underneath his jacket. It's the size of his hand, and he holds it out to me.

Even before I touch it, I guess what it is. "You made another one?"

"See for yourself." He lowers it into my open hands. Fingers trembling, I unsheathe the knife, but I already know it's a karambit—like the original one he had given me long ago, the one I had lost after stabbing Felix.

"*Fraternitas Veritas*," I whisper the inscription on the blade. "Oh, Dad, it's beautiful. Thank you. I'm sorry I lost the first one you gave me."

Dad pats my chin. "I don't consider it lost. You used it well."

I return the blade to the sheath and secure it inside my belt. "I won't lose this one."

"Lose it if you have to," he tells me and motions for us to leave. "I just hope you won't have to use it."

"Where are we?" I feel the need to whisper as Rig rows our small dingy to shore in the early morning blackness. His oars splash against the water, spraying us with a cool, salty mist.

Dad peers into the dark as if able to see the shore beyond. "Maps call it the Tyrrhenian Sea. More specifically, this place is called the Port of Civitavecchia—however you say that."

"Will our sub be safe in these waters?"

"Safe as anywhere." Dad grunts. "If there's a port authority, we'll check in. Someone's bound to discover us sooner than later, so we might as well be open about it."

Somehow, sneaking to shore at this hour doesn't suggest transparency. But I hope Dad is right, and we can declare ourselves. Maybe the person in charge can help us find a way to Orvieto without walking the whole way. Though after being on a sub for days, stretching my legs on solid ground doesn't sound like a bad idea.

A light sweeps across us and highlights the words etched inside the dinghy's frame by my seat. *Avalon*. Dad thought of Mom in all the details. That thought offers a strange calm.

"Search light," Dad mutters. "Do you see that small bay ahead? Go right."

"Are those ships?" Rig lets out a low whistle. "Monsters."

The circling beacon reveals gigantic skeletons of ships in the distance. Some sag beneath the water while others remain buoyant but in varying states of decay. Interlaced between them are smaller vessels that appear seaworthy.

I can't keep my mouth from hanging open. "What are they?"

"You mean what were they?" Rig mutters. "I thought you said this place could help us. All they've got is a ship graveyard and a light show."

"Could be a front," Dad warns as we pass through the bay's narrow opening. "Head toward that ramp on the left. There's a long structure beyond it. Could be a fort."

How Dad can keep his focus right now amazes me. I'm too distracted by the lumbering shadows in the distance.

Rig beaches the dingy on the cracked concrete ramp, and we scramble as the beacon once more flashes over us. If there's a lookout, someone must have seen us approach.

"Stay close." Dad squeezes my arm. "It's too quiet."

We bear crawl up the shallow embankment and find a series of steps. Tall weeds tangle between them, and something creeks just beyond.

The light scans again, revealing an overgrown playground. The breeze pushes at an old swing set that squeaks as if a ghost child were swinging.

I shiver as we reach it. What is this place where children once played?

Dad stretches an arm to stop me from moving forward. A stone's throw away is the jagged line of a metal gate that surrounds a dark fortress. The gate seems half sunken in the ground but still too tall to easily climb over. Strange.

Dad presses a hand on my shoulder. "I'm going to see if there's a way around it. Wait here with Rig until I signal."

"But…"

"Wait for two low whistles. If you hear anything else, head back to the sub."

Sweat breaks on my forehead as Dad picks his way across the riveted pavement. It's as if a farmer took a plow and tore up the concrete surface.

This is not at all the warm welcome I expected from Orvieto. But then, we're not in Orvieto. And the night is anything but warm.

"We should go with him," I start to say when a laser beam dots Rig's chest. He sees it just as I do and jerks us both to the ground.

"Dad! Watch out!" I cry, but the discharge of a weapon beats my words. A floodlight slams against my vision, creating a spectrum of dots that dance in the air. Rig curses and spreads himself on top of me. It's a foolhardy attempt to protect me, but the move warms my heart.

But Dad? What was that noise?

A metallic thud reverberates across the ground, followed by boots pelting the pavement, but Rig's body is too thick for me to see through. There could be four or forty men for all I can tell.

Someone kicks Rig in the side, and the boot grazes my arm. The stern voice speaks in a language I don't understand.

Rig slides off my back, and I twist for a better look. The spotlight outlines maybe fifteen men, all with weapons aimed at us. The imposing gate has sunken into the ground, but how?

Rig slowly rises with his hands in the air, and I shakily follow his example.

A man steps forward and shouts at us again.

I shake my head. "We can't understand you."

The soldier frowns and shouts something over his shoulder. One of the other guards runs toward the fortress.

"Please," I say. "We're here to go to Orvieto and see Abra Bianchi."

His eyes narrow. Is that a look of recognition or suspicion? He spews orders at his companions, who encircle us like vultures might carrion.

"Rig, where's Dad?" I call over to him as two soldiers block my view. Rig stands several inches taller than most, so he can probably still see.

"He's on the ground." Rig gestures to the men and points at Dad.

I press between the muscular bodies, but they shift to block me in. "Dad!" I scream. Maybe he'll hear me.

A guard barks at me, a clear warning to shut up. But I haven't come this far to lose my father.

There's a small gap between two of the men. It's enough for me to spot the fortress that looms beyond the dark form of my father's prostrate body.

Kristen Hogrefe

CHAPTER 20
~ Portia ~

Friday, 7.3.2150
Port of Civitavecchia

"Dad!" I gasp and bolt between the men. One catches my jacket, ripping the sleeve off the shoulder. Two others each grab an arm and restrain me. I'm on the ground, ignoring their orders and fighting the way a mongrel might for its last meal.

"Legs!" Rig's voice comes deep and loud. "They've got Abram and are heading for the fort."

The men yank me to my feet, which are about the one thing not tied. My wrists and arms scream in pain from whatever straps they've used to bind them.

A guard on each side grips my shoulders to point me in the right direction. It's a good thing, too, or I'd trip on the uneven surface—or the small spokes rimming the ground around the fort. They're all that's left of the imposing metal gate, now submerged.

I glue my gaze on Rig's beanie cap, which bobs in the spotlight ahead of me. Then, as suddenly as the light appeared, it vanishes, leaving more spots on my vision. How can these men see so well, and all I can do is keep from tripping?

Maybe they've memorized all the ruts and potholes in the

pavement, or maybe they have some secret night vision.

A sudden screeching noise sends me shuddering into the guard on my right, and I kink my neck to find its source. Behind us, the metal gate rises back to its original height, trapping us inside its perimeter.

There's no chance of escape now.

A metal door clanks open, and a yellowed lantern illuminates the path inside the fortress. The large open court inside the walls remains black, and my escort keeps me close to the wall. Are they afraid of exposing themselves? But if so, to whom?

Someone yanks open an interior door, and Rig ducks his head inside. A trim man with a moustache steps from behind a table. He's dressed in the same black uniform as the others, but somehow, he wears it differently—as if it were a badge of pride and not a thing of necessity.

The guard addresses him and gestures at Rig and me. The only word I understand is Abra Bianchi's name.

The door opens again, and a tight cluster of guards enters. The front two drag Dad by underneath his arms. His head sags to the side, but his eyes flicker.

Tears prick my eyes. At least he's alive. But what have they done to him? The guards set him onto a wooden chair in the corner, and he droops against the wall.

"Dad," I whisper and step toward him, but the soldiers jerk me back. Wincing, I glance to the moustached man. "Please, he's my father. He's hurt."

The man's dark eyes glimmer in understanding. He clears his throat. "What are you doing here?"

I gasp. Though heavily accented, his English is clear.

"Please," I start. "We're from the ASU. The chairwoman of the Orvieto Confederation, Abra Bianchi, invited us to come to talk about a possible alliance."

He narrows his eyes. "You're lying. She would have informed us."

"She didn't know if or when we would come," I hurry to explain. "The Translation cut out before we firmed up details. But she said if we came, she could give us a special modem with a secure connection. That's why we're here."

The man frowns, but some of the suspicion leaves his expression. "Why would the ASU send a girl and her father?"

I swallow. Will he discredit me if I tell him we're the rebels who have overthrown the Dome? But the truth is better than a lie. "We're part of the Brotherhood, the rebellion that's holding the capital right now. But without help, there's no telling how long we can keep the Friend and his Rosh League muscle from taking over again."

His eyes widen. "You are telling the truth?"

"Yes, sir."

"And what is your name?"

"Portia Abernathy, sir."

He pauses as if considering my words, and I sneak another look at Dad. He's so pale.

The leader spews a command in his language, and the guards release their grip. One undoes the straps on my arms, which is all the invitation I need to dive toward Dad.

I kneel beside him and cup his weather-worn face in my hands. "Dad, can you hear me?"

He groans in response, while I scan his body for injuries. I don't see any blood. Perhaps they used some type of stun weapon on him?

"He will be well." The gentler tone of the leader's voice surprises me. "However, he cannot come with us. And your other friend…" He motions to Rig whose scowl doesn't invite trust. "He will stay here. But you will come with me."

"Hey, hey!" Rig's outburst awards him a slap in the face. "I go with the girl."

"You are in no position to make demands." The man's icy tone makes Rig flush.

The leader turns to me. "My name is Générale Lorenzo, and right now, you're at Fort Michelangelo. We must leave at once if we're going to reach Orvieto before daylight. Our numbers have to be few, or we'll arouse suspicion."

I shakily rise while keeping a hand on Dad's shoulder. "You'll take me there?"

"Yes." He snaps the answer. "No one else speaks English, and I must assume responsibility if you're an imposter."

"But my dad…"

"He and your companion will be fine."

Générale Lorenzo rattles off orders in his native tongue faster than my brain can process what's happening. Rig and Dad can't go with me. I have to go alone.

I bend down and kiss Dad's forehead. I don't think he registers I'm there. "I'll be back, Dad. I love you."

Soldiers still hold Rig tightly, but he jerks his head at me. "I don't like this, Legs. They should let me go with you."

I shake my head. "I have to go. Watch out for Dad."

Générale Lorenzo motions to a guard who moves next to me

and prods me onward, though he doesn't touch me. I force a smile for Rig and follow the two men into the center court.

A flagpole clangs in the ocean breeze as we steal along the walkway, hugging the interior wall. We reach one of the corner bastions and enter. The dank interior sends a shiver down my arm where my torn jacket still hangs.

I want to ask questions, but my days working for Osborne taught me patience. I've already agreed to go with these men, so questions now will only interrupt the tremulous trust established and break the early morning's facade of stillness.

Yellowed bulbs inside metal-caged lanterns light our pathway down a narrow stairwell. The musky odors and chill remind me of my first visit to the archives. I had trembled with the excitement of exploring.

I brush my fingers against a crumbling rock in the wall. This place seems more ancient and has likely witnessed more history than an archive could contain. But fear dampens my curiosity. If these men aren't trustworthy, I'll never see Dad, Luther, or anyone I love again.

The general pauses at a low archway that appears to be another door. "We're going to take an underground passage out of the city. We'll come out in an old storehouse with several motor bikes. Do you know how to ride?"

"Uh, no. I've never seen a motor bike."

He frowns and retrieves a headlamp from a nook in the wall. Strapping it around his forehead, he flips it on and opens the door. "It's not hard. Follow me closely, because we won't be stopping until we reach the dying town."

I swipe at cobwebs that tangle in my hair. "The what?"

"Civita di Bagnoregio." The general continues his brisk pace even though the tunnel's ceiling grows shorter. "It's called the dying town because erosion has made living there too dangerous for most. You'll see. But two of our own now run operations from the abandoned town, and we have a hidden outcropping near the bridge where we keep supplies. It's a perfect break point before we reach Orvieto, but we'll have to hurry to get there before daybreak."

His tone scolds me as if talking wastes too much effort. His companion takes up the rear position, probably because he's worried I'll back out now or not be able to keep up.

But I have no intention of being left behind in a creepy tunnel or miss seeing what a dying town looks like.

I'm so focused on my footing and deep breathing that I lose track of time. The slope gradually increases, and the general pauses at a wooden panel. It reminds me of a vertical version of Lord Osborne's trap door system.

He pries it open, but there's only more blackness on the other side. The beams from his headlamp reveal the dust-laden air and some dark shadows in a corner. Maybe those are the bikes.

The subordinate pulls a tarp off the bikes and rolls the first toward a latched wooden door.

The general's hand on my shoulder makes me jump. "Wait here."

He and the other man slink into the open air. Perhaps they're scouting the area to check for any danger, though I don't know what they are so cautious about. After all, isn't Orvieto beyond the Rosh League's reach?

An engine sputters to life, followed by another. The general returns alone and presses something into my hand. It's a headlamp for me. About time.

Silently, I slip it onto my forehead and emerge into the night. Our companion sits on one motorbike with the two others idling on either side. The single-rider vehicles are shiny black, the color of a black racer snake, but it's the knobs and markings on the gear area that send me into a panic wave.

I hold up my hands. "I can't drive that. I've never driven anything before."

"Yes, you can." The general trades places with the guard. "Clutch is on the left hand. Gas is on the right."

"Clutch? Gas?" I whisper.

"Sit."

When I climb onto the seat, my feet barely touch the ground. The general takes my left hand and places it on the left handle bar. "Feel that lever? That's the clutch. Hold it down, and you won't go anywhere. Now, gradually release it."

"What's going to happen?" The words rasp against my dry throat.

"You're going to idle forward. Just don't let go fast."

I wobble forward and try to keep my balance. The general walks beside me. "The right side controls the gas. Now, pull the clutch in, use your foot to put it into first, and then slowly release the clutch while giving it a little gas. You'll be riding in no time."

This guy is crazy if he expects me to remember that.

I want to wipe my sweaty palms on my pants but don't dare let go of anything. "How do I stop?"

"Squeeze the brake on the handlebar and hold the clutch in as you come to a stop." The general attempts to make hand signals in the dark, but he looks like he's swatting at insects. I swallow a laugh. The situation would be funny if someone other than the girl who's never owned a bicycle were learning how to drive a motorized one.

"Don't forget the gear shifter." He points at my left foot. "To return to neutral, gently tip the shifter up. You'll see a green light on your dashboard, which tells you you're in neutral."

I'm going to crash and die. No, I can't. I haven't come half way around the world to end my life on this machine.

"Basically, keep driving until we stop. We can help you if you can't get the gear shifter right. Just make sure to pull back on the clutch when you need to stop."

I start to suggest I ride with him, but he turns and hops on his own bike. He and the other man idle up to where I've teetered ahead of them. "Ready?" A grin tugs at the general's moustache.

Is he serious? It's the dead of night, I don't know anything about the terrain, and I'm about to drive something I barely understand.

But he doesn't give me time to answer. He and the guard take off down the road.

"Slowly release the clutch and give it gas," I say the steps out loud. "Don't die. Don't die."

The bike lurches forward, but something's not right. Oh, the green light is still on. I'm in neutral.

I press down on the switch gear, and the bike takes off. But I'm so focused on the bike that I go off the gravel road and cut back just before sliding down a ditch.

This is suicide. I can't even see the other two bikes, though I can still hear them.

I twist the bike in the direction of the road and try again. The bike's small headlight gives off enough light for me to know where the gravel ends and the grassy terrain begins. At this rate, I'm going to be driving in tunnel vision all night.

This time when I release the clutch, I manage to stay on the road and plunge forward.

I don't dare look back to see where we've come, because the switchbacks ahead of me are so sudden and steep that it's a wonder I don't plow off the side of a cliff.

Perhaps the drive would be breathtaking if it were daylight. I can only imagine how stunning the sweeping vistas might be. Instead, I sputter forward, my eyes glued to the pavement that sometimes offers a smooth ride and other times writhes like a sea serpent.

Clearly, no one has time to maintain roads on this side of the world either.

When the first hints of daylight pierce the cold morning sky, I finally catch up with the two bikes and ease up on the gas. I have only a general idea of the time. We left the sub before 0400 hours, so the time must be approaching 0600. My nose is numb, and my arms are stiff as boards from gripping the handlebars tightly.

As I slow, the second man grabs my bike. It's a good thing, too, because I can't coax my foot to downshift, and the sloping road offers no chance to naturally decelerate. He taps the switch with his foot and then twists the key to shut down the bike. With him holding the handlebar, I gratefully climb off.

Solid ground never felt so good.

"This way." The general guides his bike down a narrow walkway and around what once must have been a tavern or dining hall. Metal tables and chairs lay strewn on an outside patio. Most are covered with vines and tangled with grass as if the earth is reclaiming what man once built.

An old stone wall offers protection from a steep ledge, and the general leans his bike against it. The impatient guard prods me from behind, and I hurry to catch up to where the general is now standing, his gaze riveted on something in the distance.

I find the kickstand and leave the bike next to the general's before collapsing onto the ground by the wall. A network of vines seems partly responsible for holding the crumbling rocks in place.

The general and guard talk in hushed tones but at a rapid-fire pace. I turn away from them to watch the golden sun pierce through low-lying clouds. The hazy sky turns shades of purple and peach, forming the backdrop canvas to the sprawling landscape before us. It looks like a child scrawled a marker across the page, and nothing was left even, least of all that ragged remnant of a city.

How had I not seen it sooner? But I had been too intent on just taking my next step and learning to trust my stiff legs again.

I want to tell those two to stop talking. Silence seems more fitting for the tragic beauty of this dying place. Buildings jut out along the edges and top of an eroded mountain, now bathed in the dawn's warm glow. A tooth-pick-like bridge marches up a steep incline toward the city and looks less than reliable.

Despite its allure, I hope the general won't waste time making that journey when we still have to reach Orvieto.

The last thing I want is to sit on that miserable motorbike for any longer than necessary.

Boots crunch on the ground nearby, and I glance up. The general gives me a tight smile. "Good news. We can safely continue to Orvieto."

"Safely?" I repeat. Was that ever a question?

His lips twitch, tweaking the hair of his moustache. "You said you're from the ASU. Is anything there safe?"

I slowly rise and rub my sore legs. "Of course not."

He steps toward his bike and kicks the stand. "Then you should know. Life isn't safe anywhere."

Kristen Hogrefe

CHAPTER 21

~ Portia ~

Friday, 7.3.2150
Orvieto

The streets of Orvieto yawn with early risers. Their suspicious dark eyes flash as our three motorbikes crawl into town.

At least, mine crawls. I don't worry any more if I lose my visual of the general. He can slow down and wait. I'm stiff, tired, and never want to see a motorbike again in my life.

I had thought the switchbacks to the dying town were steep, but the ones to Orvieto left my knuckles white. And here I had thought daylight would help. Instead, the sun's rays only created a clearer visual for how close to plunging off the road I came several times.

However, I can't deny the beauty. When we first spotted Orvieto, I thought I might be hallucinating. The city rises from atop a mountainous cliff, and parts of it seem carved into the rock wall. Houses, perhaps the edges of another fort, and pinnacles from a gigantic structure rise from beyond the wall. Although I witnessed a Simulation here, it's still hard to believe the place is real.

The town itself awakens my senses. I pass a little cafe where rich odors of fresh bread and a breakfast medley of seasoned foods tempt me awake. A green-framed chalk menu I can't read explains the morning's fare. I'd love to collapse into one of those wooden chairs and join a man reading a book over coffee.

No, I'd rather just steal his coffee.

The cobbled roads and steep buildings create a sense of tightness. No, of closeness. These people share life together. Two children dash in front of me after a hoop toy, and I nearly crash into a row of potted plants to avoid them. They don't even acknowledge me before continuing their game.

I try to imagine what growing up here might be like but can't and maybe shouldn't. My own childhood in an isolated cube seems starved compared to the rich companionship these tight-knit streets and houses suggest about the people who live here.

Lush green vines crawl up the building faces, but I focus forward, afraid I'll run over someone's child or cat if I don't pay attention.

Ahead, the narrow road broadens, and I glimpse a large structure above the housetops. Maybe the general is waiting for me there.

At the end of the road, I grip the clutch, kill the gas, and stare. Before me, a courtyard stretches as wide as the road was narrow, but its centerpiece is what steals my breath.

It's the cathedral from the Simulation. Someone painted or carved—I can't tell which from the distance—murals on the different levels. And then there is the ornate design of the windows and those flying pinnacles…

"It's quite something, isn't it?" The general's voice makes me jump.

"Yes." I close my mouth, embarrassed I've been gaping.

"It will be even more magnificent tomorrow for the celebration," he says with a smile.

I pinch myself and don't care if he thinks I'm weird. Will I actually get to witness in real time the event I'd seen through the Simulation? I'll get to be part of history, not just wish for a chance to go back in time to experience it.

But wait. Every day of my life is part of history. And my daily decisions shape it, whether in big or small ways.

I reluctantly start my bike again and follow the general and his impatient guard past other buildings until he parks in front of a narrow apartment. Maybe they'll actually let me shower and nap before meeting the chairwoman.

"Alberto will take your bike," the general says.

The scowling guard does have a name. But perhaps the scowl is not his fault. After all, I'm the reason his night shift at the port turned into an early-morning ride through the countryside.

The downstairs entrance smells musty, like the inside of my old barn-home. But any simple accommodations will make me happy.

The general leads the way down a slender hallway that stops at two wooden double doors. The shiny metal handles seem out of place, a single clue that this residence may be more than meets the eye.

He twists it open to reveal a long conference room and table, around which sit an assembly of people, all who pause mid conversation to turn and stare at us.

At me.

I stiffen, immediately self-conscious of my tangled hair, torn jacket, and general dustiness. Alexis would have made a much finer diplomat than me. But how I appear matters less than who I represent.

Straightening my shoulders, I take a breath and approach the table. A man rises and pulls out a chair for me. I smile and try to sit gracefully, but my backside feels bow-legged from that motorbike. I wince and perch on the edge.

A woman on the far ends leans forward and folds her hands. Her velvety black hair and purple glasses remain as they were during our short Translation. Abra Bianchi studies me with a look of curious interest. "I recognize you. You were the girl in the room during the Translation."

"I'm Portia Abernathy, Dar—the President's sister." I gulp and almost can't squeeze out the title we agreed on. "The Doctor Revisionary."

She cocks her head. "Interesting. Is there some nepotism in the Brotherhood?"

I frown. "Excuse me? What do you mean?"

"Nepotism." She waves her hand. "You know, favoritism based on family relationship."

I bite my tongue to keep from laughing. "Chairwoman Bianchi, sometimes family are the only people you can trust, and sometimes, not even then. However, no, there are other members in leadership who aren't blood relatives."

"But your father brought you here, no?" The general asks.

"Yes, he did. He's a brilliant Tooler and submarine captain."

"Tooler?" Bianchi arches an eyebrow.

I stop mid-breath. Have they never heard of a Tooler before? "You know, he designs and builds things."

"You mean like an engineer."

I shrug. "I suppose? Your words are different than ours."

"It doesn't matter," she says. "What matters is that you came."

"Yes, ma'am." I shift in my seat. "I came for the modem so that we can communicate with you."

"Is that all?"

Her smile unsettles me. I can't tell her that Darius didn't exactly commission this trip and jeopardize the possibility of an alliance. I need to learn as much as I can and hope he'll listen to my report.

"Chairwoman Bianchi, I'd like to get to know you and your people—to better understand if we share the same values." I rub the back of my head which has started throbbing. I'm probably just tired.

"We share the same enemy." She studies me intently. "Perhaps when you understand the scope of their choke hold on the world, you'll better appreciate why we rebels should help each other."

She certainly has a point. Nothing unites like a common enemy, but I would prefer we also share similar visions. However, this is wartime. Beggars can't be choosy.

I clear my throat and offer a smile. "I'd like to stay for your Orvieto Forever celebration, if it won't be too much trouble. That's tomorrow, right?"

Her lips purse into a smile. "Yes, and you are welcome to be our guest."

"And my crew members..." I glance at the general.

"They will be able to remain in port until your return."

I nod, but the image of my father slumped in a chair still worries me. "Can someone at the port also let me know how my father is doing?"

Bianchi's brow furrows. "What do you mean?"

The captain colors. "We thought the submarine and her convoy were intruders or spies. We stunned one of the men, but he'll be all right."

She pushes her chair away. "That explains your jacket, no doubt. Miss Abernathy, I'm sorry for the misunderstanding, but as you know, our border patrol must take precautions. Your father will recover soon enough."

I follow her example and rise. "Thank you, I understand."

"Please accept our hospitality during your stay. Get some rest, and we'll meet again later today."

A dark-haired young woman, maybe my age, appears at my side. She beckons me to follow her.

"Thank you, Chairwoman Bianchi." I give the group at the table a small bow and follow the girl who I hope will lead me to a hot bath and clean bed. Although I still know little about this strange place called Orvieto, the people here haven't stabbed me in the back.

At least not yet.

"Svegliati!" Someone shakes me, and I bolt upright. It's the girl who brought me to this room, perhaps hours ago?

She rattles off more commands. Doesn't she realize I have no idea what she's saying?

I hold up my hands, scramble off the bed, and retrieve my torn jacket from a chair. It smells and looks like something a mongrel dragged through the mud, but I shrug it on top of my new black uniform that matches everyone else's around here.

I still stand out like a sore thumb with my blue eyes and part-blonde-part-dark hair.

As we head for the stairs, I pause by a small window. The sun has crossed the center of the sky and begun its afternoon descent. The time must be well past 1700 hours. Have I really slept that long?

The girl doesn't stop chattering until we reach the conference room. Either she doesn't mind I can't respond or welcomes anyone with a listening ear.

The room is empty, except for the general, the escort Alberto, and Chairwoman Bianchi. All three stand when I enter, but their faces aren't smiling. The skin on my neck tingles.

"I—I didn't mean to sleep that long," I stammer, but Bianchi waves her hand.

"Don't apologize," she says. "Unfortunately, you have to go."

"Go?"

"Our intel has picked up a Rosh threat targeting Orvieto for the celebration tomorrow. We don't know how or where they're planning to mobilize their assault, but you must leave with the modem as soon as possible."

My chest constricts. "But I just got here, and there's so much I want to know." How could I have wasted such precious time sleeping? I wish that chatty girl had yelled in my ear hours ago.

Bianchi starts for the door. "I'm going with you to the port so I can share how I hope an alliance will benefit us both."

I glance at the general. "Does that mean…?"

He grins. "We won't be taking motorbikes this time."

However, the semi-circle of a vehicle out front doesn't look much more promising. There are only two doors, and I wonder how it's going to handle the ruts in the road.

Alberto grunts at my hesitation and claims the driver's side door. The general opens the passenger side and leans the front seat forward, revealing a small double seat in the back.

I climb in after Bianchi, and he resets the seat.

"What kind of vehicle is this?" I ask. My knees are nearly in my chest. And I'm short.

She fastens a belt across her hips and smiles. "We call it a bug. On these roads, we must travel as inconspicuously as possible. Although we can scramble much of their spyware, the Rosh League's heat sensing technology scans our peninsula routinely. We have to mobilize carefully so we don't alert them of our moves."

"That must be tricky."

"It is, but it's given us practice mobilizing under cover."

The engine sputters, and I follow Bianchi's example and fasten my restraint belt as well. "Practice for what?"

"Practice for the day we pinpoint their headquarters." She leans forward and addresses Alberto who nods and punches some buttons in the dashboard. The climate inside the car immediately begins to warm comfortably. At least the little bug has heat.

I rub my jacket against the window to clear smudges. "What do you plan to do when you find it?"

Bianchi blinks as though confused. "We'll take it out."

"Take it out? How?" I give up on the smeared window and face her.

She shakes her head. "You don't understand, do you? The Rosh League holds our continent hostage, too. They've dominated for over a century, but their grasp can't hold forever. However, they're only vulnerable when their leaders convene during summits, and even then, the always-moving location makes pinning them down almost impossible. As a result, their iron-fist rule remains intact."

"Moving? Is it a ship?"

"Sometimes it's a ship, a sub, a train—we don't know where until it's too late. Still, we're catching up with them. We're trying to at least. But that's another matter."

She presses her lips together as if to say she doesn't want to go into her offensive strategies with me.

Time to re-focus on the present issue. "How do you see us working together—once I get this modem home?"

Her smile returns. "Simple, we communicate and find ways to help each other. We're entrusting you with a modem so your team can strategize with us and identify where you most need muscle. And if you really do have surplus grain, we would welcome that in return."

Her tone is frank but holds an edge to it. This woman isn't used to asking for help. I want to ask how bad the famine conditions are but don't. "Yes, I think we can help."

Bianchi nods. "We can also offer some distractions that may take the focus off you while we continue our hunt for the next summit location."

We hit a rut in the road, and I bump the ceiling. "When's that?" I rub my head.

"Based on the static our intel is picking up, it's soon. "

Seriously? They don't know when or where this secretive meeting will take place? It sounds like they're trying to find a needle in a haystack.

But at least they're trying. "We could use a distraction," I say. "Felix—the Rosh League's puppet in charge of the ASU—is attacking us with drones. They've already bombed and burned much of our operation station."

"Then take some cues from them," Bianchi says, "and move your operations."

"But we don't want them to think we're backing down," I object.

"Right now, you're a sitting duck for them. Move or be moved."

We hit another pothole that slams me into the general's seat. "Scusa," Alberto mumbles.

I rub my head. "What language do you speak? Maybe I should try learning it."

Bianchi smiles. "Italian, but there's no need. Everyone in our committees speaks English, because that's what the Rosh League uses."

Still, I think I should learn. It would certainly help me figure out if ordinary people are shouting, swearing, or saying sorry.

Bianchi doesn't offer to help with our immediate problems, which makes me wonder how thin her resources are stretched. If they could find the Rosh League's headquarters, maybe our drone problems would go away.

The sun dips low on the horizon when we pull into Fort Michelangelo. Two guards open the metal gate, and the little vehicle squeezes right through the opening.

Now that we're here, I'm anxious to see Dad, but first, I have to keep from getting swept away by all the guards mobilizing in the center court. Bianchi didn't talk any more of the threat, but the intensity level in the fort has skyrocketed since my first arrival.

The general offers me a hand and helps me from the back seat. I'm as stiff as I was after the motor bike ride, but at least, I'm still clean.

He calls to Alberto, and the front of the bug pops open, revealing a small cargo space. The general pulls out a compact suitcase and hands it to me.

It must be the modem. Bianchi circles to join me, and Alberto all but herds us inside an office.

"This is all we need?" I ask, indicating the suitcase.

"Yes, now let me explain how it works." She takes it from me and places it in a chair.

"Wait." I glance over my shoulder. "Are my father and friend still here? I would like for them to see this."

She shakes her head. "No, they returned to the sub but know you're coming."

I watch as she unlatches both sides of the case. Inside is a solid plastic housing with a series of knobs and a wire connecting cable.

"It's very simple," Bianchi says. "Plug the cable into the audio jack of the Translator. The dials are already in correct positions, but if something gets bumped, the number sequence is engraved on the housing."

"Easy enough," I agree. The actual workings of the device remain a mystery, but Dad can probably figure it out.

Bianchi closes the case, snaps the latches, and hands it to me. "Good luck. Please contact us once you get back so we know you made it. Otherwise, we'll have to assume the worst and that the modem may have fallen into enemy hands."

My throat tightens. I hadn't been worried about our safe return until now. "Has that happened before?"

An explosion rocks the walls, and we fall to the ground. The century-old ceiling sheds powder and debris, and we crawl to the exit. There, on the far side of the courtyard, a gaping hole smolders in the fort's wall.

"I thought you had shields!" I shout above the roaring.

Bianchi pales, and she presses a hand on my shoulder. "You've got to go."

CHAPTER 22

~ Portia ~

Friday, 7.3.2150
Orvieto

I grip the case and climb to my feet. "Which way?"

"Port's that way." She indicates a gate as the general rushes to her side.

He pulls her toward the wall. "Someone took our shields down, and that missile was cloaked. We've got to get you below ground."

We both stare at him. Surely that's impossible?

His expression darkens. "Someone from the inside."

Bianchi's face drains of any last color, but she offers me one last smile. "Good luck."

The two disappear inside another wall entrance. I'm on my own. Biting my lip, I run toward the gate. Of course, she has more pressing concerns than guaranteeing me a safe escort. Her country is under attack, and someone has figured out how to breach her shields.

Still, I can't shake a crawling uneasiness that I'm as much a target as she is. I hug the modem to my chest and dart toward the exit. The hairs on my neck prickle, and I jerk my head.

Is someone watching me? A figure disappears inside another room. Was that Alberto? But I don't have time to stop and find out.

Outside the fort, the gate is down. Had someone disabled that too?

I race toward the darkening waters. With the smoke and sinking sun, the space between land and ocean blurs. Another explosion makes the ground roil. I trip and fall onto the concrete. What's left of my jacket takes the brunt of the fall. My arm burns, but it keeps the case from taking the hit.

My ears roar, and I shake my head to regain my focus. The submarine can't be far beyond the bay, but there's no way I can swim to it. Here's hoping the general or someone at the fort told Dad to send the dinghy to get me.

"Portia!" A man's deep voice calls out to me. There, by the shoreline, is the dinghy. A lone man jumps out to wave his arms at me. I wave back and scramble toward him.

He meets me half way and grabs my arm. "We have to get out of here."

"How's my father?" I climb aboard and keep the case tucked tightly beneath my arm.

The man's face puckers. It's half concealed beneath a beanie cap, like one of Rig's, and the other half bristles with a scraggly beard. "He's worried about you."

"But is he all right?" I study the man closer, trying to place him on the submarine. But my head is in such a fog right now. Half the crew look the same when they don't shave.

"He'll be all right, just has to make preparations for a quick escape. This place is a war zone, but you got the modem?" His eyes settle on the case.

My skin crawls again. How does this man know about the modem? Did Dad tell him? And if Dad's all right, why didn't he come himself or send Rig?

Another blast strikes closer, hitting the rocky side of the bay. Boulders fragment like ice cubes and fly into the sky.

In the distance, one of the slumbering giant ships catches fire and glows like a torch. I cover my ears, but the ringing noise won't go away.

The man rows harder. Through smoke, the sub's outline appears. It bobs above the water's surface.

Something isn't right. My brain screams for clarity, and I close my eyes. My fingers scrape the dinghy's inside.

"Avalon." That's right. Dad had etched Mom's name next to my seat. My fingers blindly feel for the engraving. Though dirty, the boat's interior is smooth.

I scoot on my seat to the other side and search again. Nothing.

"What are you doing?" The man's question makes me open my eyes. He stares at me with suspicion.

"Just trying to get comfortable." My voice sounds like a squeak to my own ears, as the reality hits. This dingy doesn't belong to the Avalon.

And this man isn't one of Dad's crew. The karambit inside my belt rubs against my skin. I had hoped I'd never need to use it.

"If that case is too heavy for you, put it by my feet." He glances away but rows harder. Muscles ripple under his shirt. Even with Dad's blade, I can't fight this man and take over the boat.

His fixation on the modem scares me. Hadn't Bianchi said that if it fell into the wrong hands, their secure communication system would be compromised?

The sub grows larger. I'm running out of time.

We're too far away from land for me to swim. I'd freeze before ever reaching shore, and if I tried, the man would catch me.

But the case should be heavy enough to sink.

"Oh, God, help me." I heave a shaky breath and hurl the case as far as I can.

The man explodes with cursing, as someone shouts from the submarine lookout. "What are you doing?" He roars and swings the boat around in search of the box.

Please sink. Please sink.

I grip the seat. "My father didn't send you, did he?"

His face burns a dangerous red as his eyes scan the waters.

Oh no. The case bobs above the surface. It must have some kind of air bubble.

"Gah!" I grimace and leap overboard. The icy water pricks my body like a thousand needles, but I claw frantically toward the case.

Grasping it, I fumble for the clasp, but my fingers are already numb and won't work. I grope at my waist for the blade and hammer it against the case, which punctures. Then, I push it beneath me. If the salt water doesn't destroy it, at least it should sink now.

An oar splashes inches from my face. The water burns my eyes, but I keep kicking at the case until I can't feel it beneath me anymore.

"Fool!" The man raises his oar to strike again.

I raise my knifed fist to fight the blow and try to kick away from the boat but my feet touch something else, something metal.

It's the sub.

There's shouting, and the man lowers his oar. Instead of hitting me, he jabs it toward me.

"Grab it."

I hesitate. Getting into that man's boat is the last thing I want to do. Is it better to be captured or drown?

"Who are you?" I tread water, still gripping the blade.

"Grab it." He repeats through gritted teeth.

He's no friend, but I have a crazy urge to live. As I latch onto the oar, the karambit slips from my numb hand. *Oh, Dad, I'm sorry...*

The man drags me into the boat, and my teeth chatter like a hailstorm hitting glass. Other splashes and shouting punctuate the world around me, but they grow dimmer.

The dingy lodges in place, and the man snatches me and hurls me over his shoulder. Somewhere, a hatch opens. Blood rushes to my head, blurring any clear image of my surroundings.

The throbbing stops. No, we stop. The man dumps me on the ground. At least I have enough instincts left to protect my head with my arms. I curl into a fetal position.

Someone shouts orders. The voice seems strangely familiar. Maybe I'm hallucinating—half frozen, half conscious.

Hands, not gentle but not cruel, pry my head from its hiding place in my stomach. They brush the hair from my forehead and then suddenly stop.

There's a deep sigh, followed by words so low I wonder if I hear them or dream them. "It would have to be you."

A warm, soft glow envelopes me. It's the most wonderful feeling, as if I'm cocooned in an invisible blanket.

I crack open an eye. I'm lying on a metal table and thinly covered with a satiny white sheet. Above me shines a lamp, perhaps a heating lamp? None of the lights in Crystal ever gave off this much warmth.

The sheet crinkles as I uncurl my stiff limbs.

"Leave us." The harsh voice breaks the comfortable silence. I roll to my side to catch the retreating figures of two guards. A wiry man stands with legs apart and arms crossed—staring at me.

I squint under the bright light to make out his features better. His tightly cropped hair frames his square, muscular face, which, though blurry, reminds me of someone I know. I blink again to clear my head.

A switch clicks, and the light dulls above me. The warmth disappears with it, but I can finally focus on the man who still hasn't said anything. Scars run fingers across his otherwise handsome face.

I slide to my feet. "Orbit!"

In two steps, he clears the space between us and slaps me across the face. "Insolent girl! That's no way to address the Commanding Gage."

I stagger into the table and rub my jaw as reality hits me even harder. Osborne sent Orbit to work for Felix under the facade of a Gage named Colson Crabtree. Osborne is dead. That can only mean Orbit now works for Felix.

But what is he doing here? And how did he find me?

"Gage Colson?" I grip the table's edge. A dozen questions

swirl in my head, and I grasp for the most basic one. "Where am I?"

He scans the empty hallway and seems satisfied. "You're in no position to ask questions. Or have you forgotten all your training?"

I frown. Is he really going to bring up Osborne's stupid training protocol halfway around the world?

I bite my lip. There's no point wasting words arguing. Orbit will explain when he's ready.

"Sit." He motions to the metal table. I climb back up but feel like a patient on an examining table.

"How did you come to have that modem?"

My gut twists. Had they recovered it? I gulp and focus on his expressionless face. Part of me wants to make up a story, but he knows all my weaknesses. And part of me clings to hope that despite his impenetrable facade, he still has a soft spot for me.

I take a deep breath and plunge in. "I met with Orvieto leaders to pick up the modem that would allow the Brotherhood to communicate with them."

"You've made an alliance with them?" he asks.

I hesitate. "It's not official, but it's promising."

"I didn't think Darius Abernathy would pick his sister for this kind of mission," he mutters. "I thought he had more sense than that."

"How did you know we were here?" I whisper.

He glowers at me.

"I know… I'm not allowed to ask questions," I mutter, "but none of this makes any sense."

"Shut up and listen, and it might." Orbit circles the table.

I close my eyes as a shiver runs up my spine. My shirt is still damp, and a chill has crept into the room.

"Our intelligence detected a Translation between Orvieto and a location in Crystal. Based on something your team member let slip, Felix suspected you had contacted them out of desperation. The connection was too brief to tap, but we know the Orvieto Confederation follows a strict code in its communications. It involves a modem we haven't been able to unscramble. We traced your submarine here and found an opportunity to intercept one."

"Why is it important?" I ask.

For once, he smiles, but it makes me feel colder. Orbit seems eerily in-tune with Felix's motives. "Because if we can hack that modem, we can destroy the OC's communication system, intelligence, and what's left of its crumbling European rebellion."

He chuckles. "Besides, taking out the Brotherhood's submarine makes your own rebellion even more defenseless."

"No!" I jump from the table and swing at him. I've punched him before. I can do it again.

But he blocks my blows and twists my arms in a painful gridlock. "You're getting slow, Sage." He spits the name of my old alias in my ear. "And I'm afraid your rose-colored revolution is running out of options."

I grit my teeth to keep from crying at the pain. "My name is Portia. Let the sub go."

"Can't do that."

"Dad's on it." I gasp out the words. Will he care or just think me soft?

He relaxes his grasp for a moment and spins me to face him. For an instant, there's a trace of sadness in his eyes. Perhaps he remembers the dream I confessed of one day having my family again.

His expression ices over. "War is war. There are winners, and there are losers."

"But we can fight on the same side," I argue. "Deep down, you have to know Felix and the Rosh League don't care about the people or anything but their own selfish interests. You can help us."

Orbit gives me a warning glare as if I've crossed a line. "I only take orders from one man."

"What?" I shake my head. "But Osborne is dead."

For an instant, his hard expression vanishes, replaced by genuine surprise. The next moment, it returns with fiery rage. "You're lying."

He shoves me into the table, but I bounce back. "No, it's true. After you left the arena, he came after me and tried to kill me. I exploded one of the vests in self-defense, and it incinerated him."

Even as I confess the words, I tremble. Osborne may have been a monster, but killing him was still too gruesome for words.

Orbit's eyes flash but then refocus as footsteps sound in the hallway behind us. The guards must have heard me bang into the table.

I step close to him. "You're a free man now. You decide what you do or don't do. Help us. You don't want to trade one tyrant for another, do you?"

His eyes narrow. Is that pain or an apology? Or am I a fool to think Orbit would ever help me and risk his own cover?

This time, his blow to my face comes harder, sending me crashing over the table. I land in a heap on the other side, and my leg twists painfully beneath me as I try to protect my injured face.

"I told you to leave us." Orbit's angry words sound muffled and fuzzy.

"We heard noises," another man says.

"Don't you think I'm capable of handling one wisp of a girl?"

My head throbs, and I try to straighten my bruised leg. At least nothing feels broken.

There's a muffled response, and a guard rounds the table. He reaches under my arms and yanks me to my feet. I can't resist even if I wanted to.

He drags me to where Orbit and the second guard converse, but Orbit doesn't acknowledge me. He should be ashamed of the way he's treated me. Perhaps I mean nothing to him?

"Lock her in quarters," he says. "I'll deal with her later."

The guard slowly drags me after him to the door as the second man clears his throat. "Captain requests your presence in the control room. The other sub is within firing distance. And he asked to know our next course."

I lift my head for one last glance at Orbit, and for a split second, make eye contact. *Please.* I move my lips and hope he can read them. I'll get on my knees and beg if it means saving Dad and the crew.

Orbit hardens his expression and looks away. "Deadwood," he tells the guard. "Tell him to set a course for Deadwood."

My head swims. Deadwood means Felix. Deadwood means never seeing home again.

But what did he say about the sub? Did I miss that? I dig my heels into the flooring to make the guard really work if he wants to move me.

"And the sub, sir?" the other man asks again.

"Tell the captain to wait for my command to fire."

"Yes, sir."

"No!" I scream and try to yank free. The guard struggles to keep his grip.

Orbit spins and glares at us both. His scowl is hauntingly similar to the one Osborne used before dislocating my arm. "Lock her up!"

Kristen Hogrefe

PART TWO THE
SUMMIT

CHAPTER 23

~ Portia ~

Saturday, 7.4.2150
Atlantic Ocean

I shiver awake. A scratchy blanket separates my sore body from the cold, hard floor.

Where am I? Pulling the blanket around me, I scan the dark room. A sliver of light cuts beneath a door, and I crawl toward it. But I bump something on my left, and it clatters to the floor with a thud.

The wooden handle brushes my hand. A mop? Is this a storage closet?

On all fours, I edge toward the door and squint beneath it. I can't see anything but the floor. I try the knob, but it's locked.

A faint patter of footsteps grows closer, and I retreat into the dark void.

"You locked her in there?" Someone mumbles.

"Wasn't sure where else to put her," comes the reply. "The only available beds are with the crew, and I didn't think…"

"Never mind. Just open it up."

My breath catches at Orbit's low voice. I tug the blanket tighter as if somehow, it can protect me.

The door swings open, and someone flips a switch. I tuck my face inside the scratchy fabric to shield my eyes from the sudden brightness.

There's a grunt. "Have your men find a cot and then get back here and clear out this space. I don't want anything left the prisoner could use to injure herself."

Injure myself? Does Orbit think I'm suicidal, or does he have a reason for me to be?

"Yes, sir."

I wait for the sound of receding boots before peeking out of my blanket. Orbit closes the door and then steps closer to me.

His conflicted scowl makes me flinch. Does our history mean nothing to him?

He takes my chin in his hands, but his touch is gentle, almost regretful. "It just had to be you," he mutters again. "Can't you stay out of my way?"

"Can't you stop beating me up?" I pull away and rub my head where a nice goose-egg is forming. "Let me go."

His expression hardens. "That's not my decision to make."

"But I'm of no value to you."

"Mr. Caesura disagrees."

I suck in air. "You told him you'd found me? Orbit, please…"

"Don't call me that!" His eyes flash. "And yes, I told him. He's my superior. And after he learned we'd lost the modem, telling him about you at least provided a consolation prize."

I curl up tighter into the blanket and face away from him. My voice shakes in anger. "I was a fool to ever think you were a friend of mine."

"This isn't personal. I'm doing my job."

"Not personal?" I choke on the words and still refuse to look at him. "Felix hates me. You're his Gage, so you of all people should know what he does to his enemies."

Orbit doesn't respond. I can only imagine what horrors he's witnessed at Felix's command.

"You might as well shoot me now." I stiffen and close my eyes. "What does it matter anyway? You blew my father's submarine out of the water. I might as well go down too."

His rough hands grab my shoulders. "That's not how a soldier thinks. I taught you better than that."

I whirl to glare at him. "Newsflash, Gage Colson. I'm tired of fighting."

He slaps me. "Then wake up. You're going to need every ounce of courage you can muster."

I squint back hot tears and narrow my eyes. "And I once thought you were my friend." Slowly, I turn again to stare at the wall where a variety of cleaning supplies and tools clutter the space.

He exhales behind me. "Like it or not, I'm going to keep you alive as long as I can."

If he expects a thank-you, he can forget it.

"But everyone is desperate these days. I overheard the Rosh League representative tell Felix that if he doesn't reclaim the ASU, he will never have the opportunity to rule it."

The idea of Felix being under pressure makes me even more nervous. He'll do anything to help his own interest. After all, he didn't blink at murdering his mother.

Orbit pauses and takes a deep breath. "The stakes are high for everyone."

I slowly spin to face him. "But whose side are you on?"

His jaw tightens. "I'm doing my job."

I shake my head. "That's a cop-out, and you know it. Come to grips with the fact Osborne is dead. You don't work for anyone but yourself, and you'll have to choose a side sooner or later."

His icy glare sweeps past me and scans the room. "My crew will empty out this space and get you a cot. Once we get to Deadwood, Felix will decide what to do with you."

I snort. "He won't lose any sleep over one more murder." I clutch the blanket around my shoulder and stare him in the face. "The question is: will you?"

Orbit flinches as if I struck him, but he soon plasters on his trademark hard expression. "For the record, I think you're a nice kid."

He pauses at the door. "And for the record, I did fire on the sub but didn't sink it. Sometimes, you have to be willing to take a few hits to save your cover."

I gasp. "You mean…" But Orbit jerks the door open and slams it shut just as quickly.

The thud echoes in the small room. Maybe Dad is still alive, and maybe somewhere deep inside his cold shell, Orbit has a heart.

But will he learn to listen to it?

CHAPTER 24

~ Luther ~

Sunday, 7.5.2150
Crystal

Luther slaps his alarm clock and hits the floor to begin his morning reps. These days, he can't wait to get out of bed. It's not like he's sleeping much anyway, and his worries snake their way into nightmares when he does.

But Portia should be back in two days. Maybe then he can finally get his head in the game.

Plus, by the end of this week, Gath should be able to return. Deidra's last message said that he and the other two men are healthy as "hogs," whatever that means. He still doesn't get her sense of humor, but there's no question she's hog-wild about Gath. After all, only a crazy-in-love woman would volunteer her safety to care and cook for men with a potentially lethal disease.

Does Portia care that much for him? He shakes off his doubt. Of course, she does. She's just young and deeply attached to her dad. Still, watching her choose to go with Abram rather than stay with him hurt.

And yet, he understands her fear of loss. She'd lost her dad once. And now, he knows what that feels like.

He needs to find time to visit his mom and give her Dad's message, but that trip will have to wait until Portia returns. There's no way he'll risk being gone when she gets back.

Luther tugs on a clean shirt and washes his face. Then, he holsters his ammo belt, loads a fresh magazine into his Glock, and swings his semi-automatic rifle over his shoulder before entering the deserted hallway.

Darius wanted his team to evacuate to the underground levels of the university, but Luther refused. Though he won't admit it out loud, he hates the underground. Sure, the last dormitory standing could go up in flames at any moment, but he trusts their team of spotters. By their estimates, he'll have one minute from the warning siren to take cover.

Besides, none of them knows which day is his last, and he doesn't want to miss his final sunrise because he's hiding below ground.

"Morning, Luther." Harley's voice makes him jump.

"Morning." Luther frowns at the Gage-turned-rebel. "I thought you were on night shift? What are you doing up this early?"

"I'm due for some shut eye, but Darius asked if I could find you first." Harley rubs his bristled beard. "He said it's something urgent about the OC and that you'd understand. He said to report to the portal room stat."

"Uh, thanks." Luther tips his head and changes directions. OC? Man, he really does need to sleep better. He has no idea what Darius means.

He's half way there when the shrill horn blows.

The half-destroyed steps to the library's entrance are within jogging distance, but he can't hide below ground during an attack. He had briefed the new sniper recruits yesterday, and a good leader leads by example.

Today's attack will test the strength of their plan. Luther beelines for the closest sniper station or what his defense team designated a station. It's the clock tower in the square. Sure, it's open, but the last few drones appeared to have preprogrammed targets and weren't heat sensing. And more than likely, taking out the clock tower isn't high on Felix's priority hit list.

He takes the steps by two and reaches the top just as the first few drones explode mid-air. The spotters have bought him extra time. If all the snipers reach their stations, there's a chance they can take most of the swarm out before it does much damage.

Luther regulates his breathing and watches as the sights rise and fall with the change of his breath. Once satisfied with his sight accuracy, he scans the smoke for the remaining swarm.

And then he waits his turn. There are five other sniper locations. Based on the trajectory path of the swarm, his station will fire third. His team can't risk wasting ammo shooting the same targets.

A rapid succession of three shots signals his turn. He lines up his sights on the new leading drone and fires.

The agreed rule is to fire only two magazines before passing off to the next station. Luther grips a third and debates. The whole sniper team risks jeopardizing their locations, and this swarm is larger than the last. There are still too many for the other stations to take out.

He slams in the mag and breaks his own rule. The swarm is heading for the library, as if Felix knows it holds the heart of their rebellion. They just have to hold out until Portia and Abram return with the modem, and then, maybe he can convince Darius it's time to move.

The drones drop like flies as he empties another mag. He's tempted to load a fourth when half a dozen drones break away from the pack.

And head straight for him.

"Lousy," he mutters and loads fresh rounds into an empty mag. He's too high in the tower to reach the ground before they arrive.

He picks off the first four, but then, his gun jams. His first attempt to clear the dislodged ammunition fails, and he draws his Glock 17. It doesn't have the accuracy of a rifle, but the drones are closing the distance fast.

After a first miss, he nails one on his second shot. But the final drone begins evasive maneuvers, wasting his next four shots while edging closer.

How can drones be this smart? Unless… The thought makes bile rise in his throat. Could they possibly be smart drones, capable of changing their targets and responding to stimuli?

The last drone swarm unleashed fire balls that killed five of their people. Will he be the next casualty?

"Hold it together." He grits his teeth. There are only three more rounds before he has to waste precious seconds reloading, and the drone is dangerously close.

He trails the drone's erratic pattern and then risks a rapid-fire succession. The drone explodes about a dozen meters away from the tower's edge. He covers his face to protect against the blinding heat of a firebomb.

The ground shakes, and he counts the booms. One, two, three, four… twelve, thirteen, fourteen.

That's still too many drones that reached the target but small compared to the original pack that likely numbered a hundred. Luther reloads his Glock, stuffs his empty AK mags in his belt, and evacuates the tower.

Where the library steps were is now a smoldering cloud of fire and debris. Why is Felix determined to destroy the place?

But the fool should also know there are back entrances to the underground. The closest one starts from behind the auditorium. Surprisingly, that building hasn't taken any direct hits, though nothing remains of the front doors except for the frames and broken glass.

Luther cuts his way across the rubble and down the side hallway leading to the executive office Darius had showed him. At the rear of the room, what looks like a closet door in fact serves as the entrance to a stairwell between the two buildings.

When he reaches the portal, he presses against the unlatched door and peers inside.

Oh good. Darius, Alexis, and Lydia are already here. At least they didn't get caught in the explosions. But their faces are like white sheets. Had they lost someone else?

Darius strides toward him and greets him with a back slap. "Glad to see you're still in one piece."

"The library isn't." Luther accepts a seat next to Alexis across from the Translator screen. It glows a dull blue. Why is that on?

He directs his focus toward Darius. "You know we can't stay here forever. These lower levels won't hold up if Felix keeps pounding the foundation."

"I know." But Darius says the words absently, like a child might when he confesses to not doing his homework.

Alexis and Lydia study the floor. Their puffy eyes give away that they've been crying.

Luther sucks in a breath and asks the question no one seems willing to offer. "Who did we lose? More of our militia? Or has Felix started hitting other Brotherhood targets like Randolph's tavern?"

Darius doesn't meet his eyes but shifts his attention to the screen. Slowly, he pecks at the panel for operating it.

"We received a transmission this morning from the OC."

"OC?" Luther asks. "What does that mean?"

"The Orvieto Confederation." Alexis's voice cracks.

"Orvieto," Luther repeats. "Wait, that's where Abram and Portia are."

Tears gush from Lydia's eyes, and she hastily wipes them with her hand. Luther eyes her nervously and grips the edge of his seat. "Spill it, Darius. What's going on?"

"See for yourself." Darius jabs his fingers on the keyboard, and the image of the OC chairwoman appears.

"This is Abra Bianchi, on behalf of the Orvieto Confederation and survivors of the Avalon."

Survivors. The word roars in his ears. There must be some mistake...

Her voice continues the way one might read an obituary. "The Avalon arrived in port on July 3, and your young diplomat traveled to Orvieto to meet with us. We provided her a copy of the modem, but due to an impending threat, returned her to port as quickly as possible. Our enemies staged a missile assault against the port. In the confusion, she was captured by an enemy submarine, attempting to steal the modem. She managed to destroy the device, which is no longer active, but the sub vanished with her on board— after firing on the Avalon. Though the Avalon wasn't destroyed, she suffered severe damage and casualties among the crew. We are working with them. Though this connection may not be secure, I felt contacting you was only right. I trust we will talk soon."

With that, her image vanishes.

"No." Luther grabs his head with his hands. His whole body shakes. He had allowed Portia to go. And now, had he lost her forever?

"She may still be alive." Darius's voice is almost too low to hear.

"Give me one good reason they wouldn't kill her—especially if she destroyed the modem?" Luther demands.

"Because if that submarine captain figured out she's my sister, Felix will want her, perhaps as a bargaining chip."

"No!" Luther jumps to his feet. "She would be better off dead than in the hands of that monster." He closes his eyes. "You don't know him like I do."

Darius swallows hard. "As long as she's alive, we can hope."

Luther paces the floor. "Do you think they'll take her to Deadwood?"

"Maybe."

"Then I'm going back."

"Out of the question," Darius says. "I've lost Portia, possibly Dad, and who knows how many crew. I'm hopeful the sub can be repaired. Based on Bianchi's message, I think it can."

"Come again?" Luther frowns. "I didn't hear anything about

repairing a sub."

"She said they're 'working' with the sub survivors, but the key was her ending. She said she trusted we would talk soon. That can only be possible if we have a modem and can talk securely."

Lydia sniffs. "That's some good news at least."

"In the meantime, we have to change our game plan." Darius shuts down the Translator. "Alexis has agreed to remain in the portal room to wait for any communications from the OC or Felix's camp." He gives Alexis an appreciative look. Maybe he's finally learning he needs the woman on his side.

Darius moves to Lydia's seat and gently tugs her to her feet. He wraps a supportive arm around her waist and turns to him. "As for you and Lydia, I need to talk to you both in the lab."

Luther nods and takes a last look at the slumbering screen. If only Portia would appear and promise him she's all right. But he doesn't even know if she's alive.

His feet feel like lead as he follows Darius and Lydia. The lab can mean just one thing. Their Mavens have cracked the virus.

But using it against Deadwood now can't be an option—not if Portia is a prisoner inside Felix's fortress.

CHAPTER 25
~ Gath ~

Monday, 7.6.2150
Crystal, Cube 1776

Gath prods the last of the tinder into the small flame and gently blows to help it catch. Though Deidra had cooked meals fit for a king on the small fire pit, he can't wait to take her back to Crystal. A week living in the library ruins is enough to make any man stir crazy.

The eeriness coupled with the roving mongrel threat had been enough to spook Dirk and Eddie. They had disappeared two days ago, ignoring his warning that they should stay together and be quarantined for a full week.

He hopes they found their way home and not into a mongrel nest.

At least if they're alive, they should be clean. None of them had come down with the virus.

"Thank you, Lord," he whispers and glances to where Deidra sleeps in a make-shift bookcase bed he had filled with blankets.

This is the second, second-chance God had given them. The first was finding each other after over a decade of living double lives and assuming the other was dead.

In a sense, Abel and Beatrice are dead. They aren't the same people they once were. That's one reason they had decided to keep their new names. They can't erase the past, but they can move forward.

Gath tosses the last of the beans onto the skillet and places it above the flame. As soon as they eat, they'll start for Red's hostel.

He has so many unanswered questions. Had Deadman or anyone else from the vessel survived? Had Portia and Abram safely returned from Orvieto? Had Felix launched any more drone attacks?

A soft groan interrupts his thoughts, and he swivels toward his girl. "You awake, beautiful?"

"Uh-hmm." She blinks sleepy-seed eyes at him. Their tropical chocolate-brown color melts his insides. Living in an old library for two days unchaperoned with his childhood sweetheart hasn't been easy.

She hadn't understood his struggle. She'd told him she was a big girl now and he didn't need any permission from her father. Back in the day, her open arms would have been all the invitation he needed.

But now, he's different. He knows there's a right and a wrong way to start that kind of commitment. And even if he doesn't have to ask her daddy, he still has to answer to his God.

He sucks a deep, cooling breath. He'll put a ring on her finger soon enough, and then she'll be his.

"You ready to go home?" he grins at her. "Breakfast is about ready, and then we can head out."

She lets out a lazy yawn and stretches her bare arms above her head. "I'm already home as long as I'm with you."

The passion in her eyes could make a man lose control.

Beans. He refocuses his attention and stirs vigorously. Then, he clears his throat. "I know, but I want to take you home and do right by you. And we need to help the others. I hope nothing has happened while we've been cooped up here, but I have a bad feeling in my gut."

She swings her legs over the side. "Is that why you're up early again?"

"Yeah," he mutters. "I hope I'm wrong."

Deidra slides off the edge of the frame and joins him beside the fire. "I hope so, but I'm worried too—about Portia. I don't think Luther wanted her to go on the submarine."

He reaches for her hand and squeezes. "We'll pray."

Her smile fades, but she nods and closes her eyes. One day, she'll understand. It isn't that she denies his story and the change that's taken place in his life, but she doesn't seem to see the same need in her own life.

But that's another problem for another prayer.

He squeezes her hand again and begins. "Dear Lord, thank you for this food and for keeping us safe. Watch over our friends and give us strength for this day. Amen."

Maybe he's had too many beans, or maybe he just needs to make a start. Either way, he lets Deidra finish them while he secures his pack and checks his flashlight and Glock 19.

She straps on her own small pack, secures a crutch under each arm, and follows him out the dilapidated library's entrance.

The morning shines bright and cold. Gath usually sets what most people call a breakneck speed, but with Deidra still on crutches, he settles for a slower pace. Even so, they reach the hostel right before noon.

Someone rocks in a lone chair on the front porch. The man's gaze seems fixed on an intangible point.

Gath squints at him. "Deadman? Is that you?"

He runs a hand through the stubble on his face and shrugs. "Yeah, just got cleared this morning. Guess your other two friends didn't make it?"

"They took off on their own. I'm hoping for the best." He studies the skeleton of the man before him. Maybe with a few weeks of Red's cooking, he'll look alive again. "Where's the rest of your crew?"

"Ashes and dust." He snorts. "They burned all the bodies with the boat. Mine should have been with them."

"Life's a gift, man." Gath steps toward him. "I'm sorry for your friends."

"I'm not." Deadman rocks faster. "At least they found a place to rest or rot. I'm stuck in this warped world and not sure which way is up or down."

Gath grips his shoulder, little more than bones and sinews. "That's because we weren't supposed to live this life alone. You've got new friends if you want them."

Deadman snorts. "Nobody would want somebody like me for a friend."

"Perfect." Gath grins. "Sounds like we should get along fine."

He motions for Deidra to follow him through the door.

"He's not here," Deadman calls over his shoulder.

Deidra tweaks an eyebrow, and Gath retraces his steps toward the chair. "Who's not here?"

"Your friend Red." Deadman resumes rocking. "He told me I

could make myself at home till he gets back."

"Back from where?"

"Wherever your rag-tag rebellion calls home base, I suppose." He closes his eyes. "Sounds like there's not too much left to defend."

Kristen Hogrefe

CHAPTER 26
~ Luther ~

Monday, 7.6.2150
Crystal

Luther pours himself another cup of black coffee and ignores the shaking above him. Dust falls from the cracks in the archive ceiling, and he shoves the pot back into the coffeemaker.

It's not his shift. If he's going to be worth anything to the people he cares about, he has to rest sometime.

Yet here he is, drinking coffee. Who is he kidding? He's never going to sleep again until he rescues Portia or dies in the process.

Oh, Cotton. Why you?

Only Alexis was present when Felix's Translation came through. Maybe he should be glad he wasn't there. He probably would have torn the screen apart to get rid of Felix's trademark all-knowing smirk.

At least she's alive, but what are they doing to her? The girl he loves would rather die than fight for Felix. How could he say that she's learning to see their perspective, and they should, too? Did he really expect them to lay down their arms, just like that?

He closes his eyes, remembering when Portia had promised to be his. Does she still have his ring? Does she lose sleep over him the way he does over her?

His vision blurs. He has to get her out of there before they manipulate her the way they have his father.

With a final swig, he downs the rest of his coffee. He needs to find Darius and get a game plan before he goes crazy.

A door squeaks open somewhere in the long room behind him. That back door to the archives has become the front door now that the library's been leveled to its foundations.

"That you, Darius?" he calls.

"Luther?" A voice too deep for Darius answers.

He drops his empty mug, which clatters onto the table. Hope rises in his chest, and he darts toward the voice. "Gath?"

Two silhouettes, one giant and one slender, appear between the bookcases. Luther beelines for his friend and clasps his outstretched hand. "You're alive!" Laughter and relief shake him to the core.

A grin rips across Gath's face. "It's good to be here." But his smile quickly fades. "We heard you have trouble and came as soon as we could."

"Trouble," Luther mutters. "That's an understatement. Where do you want me to start?"

"Where are the others?" Deidra speaks for the first time. She looks paler but strong. She must be in pain, but she's not leaning as much on her crutches.

Luther closes his eyes. "Darius, Lydia, and Alexis are here. Red arrived late last night to give me a break from organizing our defense." He gulps and tightens his lips to fight the rising emotion.

"Where's Portia?" Deidra presses.

"Stolen." He opens his eyes and meets Gath's penetrating

gaze. His friend must understand.

Gath motions to the table. "Sit down and tell us what happened."

Luther shakes his head. "Can't sit. I've been sitting too long. I have to do something."

Gath places a firm hand on his shoulder. "Tell us what's going on, and we'll help." He pulls out a chair for Deidra and pours three cups of coffee.

But Luther doesn't touch his. He needs a clear head, not another caffeine rush.

"Where do I start?" He runs his fingers through his greasy hair. Man, he needs a shower, too.

But first things first. He recounts the transmissions from Chairwoman Bianchi and then the one from Felix, received this morning.

"At least Portia is alive," Gath says.

Luther balls his hands into fists to fight the growing tension inside him. "But what are they doing to her?"

Gath gives him a hard stare as if daring him to pull himself together. "As long as she's alive, she's got a chance. Felix didn't kill her but took the time to rub our noses in the fact he has her."

"How can you be sure?" he demands. "What if Felix uses his mind-warping technology on her again?"

Gath's face takes on a thoughtful look. He starts to say something, but Deidra leans forward and interrupts. "Because it's Portia we're talking about. I think she's finally learned to stop underestimating herself. Now the rest of us need to give her more credit."

"She shouldn't have to keep fighting for herself," Luther

mutters. "We need to do a better job taking care of her—I need to do a better job."

Gath's eyes soften. "What happened to Portia isn't your fault."

"But what happens to her next is, if I don't do something." Luther pulls his handheld radio from his cargo pants' pocket. He needs to find Darius and get moving before someone tries to stop him.

"And what do you plan to do?" Gath arches an eye. "You can't exactly waltz into Deadwood."

"Felix brought Portia there by submarine," Luther says. "That means there must be a port somewhere."

"There is."

Of course, Gath had trained there as a Wasp.

Luther taps his foot impatiently. "Then, tell me how to find it."

"What good will that do you? Abram's sub is half way around the world," Gath says.

As if that's enough to keep him from getting his girl back? "Darius said there's more than one. Isn't that why Abram left Foxworth behind? I bet he's overseeing the others."

Gath grins. "Yeah, there's another one that's almost ready, but no way will Darius let you take it."

"He can try to stop me."

Deidra snorts. "You men—always trying to ride in on your white horses and rescue the damsel in distress. You won't last five minutes if you try to enter Deadwood through a front door like the underground port."

Gath nods. "She's right. We're going to have to be smarter than that."

Luther holds up his hands. "Okay, then what do you suggest?"

"We get an offensive plan and talk to Darius."

The way Gath says offensive makes his skin bristle. Doesn't he understand they've been doing everything they can just to keep the drones from destroying what's left?

"Talk to Darius about what?" Portia's brother steps away from the portal door. Luther had been so focused on Gath that he hadn't noticed it open.

Deidra greets Darius with a smirk. "Romeo here wants to save Juliet and get them both killed in the process."

Darius's brows crease together. "Huh? Who's Romeo?"

Deidra rolls her eyes. "You men need to read more. Shakespeare's love stories might give you some ideas for your own."

"You want to encourage suicide?" Gath winks at her.

She swats at his leg, and he tries to scoot his chair away. "You're missing the point."

Darius shrugs, looking lost. "Portia was the Revisionary. Toolers didn't have to read nonsense about lovers and suicide."

Deidra rises with a grunt. "You men are impossible. Where can I find Lydia and talk to someone reasonable?"

"She's downstairs in the lab." Darius motions toward an inside door. "Take the elevator down seven levels. You can't miss it."

"What's this lab all about?" Gath asks as Deidra disappears.

Darius helps himself to the third coffee cup Gath had poured. "We figured out the formula for Felix's Firstborn strain, which he's threatened to use on us as a last resort. I thought that if we could reconstruct the formula ourselves, we could deploy it on Deadwood first."

Gath's face tightens. Luther guesses his friend has the same reservations he has about the idea.

"We were successful, too," Darius continues, "but now, we've scrapped the idea. I can't use biological warfare against Felix when my sister's his prisoner."

"And my father," Luther adds, though Darius never seems to consider that factor.

Gath frowns. "So why is Lydia still in the lab?"

Darius rubs his temples. "Because now, we know it's only a matter of time before Felix deploys the virus on the people, and we need a strain to counter it."

"That's better," Gath says, as if to himself, "but that's not enough."

"Not enough?" Darius bristles. "What do you mean?"

"Didn't someone tell me Firstborn kills in twenty-four hours? Assuming our train tracks stay operational, there's no way we can deliver an immunization in time." Gath lets his words settle and then continues in a softer tone. "I mean, you're being proactive and preparing for the worst, which is great, but you need to step up your offense."

Darius crosses his arms. "You got any ideas? Because while you've been in isolation, I've been trying to keep the Brotherhood in one piece. Felix's drones are relentless."

"Drones." Gath cuts his eyes to Luther. "Now there's something. I want to see one."

Darius motions to the back door. "Take your pick. We've got the makings of a drone graveyard behind the library ruins."

Library ruins. Luther glances at Gath and wonders if the words pricked him, too. The library ruins of Cube 1776 were one thing.

His own civilization becoming the next set of ruins for a future society to explore makes his stomach churn.

Gath rises from his chair and meets his gaze. "Let's see these drones."

Kristen Hogrefe

CHAPTER 27

~ Portia ~

Tuesday, 7.7.2015
Deadwood

I run my finger along the rim of the tin plate to scrape any traces of last night's meal. Though I can't see well enough to tell if I've missed anything, I know I haven't. It's been several hours since the crew member delivered the oatmeal. Only insomnia keeps me interested in the plate now.

Standing, I attempt to distract myself with it, balancing it on my head and testing how long I can spin with it there before falling.

It's the lamest game I've ever invented. But solitary confinement messes with one's mind.

I haven't seen Orbit for four days—at least I assume four days have passed by how many meals I've received. Though they feed me, the isolation is more unbearable than the Warren coal mines. With nothing to do and nothing but my cot and water pitcher, my trips to the bathroom feel like social holidays. At least I see faces instead of bare walls. Those walls give my imagination too much blank space to wonder how Dad and the Avalon crew fared from Orbit's "friendly fire."

My escapes are sleep and intensive exercise routines, which I do twice a day to keep from going stir crazy and to exhaust my pent-up energy. Oh, and then there are my tin plate games, but the crew bangs on my door when I make too much noise.

My head swimming, I collapse onto the cot as the tin plate clatters to the floor. If only I could sleep! The time could be anywhere between 0200 or 0600 hours. There's no way to tell, other than the hunch my headache provides. It's early, too early for the morning breakfast and bathroom break.

And yet, footsteps sound at the door, and it swings open. Orbit stands there, along with two crew members.

He grimaces in the doorway. "It smells like a locker room in here."

I swing my legs off the cot. "You didn't give me many options for passing time."

Orbit ignores the remark and throws a jacket at me. "Put that on." He motions to the crew. "And then cuff her."

"We're here?" I stuff my arms into the faded gray sleeves and cast a last look at the slate-colored walls around me. Suddenly, they seem much friendlier. Nothing better can wait for me in Deadwood.

Orbit starts down the hallway while the two guards sandwich me between them. We reach the ladder to climb out, and one of the crew un-cuffs me while the other trains a handgun on me. "Nice and slow," he says.

As if I have any desire to be shot in the back.

Orbit stands at the exit with his own handgun ready, but the display of force is wasted on me. Another guard reapplies my cuffs as I gape at the underwater port.

I can barely breathe in the frigid air, and the spectacle

threatens to steal what little air is left in my lungs.

The vast chamber is in the shape of a dome. There's no sky above, only strange artificial lights that cast shadows and make estimating the size of the space impossible.

Submarines—at least five others—dock in an organized fashion along the port. I don't know what else to call the underground shipyard.

Is this place a manmade cave accessible only by submarine? Yet the dome-sky above me isn't earth but perhaps glass. Does it separate me from the outside? I stagger to keep up with Orbit who seems untouched by the chill. If the weather is this brutal below ground, which likely retains the average yearly temperature like the caves of Warren, what must conditions be like topside?

But I forget where I am. Deadwood lies in the Black Tundra where Wasps once trained.

I clamp my mouth shut to keep my teeth from chattering and stumble after Orbit along the metal gangway. With my hands tied and my legs going numb from the cold, staying vertical becomes my new objective.

Ahead, metal stairs crisscross upward to a platform. There have to be at least ten flights.

I stop at the base and turn to the crew member. "Will you please take these off?"

Orbit has already begun taking the stairs by two.

"Sir?" the man calls after him. "Her cuffs?"

Orbit either doesn't hear or doesn't care. Knowing him, I guess it's the latter.

The man glances to his colleague, who shrugs and keeps his gun trained on me. "She's got nowhere to go."

I sigh in relief and rub my wrists before beginning the long climb. Orbit waits impatiently at the top with his arms crossed. I'm ashamed for him to see that I'm huffing, but these freezing temperatures make breathing painful.

"Where are her cuffs?" He glares at the guard.

"Here, sir." The man cringes.

"Put them on, and then return to the sub. I'll take her from here."

As the man tightens the cold metal around my wrists, I scan the underground dome. The platform offers a birds-eye view. On one side is the port—or maybe harbor is a better word. On the other, a series of hangars store…

"Are those airplanes?" I whisper as the two crew members retreat down the flight of stairs.

"Yes," Orbit snaps at me.

I can't take my eyes off the vehicles with wings. There have to be at least a dozen. "I've only seen them in books."

"Mr. Caesura has his own fleet, not to mention all his drones."

The squeezing sensation grips my chest again. Darius has none of these resources. We have one sub halfway around the world, and who knows what damage it's suffered.

"You're outmatched." Orbit's words pull my focus towards him. I can't tell if the blank expression on his face stems from pity or resolve.

I squeeze my cuffed hands into balls. "That doesn't make what Felix is doing right."

"You don't have to be right to win."

I stick out my chin. "Maybe not, but can you live with yourself afterward?"

Orbit's eyes glaze over. "We're wasting time. Come with me."

"As if I have a choice," I mutter.

Orbit presses his finger onto a pad, and the metal wall before us parts. "You always have a choice, but that time for you is past. Now you have to deal with the consequences of your choices."

He grips my arm and pulls me next to him inside the giant elevator.

The metal door closes without a sound. "You're right." I look at his profile, complete with a strong, stubborn jawline. "We both get to choose, and maybe it's too late for me to make a difference. But it's not too late for you."

For a brief second, the tenseness leaves his jaw, and his eyes soften. "I'll do what I can for you, which won't be much."

I nibble my lip. "If you want to do something for me, be true to yourself. Deep down, the Orbit I know isn't a machine that does a master's bidding. He's a free man with a noble heart. Our world needs men like that."

His lips stiffen. "You're wrong… about me."

I lower my gaze and swallow a deepening sense of loss. "If I am, then there's no hope for either of us."

Compared to the maintenance room on the sub, my new prison is a palace complete with kitchenette, bathroom, and a luxurious queen bed. Did Orbit deposit me in the wrong place?

No, this type of showmanship suits Felix's twisted personality. He'll give me a taste of comfort and then snatch it away. He's a master of contrast and contradictions.

I nibble the cheese and crackers left for me on the counter. I'm too hungry to care if Felix means for even this detail to remind me I'm nothing but a mouse to him.

Perhaps I give him too much credit for creativity. But sometimes creative minds can be the cruelest.

"Glad you're making yourself at home, Frosty."

I choke on a cracker and pound my chest to breathe. There's only one person who calls me that stupid name. Whirling on the stool, I face the door.

The thick metal panel remains closed and silent.

Felix's laugh rakes through the room. "Over here."

I slip off the stool and stare at the large screen across from the bed. A close-up of Felix's chiseled face smirks at me. He's sporting a trimmed blonde goatee that frames his full lips. His demigod good looks might fool anyone—but me.

But his head is tilted? That's an odd angle for a Translation. He reaches to tap something… on his wrist?

"I recognize you now, but I have to give Osborne props for your disguise. I like his improvements, but I prefer you blonde." His jagged grin spreads. "Still, he had me fooled into thinking you were a dim catering maid, nothing but a pretty face."

Don't flush like a schoolgirl. He's just making you feel small.

I cautiously sit on the bed's edge. "Why am I here, Felix?"

Oh, that raucous laugh! I tighten my jaw and wait for him to finish. The screen is shaking too hard to focus on him anyway. He must be recording himself via some portable device.

"Oh, Frosty, I've forgotten what fun you can be." He sucks a deep breath and steadies his hand. "Why are you here? You seem bent on mixing with the wrong company."

I cross my arms. "I could say the same about you."

He flashes a smile, but it seems forced. "Maybe you can't help the rebel blood in your veins. But don't worry, doll. I've got the antidote. I promise you'll learn to see things my way."

Antidote? If it's anything like Eliab's chair…

I grit my teeth. "You might as well kill me now and get it over with, Felix."

"Brave words, doll." He pulls the camera closer and winks at me. Those sharp gray eyes slice at my courage. "But that spunk is the reason you're worth saving. You're going to be so valuable to me."

Cracker chunks and bile climb up my throat. No, he can't be serious. I will never…

The metal door slides open, and I grip the comforter. Felix taps a device on his wrist, and the connection on the screen breaks.

Next to him stands Orbit, his face as expressionless as the blank wall in that maintenance room.

Felix holds out a hand to me as if I were a naughty child. "Come along, Frosty. There's someone I want you to meet."

Kristen Hogrefe

CHAPTER 28

~ Portia ~

Tuesday, 7.7.2150
Deadwood

I don't know left from right anymore. The hallways all look the same. Orbit presses a hand on my shoulder to stop as Felix swipes his finger against a scanner in the wall. A double set of metal doors part before us. Antiseptic odors slap my face, and my eyes water. What is this place?

Dozens of white-clad workers mill around the factory-sized space—a laboratory, perhaps. Orbit nudges me forward to mount an open metal stairwell that leads to a second-level walkway ringing the space. Centered along the walkway is an enclosed glass room. Only, I can't see inside due to the strange thickness of the glass.

But when Felix opens the door, I tense. There's a chair. *Oh, God, please not again...*

Orbit shoves me into the chair, and I stagger against it. The room's design, if not decor, resembles the one where Eliab took me for the "treatment" that left me devoid of a personality for a month. A long cabinet and counter run across one length of the room. What instruments of terror do those contain?

Felix closes the door behind us, then thumbs through a screen on his wrist watch. Apparently, the person he wants me to meet is late.

Although Orbit doesn't bind me to the chair, there's no chance he'll let me escape. He retreats a few steps behind me like a watch dog.

I press my thumb into the leather beneath me and don't feel any metal. The luxurious thing even has a cup holder. Surely it can't be a torture chair.

But what's in those cabinets? And why does the room smell sterile?

The door opens, and a short man with a pasty complexion enters. Round, metal-rimmed glasses offset squinty, cold eyes. I tense in my seat. I know this man. He was the Rosh agent with Felix the night the Friend was murdered. What can he possibly want with me?

He surveys me through metal-rimmed glasses and then directs his attention to Felix. "You made her sound interesting. She looks like a waste of time."

Interesting? What does he mean?

"Please have a seat." Felix motions to two chairs across from me. "This woman is Portia Abernathy, the sister to the man running the rebellion."

He crosses his arms and ignores the seat. "Then execute her and send him a message." His matter-of-fact tone better fits someone ordering a meal, not suggesting a murder.

Felix frowns. "I could, but she's more valuable. I want you to talk with her and see if you agree."

"I already disagree." The man sniffs at me. "You're wasting

your breath if you think she's the candidate for the demonstration."

My heart leaps to my throat. Demonstration?

Felix doesn't respond but turns toward me. "Portia, I want you to meet Viceroy Plume."

"There's no need for introductions." Plume reaches for the door handle. "I have no interest in talking with her."

Blood rushes to my face. "The feeling is mutual," I mutter.

His hand freezes mid-air. He cocks an ear my direction. "Excuse me?"

I shrug and study the glass wall. This man can't possibly care what I think. And I don't care about the opinion of someone who encourages a son to murder his mother.

"As I was saying," Felix cuts in, "there are some good reasons she's our girl. First, she can persuade the panel that our technology is ready for use. After that, the possibilities are endless. We could send her back to her Brotherhood and use her to infiltrate their ranks. Darius will be none the wiser that his own sister is destroying his team from the inside..."

I shiver and squeeze the sides of the chair. "I would never do that."

The man steps toward me, a spark of interest in his eye. "You would if you were programmed to do so."

"You program machines, not people," I retort. "Even your personality chairs have failed miserably. I hate to break it to you, but Mary Shelley invented Frankenstein a long time before you did."

Behind me, Orbit sighs. He should know I'm not good at diplomacy.

Plume's lips twitch. "I'll take that seat after all. You may be on to something, Felix. If we can reform this one, we can reform the world."

I retreat into my chair and glance at Felix who strides to a cabinet. He pulls out a short glass cup and measures a cloudy liquid into it.

"Exactly," he says and places the glass in my cup holder without a word to me.

I eye it warily. If he expects me to drink that…

"You said her brother and father are engineering geniuses, no?" Plume taps his fingers together. "She might be valuable after all. The Rosh League can use innovative minds."

"Right," Felix agrees, "but for now, the committee has warrants out for their execution because of the rebellion. But if we can provide evidence such minds can be reprogrammed…"

I grit my teeth but can't keep from lashing out. "Do you hear yourselves? Don't you have any morals? People are individuals, not machines."

"My dear, ethics are relative." Plume squints at me. "What's wrong for you is right for me."

Felix chuckles and gives me a patronizing smile. "It's better not to worry about ethics, Portia. Worry instead that you're on the winning side. And with our help, you can be."

I glare at him. "I don't want your help."

"Careful." The Rosh agent's eyes narrow to slits. "We have yet to decide if you're worthy of our help."

Worthy? Since when does another person decide someone's worth?

He crosses his arms. "Your father and brother have a reputation for brilliance. What do you have to offer the world?"

I blink at the question and stare in confusion at Felix.

"Oh, Frosty, don't sell yourself short." He smirks and turns to Plume. "Her scores were as good as mine at the Crystal Globe. They may have even been better. She's brilliant at deception. Why, the little snake fooled me twice and gave me the scar to prove it."

Brilliant at deception. The words slice through my gut. Have I really become so well-versed in lies that I have a reputation for them?

"But I think her real strength lies in diplomacy," Felix continues.

I nearly choke. What is he talking about?

"After all, her Brotherhood risked sending her halfway around the world to secure an alliance. She might have succeeded if Gage Colson hadn't intercepted her."

Plume stares into space as if considering Felix's words. "You have two weeks to make her ready for a demonstration at the summit. If you fail, you won't get any more funding for your pet project, and the summit will vote to launch Firstborn immediately. If we can't reform them, we wipe them out."

Demonstration. Summit. Council. Firstborn. The words blur in my head like a horrible nightmare. Is this the secret meeting that the Orvieto Confederation is trying to find? What does he mean that if Felix fails, Firstborn launches?

Felix rubs his hands together. "Excellent." He returns to my side and pries one of my hands off the seat I've been gripping. He rubs his thumb along my skin, sending pricks of terror up my arm. "We're going to make a great team, you and I."

I yank away. "I'll never help you."

"Oh yes, you will." He laughs. "You won't be able to help

yourself. Our technology may have failed you once before, but we've made advancements since then."

He looks past me to Orbit. "Call the Mavens and let them know she'll be ready in half an hour for the procedure."

"Procedure?" I shrink away from him.

Felix retrieves the glass from my cup holder and holds it out to me. "Don't worry, Frosty. You won't feel a thing."

I shrink away. "No."

He glances between the cup and me. "You can drink this like a good girl, or we can pipe it into you some other way."

Felix shoves the glass into my trembling hands. "Drink up... cheers!" He laughs at his own joke.

But I'm not laughing. I jerk my head to catch a glimpse of Orbit. He refuses to meet my gaze. I'll find no help there.

I study the glass. It makes me wonder if the poison Felix gave Julianna was kinder.

Shakily, I raise it to my lips, close my eyes, and breathe a last, desperate prayer. *Dear God, please help me.*

There's a quiet glow above me somewhere. My whole body is warm, relaxed, as if I've woken up from a long nap with a fuzzy blanket.

But there's something like a dull ache, too. If only I could latch on to the discomfort to pinpoint its source. I try to reach out but can't move.

Tilting my head to the side, I see why. Straps wrap around my elbows and attach to the arm of a chair. I peer down at my waist and legs, which are also cinched to my recliner.

My chest pounds. Where am I? I close my eyes and take a series of deep breaths to stop the panic that threatens to burst inside me.

Fuzzy faces form in my memory. Orbit's appears first. At least in him, I have a friend. But then I remember the submarine and where he brought me. No, he delivered me to Felix and that other horrible man.

Felix's face flashes before me and awakens a sense of uneasiness. He had brought me to this room. But why am I like this? What had happened after that?

I tug at my legs and arms, but the constraints don't budge. Next, I try twisting. My wrists are tiny. Maybe I can…

"Relax, my dear. Don't hurt yourself."

The man's soothing voice comes from behind me, and I let out a little shriek.

"Don't be frightened." There's a clicking noise as if he's entering something on a tablet. "Your vitals are strong, and the connection is successful. You have nothing to worry about."

Connection? What is he talking about?

"Why am I latched down?" I croak out the question. Ugh, my throat is like sandpaper.

"It's a precaution." He pats my shoulder. "Here, let me unlatch this one so you can drink some water." He frees my right hand and elbow. Then, he presses a paper cup into my hand.

He might as well have zapped me. The cup stirs my memory. Felix had made me drink something—had done this to me.

Hands trembling, I sip and swallow, but something about my

neck doesn't seem right. Maybe my throat is swollen? There's that dull ache again.

I drop the cup into the holder and touch my skin.

Only, it's not my skin. It's cool, thin, and hard to the touch, like a plastic choker necklace might be.

I run my finger around my neck. Sure enough, the foreign material traces all the way around. On either side of the ring, my skin feels puffy. What have they done to me?

Biting my lip, I scan the room for a mirror. There is none, but above me, the metal framing of the surgical lamp offers a dull reflection and confirms my suspicion: I have some kind of collar on my neck.

"I'm not an animal," I mutter and cover my throat.

"What's that?" The man grunts behind me.

"I'm not an animal!" I scream and slide a fingernail between the material and my skin. Warm liquid oozes between my nail. That must be blood. My blood.

"Hey, stop that!" The man bends over my shoulder and snatches at my hand. "You'll hurt yourself."

I grab his wrist and yank. He staggers forward, half falling over me and half trying to break my hold. Panic spreads across his face as if he's stunned by the intensity of my rage.

When I release him, he slides off the side of the chair and to the floor. Meanwhile, I snatch at the other constraints, freeing my left arm and waist.

"Stop!" He taps furiously on his watch and raises his wrist to point it at me. Is he trying to record me? Who cares. I'm not afraid of a man's wrist watch.

But then I focus on his face, and in an instant, realize there are other problems bigger than my own. I know this man.

"Mr. Danforth?" I gasp. "What are you doing here?"

For a few seconds, we stare at each other, mouths gaping. Surely, he must recognize me.

His lips tremble, and a flicker of doubt crosses his face. "How do you know my name?"

Oh, right. He doesn't recognize me because of the way Osborne disguised my appearance.

I smile eagerly. "It's me, Portia Abernathy. I look different now, but I'm the same girl who used to live next door."

The confused lines on his forehead deepen. "How do you know my name?" he asks again and slowly backs away from me toward the counter.

I open my mouth to protest. Maybe he'd forgotten about me after Dad and I moved.

"I'm the girl who used to live next door," I say, softer this time. "Luther and I went to school together."

His brows crease in concentration, and he grips the ledge with his hands. "Luther? Young lady, what are you talking about? We just met a few moments ago."

My throat goes dry, and a shiver snakes its way down my spine. Perhaps Mr. Danforth doesn't remember me, but how can he forget his own son's name?

And then I see it. In our scuffle, the top button of his collared shirt had come loose, revealing trace edges of a metallic black collar underneath.

Dear, God. He has one embedded in his neck, too.

I have to get out of here. Bending at the waist, I snatch at the last two constraints holding down my legs. Once free, I can outrun this shadow of the man who seems to have forgotten he's Luther's dad.

There. My fingers fumble with the last clasp, which breaks open. I swing my legs off the table, but a tight hand squeezes my shoulder.

I jerk away. "Let me go!"

He releases his grip, and too late, I see the syringe in his other hand. He stabs it into my arm.

I shriek as he shoves his finger on the applicator, and the syringe's contents burn beneath my skin. I writhe and shove him away at the same time. He loses his fingering but leaves the syringe in place.

With a shaky hand, I yank it out and fling it across the room.

"Stay put." His voice sounds frightened. "You won't be able to…"

I fall off the side of the table and break my fall with my shoulder. It throbs as I roll to my knees and crawl toward the door.

Why is it moving? My head swims, and my vision goes double. I reach for the door knob and come away empty. Why can't I grab it?

Now, it's blurring even more, growing darker and farther away. I must be losing control to the serum.

"Please, no." I choke a sob and curl up with my head tucked inside my chest. There is no way out but through the hovering blackness.

CHAPTER 29

~ Portia ~

Wednesday, 7.8.2150
Deadwood

There's light on the other side. I squint through a fog that seems to hang over my senses. Why is everything blindingly white? Or, maybe everything seems white compared to the black hole that engulfed me.

I retreat behind closed lashes and breathe deeply, hoping to ward off the ache pounding in my head.

Where am I? What happened?

I pinch my sheet. It's starchy and smells like disinfectant. Maybe I'm back in the sub's quarantine room with those friendless walls. No, it's too cold for the sub.

Shivering, I pull the sheet to my chin, and my fingers brush something cool, metallic, and foreign on my neck.

My eyes flash open, half expecting a snake to have slithered around my neck. But no fangs clamp down on me.

I touch the serpentine smoothness again and trace it around my throat.

And then I remember. I had been strapped on an operating chair, and Luther's own dad was responsible for me being there.

What horrible nightmare am I living?

Sucking a breath, I brave up and survey my surroundings. I'm back in the room where Orbit first left me. The queen bed, though starchy, is comfortable enough. Beyond it, there's a screen. I just hope no one is watching me through it.

On the other side of the room is a small kitchen and a door, which I assume must be a bathroom.

Bathrooms have mirrors.

Cautiously, I touch my feet to the floor. It seems level enough. Swaying with arms outstretched for balance, I work my way to the bathroom and fumble along the wall for the switch.

It snaps on with blinding brilliance, but I'm too transfixed on the mirror to care. A collar fastens around my neck. It's a delicate, black band and looks like a choker that a wealthy woman might wear to a dinner event.

But it's also translucent. Holding my breath, I step right up to the mirror. Sure enough, tiny corpuscles float inside the collar.

What will wake them? With the chair, Eliab had only to program the controls. But what controls this collar? Gingerly, I trace a finger around it. There doesn't seem to be any button or clasp.

The chair was one thing. But this—there's no way to get out of it without surgery. My skin around it is still pink and puffy from where the Maven embedded it. Dried blood coats one corner where I had tried to claw it off.

Hot tears burn inside my lashes. How could Luther's dad do this to me?

I choke them back and hold my breath, half expecting a pin-pricking sensation to start any moment. Perhaps the collar wakes up shortly after I do?

But nothing happens. I tear my gaze away and slap on the faucet. Splashing cold water on my face helps, but I can't shake a persistent dizziness. Perhaps it's a side effect of the collar.

After mopping my skin dry, I return to the rest of my living quarters. Granola bars and some other snacks perch on the kitchen counter, but I ignore them. Right now, I just feel sick.

There's a subtle beeping sound, and the metal front door slides open. I retreat behind the tall counter-top as the wiry but muscular Gage enters.

I narrow my eyes. "Orbit."

He ignores the name. "I'm Gage Colson, here to escort you to breakfast."

Breakfast? How long have I been out?

"No thanks." I use my foot to tug a stool out from under the counter. "Not hungry."

He folds his arms. "Not optional."

I plant myself on the stool and cross my arms. "Not budging."

Orbit steps into the kitchenette. "Don't push me."

"Oh, because I'm the one doing the pushing here?" I flick a granola bar across the counter-top at him. "I'm not the one who planted a freak collar on someone's neck."

He steps on the granola bar and moves to the edge of the counter. "It's time to go. This is the last time I'll ask nicely."

I jump off the stool and shove it toward him. It clatters on the tile by his boots. "Nicely? There's nothing nice about any of this…"

The room spins again, and I lean into the counter. Squeezing my eyes shut, I try to regain my sense of balance.

His firm hands squeeze my shoulders, but his grip isn't unkind. "Get your head in the game," he mutters in my ear.

"Game?" I sniff and squint at him. "Is that all this is to you?"

"Lose the pity party, Portia," he growls and pushes me toward the door. "I can't help you when you're not willing to help yourself."

Help me? Is he even considering that?

Orbit keeps his arm locked in mine so I don't swoon in the hallway. My dizziness must be a bad combination of the drugs and lack of food. How long was I unconscious?

When we reach a double door, he presses his thumb onto the scanner and pulls me inside what looks like a dining room. People in uniforms side step around me without as much as a curious glance.

Orbit guides me to a private room where a small round table is set with a simple breakfast. "Eat. I'll be back in ten."

I survey the plate, complete with bacon, a hard-boiled egg, and a pancake. "Where's my fork and knife?"

His lip curls with the trace of a grin. "Sorry, can't take that chance with you. Finger food it is."

I huff as he disappears. Do they think I'll try to kill myself or rip this collar off my neck?

Not bad ideas, either of them.

My conscience pricks as I gnaw on some greasy bacon. Orbit is right. I have to stop feeling sorry for myself. I'm a fighter.

But how long do I have before this collar starts working and I forget who I am and who I love—like Mr. Danforth has?

I eat the pancake like a wafer, but it sticks to the roof of my mouth. I choke it down with the glass of water and then push back my chair.

There's no place to go. The boxed eating room contains the center dining table and a long table along the wall. On it rests a fresh coffee pot. Does Orbit know I adore coffee? I can't remember if I ever told him.

Perhaps there's a chance he doesn't completely hate me.

I pour a generous cup and stir in a packet that reads creme. Odd. It must be dehydrated or something.

The door clicks open behind me, and I whirl. Orbit has returned with Felix. He smirks. "Making yourself at home, I see. That's good."

I almost toss my coffee on his shirt, but that would be a waste of perfectly good brew. Instead, I squeeze the cup tighter and level my gaze at him. "Coffee appears to be the only remnant of civilized society around here."

Felix snorts and takes a seat, while Orbit guards the door. "Civilized? Oh Frosty, we're much less primitive than your backward Brotherhood."

"You call this civilized?" I jerk a finger at my neck. "You've treated me worse than a mongrel. Is this supposed to be my zap collar so you can keep me in line?"

He throws back his head and laughs. "No, no, no. We're not savages here. Sit down, and let's chat."

Sit down. That sounds like a mongrel's command to me.

Biting my lip, I fall into a seat, which rolls me closer to the table. I didn't realize the thing was on casters.

Felix stares at me expectantly, but nothing I have to say will sound pleasant.

He frowns and slides toward the counter to pour himself a cup.

"You're not very fun when you're cross."

"Fun? Who's having fun here?" I spit the coffee out of my mouth to keep from choking. "If this is some game to you or a match to establish your dominance, then congratulations. You win. Now can you please take this thing off me?"

He spins his chair and claps his hands as if laughing at a joke. This man is deranged.

When he finally catches his breath, he pulls the chair closer to the table and leans in. "Frosty, that collar is there to stay. It was surgically added and would have to be surgically removed."

My hands fly to my neck. How long had it taken to embed it in my skin? How hard would it be to remove?

"Why, don't you like it?" His smirk darkens. "I made sure you received the latest model—It's quite stylish, actually. You'd make quite the call girl in a negligee and your sassy choke collar."

I snatch my mug and fling the rest of its contents in his face. Too bad it isn't scalding.

Felix recoils and curses at me while trying to wipe his dripping face with the table cloth.

I shove my chair back and storm past the table toward him. "How dare you!" I shove my finger in his chest while he staggers for balance. "You—you—" I sputter, discarding all the words that come to mind. None seems strong or vile enough to describe what Felix has done to me.

Orbit squeezes between us and drags me to the door. "I'll take her to her room, sir."

"No!" Felix tosses the stained tablecloth to the floor. "If she wants to act like an animal, we'll treat her like one. She has to learn respect if I'm going to convince the viceroy she's worthy of our time."

Orbit stiffens, but his grip lessens. Is he giving me an out, or is he forgetting he trained me how to fight?

I stomp on his boots and elbow him in the gut, then twist and leverage all my weight to slam into him and catch him off balance. He crashes into Felix who hits the table. There's a crack as if something split.

Wasting no time, I bolt through the door. Though this chase can only dead end, running makes me feel stronger.

I dodge gawking onlookers in the main cafeteria and slide after two others who exit through the metal door. In the hallway, I restrain the urge to bolt full speed. That would just draw attention to myself.

Think, Portia.

I straighten my uniform, stick out my chin like the rest of these snobs, and speed walk through the busy halls. An elevator opens to my left, and I slip into it.

Right behind me, a man pushes a cart and hedges me inside the elevator by the control panel.

Don't panic. He's just a custodian.

His moustache twitches, and he eyes me warily as I press the highest level the elevator has to offer. The only way out is up. If I can get back to the port that brought me here, maybe I can...

I stop the thought. One step at time. I have to find the port first.

"You lost, girl?"

I shift my attention to the custodian. He looks too crusty to care if I'm lost or not.

"Nah." I shove my hands into my pocket.

He grunts and nods toward the button I'd pressed. "You want to go to the garbage dump?"

My jaw drops. "I—uh—thought that was the port level."

He jams his finger into the number below it. "This one's the Gateway."

The port has a name?

"You part of a new sub crew or somethin'?" he asks.

I jut out my chin. "Don't I look like one of the crew?"

His eyes flicker as his gaze rests on my neck. Does he notice the collar under my shirt?

He wraps gnarled hands around the cart and glances away with tired eyes. "You look like you could be whatever you wanted."

His words knock the breath out of me. Does he see through my thin veil of an act?

The elevator reaches the second to highest level. As the door begins to part, a red light at the top flashes and shrieks.

Crusty's eyes widen, and he pulls up his sleeve. He's wearing one of those watches, too.

"Escaped prisoner, female," he mutters and then stares right at me. "That you?"

My mouth goes dry. Will this man turn me in?

I'm not waiting to find out. I dart through the crack in the elevator and nearly trip on the platform. Beyond is the winding staircase, and below, the submarines and planes.

I take the stairs by two and grip the railing for balance while mentally ticking off all the options that won't work. I can't swim. Escaping by sub is too slow, and surely, Felix can track this stupid collar.

When I hit the ground, I veer toward the planes and the glass-like ceiling that separates it from the outer world.

I barely know how to drive a motorbike, let alone fly a plane, but there's no time like the present to learn.

Compared to what's waiting for me back with Felix, crashing and burning seems the friendlier risk.

Somewhere to my left, there's shouting. I ignore it and focus on a male pilot who sits inside a small cockpit a few meters away. His engine is running, and even if it weren't, he's too focused on his dashboard to hear the ruckus breaking loose around him.

No, wait. His engine isn't just running. His plane is moving. The cover to his cockpit slides closed, and I run harder. In my upper peripheral, I watch the thick ceiling part.

This might be my only chance. My lungs scream for more air, but I focus on the wings. As I run parallel to them, my chest tightens. They're too tall for me to reach.

The wheels are another story, but the plane has begun to lift off the ground. It's now or never.

With my last burst of energy, I lunge toward the left wheel and grab on to the framework above it. My feet drag against the cement ground, and moments later, I'm not touching anymore.

Hold on, girl. I hug the framework with every ounce of strength as a frigid gust slams into my face, leaving a prickly, tingly feeling.

Panic rises inside me. How long can I hold on in sub-zero temperatures before my hands go numb? What if the pilot isn't going south but doing a test run? What if he circles right back?

The ceiling grows closer, and I refuse to look down. If I fall now, I'll be mush. The custodian would have to scrape me off the pavement.

Blood roars in my ears as we clear the exit. Even if for a moment, I'm free.

The sun on the horizon sears my vision and reflects brightly off the tundra. Snow blindness is the last thing I need.

The plane suddenly drops, and I almost lose my grip. Has the pilot noticed me, or am I affecting the plane's weight distribution?

The tingling sensation all over my skin turns to burning. This wind shear is going to rip the skin off my face.

It's all I can do to keep from screaming at the agony. But it's not just my face anymore. It's as if someone is jabbing hundreds of needles into my body.

My eyes flash open in horror. No, that's not the cold, brutal though it is.

That's the chair.

That's the collar.

That's Felix.

CHAPTER 30
~ Portia ~

Wednesday, 7.8.2150
Deadwood

A gust of wind smacks the plane, which dives low to avoid the repelling gust. Is that a snow bank we're hovering above? But I can't tell up from down anymore. Pain streaks fingers across my vision.

I try to lock my arms in place while my body writhes from the collar's curse. But my arms don't even feel like they belong to me anymore. They're slipping—I'm slipping.

The plane continues its course, but I'm no longer with it. For several seconds, I free fall. Maybe this is what death is like?

Powder engulfs me, but I can't tell if I'm hurt from the fall or not. All of my nerve endings are already on fire. If only I would black out and find relief somewhere.

I groan. I cry. I scream. I claw at the collar around my neck, but my fingernails shred my skin until the snow turns red around me.

"Oh, God," I gasp through the tears. Will this torture never end?

A dull ache replaces the sensation of daggers slicing through me. The sub-zero temperatures must be killing my nerves. If I could only keep walking, but the collar has debilitated all control I once had over my limbs.

Given my options, freezing to death feels kind of friendly.

My teeth stop chattering, and my mind blurs. Maybe this is my last chance. I can't move my lips, but I whisper in my mind. *I'm sorry, God. For failing my friends. I've failed you, too, but don't leave me now. Whatever is on the other side, I want to find you there.*

There's a roaring in my ears. Maybe that's the last of my senses to shut down. It's strangely comforting. The pain is all but gone now.

Lashes closed, I sink into the snow bank. It pulls away.

I shiver as something less soft slides between me and my snow tomb. The roaring continues in the background, like someone forgot to turn off a blow dryer.

Shut it off and go to sleep.

The other side is warm and dry. There's a dull light that silhouettes the small space.

More walls? A casket? But where is the light coming from?

I squint at the glowing object next to me. A lamp. I don't have many guesses about what the afterlife will be like, but I never imagined electricity being a part of it.

Familiar starchy sheets cover me to my neck, which I can hardly turn. I try to move my arms, but they're trapped under something.

After blinking a few times, I strain my eyes across my chest. *Constraints.*

No, this isn't the afterlife but a bad nightmare. Only a bad nightmare would take me back to a bed like the ones in Deadwood.

But I've never been this aware in a dream before. And usually, once I figure out where I am or what's going on, I wake up.

Maybe if I roll over, I will. But I can't. There's a strap across my chest.

Panic rises through me. Simultaneously, a beeping noise begins as if racing to keep time with my heart.

Something scrapes nearby, and footsteps tap toward me. "Whoa, take it easy. You're safe."

I roll my eyes toward the man's voice. A fuzzy figure stands over me, and I can't clearly make out his features. But that voice thuds in my memory.

Something warm seeps into my arm, and the beeping slows. "Rest now."

If I could cross my arms, I would. Instead, I glare at Orbit. "You told me I was safe."

He rolls his eyes. "You're alive, aren't you? That's safer than freezing to death in the snow."

I'm not sure. Being back in Felix's domain is the least safe place on the planet, as far as I'm concerned.

"Besides, I've convinced Felix and the viceroy to begin your training, told them how gutsy you are, and to imagine that kind of energy working for them. Your crazy escape attempt actually played in your favor."

I grit my teeth. "I don't want their training. I'd rather be dead than lose my mind."

He snorts. "Now that's gratitude. I save your skin, and you hate on me."

I slide up straighter in the elevated bed and lean forward as much as my constraints will allow. "You'd do the same if someone were reprogramming your mind."

Orbit hesitates and glances over his shoulder. The metal door remains closed. It's just us, for now.

"Portia, you've been in and out of consciousness for two days. Meanwhile, your treatments still go on every night."

I shudder and shrink away. "You mean… This collar works on me while I sleep?"

Orbit bites his lip. "Yeah, that's why Felix said it's civilized. Because when you're asleep, you don't notice the pain—or at least, only your subconscious does."

"But wouldn't I wake up?"

He shakes his head. "No, don't ask me why. It's how the thing's designed."

I look at my hands. They're bandaged, probably from frostbite. So much of me is bandaged, and yet inside, I don't feel any different. But if this collar works while I sleep…

Pressing my lips together, I ask the question that makes my stomach sick. "How long do I have—have before I forget everything?"

Orbit grins in response. Oh, if I were free, I'd punch him.

"That's just it, Portia. You should be noticing the effects now. You should be less passionate, more subdued, not as upset about the collar. The first stage is acceptance that it's a device meant for your good." He pauses and lowers his eyes to my neck. "Yet you've already done plenty of damage to yourself trying to be free of it. And if I undid your arms, you'd probably try to tear the rest of your neck off to get rid of it."

I frown. "What are you saying?"

He lowers his voice. "I'm saying that the collar isn't working on you."

His words take a moment to sink in. But that's impossible. Why would the collar not work on me? It's destroying Mr. Danforth. Who knows how many other people's minds it's mummified?

I meet his gaze, feeling hopeful for the first time in days. "Do you mean that you disabled some feature of my collar? That there's a flaw with it?"

Orbit scratches his chin. "Wish I were smart enough for that. I don't have any idea why it's not working. Your collar is the same as all the other ones manufactured."

My heart drops, and I look past him to the white wall. If there's nothing defective with my collar, then it's only a matter of time before my mind becomes like that wall: blank.

Orbit stands and straightens his uniform. "Listen, I have to report to Felix that you're healthy enough to meet with him. He's going to start testing the results of that collar, and you're going to have to play along—pretend that Darius and the Brotherhood are the real enemies here."

My throat tightens. "But what if I start believing that? If I do,

Orbit, you have to promise me you'll tell them what's happened…
or put me out of my misery before I say something I don't mean."

His lips twitch. "I'm not killing you, Portia. I risked my neck
to save you—again."

I jut my chin forward. "Then save the most important part of
me and get this thing off."

He runs his hand over his face. "Can't do that without giving
away who I am."

"And who is that?" I demand. "Someone's puppet or your own
man? I've told you Osborne is dead. You have to decide for
yourself where your allegiance lies."

His eyes flash, warning me that I've crossed a line. "You don't
know everything. Do your friends a favor and stop thinking of
yourself as a lost cause. Maybe you can do them some good."

His words cut. How can I do anyone good if I forget who I
am? But maybe Orbit is right. As long as I remember, I can do
something.

Orbit presses his thumb into the door scanner, and it parts for
him to exit. He twists his neck. "Expect a Healer within the hour
to complete your medical release. Once you're free of those tubes,
an escort will take you to Felix. Be ready."

With that, he's gone.

Be ready.

CHAPTER 31

~ Gath ~

Thursday, 7.9.2150
Crystal

Gath massages his temples and tries to shake off a nagging headache. The sun's glare off these junk drones doesn't help, but he's convinced the offensive answer they need is buried in the mess of metal before him.

He had ordered the militia to collect and deposit any drones they found behind the library's ruins where many discharged drones already littered the ground with debris. That way, when he needs a breather from mediating arguments between Darius and Alexis, he can retreat through the back passage and catch a silent break with the remains of the metallic detonators.

He almost prefers the mangled metal to political talk. Frankly, he could care less about structure. He's a man of action.

But he's seen enough leadership to know there has to be organization. He'd just rather not be the one to hash out the messy details.

He picks up his hatchet to resume dismembering these machines. There's got to be a clue somewhere in the mechanism's parts.

"Gath? You there?" Gil's voice calls beyond the mound of metal.

"Yeah, over here." Gath squints as his colleague hauls a plastic sack behind him. He drops the hatchet and runs over to give him a hand.

"Whatcha got?" Gath snatches a corner of the plastic to help him drag it.

Gil grunts. "Wait till you see what my team found lying in an empty field—doing absolutely nothing."

They reach the twisted collection pile, and Gil unties the rope he'd been using to secure the giant, make-shift sack.

Gath whistles. Though jumbled from the haul, a dozen perfectly intact drones appear. Fighter instincts kick in, and he motions for Gil to step back.

But his friend shakes his head. "No, they're off. We looked for a switch, anything—but couldn't figure out why these ones aren't working."

Gath snatches up the hatchet he'd been using to dissect the drones. "I don't buy it. It's only been a few hours since the last drone attack. These are either leftovers from that barrage or part of a new cluster waiting to hit us again."

With a few swift swings, he cuts off the drone arms until the dozen look like decapitated grasshoppers.

Gil raises an eyebrow. "Really? I bring you perfectly good drones and the best you can do is dismember them?"

"Rule number one of war," Gath says, while wiping perspiration from his forehead. "Never underestimate the enemy."

The words no sooner leave his lips than a humming sound begins, and the drones start vibrating.

"What…?" Gil steps toward the drones for a closer inspection.

"Get back!" Gath yanks him away, and they dive behind the massive pile.

A moment later, the ground shakes with a succession of booms. His headache is never going away. The explosions stop, only to be replaced with the pungent smell of burning metal.

Gil huddles in a tight ball, and Gath plants a hand on his shoulder. "Coast is clear."

The man is visibly shaken. "Dude, you just saved my life."

He squeezes his shoulder and offers him a hand up. "Let's go check out what's left."

They fan away the smoke and kick at the still-hot metal. He'll have to wait to inspect these until they've had time to cool.

"Look at that!" Gil points on the far side of the debris. "One is still intact."

Gath frowns. Is it a delayed reaction? Or is this drone different? "Stay here."

"Don't go, man. It's dangerous."

Gath ignores him. "I don't think so, but wait here in case." He steps cautiously over the shreds of metal and picks up the drone.

Something is different about it. Didn't Gil say he couldn't find a switch or anything to activate the drones? Yet, there's a clear latch on the bottom of this one.

Bracing for an explosion, Gath clicks the latch open. Nothing happens. He inserts his hand and finds a wire leading to a palm-sized device. He tugs it free and inspects it.

"What did you find?" Gil calls from a safe distance.

"I don't know." Gath flips it over in his hands. There's a button on the side. Is it some kind of recorder?

He presses it and holds his breath.

This is Deadwood. Congratulations if you've figured this out. I'm not Felix, and I'm not a friend, but you deserve a fair chance. Write this down. Here's the next ten drone strike times and locations...

Gath grabs a piece of sharp metal and scrawls the numbers in the dirt. What if this recording only plays once?

When it finishes, the recorder clicks. Gath stares at the sets of numbers in unbelief. Is this a trick, or are these real? There's one way to find out.

"What's going on?" Gil finally joins him. "Whoa, what's all that?"

"Get something to write with, and copy those numbers down, exactly." Gath darts for the underground entrance to the library. "I've got to find Darius."

Clutching the recording in his hand, he rushes down the tunnel through the archives and into the portal.

"... We've got to listen to each other!" Alexis all but shouts at Darius.

"But nobody's listening to me!" Darius waves his arms in frustration.

Gath clears his throat. Looks like he's been gone too long. "Time out."

Alexis and Darius spin to face him, their faces red from arguing.

"I found something you need to see." Gath holds out the recorder in his palm and recounts the story.

"Should I bring in Red and pull our snipers' focuses to these coordinates?" Darius asks.

Gath shakes his head. "No, I don't know how old these are. I need to map them out and compare them to the latest hits. Until we figure out where we currently stand in this list of targets, we need Red to stay on defensive alert." He sucks a deep breath. "Actually, with your permission, I'd like to start a new offensive plan. Leave Red and Luther as alternates on defense."

Darius nods. "I'm listening."

"Not only do I want to map out all the strikes and compare them with these coordinates, but I also want to organize scout teams. Gil said they stumbled upon these sitting drones by chance. But why were they sitting? Were they recharging? Waiting? I need intel and research teams on this. I also need hands to help me dig faster through the junk pile in the back. Maybe there's another recorder in there."

Gath pauses to breathe again. "Whoever this person is, we need to find out if he's actually helping us or feeding us wrong intel. And then, we need to figure out why."

Darius grins. "Gath, this is what I love about you. You shoot strait. By all means, organize whatever teams you need. Talk to Red and Luther and figure out what men we can spare to pull off other shifts."

"Thanks." Gath cuts his eyes toward Alexis who's been listening quietly this whole time.

She steps forward and claps her hands. "Bravo, that's exactly how a president and his Commanding Gage should communicate."

Gath grits his teeth. "With all respect ma'am, I'm not a Commanding Gage anymore. And I have no desire to be."

She clears her throat. "Well, I didn't mean anything by it. But you certainly have a military head on your shoulders. Maybe we can call you…"

Gath holds up a hand. "I don't need a title. I just want to do my job."

"Sounds good, general." Darius slaps him on the shoulder.

Politicians.

"Wonderful!" Alexis smiles. "And all I meant is that you two work together the way a leadership team should."

Darius bristles. "It's easy to work with people who listen to each other."

"Then let's start over and give that a try, shall we Mr. President?" She holds out her hand in a truce-like gesture.

His friend snorts. "What good is a president if his own sister goes around his back, and then he's powerless to keep her safe? And now, she's a prisoner of war."

Gath's chest tightens. "You and Portia are having a rough patch, but don't quit now. She's still alive."

"As far as we know."

An idea sparks in his mind. "Darius, what if we could send a response to this person? Maybe he can tell us something about Portia."

Darius rubs his jaw. "It's a stretch but worth a shot." He hesitates. "But as much as I love her, I'm not the one to send that message. Luther is beside himself."

"We all want her back, Darius. But yes, let's get Luther."

"Would you like me to get him?" Alexis volunteers.

Darius's shoulders relax. "Thanks, Alexis. I'd appreciate that."

"Yes, sir." She strides to the door, then pauses. "We've made a lot of mistakes already, but that doesn't mean we can't work through them. Luther shouldn't have sent Portia without consulting you, and Portia shouldn't have gone, but that's water under the bridge. Next time we have to make a big call, we need to vote." She gulps. "And your vote, Darius, counts double."

Darius's shoulders sag as if a weight falls on them. "It's not a bad idea, Alexis, but right now, let's take one thing at a time. Get Luther, and let's see if we have a shot at saving my sister."

Gath grins. His heart hasn't felt this hopeful in days. "And stopping these drones."

Kristen Hogrefe

Chapter 32

~ Portia ~

Friday, 7.10.2150
Deadwood

I sit on my hands, which sink further into the red plush chair. Before me, a wide screen spans an entire wall. The room uncannily resembles the portal in Crystal.

The guard had delivered me to Felix, just as Orbit had said, but Felix hadn't even acknowledged me when I arrived. Instead, he waved the man off, not that his absence matters. I've counted at least two other silent watchers in the back of the room.

Part of me wants to smile. Does Felix consider me capable and enough of a threat to merit such supervision? But then, I did nearly escape a few days ago.

Nearly. If only I had succeeded, I wouldn't be here.

"You're looking—better." Felix peers over his podium at me. His voice holds a suspicious edge.

But what am I supposed to say? My gut reaction is to tell him that it's no thanks to him. That won't do, so I settle for my second choice: silence.

The corners of his mouth tighten. "Hello? I'm talking to you, Frosty."

Ugh, do we really have to make conversation? Glaring at each other would work fine for me, but Orbit's warning rings in my ear. I draw from my lip-service experience with Osborne.

"Yes, sir," I say.

"Hmm, and how are you feeling?" His eyes narrow as if inspecting me.

"Fine, sir." I keep my voice at a monotone.

"Well enough, I guess," he mutters and taps on his screen. "We'll begin your training today."

"Yes, sir."

He flashes a forced smile. "I'm not buying the act, Frosty. You can't have gone from a rabid rebel to a compliant robot in a few days, unless you hit your head. And I didn't see any notes about a concussion on your report."

Something twists inside me. I can't fight Felix the conventional way, but I'm going to play the fool... and perhaps make a fool of him in the process.

"You were right," I say flatly. "If we can't beat you, we should join you. I was out of line the other day. Call it a near-death conversion, but I'm here to cooperate."

Felix grunts and studies me harder as if unsure of my motivation. Does he distrust the effectiveness of his own collars? Or perhaps I'm laying the act on too heavy for day one of training?

"For your sake, I hope you've learned." His lecturing tone reminds me of Professor Mortimer. Wouldn't the old professor be proud of his young protege now? "Viceroy Plume was very hesitant to let me waste my time on you, but he's approved one final chance."

"Thank you, sir."

"Don't thank me yet." The familiar glint returns to Felix's eyes. "You can say pretty words all day, but I want to see some evidence."

His gaze sweeps past me as the faintest click sounds from the rear of the room. Who just entered? I force myself not to look. Portia would look. Zombie girl wouldn't be interested.

Felix bows his chin slightly to acknowledge the guest. Twenty-somethings nod down to acknowledge older people but do a head-up for peers. This person is older or a superior.

And the other person who seems to have some stake in my "success" is the viceroy.

A knot twists in my stomach. But what is there to watch? What kind of training is this?

Felix returns his attention to his keypad, and the screen turns a light blue. He's preparing for a Simulation, but where does he plan to take me?

My hands start to sweat. This is like my Simulation class with Professor Mortimer all over again. What traps has Felix laid for me?

"Remember one thing," Felix says as the blue hue envelopes the span of our two seats. "You work for me now."

I gulp, not trusting my voice, and blink at the brightness.

Suddenly, the world goes dark, cold, and wet. The air is spiced with a salty scent, and waves break against a nearby wall. My boots land on uneven ground, and I thrust out my arms to get my balance.

Someone catches them with rough, but not unkind, hands. "Get on your land legs, Legs," a voice snickers.

I jerk my head toward the voice. "Rig?"

He snorts. "Who else? This might be a ship graveyard, but I

ain't no ghost."

"Shh!" A dark, lumbering figure in front of us swings his head around as if to scold two children.

Dad. It's a good thing Rig's holding my arm.

The reality of the Simulation hits me like those waves crashing against the sea wall. Felix didn't take me back to a date in distant history. He took me back to the Port of Civitavecchia on the night Rig, Dad, and I beached the dingy to scope out the place.

That night fast became a nightmare, with my dad lying unconscious on the ground, and all of us taken prisoners. At this moment, we had no idea what lay ahead.

I shrug off Rig's hand and step closer to Dad while scanning the area. There's no sign of Felix. But didn't he come with me? Where is he hiding?

"It's too quiet." Dad's voice pulls me into the moment. He presses a hand into my arm. "Stay with Rig until I signal."

"No, wait!" I whisper urgently. "It's a trap."

Dad frowns. "We don't know that. Now wait for two low whistles. If you hear anything else, head back to the sub."

I try to protest, but Rig again catches me from behind. I don't remember him being this clingy.

I squirm out of his grip. "Rig, we have to stop him. Just listen. We're going to get ambushed. We have to save Dad."

He rolls his eyes as if I've gone crazy. "Get a grip, Legs. No one has a peephole into the future."

His words slam against my heart. If only I could make him understand that I do, because this moment is in the past. This horrible moment…

"We should stay together," I try again, but at that instant, the laser pointer hovers over Rig's chest. How had I forgotten about that?

Before he can reach for me again, bullets rip open his chest.

I scream as he falls into the dingy, nothing more than a mangled corpse.

No! That's not what happened. Rig isn't dead. He can't be dead.

Noises from above draw me back into the nightmare, and I scramble over the uneven, broken pavement. Somewhere beyond is Dad.

The scene unfolds like a distorted dream in slow-motion. The port guards appear out of thin air. They hustle me, but instead of blocking my way, they propel me forward.

"Dad!" I squeeze between thick, sweaty soldiers.

Finally, I break through, but I'm too late. Dad's already on the ground, unconscious.

And now, Felix gloats above him with a rifle aimed at his head.

I slam my boots into the concrete to stop and suck in a desperate breath. Swallowing hard, I glance between Felix and Dad.

Felix wears the same uniform as the other Orvieto guards, but his blonde hair and fair features stand in sharp contrast to the olive-skinned, dark-haired Italians. He shouts something to one of them in a foreign language. Wait, how can Felix know this foreign tongue?

Rough hands push me toward him, and I stagger forward. Maybe this is a bad dream and not a Simulation. This isn't at all how this day in history went down.

But I'm not thinking straight. All I can focus on is Felix's rifle aimed at Dad's head.

The guards stop shoving when I'm standing above Dad an arm's length from Felix. Smirking, he turns the butt of the rifle toward me.

"Take it. And finish off this traitor."

Something like panic threatens to choke me. I can't shoot my dad. Surely, he knows that...

I snort air through my nose to keep from hyperventilating. The roaring in my ears threatens to drown me.

We're reopening history's pages, not changing it. The only change we hope to accomplish is in ourselves.

Professor Mortimer's words whisper in my memory, reminding me that a Simulation isn't real life. It's a test. And if I want a chance to help my family, I have to pass it.

I steady my hand and accept the weapon from Felix. Strangely, it makes me calmer. No way in real life would Felix hand me a loaded gun that I could easily take and shoot him with.

My finger scratches the trigger while the gun's still aimed his way. I'd very much like to light him up.

He knows it, too, because he stands there with arms crossed and a taunting glint in his eyes.

I lower the rifle from him to Dad's prostrate form. At least his face is down, and I can't see him.

Pretend he's nobody. But even nobody to me is someone to

another person. This is crazy. I'm not a soldier or an assassin, yet Felix expects me to shoot...

Yes, he does.

Come on, Portia. Get it over with.

After one more deep breath, I raise the sites to my line of vision and aim.

"Wait." Felix's hand comes down on the barrel. He motions to another man. "Turn him over. Make sure we have the right man."

My stomach knots. Can he really be this cruel?

The guard kicks Dad over, and he lets out a groan. There are scratches across his face, and his eyelids flutter.

Everything inside me wants to drop the gun and throw myself on top of him so these men can't mock him in a Simulation.

"That's better." Felix clears his throat. "Go ahead, Frosty. Put him out of his misery."

I bite my lip. I can't do this. I can't pretend. I can't...

"What's the matter, Frosty?"

"I—I've only killed someone once before—in self-defense." I don't have to fake the trembling in my voice.

"This man is an enemy of the ASU." Felix glares at me. "You're executing justice. Now, on my command, fire."

I nod and raise the rifle again, aiming at Dad's head. At least it will be swift and painless.

Fingers trembling, I slowly squeeze the trigger. The next second plays in slow motion. Dad's eyelids flutter open, and his warm brown eyes lock on mine. Confusion, betrayal, and horror flash in his expression as the round explodes and tears through his skull.

I drop the rifle, scream, and cover my eyes. But Dad's last image is now seared on my memory.

Strong hands grip my arms, and someone slaps me. "Get yourself together." Orbit's low voice growls. How did he get here?

I lower my tear-stained hands. Dad's gone, and I'm back in the training room. Felix leans forward in his chair, studying me intently, while the figure in the rear of the room snakes toward us.

It's the viceroy. "Worthless." Impatience etches his tone. "She's nothing but worthless. I'm beginning to question the efficacy of your technology—and this whole plan."

Felix rises and frowns at me. "She's only had three—or four—treatments. And she did shoot her father. If you knew her as well as I do, you'd realize what a feat that was. Four days ago, I'd have to skin her alive and still she'd never pull that trigger."

My heart pounds as fresh tears pour down my cheeks. Is Felix right? Have I already changed? Or am I still in control of my own choices?

The viceroy grunts and glances at me. "Call me when she's ready for a real demonstration—one that doesn't end with her dissolving into tears." With that, he stalks up the aisle and disappears out the door.

After he's gone, Felix crouches in front of me. He jerks his thumb on my cheek and flicks away a tear. Then, he presses his finger deeper into my cheek until it rubs painfully on the bone.

"Plug the waterworks, Frosty. You're made of tougher things, and if you want to stick around, you'd better perform."

I bite my lip from the pain and steady my voice. "Yes, sir."

"Better." He moves his thumb to my chin and tweaks it. A devilish smile plays across his lips. "Besides, you and I have something in common now."

Someone's breath catches behind me. Is Orbit still there? He must be. But why is he holding his breath?

Felix squeezes my chin tighter. "Now, we're both responsible for the death of a parent."

I grind my teeth to keep from reaching out and strangling him.

He throws his head back and laughs. "Of course, yours was just training now. But one day, you'll do this for real."

Orbit's hand comes down hard on my shoulder. "Should I return her to her room?"

Felix frowns at the interruption but glances at his watch. "Yes, we'll train again tomorrow."

His words pound into my head. How can I train like this day after day and keep pretending? But more frightening is another thought: How much time do I have before I stop caring?

Kristen Hogrefe

CHAPTER 33

~ Portia ~

Friday, 7.10.2150
Deadwood

Orbit escorts me down the sterile hallway. I hate the sanitized feel of this place. It's so impersonal, like someone wiped it down with antiseptic spray, the way Felix hopes to wipe my personality and memory for good.

I long for a little dirt, something that reminds me that real living is messy, not a manicured menu of someone's agenda.

Already, I'm becoming familiar with the maze of hallways, which aren't as extensive as they originally seemed. I always go left to get to my quarters.

Orbit reaches for the crook of my arm and tugs me right. "We're going this way."

I study his face, which remains impassive. He's taking me somewhere else.

For a split second, I hope it's a secret way out. Maybe he realizes Felix is a monster. He's going to come with me. Perhaps he'll help us...

Orbit presses his thumb onto a door scanner, and the thick metal door parts. I hurry to catch up but stop in my tracks. Before me, hundreds, if not thousands, of drones line racks.

This must be a hanger where the drones are kept or built before being launched. If so, then there's a door.

But there's nothing to fly or drive here that's larger than these tube-sized drones the size of mutated, elongated watermelons.

Not that they look like watermelons. But that kind of surface area isn't going to help a girl like me get out of here.

Orbit walks past the rows of drones toward the far side of the room to a pile of twisted metal. "What are we doing here?" I follow, muttering.

"I have something to show you," he says.

And I'm supposed to be the one losing my mind.

Reaching down, he pulls a drone casing out from behind a large stack and holds it out to me.

I arch an eyebrow. "What am I looking at?"

Orbit rolls it over in his hands. "It's a drone, genius. But do you see that casing underneath? That's where we usually place the detonator."

I step away from him. "You mean it could explode any moment?"

He shakes his head. "No, this drone is different. It never had a detonator in the first place."

I edge closer again. "Then what was it supposed to do?"

"There are different types of drones—messenger drones, explosive drones, reconnaissance drones." He toys with the underside latch.

I'm still stuck on how this stupid piece of metal even works. "But if it's not an exploding drone, how does it know to come back?" I brush my fingers against the smooth outer shell.

"Each drone has a tracking device embedded in its design that matches the signals of a receiver here in Deadwood. The drones are solar-powered, so once they recharge post mission, they return here."

I've heard of carrier pigeons but carrier drones? "So they come back—except if their mission is to explode and kill people?"

He shrugs. "War is war."

I still don't understand his point. "What does this drone have to do with me—with anything?"

Orbit flips it upside down again to expose the empty casing. "I'm in charge of the drone offensive, and I monitor the reconnaissance recordings. This is the first that's ever returned with its recorder tampered with."

"Recorder?"

"Yes, we equip select drones in a swarm with recording devices to gain some intel or reconnaissance while the detonator ones do the distracting."

I cross my arms. "If you're not trying to kill us, you're spying on us?"

He opens his mouth, but I cut him off. "I know. War is war."

Orbit smirks. "I thought you might be interested in this specific recording. I'm just glad I had the chance to listen to it privately instead of during an intel meeting."

While balancing the drone in one hand, he reaches inside the underside and retrieves a narrow black object.

I squint as he holds it out to me. "And what's that?"

"The recorder." He holds it up for me to see. "It's a USB pen drive with audio voice recording. The recorder is typically triggered after a set number of explosions, but this one was triggered manually."

Orbit strides toward a small cubicle in the back of the room. It must be a workstation for whatever personnel take turns working in this area.

I trail him like a nervous puppy. The metal door remains sealed, but what if someone were to find us here? Would Orbit get in trouble?

He inserts the drive into a laptop device and taps so rapidly on the screen that I can't keep track of his actions.

I'm about to ask him what he's doing when the audio starts playing. "Whoever you are, I don't know what game you're playing."

My throat constricts. Luther!

Orbit snorts. "Took them long enough to figure out my messages."

Messages?

"You seem to be telling us where the drones will strike—as if you're helping us—but who's to say you aren't trying to divert our resources to attack us where we least expect?"

"Wait, is he talking about you? Did you…"

Orbit shushes me. "Just listen."

The recording continues, "And if Portia really is alive, I want proof."

My eyes water, but I blink back the tears. "You've been contacting my friends—helping us?"

Orbit's face tightens. "Who's to say his accusation isn't correct? That I'm only helping them to build their trust now and make them vulnerable later?"

I gulp. "Because you're a better man than that."

He shakes his head. "I'm not a better man."

I press my hands on the desk corner and lean toward him. "Then why did you show this to me?"

His tired eyes meet mine. "Because he asked about you, and—if you are going to forget who you are—I thought…" His voice trails off. "I'm an idiot. Never mind." He jerks the drive from the laptop and shuts the device with a snap.

"You thought what?" I'm inches from him now. "Please."

He bites his lip as if embarrassed to admit his thoughts. "I thought you might want to say goodbye."

"Orbit, I…"

He shoves the drive into my palm. "There's space for a one-minute recording. Give it to me when I pick you up tomorrow morning, and I'll see that it gets in a drone."

Once more, he snatches my elbow and marches me toward the metal door. In an instant, he's transformed from someone who seems like my friend to the no-nonsense Gage Colson.

I do the double step to keep pace with him. When he opens the door to my prison-room, he closes it without even a goodbye.

I stare after him and then unclench my fist to study the drive. I can send my own personal message! I don't care what Orbit says. He's helping me.

After slipping the drive in my pocket, I collapse onto the bed and study the ceiling. What can I say to Luther in sixty seconds that could possibly help him understand what's going on?

Luther, it's Cotton. I'm alive, and I love you. But they're trying to make me forget who I am…

Forget. I'm not the only one here at risk of forgetting who she is. There's another person's story Luther needs to hear before it's completely wiped away.

CHAPTER 34
~ Portia ~

Friday, 7.10.2150
Deadwood

Staring at the metal door won't make it open. I'm going to have to annoy someone for a chance to get to the laboratory.

With a determined breath, I press my thumb onto the access panel. It flashes red, and the door remains solid.

I try again. And again. Over and over. The red light flashes so many times I start to see spots, and I wonder if I might become the new beta tester for technology failure.

For the hundredth or more time, I slide my finger in place. The door whooshes open, and I stagger back—more from shock that my idea actually worked than fear of what the consequences will be.

A Gage—or some other guard—stands there with a scowl on his face wide enough to belong to Felix himself.

He steps inside, and the door clamps shut behind him. "What's going on?"

"I-uh." I swallow. I should have thought about a response on the off-chance my crazy idea actually worked.

"I don't feel well."

"Sleep it off."

I gulp. "No, it's my injury. It started oozing, and…" I tug my shirt loose from the belt and slowly roll it up, hoping against hope he won't be a pervert and actually want to see my skin.

He grimaces and holds up a hand. "Come with me."

I let the shirt fall un-tucked over my belt and resist the urge to run after him. A convalescent wouldn't run.

Instead, I hug my stomach and teeter behind him. What seems like an eternity later, I stagger inside the laboratory doors. However, instead of the examination room at the top where Burke Danforth implanted my collar, the guard guides me into a smaller office on the ground floor.

"Sit." He motions to a shapeless chair and calls for an attendant.

My heart races. What if someone other than Burke comes to examine me? How will I bluff my way out of this one?

The guard returns moments later with a trim woman in a lab coat. She frowns at me like I'm a disobedient child. "What's wrong with her?"

"She said something was—oozing." The guard glares at me. "Patch her up quick-like, because my shift ends in fifteen."

She snaps on latex gloves and approaches me with probing eyes. "You can't rush remedy. Now wait outside while I have a look—if you have a queasy stomach."

The guard mutters under his breath and steps outside, though still within earshot. There's no escaping, but I might have a chance.

I flash her a fake smile and rub the collar around my neck. The skin around it is tender to the touch. I rub harder. It needs to look as irritated as the guard outside.

"Where's the problem?" she asks.

"Oh, my stomach. It's where I fell. It's oozing." I groan and hug myself.

Her brows furrow. "Let's have a look."

"It's from when I fell," I say again and roll up my shirt. Closing my eyes, I jab a finger to the left of my belly button. "Right there. Please, make it stop."

"Um…" She clears her throat. "Nothing is oozing."

I flash my eyes open. "Oh, yes, it is! Isn't it? Oh, but it feels like it's oozing." Again, I rub my fingers against the inflamed skin of my collar. "My skin crawls sometimes."

The woman steps back, and her gaze finally rests on my neck. Her expression is unreadable. It's either suspicion or concern.

"Wait here." She steps outside, mutters something to the guard, and strides away.

I hold my breath, expecting the man to return any minute and slug me for lying to him. But to my surprise, he stays outside. Then again, I can't blame him. I'd want to steer clear of an oozing mental case.

Minutes later, she returns with another man. I drop my gaze to the floor to hide my relief. Finally, Burke Danforth is here.

"Hmm." He steps closer, and I dare to meet his stare. There's no sign of recognition, only clinical compassion. "Help me get her to the operating room. I need to take a sample and get some bloodwork. There could be an infection."

At the word infection, the guard reappears at the door. "If I'm not needed here…" The look on his face reveals he'd rather be anywhere else.

Burke waves his hand. "We can handle this. I'll call another escort when she's ready to go back to her room." He then interlaces his arm with mine. "Come, dear. We're going to take care of you."

The other woman grips my arm on the other side, and I don't resist. Somehow, I have to get Burke alone.

When my skin brushes the thin, paper-like sheet covering the operating table, I second guess my idea. The last thing I want is Burke to clasp me in constraints or worse, put me under.

"Really, I'll be fine," I murmur and slide out of the woman's grasp.

"Yes, you will," she soothes and tries to push my shoulders to make me lie down. But I firmly resist and stay seated.

She studies me with the same nervous expression and doesn't try again.

That's one good thing about impersonating a crazy person. At least I have the element of surprise.

Burke turns from his prep table and approaches me with thin tape. "Now, I'm going to wrap this around your arm and see about a vein."

Great, Portia. Just great.

He taps on the inside of my arm until he's content with his search. Then, he reaches for a syringe. "Now you're going to feel a little prick. Keep your eyes on my face, and it'll be over before you know it."

I obey and study his face. The weary lines around his eyes remind me that he once used to smile. His firm nose and square jaw mirror Luther's, but Burke's eyes aren't anything like his son's black ones. They're gray, almost clear—almost lifeless.

There has to be something left inside him, something that hasn't been erased. And whatever it is, I have to save it for Luther.

I wheeze and catch my breath. "The room's spinning," I lie.

"Get her a peppermint," Burke tells the woman without glancing up from my vein.

"We don't have any in here, sir," she says.

"Well then, go get some! Her blood sugar is probably low." Burke removes the syringe, and I wobble on the seat. "Now, Ingram!"

She dashes out the door and down the steps to the floor of the laboratory. This might be my only chance.

Burke places a cap on the syringe and returns to press a gauze swab against the bruised vein.

I grab his hand with mine and force him to meet my gaze. "Burke Danforth, don't you remember me?"

He tries to pull back, but I don't let go. Perhaps he still thinks I'm crazy.

"Do you remember your son, Luther?" I squeeze tighter and retrieve the drive from my pocket with my other hand.

"Luther?" He repeats the name like a question.

"Yes, Luther, your son. Think hard. You must remember him."

He presses his eyes shut. "Yes, Luther."

I swipe the recorder on and hold my breath.

Burke squeezes my hand, and I wonder if he envisions that I'm Luther. "Oh, Luther, my boy. I'm sorry. So sorry. I was wrong, wrong. Tell your mother... But the virus, it will kill everyone. You have to get her to safety. You don't have much time."

"Mr. Danforth, what do you mean?" I ask and gently squeeze his hand. "Stay with me."

Heels click on the floor, and I swoon onto my side, shoving

the recorder into my pocket.

"Here are the mints, sir."

"Mints?" Burke mutters.

I suppress a smile as she stammers on, "You—you asked me to go get them?"

"Oh, that." He retraces his steps to the prep table. "Then, give her one! I still need to clean her neck."

"I can do that," the woman says. "Is there anything else wrong with her?"

Burke rubs his jaw. "Can't know until I test the bloodwork. For now, use a disinfectant and add some balm to the irritated skin. Then, give her a pill to take so that she sleeps."

"Yes, sir."

"And leave one out for me, too." He rubs bloodshot eyes and gives me a distant look, as if he's never seen me before. "I could use a good night's sleep, one that doesn't involve nightmares of strangers who say they're my friends."

When a different guard returns me to my room half an hour later, I eagerly escape into my prison and welcome the closed door. Legs still wobbly from my success, I collapse onto the bed and squeeze the USB recorder.

My plan worked. It actually worked. Not much has for me lately.

I squeeze my fingers around the drive and roll face down on the bed with a pillow pumped against my head. If there's any room surveillance, it will look like I'm crying, not replaying the message.

It's all there—what may very well be Burke Danforth's last recorded memory. It's a precious gift I can offer Luther about his

Dad.

And at least he can hear my voice in the recording and know that, for now, I'm still alive.

With a flushed face and a sour expression, Felix greets me as I enter the training room the next morning. "What is the meaning of this report? I didn't authorize any visits to the lab."

"I wasn't feeling well," I say and slump into the closest chair like a disobedient child. I brace myself for his tirade and shut him out. All that matters is that Orbit has the drive and promised to send it out in the next drone swarm.

Felix snaps his fingers in front of my face. "Are you listening?"

I blink and rub my head. "Sorry, I'm still a bit off. The doc said I might have an infection."

He snorts. "And whose fault would that be? You're the one who almost clawed your collar off."

A retort rises in my throat, but I swallow it. I want him to think I'm reformed, submissive.

"What's on the agenda for today?" I ask and focus absently on the screen. But even at my own suggestion, my heart beats faster. If he takes me back to see Dad again, I don't think I can hold myself together.

Felix grunts and retreats behind the podium. "You like history, right? Today, you get your fix." He pecks at the screen with such ferocity I wonder that it doesn't crack.

History. That's safe, right? But I've had enough experience with Simulations to know that I don't react well to emotionally charged situations.

I shift in my seat and glance at the door. Another guard, not Orbit, stands there. Part of me wonders why Orbit hasn't appeared, but I dismiss the thought. Maybe Felix has him on another drone-related errand today.

"Wait and see." Felix smirks and taps a final command with flourish. The floor around me illuminates, and I clutch the armrest. Will I end up in a snowstorm? A battle?

I blink, but I'm still sitting in a chair, a plush chair not all that different from the private one back in the training room.

I'm in an auditorium? Voices project while someone to my left sneezes. It's a woman. The man next to her offers his handkerchief and leans forward again in his seat, face rapt with attention.

We're watching a play. This must be some kind of theater or convention hall.

There's a flyer on the man's lap, and I tilt my head to read it. The lights are dim, but I can make out the largest words.

Our American Cousin.

CHAPTER 35
~ Portia ~

Saturday, 7.11.2150
Deadwood

I sink lower into my seat and study the characters on stage with their hoop skirts and pinstripe suits. Why would Felix send me to a play? This feels too normal, too enjoyable.

The audience laughs at something a character says, but I can't spend my energy trying to follow the play. I have to figure out why I'm here.

I crane my neck to survey the crowd. I'm on the lower level, and there's a balcony above me. To the far right is a box seat, probably reserved for someone rich. There are two couples sitting there. There's nothing singularly interesting about the women, but the two men stand out. One wears a uniform, perhaps military. The other wears a suit, but there's something about that long face and black beard that seem familiar.

Someone taps me on the shoulder. "Excuse me, sir, but I believe you're in my seat."

Sir? Oh, right. I'm dressed in a uniform, not a skirt. In the dim lighting, he's mistaken me for a man or perhaps a youth. His tight tone suggests that *sir* might be a stretch and simply a way to get my attention.

"Sorry." I stand and dart past him, keeping my head low. The last thing I need is someone calling me a cross-dresser. Crystal might condone that practice, but I doubt this society would. The women aren't even showing ankle skin.

I twist my hair into a pony tail like some of the men here and hesitate in the aisle, unsure where to go. I circle to the back of the auditorium when an attendant steps in front of me.

"Can I help you?" The usher surveys me with arms crossed.

I stuff my hands in my pockets and glance away. "Um, I think I was in the wrong seat."

"Where's your ticket?"

I dig deeper in my pockets and then pull out my hands, holding them out empty. "Sorry, I must have dropped it. Maybe I left it in the bathroom. Which way to the—men's room?"

The man's brows knit deeper in suspicion. "Outhouses are out back."

"Outhouses," I repeat. That's right. I'm not in Crystal anymore with its indoor plumbing luxuries. "Well, I'll go check."

He shadows me to the entrance. "You won't get in without a ticket."

"Of course." I plaster on a fake smile.

I stop outside the entrance and blink. The dark night surprises me, though it only makes sense for a play to take place in the evening. Still, there's something unsettling about the darkness.

Why am I here? And what does Felix expect me to do?

Laughter pulls my attention toward the dimly-lit street. Two men stride toward me, arms wrapped around the other's shoulders as if co-conspirators.

There's no mistaking Felix's blond hair and swagger, even in the night. The other man is harder to make out. His hair is dark, but he's as athletic as Felix.

My gut twists. Whatever reason I'm here, I'm about to find out.

Felix waves me toward them. Everything in me wants to run the other direction, but my feet obey. I hate the power Felix holds over me, and I hate that I have to be his pawn.

I fall into step with the men. "Hey, Felix."

"Perfect timing." Felix slaps my back, harder than necessary. "Frost, I want you to meet Booth. Booth, Frost."

Frost? Really?

"Nice to meet you, son." Booth leans in and grabs my hand. His breath reeks of liquor. They've been drinking?

Booth tweaks his moustache and gives me a once-over. I'm suddenly grateful for the dark.

"He really wants to pull the trigger?" Booth's voice lilts. "I can't risk any mistakes. I might not get another chance like this."

"Frost will pull the trigger all right." Felix stops walking and slides something cold and metal inside my belt. It must be a gun.

He leans close so that his breath comes hot against my ear. "Untuck your shirt."

My heart nearly pounds out of my chest. Who does he expect me to shoot?

I snap myself to the present. If I don't pay attention, I'll never pass whatever test Felix has planned for me.

He's resumed talking with Booth. "... and you've got the cash. Besides, you'll be right there. If the kid misses, you can finish the job yourself. But Frost won't miss."

We're back at the entrance to the theater, and my heart sinks. Whoever I'm supposed to kill must be inside. And so is that suspicious attendant. He's never going to let me get past him—unless Felix has tickets?

But when Booth opens the door, magic seems to happen. Sure enough, the attendant is right there, but his expression transforms from scowling to sunshine in a split second.

"Good evening, Mr. Booth!" His smile spreads from one corner of his mouth to the next.

"Evening." Booth nods in return and waves a hand at Felix and me. "My guests."

And just like that, we score a pass, free and clear. Who is this Mr. Booth?

Felix grabs my hand and tugs me after Booth who's already started up the stairs. Felix and I can barely keep up. This man is crazy determined or perhaps plain crazy. Is this a mission of revenge? Of an enraged lover? What is driving this man to commit cold-blooded murder?

Booth pauses only once at the top of the stairs and grabs my shoulder. "There may be a guard. I'll take him out, and you shoot the president."

President. I recoil, but Felix tightens his grip on my hand. I'm supposed to be an assassin?

I try to steady my voice. "What does he look like?"

Booth's eyes widen as if I'm the one here who's insane.

Felix squeezes so hard I think he might break my hand and spits in my ear. "He's the one not in a major's uniform or wearing a dress."

Booth snorts. "Ready?"

Hands shaking, I retrieve the gun Felix tucked inside my pants. It's the smallest handgun I've ever seen, but I suppose anything point blank can kill a man.

And since I'm about to shoot someone from the back like a coward would, point blank shouldn't be a problem.

We reach the box seat area. All that separates me from murder is a curtain. From the stage, a male actor's voice calls out, "Don't know the manners of good society, eh? Well, I guess I know enough to turn you inside out, old gal—you sockdologizing old man-trap..."

The audience bursts into laughter as Booth whips back the curtain. There's no guard.

I'm a few feet away from the man with the dark hair and beard I saw earlier from the lower level of the auditorium.

I raise the handgun. Does murder count against me if it's not real? But now is no time for a philosophy debate.

I pull the trigger, and as the president slumps in his seat, my heart condemns me. This man may not be my father, but doubtless he is someone else's. Yet I didn't hesitate to kill him.

What kind of monster is Felix making me? No, what kind of monster am I allowing myself to become?

Amid screams, Booth slashes past the other man in the box, climbs the rail, and jumps onto the stage.

"Sic semper tyrannis!" he projects from the stage like a seasoned actor. "The South is avenged!"

Fragments from my undergrad Latin class help me piece together his meaning. *Thus always to tyrants!* Could this president have been a tyrant? But it doesn't matter. One wrong deed doesn't deserve another.

I drop the pistol and stand frozen in place, staring at the limp form of the unconscious president. The woman next to him shrieks and gapes at me as if I'm some sort of demon.

Maybe I am.

"Now it's your turn." Felix whispers in my ear. I hear a click next to my head. He takes my hand and wraps it around a gun stock, guiding my finger to the trigger.

He wants me to shoot myself? Why doesn't he just do it?

But I can't bear that woman's screams anymore. This man must have been her husband.

I close my eyes. *Do as your told. It's only a Simulation.*

I pull the trigger.

The room blurs into focus but seems to take longer than usual. Maybe it's because my own head is still reeling from the awareness I murdered a president and then committed suicide.

But here I am, alive. Or am I?

I run my hand across my face to wipe away the sweat droplets. Somewhere behind me, there's a staccato clapping, as if one member of the audience had enjoyed watching the spectacle unfold.

Yet only a twisted person could.

Felix remains perched on his stool and rubs his hands together. He looks past me with a triumphant smile. "She'll be ready!"

In response, the door's latch clicks as the silent observer makes his exit.

Throwing his head back, Felix laughs and relaxes his shoulders. "Oh, Frosty, good show! I knew I could tame your rebel heart."

Bile burns my throat, and I swallow hard. I can't focus on my emotions right now. I need to use this opportunity to learn what is actually going on here.

I stretch my neck as if recovering from a long, boring presentation. "Was that person—that president—real?" I ask.

"Real?" Felix slaps his thigh and slides off the stool. "Why, of course, he was real! That was Abraham Lincoln, sixteenth president of the past civilization."

"Was he really assassinated? I mean, did I kill him?" I scratch my head. "I'm trying to understand if I'm in a Simulation or a Translation."

Felix strides toward a white board next to the projector and snaps a marker between his fingers. "You're in neither."

His words send a shiver down my spine. After the horrific encounter with my dad in yesterday's training, I knew I was dealing with something new here. But I still don't understand it.

"Yes, he was assassinated, but not by you." Felix uncaps the marker and draws three circles on the board. "Our friend Booth did the job."

I lean forward and attempt my best innocent expression. "But I shot him."

"Only in the Fabrication." Felix writes in each of the circles. In the first, he scribbles Simulation; in the second, Translation; and in the third, Fabrication.

"Fabrication is a modified technology we developed for training purposes. It allows us to use the resources of a Simulation but insert our own personas. The programming is a lot more involved, but our developers continue to find new ways to make the interactions more seamless and lifelike."

My hand twitches just remembering the handgun, and my ears still ring with that woman's screams. How much more lifelike can they design it?

"It seemed perfectly real." I hope the low tone of my voice helps conceal the trembling I feel.

"That's because you're too absorbed in trying to figure out what's going on." He taps the blunt end of the marker against his head. "Your mind pieces together what's missing, much like it does in a dream world."

Dream world? Does he mean a nightmare? This program has a lingering effect on the real world that makes me uneasy. What if I stop being able to recognize where Fabrication ends and reality begins?

Felix draws an arrow from Simulation to Translation to Fabrication on the board. "You see, we've taken the historical realism from a Simulation with the immediate nature of a Translation to create a module where alternate histories become possible. It's a great way to train test subjects to see how they would have responded in the very situations we want to prepare them for. It's also a fascinating exercise in *what if.*" He lets his words hang suspended.

"What if?" I repeat and force myself to focus on his twisted face.

"That's right." He caps his marker and slowly starts toward me. "What if you had assassinated Abraham Lincoln? What if you had then killed yourself?"

I bite my tongue. *I wouldn't be here.* That would almost be a mercy.

"What if you had never made the poor choice to join your brother's antics?" His hot breath on my face snaps me to the present, and I jolt straighter in my seat.

Does he really think I would ever have chosen him over helping Darius?

I slant my gaze toward the screen and ignore how close he is. The screen is now blank. Is it only a matter of time before my personality becomes the same way?

"When do we train next?" I ask.

"Every day." He steps back and follows my attention to the screen. "Every day until you're ready."

"Ready for what?"

"Ready to do whatever I ask."

Kristen Hogrefe

CHAPTER 36

~ Luther ~

Sunday, 7.12.2150
Crystal

Luther stares at the drive in his hand and sinks into the portal chair. He'd listened to the message half a dozen times until Darius asked him to stop.

He should be relieved to know his father and Portia are still alive. His heart should be happy to hear her voice, but instead, he feels cheated. The message sounded more like goodbye, and he's not ready to say his.

But now is not the time for self-pity. "Is Abram going to join us for the modem test?" he asks.

Darius shakes his head from where he and Alexis monitor the receiver for the Translation from Orvieto.

"No, he's resting. Can't blame him."

Luther nods. The man had appeared as if from the dead on the early morning train with the ragtag remnants of his crew. Their unexpected return felt like a victory punch in the arm, except that not everyone had come home.

Abram had delivered the modem from Orvieto and asked to be left alone to rest. His story would come out later, but right now, they need to hear from the OC.

"They're transmitting." Alexis leans forward in her seat as one figure gradually takes form before them.

Abra Bianchi appears at the screen with her characteristic purple glasses. A clip pulls her bobbed black hair away from her face, which looks more taut than usual.

"I'm glad the modem made it safely to you," she begins, "because we don't have any time to spare. Our intelligence has confirmed the next Rosh League summit is July 21. We need to determine the location and strike. Their forces have started a new assault against us, and we can't hold up against this type of relentless warfare."

"Where do you think they're meeting?" Alexis asks.

"That's the million-dollar question. We don't know. Even our intel on the inside hasn't figured it out."

"Maybe our person on the inside can." Gath interrupts from the back.

Luther's stomach twists. "Gath, you don't know what you're saying."

Gath ignores him and moves closer toward the hologram of Bianchi. "Portia, our diplomat who was kidnapped by the submarine in your port, is still alive and at Deadwood. We've successfully sent and received a communication through one of the ASU's own drones."

"I'm listening." Abra's face pinches in concentration.

"We may have someone inside Deadwood, but there's no way to track her or anyone else for that matter," Luther cuts in. "Just because we've been able to communicate with her through a rogue drone doesn't help your problem of figuring out the location for the next Rosh League meeting."

"Actually, it might," Abra says. "Are you still able to send her messages through the drone?"

Luther looks to Gath who stands with arms crossed behind Alexis. "We still have the drone and can send it back. Assuming Portia still has the means to retrieve it, I'd say yes."

"That's a big assumption." Luther rubs his jaw. "Someone has to be helping her. How else can she get access to the drone arsenal? Portia may be smart, but there's no way she could pick one drone from a hundred. It would be like finding a needle in a haystack."

"If someone is helping her, that's even better," Abra says.

"Assuming their luck doesn't run out," Luther mutters.

"If I sent you something, could you get it to Portia?" Abra asks.

"Send us something?" Alexis repeats. "How can you possibly send us something? Abram's sub just returned with your modem, and that took days—and an incredible risk."

"We can send you a drone of our own which will travel much faster," Abra says. "I can have the chip to you by tomorrow."

Darius's jaw drops. "You have your own drones? What chip— what do you mean?"

"Remember, we haven't been in the technological dark ages like you have," Abra explains. "Our tracking chip is traceable via our computers. Get a message to Portia. Tell her to plant that chip on a sub leaving next week for the conference."

Luther shakes his head. "I don't like it. Sounds like you're asking the impossible of her. Remember, she's a prisoner inside Deadwood. She could get herself killed trying to get access onto a submarine."

Abra starts to say something, but he rushes on. "How do you know a sub from Deadwood will leave for the summit? Sounds like speculation to me."

She offers a patient smile. "Deadwood is one of the Rosh League's ports, and since your rebellion, they've clamped down on their ASU leadership. Our intel shows one of their own viceroys is there right now, and he'll have to attend the summit."

Luther bites his tongue. There's no arguing with this woman. She has an answer for everything.

Abra continues, "If she's figured out how to communicate with you via drone, she's more resourceful than you give her credit for. Besides, we don't have any other options at the moment. It's worth a risk."

Worth a risk to whom? He'd like nothing more than to find his own way inside Deadwood again and break Portia free. The last thing he wants is creating more possible problems for her.

Another thought gnaws at him. How does Portia have the freedom to move about, and who would help her?

He thinks of her transmission. His dad is being brainwashed, but perhaps he's still lucid enough to remember the girl next door. Could his dad be their saving grace?

But how much longer does the man have before he forgets who he is? And after that, Portia will be friendless inside the enemy fortress again.

A hand squeezes his shoulder. Gath has moved to his side. "Come on, we need to get that drone ready. And I need your help wording the message."

Luther tears his gaze away from the screen. Darius and Alexis don't need him to finish their diplomatic Translation.

He's heard about as much as he can stomach anyway. Everyone seems to be forgetting that Portia's the one who needs a rescue mission, not another burden on her shoulders.

Gath leads the way out the door and down the long archive aisle. "You seem about ready to self-implode. Tell me what's eating you, man, or it's going to consume you from the inside out."

Luther grits his teeth. He doesn't need a lecture from Gath right now. He needs a punching bag with Felix's face on it.

"I just—we're no closer to breaking Portia out of that prison and actually helping her." Luther opens and closes his fists to relieve some of the tension.

"But maybe she's exactly where she needs to be to help us," Gath says. "If we can find the location of the Rosh League summit and the OC can make good on their promise to blow the leadership team out of the water, then maybe breaking into Deadwood will be a moot point."

They reach the back door, and Luther stops short. "Do you hear yourself? You're a military man, Gath. What happens when the enemy loses a war? What do they do with their prisoners before they can be rescued?"

Even the dim lighting can't hide the tightening lines on Gath's face. "They kill them."

"Exactly." Luther folds his arms. "I don't want Portia to have to be a hero anymore, Gath. I want a life with her."

"But we won't have the chance at a life if the Rosh League continues to dominate the globe—and you're forgetting the Firstborn threat." Gath twists the metal door. "If we don't give Felix a reason to surrender, he's going to use it on the citizens sooner or later. And in that case, you won't be here—and there will be no home for Portia to return to."

They climb silently through the tunnel system until the hallway opens out back behind the destroyed library. The sinking sun reflects off the contorted metal that composes the drone graveyard.

Luther taps his foot impatiently. "Why are we here? I thought you took the communication drone to the workshop."

"I did." Gath's giant form stands just outside the door frame.

Why is he risking this exposure? They've had problems with sniper drones recently—and there's always the disgruntled citizen who's angry the Brotherhood hasn't provided a bread factory. But overturning a tyrant doesn't mean a better life overnight. These people have to take ownership for their condition, too.

Luther sighs and rubs his temples. There are too many problems and no easy answers. "Why are we here?" he repeats.

"Because I don't want you to miss this."

Luther heaves an exaggerated sigh. "Miss what?"

"Are you blind, man? The sunset catches that mound of metal and changes an ugly mass of gnarled warfare into a blindingly beautiful reflection."

Luther shields his eyes. "It's blinding all right. But yeah, the metal does seem to change color from orange to pink as the sun goes down. It's pretty enough, I guess."

"I'm glad you can finally see it."

"See what?"

"The sun transform twisted ruins into something beautiful."

Gath's words sink through his skin. His friend isn't talking about the drones anymore.

Luther hesitates. "You think there's still hope for our world?"

"Our world, yes, but I was talking about you."

Heat floods his cheeks. "What do you mean?"

"I mean what I said. Until you realize that you need God in your life, it's going to be empty—with or without Portia. You can only reflect his love when you first accept it."

"Sounds like something Portia would say," Luther mutters.

"That's because Portia lives like God is real. If you start living that way, you'll stop trying to hold onto things you can't control and make a difference where you can."

"You think I should let her go? Just give up on ever having a future?" Luther chokes out the last words. Why does it feel like someone is squeezing his heart?

"I didn't say that." Gath shakes his head. "I want Portia home, too. But you need to stop trying to control things you can't. If you believed in God, you'd realize that He can use even the most out-of-control situations and bring about good. Who knows if Portia is in Deadwood at this specific time for this specific reason? You need to start praying and believing that there's a God who can turn the world upside down on its head if he chooses—and he doesn't need you or me to do it."

Luther swallows as the fading light casts darker purple and then gray shadows on the metal. "Then what do you suggest we do?"

Gath stares into the growing darkness, but the sunset's glow still radiates on his face. "We pray. We have faith. And we act. We act like everything depends on us but believe that everything depends on God."

Kristen Hogrefe

CHAPTER 37

~ Portia ~

Thursday, 7.16.2150
Deadwood

Sweat drips down my face, but I steel my eyes so that Felix can't see the rage burning behind them. For the last five days, I've performed flawlessly in Felix's Fabrication sessions. I've murdered my brother and George Washington, as well as torched a city called Atlanta on some crazy man's march to the sea, leaving the people to starve in the decimated aftermath.

Felix has done everything short of ask me to poison my own mother in a module, but maybe his conscience stings from murdering his.

I doubt it. I half suspect his heart is made of metal, or he's sold what's left of his soul to the devil. I refuse to believe that anyone short of a psychopath could invent the cruel tricks he's played on me.

I hate that self-satisfied smirk, the smirk that tells me he's proud of the well-oiled machine I've become—or that he thinks I've become.

"You're ready and just in time." Felix makes a mock bow toward the audience of one who has silently observed all my trainings. "Did I not say she would be brilliant?"

Staccato applause rewards Felix. "If you can deliver a performance like that to the council, no one will question your reforming abilities and technology again." Viceroy Plume's words slice at my heart. I don't want to be Felix's demonstration doll. The last thing I would wish on anyone is to endure the humiliation of a collar embedded in her neck so that some political puppet can solidify his position of power. I don't want to promote his methods. I want to end them.

"Gage Colson, take her to her room." Felix snaps his finger toward where Orbit waits by the door. "See that's she's well rested before we leave tomorrow morning. I can't have our star sleep deprived."

"Yes, sir." Orbit steps forward, my cue to stand and follow him. Has he enjoyed watching my descent into depravity? Though the only real kill on my hands is Osborne—and that was self-defense—I can no longer excuse myself as innocent.

No one who acts out murder and mayhem in such graphic detail can claim a clear conscience. Doesn't the Bible say that if I hate someone in my heart I've essentially murdered him? But I don't hate these people. I'm just commanded to kill them. Is that war? Or is that inexcusable?

I shiver as Orbit leads me down the hallway. Can God forgive what I'm becoming?

Yes, His blood covers you, covers all your sin. Were it not for Gath's words that ring in my memory and his own confident faith, I might fall into self-loathing.

But am I right to keep pretending, to participate in this act? Or should I come clean and let Felix kill me? Isn't that what he's going to do eventually?

Orbit tugs my arm and pulls me out of my impossible questions. He's leading me away from the hallway that drops me off at my door.

My chest tightens. If he's taking me somewhere other than my room, he's directly breaking Felix's order, which can only mean he's helping me.

I match his stride as we detour up several levels. Before the elevator deposits us on the floor, I recognize the level number as the drone assembly floor.

My heart skips a beat. Maybe there's another message for me.

The elevator door slides open, and a uniformed man barges inside the elevator, bumping into Orbit. His eyes widen as he spots me.

Jotham Danforth! I grimace and step past him into the hallway.

He blocks Orbit from exiting the door. "What's she doing here?" Jotham demands.

"Training exercise." Orbit sidesteps him. Though his face is blank, there's a hint of fear in his eyes. Why is he scared of Jotham?

"What can she possibly..." But Orbit slams his hand onto the door's closing button, and the elevator slides shut, cutting off Jotham's question.

"Hurry." The urgency in Orbit's voice makes me quicken my step. Orbit rushes toward the large metal doors and swipes his thumb across the scanner. They snap open, and we slip inside. Is he worried Jotham will try to follow us?

But I can't think about Jotham now. Orbit has brought me to

the drone warehouse, which must mean there's a message for me.

Orbit guides me toward the cubicle and flips open the laptop. His fingers fly over the keys, and then he jerks another drive from his pocket and inserts it.

He reaches for my hand and slides something flat and cold against my palm. "Take this, and don't lose it."

"What...?"

"Just listen." He nods grimly toward the screen and casts a furtive glance over his shoulder.

"Portia, if you get this, thank you for your message. We have one for you that might change everything for us—for the OC." Luther's voice sends tremors up and down my body. His voice reminds me of the home I ache for.

But I have to focus. The OC? The Orvieto Confederation? What is he talking about?

"The Rosh League summit meets next week, and the OC needs to know the location. Take this chip—guard it with your life—until you can smuggle it on board the sub leaving for the summit. That way, we can trace Felix's movements. I know it sounds like an impossible request, but can you do it? We believe you can since you've somehow discovered how to hack into a communication drone."

I look up at Orbit. I can't take credit for the communication drone. If it weren't for him, I'd never know such things existed.

Orbit doesn't meet my gaze. His eyes seem glued to the screen, even though it's blank, except for the audio player.

"Succeed or fail, Portia, I love you. And I'll never stop fighting for you." His voice catches, and the recording stops.

I blink back the moisture behind my eyes. I can cry in my

room, not in front of Orbit.

"What—is this?" I hold up my hand, but he doesn't seem to hear me. Instead, he types furiously at the keyboard, perhaps to erase the history, and then ejects the drive.

"Orbit—I mean, Gage Colson—what am I...?" But he slams the drive onto the floor and crunches it with the heel of his boot. Then, he retrieves it and hurls it into the junk pile of mangled drones.

"If anyone asks you what you were doing on this level, tell them..." His voice trails off. Surely, he's thought this through? Or has he just taken a huge risk for my sake?

"I'll tell them you wanted me to identify footage from a drone for your reconnaissance work," I say.

He blows out a breath and grabs my hand in a rare gesture of agreement. "Yes, that will do fine." He lets it go and nods toward the exit. "C'mon, we've got to get you back to your room."

"Orbit." I hesitate. "Thank you. I don't know why you've decided to help me or if we'll survive long enough for this to matter, but thanks."

"Don't thank me." He snorts. "Watching what Felix has done to you and knowing I could have stopped it..."

"I'm the one who could have stopped it," I say. "All I have to do is tell him the collar isn't working, and I still loathe him with every fiber of my being."

"But then you could never help your brothers."

"Maybe." I sigh and stare at the ceiling. "Or I'm a coward and don't want to die."

"You're not a coward." He shakes his head and swipes his finger against the door access panel. "You're the bravest woman

I've had the privilege to know."

The next morning, I tug on a black turtleneck and curl the fabric as high up my neck as possible. Covering the collar helps, but the skin around it still itches from healing. Are my treatments still happening while I sleep?

Regardless, it's not working. That's good if I escape some day and bad if my acting skills collapse under the weight of whatever pressure-cooker Fabrication Felix has invented for my demonstration.

I've racked my brain for an explanation. The logical one is that the antibiotic Gath gave me to counteract my first treatment has somehow made me immune to future ones. The inexplicable one is that God is sparing me. But for what, I don't know.

I tuck the plastic chip-card from the drone inside my socks and tie the boot strings extra tight. I can't lose the thing that finally gives my imprisonment purpose.

Last night while I stared at the ceiling, I put two and two together. The OC must want to target the Rosh League summit with a missile or something. How does that saying go? Take out the head, and the body will die. Although destroying the council might not completely solve our problems, it would give the remaining figure heads enough of a mess to cleanup. Maybe we could get our bearings against Felix's forces and the international choke hold this group seems to have on every country.

If I can be the blip on the screen that tattles on this summit's secret location, I will be the happiest blip there ever has been—even if it means getting blown to bits with the bad guys.

It's a good thing Luther doesn't know. He thinks I'll find a way to smuggle the chip onto the submarine. In that sense, he's right.

I'm going to smuggle it on with myself.

Slipping my arms into the uniform jacket, I look around the room. I have nothing to pack. It's not like this is a pleasure trip, and nothing in this room belongs to me. I figure somewhere along the way, I'll get to shower and eat.

I edge onto the stool and wish for a clock—anything to tell me the time. Somehow, I seem to wake up with time to shower and dress before Orbit collects me each morning. Perhaps there's a built-in timer with my collar I don't know about, but there's really no way to know if it's three in the morning or almost six o'clock.

The door opens, and I smile with relief. Seeing Orbit's familiar face each morning is the one...

I tense half way off the stool. Orbit doesn't enter like he usually does. Instead, another guard waits outside the room. I don't recognize him.

My smile vanishes, and a dozen questions prick my mind. I can't ask any of them.

Instead of the usual route to the mess hall, the man escorts me into an elevator and presses the button for the second floor.

My stomach growls, but I ignore it. Breakfast is not the worst of my problems. Where is Orbit? Surely Felix's right-hand Gage would be going to the summit with him.

Breathe, Portia. Perhaps escorting me would be the least of his priorities. Yes, that's reasonable. Maybe he has other more important errands to oversee.

That thought helps calm the pounding in my chest. I'm just part of the cargo, and this guard's job is to see I'm loaded properly.

The elevator door parts, revealing the metal platform. The sight of the underground port again gives me chills. There's something lonely about the sunless glass ceiling. The harsh lighting may illuminate the space adequately but leaves it feeling hallow and cold. Somewhere, the dome meets the frigid ocean water, but the darkness conceals where nature's waters touch man's brittle efforts to cage it.

"This way." The guard's boots clank against the stairwell, but the hustling bodies below soon drown out the clatter. The gangway groans with the weight of men and women coming and going, loading crates and luggage, and checking clipboards.

I very much want to ask when we're leaving, but I bite my tongue. Orbit wouldn't want me asking any questions right now.

Behind the guard, I climb down the ladder and enter the submarine. My throat tightens in the cramped space and heat from all the people brushing past us. It's too much like the Avalon.

"Oh, Dad," I mutter. What I wouldn't give to be on a submarine where he's captain and not some stranger working for Felix.

The guard grunts. "You say something?"

"No, sir." We enter a room lined with tables and chairs which must be the mess hall. Though it's empty, the smell of bacon grease and breakfast wafts from somewhere nearby.

"Sit and wait here." My companion points to a hard-backed chair, and I settle stiffly into it. Maybe this means breakfast.

He returns moments later with something small and tightly

wrapped in foil. "Let's go." He pushes it into my hands.

The heat from the contents radiates warmth. Even if it's tasteless, it's fresh. At least Felix feeds me better than the Wasps at Warren did.

We pass the open bunk room for the crew, and the guard nods toward a series of narrow doors. "Bathrooms." He taps on one and keeps walking.

Am I staying with the crew? Surely Felix doesn't trust me with that kind of liberty.

He doesn't. After winding through the maze-like corridors, we reach another long hallway of narrow doors. These are spaced slightly farther apart than the bathrooms, but there's another difference. The doors are sheets of metal.

The guard enters a code on a square keypad embedded in the wall, and the door slides open, like my room back inside the fortress. Apparently, I won't be staying in a make-shift maintenance room for this voyage. This sub comes equipped with prison quarters.

I shrink away from the space. It's no more than the size of a closet with room only for a cot the length of the wall and floor space wide enough for me to do push-ups.

The walls, ceiling and floor are a gloomy gray which makes the area look even tighter, like the claustrophobic caves in Warren. I'd gotten used to them, but this place—it makes me feel like a rabbit in a hole all over again.

"Get in." The man nudges me forward.

"Please." I clutch the foil wrapper. "It's so…"

But movement at the very end of the long hallway draws my focus. A three-man escort hustles one person into his own closet prison. The man groans and seems to collapse inside the space.

I can't see the prisoner's face, but something about the scene seems off. Why would Felix be taking another prisoner on this trip?

My guard shoves me inside before I glimpse anything more, and the metal sheet seals the space like a tomb. The only lighting is a half burned-out fluorescent bulb caged into the ceiling. The side that works flickers like it has epilepsy. Any moment, it could quit trying and plunge me into blackness.

Don't cry. Fingers shaking, I focus on the foiled food and unwrap a bacon and egg breakfast biscuit. I pick the muffin apart into tiny pieces to make the distraction last as long as possible.

But the bread and bacon clump in my throat, and I gag it up. Who am I joking? I'm never escaping. Felix doesn't believe in the capability of his own technology, and even if I pass his test, what will he do with me?

Lock me up until the next freak show request.

I jerk my head up. Do I imagine it, or is that sobbing? Or moaning? I don't blame the person, whoever he is.

But I bite my lip. No, I won't cry too. It's not hopeless. I'm on this sub after all. And that little chip in my sock might buy the people I love the chance at a new life.

That's something worth fighting for.

CHAPTER 38
~ Portia ~

Monday, 7.20.2150
Undetermined Location

My clock once more revolves around bathroom breaks and meals, but I've stopped trying to track time. Unlike the last voyage, my goal isn't to figure out how long I've been at sea. It's to trick myself into sleep and a temporary escape from my claustrophobic prison.

But right now, my mind is too wired for sleep, and the empty sheet-like walls fuel a desperate need to do something.

There's nothing in the space but a blanket, water bowl, and emergency chamber pot. But the walls taunt me like a blank slate, and verses spin in my head like they haven't done since I wrote them for Gath.

I used to write them for him, because I thought I'd never see him alive again. The verses were my way of telling him how I felt, even though he wouldn't ever see them.

Now, there's so much I want to tell Luther.

I break the zipper off my jacket. If I pinch it between my fingers, the slender metal becomes a marker in my hand.

Pursing my lips, I sit cross-legged on my cot and face the wall.

No more
Do I fear the
past's shadows. The future
May never come for me but can
for you.

As I write, tears of relief trickle from my lashes. I read once that writing can be a catharsis, a purging of my emotions. Letting go of the people I love and the home I always wanted back is—is a catharsis. But maybe through it, I can find the last shred of courage for my ordeal.

Love on
when I am gone.
Look forward to sunrise.
Promise you'll find your way to me
Again.

Oh, Luther. Will Gath show you the way as he did me? Gath is the truest friend, like Darius said. He won't let Luther and my brother stumble blindly through this life. The empty places in my life—and oh, there are so many—are only bearable because even in them, I know my God is near.

Just like he was with Washington in Valley Forge.

Just like he'll be with me at the summit.

And somehow, he'll forgive—has already forgiven—all the things I regret and may yet have to regret.

Something drips onto my leg, and I glance down. It's blood. I squint in the lighting at the zipper, now mangled, and half of my fingernail that's broken along with it.

I slowly tear the split edge off and then lie on my back while squeezing my thumb with my other hand.

My finger throbs like a heartbeat, and I close my eyes. I've told the lonely wall my heart. There's nothing left to do but sleep and wait.

"Get up." Someone swats my shoulder, and I bolt upright. But my head feels fuzzy, and I flinch at the sudden light from the hallway. I didn't hear my door open.

I shake my head to clear the fog and stumble after the guard. How long have I slept this time?

He escorts me to a bathroom and shoves a tightly folded pack of clothes into my chest. "Clean up and get changed. You've got five minutes."

The door clicks behind me, and I squirm out of my clothes and into the tight shower. At least I have a private stall.

The water has no time to warm up, and I'm shivering when I twist it off. The shower did less to "clean me up" and more to simply wake me up.

Redressing, I rub my hair with a small towel I find under the sink. There's a rough rap on the door. My five minutes are finished.

The guard grunts at my soppy hair. "There's a comb in the medicine cabinet behind the mirror. Use it."

I reach into the space and pop the mirror open. Sure enough, there's a comb. I hesitate for a moment. Who knows how many sailors have used this comb, but a fear of lice should be the least of my worries.

"Better. Now hurry." The guard waves me after him, and my heart lifts. We're not going back to my cell like we usually do.

Instead, we reach the mess hall where several dozen sailors wolf down breakfast. A few glance at me and then just as quickly return to their food. Maybe there's an unspoken understanding that I'm a prisoner.

The guard puts a hand on my shoulder and pushes me into a chair in a corner. "Wait here."

He returns with two foil-wrapped objects and hands one to me. "You can eat on the way."

Way where? But again, I bite my tongue. I'll find out soon enough.

We weave through the hallways and upwards. As we do, a weight falls off my shoulders, only to be replaced with a tightening dread. I'm leaving that lonely cell but for what?

A group of guards huddle in the space below the ladder leading topside. I tear open the end of the foil and nibble on the breakfast muffin. They're all staring at me as though I'm some sort of dangerous weapon.

Another man appears and addresses the group. "Everything's loaded but her."

My escort nudges me toward the ladder after two of the guards ascend first. I stuff the rest of breakfast into my jacket pocket and focus on grabbing the rungs.

When I reach the surface, a cold breeze whips against my face. Thick fog cloaks what little visibility the sun affords. I squint at the sky and guess it's early morning. But this frigid dampness that hangs like a cloak about me is like nothing I've ever felt before.

"We'll take the dingy to the Southend shore." The man in charge speaks to my escort.

"There's an airport there, right?" He squints across the water.

"There is one on an island in the estuary, but you're taking this one by boat. Only the dignitaries are riding the plane. Follow the tracking to shore, and another boat will be waiting for you."

"Yes, sir." He accepts a palm-sized device, which must be the tracker, and nudges me toward a metal dingy where four guards already wait. One revs the motor on the back as we step inside. Two guards hedge me in on either side, but there's no need. Nothing could tempt me to jump into those dark waters.

We're in another port, of sorts, though this one appears less like a ship graveyard than the one in Italy. It's still in functioning order, though there's a hushed nature about it that makes me wonder how secretive its existence is.

Minutes later, we reach another gangway where my escorts herd me onto a ferry. Apparently, the "cargo" travels by boat while the important "dignitaries" fly by plane. I wiggle my toes in my boot and rest assured I'm still doing my job. Soon enough, I'll see the location of this summit for myself.

One of the guards handcuffs me to a hard-backed bench under a canopy on the deck while the others on the shore carry crates below.

"Where's the other prisoner?" One mumbles as he glances my way. "I thought there were two."

"There are. He's below deck."

"But that's just storage."

"There's enough air to breathe."

I shiver and curl up as tightly as I can, imagining that confinement below deck must be worse. At least I can see the water and earth. Who is the poor soul caged in storage?

But when the boat finally departs, I almost wish I were below. The wind off the water bites through my uniform, and I shake uncontrollably. With the little freedom allowed by my cuffs, I recline on the seat in a tight ball, at least partially shielded by the seat in front of me.

The guards not on watch huddle around a table in the back, absorbed in a card game. They all look the same in their identical gray uniforms and cropped hair cuts. The only differences are the shapes of their faces and hair color, most of which are some shade of brown.

The one pacing the deck by me sports a darker complexion with jet-black cropped hair, but his hardened expression makes the differences hardly noticeable. He grunts when he catches me studying him.

"Hey, worthless up here is freezing." He calls to the others. "Where'd we put those blankets?"

"They're below—if you want to waste a trip to keep the chick happy." A coarse laugh follows, and someone bangs on the table.

I squeeze my eyes shut. I'll be better off if they ignore me than make me the butt of their jokes.

The guard doesn't say anything else, but his boot-steps recede. Maybe he'll forget about me, and maybe if I sleep, I'll forget the cold.

But minutes later, the metal floor again creaks under someone's weight. Something scratchy and bulky falls on me. A blanket?

I flash open my eyes. Behind the guard's glowering eyes is something like pity.

"Thank you." I mouth the words and stretch out the blanket with my one free hand. He marches away as I pull the edge of it over my head and close my eyes once more.

I twitch my nose against the blanket. What is all that noise? Curling my fingers around the fabric's edge, I peel it back and blink in surprise. The sun has long since penetrated the fog. The bank I'm facing boasts large, crammed structures and passing vessels.

This place must be a hub, a mega-city perhaps. A look over my shoulder reveals the guards have long since abandoned their cards. They stand as if on alert, as if their every movement is monitored.

We must be getting close.

I crouch in my seat to study a strange wheel-like structure that appears on the left side of the river. Yes, it's a wheel. I don't know what else to call it. But it's giant with identical basket-like levels all around it as if to hold—passengers?

What is this strange place that combines Gothic-like architecture with bizarre inventions?

Shortly after passing the wheel, a long, multi-storied building with pinnacles—or are those buttresses—demands my attention on the other side of the river. It looks old enough to crumble but seems manicured. Beyond it, an even stranger monument appears. In the same style as the building is a clock tower, for there, on the face, is a giant clock. I squint to read the time, just after 1000 hours. How have I slept this long? But then, time has meant nothing to me, and sleep has been my only retreat.

I'm so absorbed in studying the architecture that I don't notice the shoreline growing closer until we dock. The guard who gave me the blanket returns for it and tosses it in a barrel on deck. Then, he unlocks my cuffed hand from the armrest and nudges me toward the gangway.

"Where are we?" I dare to ask. I can't be faulted for wanting to know.

He clears his throat as he locks the cuff again. "You don't know? But then, I guess you don't know anything about the real world."

I force a smile. If the real world is anything like Deadwood, I'm not missing out.

"We're in London." He points to the clock tower. "That's Big Ben, next to what used to be Parliament."

I blink in surprise that he bothered to acknowledge my question, let alone answer it. "Parliament?" I hope for more clues to my location.

"It was the seat of politics around here, but it's been disbanded. The Rosh Council takes care of everything now, and they never meet in the same place twice."

Only a hated government would have to operate under such secrecy. "What's the building used for now?"

"Poor house, I think," he mutters. Another guard calls over to him, and the man talking with me quickens his pace until we reach a vehicle idling on the road. A door opens, and I have no choice but to duck inside.

"Get in—and good luck." The dark-haired guard slams the door after me. Why should he show any kindness toward me? Does he know who I am?

I shift in my seat to face the man beside me and then shrink back. Jotham Danforth greets me with a smirk.

"Right on time." He crosses his arms and frowns at me. "We can't have you looking like that." He reaches down and tosses a small bag next to me. "There's a comb and compact in there. At least make yourself presentable."

Fingers trembling, I pull out the comb and stroke it through my hair. How can Jotham be so unkind? Doesn't he care in the slightest what he did to my brother—what he did to me?

But should I even pretend to know him? I have to act like my collar is working.

"Don't you recognize me?" He studies his nails and presses down a cuticle.

I swallow and concentrate on combing my hair. "I'm sorry, but should I?"

He laughs softly. "That collar is a miracle indeed."

"What's that?"

He clears his throat. "We were neighbors once."

I set the comb aside and click open the compact. "Funny I don't remember you."

Jotham turns to look out the window. "Yes, funny indeed."

I sneak a glance his way. The creases around his eyes tighten as if he's seeing a memory. "Were we friends or just acquaintances?" I ask in a flat tone.

"I guess you could call us friends," he says. "Your brother and I were anyway."

My throat tightens. "My brother? Well, that's nice you two stay in touch."

He snorts. "No, we had a falling apart and went our separate ways."

Doesn't that sound nice. What he means is that he cheated his way into a Dome seat and sent my brother to a satellite.

My pulse races. I want to say many things but can't. "I'm sorry, but then why am I here?"

He opens his mouth, but the device on his wrist buzzes. Jotham scans the screen as if reading a message and then taps to speak. "Yes, she's here. Are you ready for her?"

"Yes, we're all set." Felix's voice transmits his reply, but it's muffled, or there's too much background noise for him to transmit clearly. What kind of space would echo like that?

"Very good. We'll see you soon." Jotham taps on the screen again and grins at me with a crooked mouth. "You're here, Portia Abernathy, to put on a good show."

CHAPTER 39
~ Luther ~

Tuesday, 7.21.2150
Crystal

Luther wills one foot in front of the other. Running has always been his outlet. It's never felt this way—like he has two dead weights strapped to his feet.

He sucks in air and slows on the missile-pocked track, careful not to twist his ankle in any of the holes. If he closes his eyes, he can almost imagine Portia running beside him like she used to.

But as soon as he opens them, she vanishes. He places his hands on his knees. His feet are fine. His heart's another matter.

Taking a deep breath, he straightens and starts jogging again. If only he could run in reverse and rewind the last year, no, more like a lifetime. If only he could go back and somehow prevent his brother from turning on Darius, from tearing apart what was left of the Abernathy family and ripping Cotton from his life.

But he couldn't stop Jotham then, and he can't stop him now. He grew up in his brother's shadow, and where did that get him? Not his father's favor. And though Luther is a man now, he can't stop falling short.

His head pounds, and again, Luther pauses to a slow trot.

Hating on his brother won't give him anything but high blood pressure. If only there were some real action he could take... but instead, he's stuck playing defense to Felix's drones while the Brotherhood banks on the OC cutting off the snake's head.

Again, he picks up his pace and turns his thoughts to the reason he'd come to run tonight. Pretending he had to burn off anger toward his brother seems at least a reasonable excuse, but to confess the real reason makes him seem like a jealous failure.

Darius had found him flipping through the Bible Gath had left by his cot. Not that he had been making any sense of it. "I have some good news to share for a change," his friend said.

Hope surged through him. "Really?" Luther's eyes must have betrayed his heart, because Darius's smile faded. "Still no word on Portia, but we just received a message from Foxworth."

"Everything okay in 'Prase?" Luther asked.

"As peachy as usual, but that's not the news." Darius laughed. When was the last time he had done that?

Luther grinned. "Are you gonna make me guess?"

"No, because you wouldn't figure this one out in a million years." Darius laughed again and stared at the ceiling, shaking his head. "Portia said she saw it coming, but I hadn't believed her..."

His chest tightened at her name.

"I'll just tell you." Darius lowered onto the cot across from his and rocked forward. "Foxworth and Jael got married."

"What?" Luther nearly face-planted. "Married? They weren't even..."

"I know." Smile lines creased Darius's face. "They skipped engagement altogether and took the plunge. Spunky, those two are. But I'm happy for them. Man, it's nice to be happy for someone for once."

Darius pushed himself up. "Anyway, I thought I'd tell you first since you were here. I'm going to find Lydia. She's going to be so excited."

Was that a blush creeping up Darius's neck? Maybe the reason his friend beamed had less to do with Foxworth's and Jael's news and more with his own love life?

Luther cleared his throat. "Any news from Gath on the last round of drones we shot down?"

Darius frowned as if annoyed Luther pulled him back to present problems. "Not yet." He raised an eyebrow. "Kind of surprised you aren't there with him now."

Luther's face warmed. "He kicked me out—told me to take a break and clear my head."

Portia's brother glanced at the Bible he'd let slip to the floor. "How that going for you?"

"It's not." Luther raked his fingers through his hair and forced a smile for Darius's sake. "Hey, but thanks for sharing the news. Those two deserve to be happy."

"Yeah." Darius started to say something else, then closed his mouth. "I'm going to check on Lydia now. Take it easy before your next shift."

His friend left in search of his own budding romance, and Luther tugged on his shoes, unable to stomach his own loneliness. And so, he had ended up here, running on a track that barely resembled a track any more.

Luther heaves another deep breath and begins a last attempt at running. Good for Jael and Foxworth. They deserve to be happy. And he can't grudge Darius for wanting his own chance at love.

But right now, his own life feels so lonely he'd scream if his exhausted lungs would let him.

He can't—won't—imagine life without Cotton. Not until he's turned over every stone in Deadwood will he give up hope of finding her. He'll have to convince Darius to let him go. There's no way he can live with this ache any longer.

But what had Gath said? *Until you realize that you need God in your life, it's going to be empty—with or without Portia.*

God? How is he supposed to stuff God into his life when that book doesn't make any sense? None of this religion business makes sense to him.

But it does for Gath and Cotton. How is he supposed to find it, to get it? Can't someone spell out a checklist for him to do? Surely this God is orderly and just. He can't simply give out freebies, no strings attached.

Luther's read enough court rulings and Codex laws to know justice doesn't work that way.

He closes in on lap one, lap two. His body finds its rhythm. Though the world isn't right around him, at least he can control…

His left ankle plunges into a rut, and Luther flails to catch himself. His foot twists, and he barrels to the ground, rolling to his side to ease the impact. He jerks his ankle toward his chest in a protective impulse and feels for breaks. Good. It's probably just a muscle spasm, worst case, a sprain.

Stupid drones. Stupid, stupid…

"Thought I might find you here." Gath's voice startles him, and he jumps to his feet. But his ankle shoots a million protests to his nervous system, and he collapses to a seated position.

Gath, with his tough love and answers for everything, is the last person he wants to see when he's miserable.

"Need a hand?"

Even without looking, Luther senses Gath's outstretched hand. He wants to slap it away, but it's not fair for him to take out his frustration on the man.

"Thanks." Luther accepts it and hobbles on his feet. "Just twisted it."

Gath crosses his arms. "Why don't you let Deidra be the judge of that?"

"I'm fine." Luther retracts his hand and applies gentle pressure on his ankle. He grimaces and grits his teeth. Great.

A steadying hand presses against his shoulder. "I was going to see Deidra anyway but wanted to tell you the news first."

"News?" Luther hops forward. If Gath has come to tell him about Foxworth and Jael too…

"I found another communication drone."

He loses his balance and flails again. Gath reaches toward him and grips his shoulders. "Look, man, you can either use me as a crutch, or I can fireman carry you. But we have work to do, so drop the macho I-don't-need-anyone chip on your shoulder."

In spite of himself, Luther laughs. Gath doesn't take attitude from anyone.

He angles his arm over Gath's shoulder. "Okay, tell me what's going on."

Gath grunts. "The insider gave us the exact schedule and location where Deadwood releases its drones. It's a vulnerable moment for the facility, and if we can get the OC to time a missile just right, we can destroy the fortress."

"What?" Luther clutches Gath's shoulder more tightly as they pick their way across the mutilated track. "What insider? You mean Portia, right? But how could she possibly know that information?"

Gath heaves a sigh. "I don't think Portia is the one sending us messages."

"But that drive with the recording—that was her voice."

"Yes." He hesitates. "Someone sent that for her. When you hear the rest of the message, you'll believe me."

They reach the edge of the track. "I'm not going to like this, am I?"

"No."

"Wait." Luther stops and adjusts his grip to steady himself. "We can't send a missile to Deadwood. Portia's there, and so is my father."

Gath reaches over to clasp his hand and stare him in the eyes. Is that pain or sympathy in his expression?

"Portia's not there anymore."

Gath's words make his knees wobble. "I'm sorry... what?"

His friend strides forward. "I'll tell you once we get to Deidra. At the rate we're moving, we'll be sitting ducks for drones if we don't get off this track."

Luther swallows a protest. There's no point arguing with Gath. The sooner they reach the make-shift infirmary, the sooner he gets answers.

The pile of debris scarcely looks like a hospital, but that was Gath's reason for choosing it. If the building already appears destroyed, maybe the drones won't target it again. What an aerial drone can't see is the intact story below ground.

One of their guards, all but hidden behind a man-sized piling, steps out and lifts the edge of a plastic tarp that serves as a door.

"Thanks, Carl." Gath nods at the man whose tired face glows at the mention of his name.

How Gath manages to remember the names of every shift guard amazes him, and it certainly makes the men respect him more.

They teeter down the steps, which end in a long, open room where Deidra and her crew have reassembled what little survived from the hospital attack. They've lined classroom chairs facing each other and covered them with dorm comforters to create makeshift beds. Window curtains from the few dorms that didn't burn form privacy areas for the seriously ill.

Deidra spots them right away and beelines for Gath. It's like those two are magnets or something.

She greets Gath with a kiss on the cheek and then seems to notice Luther. "What's this about?" Deidra frowns.

Luther sighs. "I was running on the track and twisted my ankle."

Gath helps lower him into a wobbly chair. "I think it's more than a simple twist, but Mr. Optimist here says he's fine."

"I'll be the judge of that." Deidra bends down and unlaces his boot.

Luther cringes as she gently tugs it off his swollen foot. "Ahh." He bites his teeth as she probes with her fingers.

Deidra's thumb leaves a temporary imprint in his skin. "This is already pretty swollen, and from your reaction, I'd say it hurts."

He grunts. "No joke."

"I don't think it's broken, but you've got a nice sprain." Deidra stands and pulls another chair over. "Keep it elevated while

I get something to wrap it." She glances at Gath, and her eyes soften. "Could you get some ice? When the temperatures dip at night, we fill some buckets with water so we have ice each morning. Ask the guard at the door to show you where you can find it."

Luther holds up a hand. "That's not necessary. Gath has some news, and this ankle can wait."

Deidra narrows her eyes at him. "If you don't take care of this, you'll prolong your recovery. Gath can tell us his news while we ice it."

Gath gives Deidra a secretive smile before disappearing back the way they came. Seriously? Is this a conspiracy against him?

No, there's no wedging his will between those two. It just doesn't seem fair that the world keeps smiling on lovers but excludes Portia and him.

Luther lowers his gaze as Deidra returns with some make-shift fabric bandages. She drags another chair next to his foot and starts wrapping.

He shouldn't think that way. He should be happy for their sake, but the ache in his own chest only encourages envy.

"What's on your mind?"

Luther glances into her probing eyes. There's no judgment there, just concern.

"Portia." It's a one-word answer with paragraphs of meaning he doesn't want to explain.

"You don't think you'll see her again?" Deidra's words cut his heart in two.

He grits his teeth and stares at the ceiling. "There's no point living if I don't."

She cuts the fabric and secures it with a safety pin. The wrap is firm but not too tight. "I thought that way once. When that ship took Gath and all my girlish dreams with him, I wanted to die."

Luther lowers his gaze to meet hers. "Portia told me your story."

Deidra folds the remaining fabric. "I know what you're thinking. You see the happy ending—if you can call this situation happy—for Gath and me."

She pauses and looks right into his eyes. "But you can't see any hope for your own."

"No, I can't." Luther wants to look away. Having this woman see straight through him is unnerving.

Deidra pats his knee. "I couldn't find any hope for my future either and look where that got me: a life full of regrets."

Luther shakes his head and feels his chest tighten again. "But what is there to hope in?"

"Gath says the answer is God."

"And do you believe that?"

She chews her lip. "I'm starting to. I know. This God-business all sounds crazy—but it's a reasonable crazy. Is there any better explanation for how changed Gath is and how good could come through the horrible choices I made working for Osborne?"

Her chocolate-brown eyes seem to brighten. "It's like I've got another chance at life, a chance to start over. The scars are there, but so is mercy."

Luther sighs. "I'm happy for you, Deidra, but what if there is no second chance for me?"

She glances behind him, and her eyes shine. Gath must be returning.

Deidra rises and places a hand on his shoulder. "Gath says that's where faith comes in."

"What is this that Gath says?" The giant ex-Gage's voice booms from behind him. Luther tenses. He doesn't want to go into this with Gath, not now. Talking to Deidra is bad enough.

"Your girl's just bragging on you." Luther cuts in before Deidra can reply. "Now that you're back, tell us about that message you received."

Gath hands the plastic-wrapped ice to Deidra who presses it into a flat package and places it on his ankle.

Luther grimaces at the cold, but at least it's a welcome distraction from the shooting pain.

His friend motions to Deidra to sit again and stands behind her. "Like I said, I found another communication drone. I ran into Darius on my way to find you and gave him the message. He was going to find Alexis and send an urgent Translation request to the OC and said I might find you on the track."

Luther grips the sides of the chair. "Then we need to join them."

"Yes, but I'm sure they started the call without us."

Luther closes his eyes and tries to breathe. His world is moving too fast, and he can't keep it from spinning out of control. Flashing open his eyes, he glares at Gath and spits out the words. "What. Did. That. Message. Say?"

Gath studies him a moment. "The insider at Deadwood gave us the exact coordinates and time when the fortress's concealed airplane strip will open its otherwise impenetrable ceiling. If we can get the OC to send a missile, we can destroy Deadwood and lock in the drones with the Firstborn strain."

Luther waves a hand. "You told me that already. What did the message say about Portia?"

Something like resignation fills Gath's eyes and sends a shiver of dread through him. "She's on the sub going to the Rosh League summit."

"What?" Luther jumps to his feet, ignoring the pain. The plastic ice pack falls to the floor and breaks open, sending ice pouring through the cracks.

Deidra groans and falls to her knees to salvage what she can, but Luther keeps his eyes glued on Gath while leaning against the chair for support. "She was supposed to plant the tracker on the sub, not take it herself."

"Sit down, Luther." Gath's steely tone nettles him. "I don't know what happened or what changed, but that's all the message said about her."

"And that's supposed to be good news?" Luther can't keep his voice from rising. "Either way, we're asking the OC to aim a missile at her."

Gath steps toward him. "If we don't destroy Deadwood, that virus could wipe out our population. And if we don't find and destroy the Rosh League leadership team, they'll continue their stranglehold on the world."

Luther drops into the chair and covers his face. "I know all that. But my heart doesn't care."

"I hate losing Portia, too. There are few truer friends, but you know what she would want you to do."

"It's not fair." His throat chokes on the words.

"God forsaking his own Son to save a wretched world wasn't fair either."

"But he's God, and I'm not."

"He's not asking you to turn your back on Portia. He's asking you to do the right thing and trust him with the outcome. And regardless, he's offering you his love and presence through it all. That's more than he gave his son when he abandoned him on the cross to pay for mankind's sin."

Could this God's love really be enough to see him through the horror of losing his girl?

The chill of an ice pack brings him back to the worried faces of his friends. Resourceful Deidra used the gauze wrapping to secure the ice to his ankle.

"Thanks—both of you." He pats Deidra's arm and squares his shoulders. He hobbles toward Gath. "If you give me a hand, we can maybe get to the portal before the call ends. I want to be there. You know Darius will want to take a vote."

"I know," Gath says softly. "All our votes matter."

Luther swallows hard. "I won't let our people down."

He and Gath start for the door. "Wait!" Deidra calls from behind them. "I have something that will help."

She disappears and returns moments later holding crutches. "If I can learn to use these, you can too," she says.

"Thanks." Luther nods.

"One more thing." Deidra tugs something from her pocket. It's a small Bible.

"Portia gave me this to read before she left with Gath when I was still in the infirmary myself. I think she'd want you to have it." She holds out the worn, leather-covered book to him.

Tears sting at Luther's eyes, but he blinks them away. "Thank you."

Luther slides the book into his jacket pocket. Right next to his heart. That's where Cotton will always be. Maybe somehow the God she'd grown to love can do something with all his wrecked dreams.

He crutches after Gath. Yes, he'll vote to destroy Deadwood, even though there's a slim chance Portia is still there, even though his father and brother are too.

He still has his mother, and he'll take care of her. Somehow, they'll find a way to get past all the grief.

Somehow, they'll rebuild, and so will their land.

Kristen Hogrefe

CHAPTER 40
~ Portia ~

Tuesday, 7.21.2150
London

I press my face against the window and turn my back to Jotham. If I can't distance myself from him, I can pretend for a moment he's not there. Oh! What I would give to find that he's a mere hologram and that instead, Luther is sitting beside me. I would curl my fingers around his and tell him…

Luther's not there. Stop being ridiculous. But Felix's trainings have started to blur the line between fiction and reality, and confinement in my cell didn't help.

I peer through the glass at the confusing mix of grandeur and gloom that London presents. Trash and debris line the streets below the magnificent architecture. Citizens in rags huddle in clusters on the sidewalks to keep warm while we drive past them in a polished black vehicle.

Was life here always this way? Or was it better when the people governed themselves through the Parliament?

If my personal experience with the Rosh League's viceroy is any indicator, I'd wager life was a good deal more bearable before this mysterious council took over.

I wiggle my toes in my boot and shift in my seat as an unsettling thought strikes me. Destroying the satellite camps and ousting the ruling Dome resulted in riots back home. Even now, Darius still has his hands full trying to maintain a semblance of order in the absence of a clear figurehead.

Will the same happen here? Can people adapt from no freedom to perhaps too much too soon?

The chip presses against my foot. I just have to believe that the OC has a plan. At least I know my piece in it.

The driver pulls up against a curb by another tall building, and Jotham opens his door. I wait until someone opens mine.

It's the same olive-skinned guard who saw me to the car in the first place. He must have been in the front with the driver, concealed by the dark window that separated the back seat.

I crane my neck to look upward. Broken glass windows appear like jagged mouths in the structure above me. I follow Jotham and the guard toward a blue and white sign that reads Westminster Station. Jotham flashes a badge at the men who seem to be guarding the stairwell and kicking at homeless people who try to seek shelter from the cold wind.

I grip the cold metal railing as we descend. What is this place, and what is that noise coming from below ground?

A cracked, electric sign greets me at the base. It's a red circle with a blue banner across the center that reads Westminster. The space itself feels like a tube with its rounded ceiling. It's as if a giant mechanical earthworm bore a hole in the ground.

My gaze shifts to the tracks that line the far side. An underground train?

A thundering noise fills the space, and the red-colored front end of an enclosed train appears. Two glowing lights dot the front.

I back against the wall to stay as far away from the slowing train as I can, but Jotham grabs my hand. "Come on. This one's ours. The council is waiting."

Felix is on that thing? I swallow hard and shake away Jotham's hand as we cross the threshold through the open sliding doors onto the train.

An intricate map on the ceiling catches my attention. "What are all those colored lines?" I ask.

"Oh, those?" Jotham beckons me onward toward a glass door separating our car from the next. "Those are the different tube lines."

"We're on yellow?"

"Right, the Circle Line. Now, come on."

I glance at the seats lining the insides of the car. They're all empty and facing each other, but I can imagine that at one point, they were full of passengers. The seats are worn and faded, even dirty.

The glass door in front of us doesn't seem to belong with the train. If this is simply a passenger train, shouldn't all the cars be identical?

Yet the glass seems spotless, new. My gut twists as I suspect this particular train has been modified.

Jotham pauses at the entrance. "This is where we part, Portia. Sorry I'll have to miss the show." He nods at the guard who takes my arm and pulls me through the entrance.

I gasp at the display before me and would have turned back if the guard weren't squeezing my arm tightly.

This car, though as narrow as the previous one, has a long

mahogany table on the far end. I count ten people seated around it, and though it's rude to stare, I can't help myself.

The men and women look like someone stirred a pot of DNA, and they emerged. From a red-head with pale skin to a woman as dark as midnight, the group has nothing in common except for the black robes they're wearing.

This must be the council.

Viceroy Plume stands behind the man at the head of the table whose white hair and pale skin contrast against his robe. His matching beard and the whites of his eyes send shivers racing up my spine. That must be the leader of the Rosh League.

Felix and a few others perch in hard-backed chairs along one side of the train car. He somehow seems smaller in this space. Across from him stand the entourage of body guards with weapons drawn. I spot Orbit's face among them, and my knees wobble in relief. At least I have a friend here.

But something seems off. His eyes and mouth twitch, and he doesn't look my way. Is he nervous for me? Does he know what's about to happen?

I glance down and see I'm standing on a blood red rug. To my right, an icy-thin screen covers half the wall.

It must be for the Fabrication. I stiffen, even as the guard tugs me toward a lone chair set in front of the screen.

The train starts moving, and were it not for the man's grip on my arm, I would teeter over. He helps me to the chair and spreads his legs apart and stands behind me as if the movement were perfectly normal.

Most of the members ignore me entirely or frown at me with quiet interest. Some peer into small, flat screens that angle toward them at their places around the table.

"The next part of our summit will require a vote on our action toward the rebellious ASU." The viceroy moves toward a podium as if to moderate. However, most of the members don't look at him but into the screens. Are they deaf?

Then I remember the language barrier I faced in Italy. Perhaps they all speak different languages, and the screens translate for them. How strange that the technology that separates the haves from the have-nots now unites the communication among this group.

"Since their little revolt, the acting Friend has developed two solutions for dealing with them. The first is a lethal Firstborn strain that will decimate the population, making room for new slaves to manage its resources and allow us to harvest its crops. The downside is the transition period and cleanup required. All the bodies must be burned, and shipping that kind of manpower from, say, South America, is going to be costly."

I want to vomit. Do they really consider our people's lives so cheap?

The viceroy takes a sip of water from his glass before continuing. "The second solution is mind-manipulation technology we're calling Reborn. And for this, I ask you to give your attention to a demonstration."

Reborn? My skin turns to gooseflesh. Only God can make a person new. What they've done to me is monstrous.

The viceroy nods at Felix who stands and joins him at the podium. "Mr. Caesura, will you please introduce the subject and explain the technology."

The subject… that must be me. Does the fate of my people

hang on my performance? I sit straighter in my chair and plaster a stoic stare on my face.

Felix smooths his white satiny shirt and shakes the viceroy's hand. "Ladies and gentlemen, thank you for your time." He flashes a charming smile. Apparently, he's not aware no one is watching him. "Today, I present the latest in the ASU's technological advancements. You're aware of our progress in personality reprogramming, but we've refined the—shall we say, cruder—methods into something more sophisticated, something that offers a humanely sympathetic approach."

He pauses and waves his hand toward me. "Portia Abernathy is the sister of the Rogue leader responsible for the destruction and interruption of order in the ASU. We captured her and instead of executing her for her crimes, gave her a second chance." Felix snaps his fingers, and I nearly shriek as the guard places his hands around my neck. I close my eyes and try not to shudder as he unbuttons the top of my shirt and pulls the fabric open to showcase my neck.

"We surgically implanted a biochemical collar that conducts the treatment. It's designed to reprogram the subject's brain, specifically, the prefrontal cortex. You see, as we age, the prefrontal cortex solidifies, making us less likely to adapt and change. By rewiring this portion of the brain, we use the treatment, coupled with suggestion, to redefine the subject's affections and loyalties."

Felix shifts his gaze to me, and my skin crawls. If only the OC would hurry up and send their missile, I wouldn't have to pretend any longer. I'm not okay with any of this. Better to die my own person than play Felix's pawn.

He rotates at the podium to address the council. "The humanity of it all is that the treatment takes place when the subject is asleep so that she has no memory of the intense discharges, nor of the subliminal message recording, usually delivered through a screen or panel in her room."

The guard tugs me to my feet, and I wobble to find my balance. Of course, I'm not used to the motion of a moving train.

A moving train!

A sickening feeling wraps around my heart. What if the OC is waiting to fire the missile until the tracker stops? What if they think I'm still traveling to my destination?

Something like panic threatens to override my stoic expression. I close my eyes and plead. *Oh, God, don't abandon me now.*

"Without further ado, I present to you Portia Abernathy in what will be the most emotionally charged Fabrication of her life. She will follow my orders without flinching and prove that our technology can now reform a Rogue into a model citizen. Consider the potential. We can take our enemies and transform their deranged genius into tools in our hands."

The members murmur and exchange nods with each other. Then, all eyes shift toward me.

Felix taps on a keypad embedded in the podium, and my guard positions me directly in front of the screen. If only he would let me sit in the chair again.

But though the chair remains within range for the Fabrication, he does not invite me to sit in it.

The blood-red carpet dims to a translucent blue, and I risk one last glance at Orbit. His facial muscles still twitch, and the expression in his eyes terrifies me.

It is not the look of a fighter like the Orbit I've always known. Is that defeat? Or an apology? Or a farewell?

I grasp to understand the change in him, but the scene before me vanishes, replaced with one I recognize.

Where Orbit appeared moments before, the impatient usher from the theater stands. He's gritting his teeth at me as if I'm an imposter.

"They're with me." Booth's voice calls from the base of the stairs.

I spin and face Felix, who's watching me with a crooked grin. "Hurry up, Frost."

I gulp and take the steps by two. Why would Felix call this my most emotionally-charged Fabrication yet? I don't want to assassinate the president again, but I know the scene is fake. If I've shot him before, I can shoot him again.

Like last time, Booth pauses at the top of the stairs and grabs my shoulder. "There may be a guard. I'll take him out, and you shoot the president."

I reach for the gun I assume Felix has once again tucked inside my pants. Yes, the small handgun is there.

"No." Felix puts a hand on Booth's shoulder. "There are five rounds in Frost's chamber: one for the guard and four playgoers."

Booth frowns but mutters something about having my back.

Why is Felix jumping right to the climax of this Fabrication? Doesn't he want to put on a show?

We reach the box seat area as a male actor's voice calls out, "Don't know the manners of good society, eh? Well, I guess I know enough to turn you inside out, old gal—you sockdologizing old man-trap…"

I breathe deeply. This whole thing is rehearsed—from the little handgun in my hand to the audience bursting into laughter. It feels easy, too easy.

Booth whips back the curtain.

But something is wrong. This time, there is a guard. My chest tightens, and I raise the gun with a shaking hand.

Orbit stands behind the president's seat and stares at me with the same mournful eyes from moments before.

"Shoot." He mouths the word with his lips.

For a hot second, I hesitate with my finger on the trigger. That's odd. Why would Orbit tell me to shoot him? Surely the guard by the president would attempt to fight me.

"Shoot." This time, Felix whispers the command in my ear.

Orbit is nodding at me and steps closer to narrow the gap between us.

I can't breathe. *It's just a Fabrication.* I aim for his head and fire. The handgun, though weak, is no less deadly at such a close range. He collapses onto the floor, and I step over him, but my ears are ringing. Was the discharge that loud last time? I shake my head. I have to focus. I have a job to do.

I expect the president to jump out of his chair, but the two couples in the box seats are laughing at the play, oblivious to our presence.

How did they not hear the shot?

Felix bumps into me and breathes in my ear. "Finish the job."

But the president with the dark hair and beard isn't sitting in the seat before me.

My father is—and next to him are my mother, my brother, and

Kristen Hogrefe

my sister.

CHAPTER 41

~ Portia ~

Tuesday, 7.21.2150
London

A cry rises in my throat, for there, in front of me, is my whole family, together. I've almost forgotten what Mom looked like, but the memory of her profile rushes back in an instant: the gentle curve of her red lips, the firm jaw, the cascade of reddish-brown hair, so much like Darius's.

To her right is my deceased sister Candace, laughing with all the vitality of one very much in love with life—not one wanting to end it because of her compatibility test's political results.

With a start, I realize how much I look like her. She had been older, a teenager, when I was a child. I'd always thought her beautiful. Would we have become best friends? What if she had married her childhood sweetheart instead of dangling at the end of a rope? Though I was only seven when I found her body, that image will forever be seared in my memory.

"What are you waiting for? Assassinate them." Felix's command sounds different this time, as if I'm hearing him through an ear piece.

"The president, you mean?" I focus my attention on Dad,

sitting where the president had been.

"All of them." I don't have to see Felix to know he's smiling at his own cruel cleverness.

My hardest Fabrication yet? No wonder. He wants me to murder my entire family.

But you can't murder people who are already dead. The ASU killed my mother by not providing the common people with access to proper medical attention, and they killed my sister by demanding compliance with a compatibility testing system that tried to take the place of God.

I will always love you. I aim and close my eyes as I shoot at Mom and then Candace. I hesitate before firing at Dad and Darius, just to make sure that somehow, this isn't a twisted reality. But the representations of them are old. Darius looks young and youthful, not like the aged version of himself I'd last seen. And Dad is much grayer than the dark-haired man seated before me.

Pulling the trigger still feels like cutting out my heart, but it's what Dad and Darius would have told me to do if they knew why I kept pretending.

But then if they knew why, they would never have let Luther send me that letter and tracker.

The green light reclaims the space, and I'm again in the train car, standing like the guard had been with my feet spaced apart. But why am I still holding the handgun?

"Bravo!" Felix claps behind the podium. "Well played, Miss Abernathy."

I step backward, hoping to find the chair, and trip over it instead. Dropping the gun, I brace myself for a fall.

But it's not the chair. It's a body. It's Orbit.

Blood cakes his head where I shot him with the handgun. *Where I shot him.*

But no, that's impossible. It was only a test. Nothing real happens in a Fabrication.

I crawl closer to him and touch his forehead. "Orbit?" I whisper. "Wake up." Not caring who's watching, I press my fingers against his wrist.

There's a faint pulse. I gasp in relief and lean in closer. "Orbit. It's me, Portia. Can you hear me?"

His eyes flicker but don't seem to focus. "Portia?" His lips tremble.

"Yes." Tears gush from my eyes. "Did I—Did I do this?"

"Not… your fault."

"But I shot you? Oh, Orbit, I didn't…. Please forgive me." I bow my head and weep, cradling his bloody head in my hands.

"Nothing to forgive." He strains to form the words. "That bullet… the last kindness you did me. They would have…" He closes his eyes.

My heart stutters. He can't be gone. He can't.

Shock racks my body as Jotham's face flashes in my memory. He had been in that elevator and seen us. He must have discovered that Orbit was interfering with the drones and told Felix.

There had been another prisoner on the sub and the ferry. Felix had brought Orbit here—for me to execute.

"Orbit." I choke. It's probably not even his real name. I'll never know his real name.

"You were right." He swallows hard and blinks his eyes again. "I chose my side. I chose… you." The pulse disappears as his eyes take on a death-like stare. He's gone.

His blood stains my fingernails and coats my hands. I'm a murderer. Felix made me a murderer.

I scream, a shrill pained cry that sounds more animal than human. Releasing Orbit, I twist on the floor to face my audience, to face Felix.

"You!" I jump to my feet and lunge for him. The guard can't catch me soon enough.

I ram my stained hands into his satin shirt and then grab his neck. "This blood belongs to you, too." I spit in his face. "How dare you make me into a monster! How dare you make me believe a lie!"

Felix tries to choke me back, but my rage is stronger than his. The guard pulls me off and throws me to the ground.

Behind them, the viceroy stands. "Get her out of here. This whole experiment is a failure."

Felix turns crimson. "She was surprised. That's all. She obeyed orders."

"And then she tried to strangle you." The viceroy returns dryly. "She isn't reformed. She's a fraud. And I'm beginning to think you are, too."

He motions to the council. "Cast your votes now. I urge you to consider extermination."

The screen behind me blinks, showing an image of the drone fleet, waiting to launch. Are they really going to broadcast the genocide of an entire population?

Oh God, forgive me. I've failed. I wasn't a good enough actress. I couldn't stop them.

The guard yanks me to my feet as Felix marches toward me. The blood smeared on his shirt matches the violence sparking in his eyes.

He grabs my throat. "Worthless!" He slaps me until my vision blurs and skin burns. Then, he twists an arm around my neck.

I can't breathe. Is he going to strangle me?

His breath comes hot next to my ear. "You've ruined me, but there's no escape for you either. We're going down together."

Something flashes in my peripheral. I squint my eyes to focus through the pain.

Dad's karambit.

"Remember this?" He presses the blade against my cheek until warm blood trickles down my neck. "I've kept it with me ever since you sliced me up and left me to die in the archives. Let's bleed out together, shall we? You may have escaped me in life, but you won't in death."

He tips the blade toward my throat.

"Fraternitas Veritas." I spit through my teeth. His face twists with rage.

Someone screams behind us, and the guard reclaims his grip on me, yanking me away from Felix. The council members rise and point angrily at the screen.

The drones are on fire? Exploding? Booms and flames fill the screen.

And then an ear-splitting blast rocks our own, and the train twists onto its side. Is this another Fabrication?

We slide toward a window, but my guard doesn't let go. He

slams into the glass and grunts as I crash against his chest. Is he buffering me?

I wipe the blood from my cheek and survey our car. Bodies pile on top of each other. Many council members appear unconscious.

Felix lies in a heap against the shattered big screen. Shards of glass stick through his arms, while larger slices flay his torso. Groans escape his lips.

He's still alive. An object glints by his feet. He must have dropped Dad's karambit.

I push off the guard and stagger toward it, my blood pumping hot in my own ears. He deserves to die. He deserves…

Another boom rocks the ground, and a voice behind me whispers. "Hurry! Come with me."

It's the guard. Though his own forehead is bleeding, there's an intensity in his eyes. He's asking me to trust him. He's asking me to choose life, not hate.

I forget Felix and the blade and plunge after him through the sideways door that first brought me to this space.

We jump off the mangled train and hit the platform's cracked concrete. Dazed, I shake my head to get my bearings, but the man grabs my arm. "Run—for your life!"

Then, I see it. A fireball inside the tube tunnel races toward us.

He shoves me into a stairwell, and we bolt up the steps and down a hallway. Perhaps there's a connecting line. Please let there be a connecting line.

The space opens to another set of tracks, marked by a circle sign that reads Gloucester Road. A train's rumbling sends reverberations through the space where a few other passengers climb aboard the stopped train. They turn and stare at us.

No wonder. We're covered in blood and probably look like zombies on the run.

We reach the platform as the doors start to close.

"Go!" The guard screams as the air on the back of my neck pricks. We're almost out of time.

He doesn't have to tell me twice. I lunge through the narrowing door and wedge my boot to keep it from closing on him. He plunges inside and yanks me free.

The passengers inside shrink away from us, but the fire show racing behind us draws them to the windows. Shrieking, they point frantically at the flames engulfing the space we just left.

The guard wraps his body over mine as if to shield me. For several seconds, we hold our breath. Is the train fast enough to outrace the slowing fireball? Or will it melt the back of the train and consume us?

Slowly, we untangle ourselves and climb onto two empty seats. The rest of the passengers huddle on the side of the car farthest away from us. At least we have some space.

I slump against the seat and close my eyes. Orbit is gone. The viceroy and council are gone.

Felix is gone.

And if I had tried to avenge him myself, I'd be dead too.

I tuck my chin against my shirt and shut my eyes. "Oh, God, forgive me for hating that man." For several moments, I stay silent until my pulse stops racing and the train's rhythm helps distract the spasms in my heart.

"You okay?" The guard touches my arm.

"Yeah." I open my eyes and let out a breath. "Thanks."

"You're welcome."

I study the gash that runs along his temple into his dark hairline. "You're OC, aren't you? You followed the tracker in my boot."

"I followed you and got lucky to get in the right place, at the right time to make this mission a rescue one."

Luck. If only he knew luck had nothing to do with this.

I follow his gaze out the glass. "Where are we going?"

He seems to study the window pane as if mapping out his plan. "We'll take the train to the Heathrow airport."

He might as well be speaking Greek. I don't know where that is. "And from there?" I ask.

The man offers a small smile that fills me with hope. "Home."

CHAPTER 42
~ Portia ~

Friday, 7.31.2150
Orvieto

With a last glance inside the quiet apartment, I latch the door and twist the house key. If my host Maria is still sleeping, I don't want to wake her for my early morning ride.

Skipping down the front step, I unlock the pasty white bike from the rack and stuff the lock into my pocket to use later.

The world might be free, but it's not perfect, though I still have a hard time accepting that thieves could belong in my Orvieto haven.

I flip the kickstand and slide onto the narrow seat, careful to tug my scarf high around my neck. The world is still cold, too. Maybe one day, the climate will moderate again as people say it once was in the past.

But I don't mind the cold, really. I don't mind much when I have free air to breathe.

The gauze bandage around my throat catches on the scarf's fabric, and I wince. That's twice now I've forgotten to be careful, and the last time, some stitches worked free. My nurse, *infermeria*, was not happy with me at all.

I gently separate the scarf from the gauze and press the bandage back in place. I'll replace it later when I clean the wound. I'm going to have a hideous scar, but that wretched collar is gone.

Breathing deeply, I peddle up the uneven road's incline. It's the same route I've taken since Maria—the young woman working at the OC apartment—invited me into her home. Though we met briefly on my first visit, she offered to let me stay with her. She can't speak a lick of English, but somehow, we bonded. Maybe it's because someone told her everything I'd lost. Looking at the pictures on her wall, I can tell she's lost her share of family, too.

I swallow. My short Translation with everyone back home after my rescue had been surreal. If only I could have reached through the screen and touched them! And then the session ended, and I hadn't said a fraction of what had happened. I couldn't put words to my story. There's so much horror I want to forget.

Maybe they feel the same way. Luther had looked pale when Darius explained the OC had launched a successful missile assault on Deadwood. I want to understand more, to talk with them again.

But since my surgery and recovery, Abra Bianchi hasn't invited me to any of her meetings or even contacted me to share when my father might come for me. Not that I can blame her. She's likely spending every spare second trying to reorganize and reconnect the broken communications among the nations previously smothered by the Rosh League. Civil wars, riots and political unrest are probably sweeping those confused nations. Restoring government at the national level will take time. People who've forgotten how to govern themselves don't step into democracy overnight.

And of course, the Rosh League's remnant leadership won't

relinquish its regional grasp without a fight. The USA might still be at risk of attack.

I suck in more air and finally reach the top of the road, thankful for the downhill stretch.

USA. United States of America. The name sounds strange to my ears, but American Socialists United doesn't fit anymore. Though we're hardly unified, we're not socialist anymore. Darius is struggling to maintain a semblance of order, at the moment, but maybe with Alexis's guidance, we'll one day rediscover what a Constitutional Republic actually looks like.

There it is. The cathedral's buttresses fly into view, and I peddle faster. The massive building has become my sanctuary, my place to start the day.

But I stop peddling as I reach the structure. How hadn't I heard that ruckus before? Dozens of people climb the cathedral's steps outside the door. Some bark orders, while others construct a stage. Others run wires and place equipment I've never seen before.

My heart sinks. So much for my quiet haven. But what are these people doing?

I peddle slowly toward a woman dressed in black who's assembling some kind of speaker. "*Mi dispiace. Non parlo italiano.* English?"

Maria had taught me one Italian phrase, simply to politely convey that I'm sorry, but I don't speak Italian.

The woman smiles but shakes her head no before refocusing on her task.

I try another man on the other side of the stage, but he shakes his head as well. I close my eyes and try to remember any Italian words that might express my question.

What is it Maria always says when I forget and try to talk to her in English?

"Che cosa?" I blurt out.

The man tilts his head. At least he's listening.

"Che cosa?" I wave my arms at the stage—everything that wasn't there yesterday.

He nods and bends down as if to search for something. "Ahh!" The man grips a long tube and smoothes out a banner. With a smile, he motions for me to take one end and help him unroll it.

My breath catches. The fabric is a dark blue, and printed on it are the words, "Orvieto per sempre, Luglio 2150." There's a name below that, but it's the combination of American and Italian flags that catches my eye.

"Oh, it's the July 4 celebration!" I say and smile at the man. His expression goes blank, and he shrugs again.

"Uh, grazie," I say and hope that really does mean *thanks*.

I return to my bike and hurry back to Maria's apartment. Does she know the celebration has been rescheduled? Is it for today? The idea of getting to see the event in person spreads my smile so wide it hurts my cheeks.

I forget about the bike lock and fumble with the house key in my pocket. "Maria!"

She rounds the corner. She's curled her pretty dark hair into a single pony tail and added a splash of red to her lips. "Eh, Portia?"

I love how she says my name. After all, Shakespeare's Portia was Italian. At least these people understand my name.

I'm gesturing but not talking. Poor Maria must be confused. "Uh, Orvieto per sempre, Luglio 2150." I spread my hands, hoping she can imagine the banner.

"Si, oggi." She smiles and claps her hands together.

"Oggi?" I have no idea what that means.

She taps her wristwatch with her fingers and stomps her foot. "Oggi."

"Time… today?" I can only hope I'm right.

Maria twirls in a cotton black dress as her dark eyes sparkle. Today must be special, because she isn't wearing her work uniform. Perhaps it's a holiday?

But then she studies me, and a frown creases her brow. She clucks her tongue and crosses her arms.

What is she staring at? I look down at my dull uniform. It's hardly pretty, but it's clean.

With a grin, she grasps my hand and tugs me into her room. She motions for me to sit on her bed while she opens her wooden wardrobe.

My eyes widen. I've never seen such a lovely array of colored clothes. Granted, her closet isn't big, but to a girl like me, it's a wardrobe of wealth.

She snatches a deep blue dress with long sleeves and a cinched waist and holds it out in front of me.

"It's beautiful." I smile.

"Bello." She drapes it over me. "Sí."

I blush with pleasure. She wants me to try it on? Maria digs out a pair of black leggings and chucks a pair of dark boots at me. I'll be amazed if anything fits, but she is petite like me, though taller.

The neckline is lower than I'm comfortable with—no one wants to see my stitches and raw skin—but I'll hurt her feelings if I don't try it.

I unwind my scarf and slip out of my uniform. Maria unzips the dress for me to step inside and then pulls the zipper back up.

It fits like a charm, though knee-length for her is shin-length for me. But I don't care. Have I ever worn a dress like this before?

Maybe when I was a little girl. But I don't remember.

With the leggings, slightly big boots, and a gray jacket, Maria completes the outfit.

We laugh like schoolgirls as we survey the results in her mirror.

And then I see it. Luther's ring glistens at the end of the cord, which hangs just above the low collar. It's been concealed for so long I'd almost forgotten it was there.

Maria's eyes soften as she sees it, too. Does she guess? How can I tell her? I slip it on my ring finger and brush it with my lips.

Tears trickle down her own cheeks, and she reaches to squeeze my hand. "Amore."

"Sí, amore," I say and swipe at the tears. Today isn't for being sad. Even if I have to keep waiting to go home, today is for celebration.

I squirm on my seat in the cathedral and study the stained-glass windows on every side of the massive interior. From narrow windows to rose-shaped ones, their ornate beauty is unmistakable even in the dull evening lighting. From there, I shift my gaze to the vaulted, pillared arches that frame both sides of the long aisle, empty except for me.

Why is Maria taking so long? Why did she leave me in this vast emptiness by myself?

Strange. I had wanted my quiet time in the cathedral this morning, and now, I want to join the crowd of hundreds—if not thousands—forming out front of the structure for the celebration. I don't want to miss a single minute.

The day had flown. Maria showed me how to make a pasta and chicken recipe for lunch with some heavenly sauce she called marinara. We'd walked to the coffee shop, visited shops and street vendors, and even explored some underground tunnels. Through a translator, she explained that they had once been a place to keep animals, store water, and raise pigeons for food. More recently, they served as bomb shelters. I hope the people won't need them for that purpose again any time soon.

Though our explorations were fascinating, I now have blisters on my feet from her over-sized boots. I should have worn my old ones, though they'd look ridiculous with the dress. I wish we had also made time to visit her work, just once, so I could have had a chance to seek out Abra. She must have some news by now from my family.

The sickening thought that something is wrong grips me. I've tried to push it aside the last few days, but in the silence, the fear grows. Maybe Dad and Luther haven't come because they can't. Maybe the OC targets weren't as effective as they had hoped, and the USA is still at risk of being pummeled. What if the Rosh League's secondary leadership has a firmer hold than we'd hoped?

I fold my hands in my lap and try not to pick at my cuticles. "Dear God, please let them be safe. Please…"

The clicking of footsteps echoes in the expanse behind me.

"It's about time, Maria…" I twist in my seat and then cover my mouth to keep a cry from escaping.

The person walking—no, running—toward me is not Maria. It's Luther.

Before I can get my wobbly legs to work, Luther reaches me and lifts me into his arms in an embrace I never want to end.

"Cotton, oh, Cotton." He breathes into my hair and then pulls back to see my face. "It's really you."

I lean in and kiss him on the lips. Words can wait. I have missed this man.

He presses me tighter against him and deepens the kiss. He cradles my head with one hand, while his fingers caress the skin below my jaw with the other.

My scarf slips, and I wince. "Sorry." I gasp, feeling my face flush. "It's just the wound still hurts to the touch."

"Wound?" His gaze drops to my neck.

My fingers tighten around the scarf, and I tug it higher. Will he think me hideous when he sees the stitches and puffy skin?

He slips his hand over mine. "Baby, what is it?"

I nibble my lip and look away. "It was Felix. Remember that collar he threatened to use on me at the Warren mines? Well, he…" I swallow the lump in my throat. Worse than the collar itself was the dehumanization it represented.

I suck another breath. "The Orvieto Healers—doctors—were able to remove it last week, but it's going to take time to heal... and it's going to leave a scar."

"Cotton, I don't care about scars. I care about you." His dark brown eyes search mine. "I'm sorry for whatever happened, but we're not looking back, remember?"

A tear runs down my cheek as I hold up my hand.

"You still have it." He clasps my ringed finger.

"Forever." I nuzzle against his cheek. "That's what I want with you—if you still want me, scars and all."

"I've always wanted you. A couple stitches won't change that."

"There are some scars you can't see." How will I tell him about Orbit?

"But God can, and He can heal those too." The tenderness and meaning in his words undo me. I lean against his chest and sob.

"There, there, you can't be bawling like this when your dad walks in." Luther dabs at my face with his sleeve. "He'll think I said something to make you cry—and I can't have him changing his mind about us."

I sniff and force a smile. "Dad's here, too? What about Darius and Gath and…"

He brushes my hair from my face. "They had to stay to work with Alexis in organizing local leadership among the squares and the response team to Deadwood."

"Response team? What do you mean?"

Luther pulls me down onto a seat next to him. "It was actually Lydia's idea. Her team is pretty confident they created a vaccination to counter the virus, and she wanted to head a team to see if there were survivors from the blast. If so, her plan is to proactively vaccinate them in case they were exposed."

I snort. "There's no way my brother said yes to that."

Luther tweaks my nose and smiles. "Your brother has a heart, though you've been too angry with him to notice it for a while. He would have gone with Lydia, but Alexis insisted that wasn't the president's place."

The words sink in. My brother is our new president, our new leader. But can he mend a country, let alone our broken relationship?

It's as if Luther reads my thoughts. "Trust me, he's as eager for you to be home as I am."

I hope he's right and plant another kiss on his cheek. "I'm here with you, Luther. I'm already home."

"But he said to tell you that our leadership team isn't complete without its Doctor Revisionary."

Doctor Revisionary. How can I ever fill that title—the title I had once wanted so badly?

The simple answer is that I can't on my own. And maybe that's the point. No leader in any role should try to lead like an island.

I pat Luther's cheek. "I'll do what I can as long as our Chief Court Citizen helps keep everyone in check."

He winks at me. "Keep you in check? As if that were possible."

I want the levity to last, but another thought twists my heart. "Wait, what about your dad? He would have been inside Deadwood."

Luther's smile fades. "As far as I know, he was. I can only hope that he is..." He sucks a deep breath. "That he and Jotham are okay."

The struggle behind his words isn't lost on me. His brother has wronged his own family, not just mine. I touch his arm. "Luther, Jotham wasn't in Deadwood. Jotham was in England. I don't think he was on the train, though, so maybe he survived."

Luther bites his lip and stares past me. "If he did, I hope—I hope he finds better company to keep."

I squeeze his arm and lean my head against his shoulder. He closes his hand around my fingers. Somehow, the unknown seems bearable together.

"Portia?" Dad's voice booms in the space behind us, and we spring to our feet. Luther tucks me into his side as we stride to meet my father half way up the tiled aisle.

"Dad!" I reach for him with open arms, and Luther lets go. Yes, he still has to share.

"Well, if it isn't Legs." Rig's voice interrupts the reunion.

I squint around Dad's lumbering form. "Rig? Is that really you?"

He snorts, but there's a twinkle in his eye. "Who else could they sucker into making this trip twice?"

Heels tap the floor, and we spin to find Maria standing there and pointing at her wristwatch. "Oggi," she says and motions toward the door.

I laugh at everyone's confused faces. "I think that means today—as in if we want to watch the show today, we'd better hurry."

Luther slips a hand around my waist as we follow Maria out a side door and around front. Near the orchestra is a row of five seats. Waiting for us at the end of the row is Abra Bianchi.

She greets me with a warm handshake. "I'm sorry I worried you, but isn't this the best surprise? The day we celebrate liberty starting over, you can enjoy it with your family and friends—our family and friends."

"Thank you." It's all I can say.

"What is this celebration?" Luther asks.

"We call it Orvieto Forever," Abra says. "It started all the way back in 2013 to celebrate the ideal of liberty for all. We've celebrated ever since and don't plan to stop—though this year is the first we've celebrated on a new day."

"July thirty-first instead of July fourth," I say. "I'm okay with a new re-birth date for celebrating our country."

"For celebrating freedom beyond borders," Abra adds. "After all, that's part of our mission statement: Looking ahead and continuing to build bridges."[iii]

"I like that," Luther says, "but we sure have a lot of bridges to build—and rebuild."

Music rumbles before us, signaling the presentation is about to begin. Abra smiles and moves to her own seat. Luther slides into one beside me, and I squeeze his hand.

"Yes, we have a lot to rebuild." I nuzzle closer. "But there's no one else I'd rather partner with to face it."

He tugs me onto his lap and wraps his arm around me. He doesn't need to say anything for me to know he feels the same way.

A vocalist begins singing "Amazing Grace," and the audience stands. Luther raises me to my feet but doesn't release my hand. We listen in awed silence as the tenor gives wings to the timeless words, the same ones I heard during my Simulation all that time ago.

I bow my head as the lyrics sink into my soul. "'Tis grace has brought me safe thus far, and grace will lead me home."

Notes:

[i] Matthew 24:28
[ii] Exodus 14:13
[iii] "Orvieto Legacy." www.orvieto4ever.com/legacy/

DISCUSSION QUESTIONS

1. The Orvieto Forever tradition that began in 2013 inspired the setting for the Brotherhood's international ally and the thread of hope for "liberty for all" even in Portia's dystopian world. Visit www.orvieto4ever.com/ for a preview of what this incredible celebration is like.

What American and family traditions do you celebrate in your home? Take a moment to remember *why* you do them and be grateful.

2. Portia and her brother Darius have a falling out after she discovers he lied to her about their father. When her fiancé Luther thinks about the strife between these siblings, he considers that *the fastest way to kill love is with lies.*

Have you ever experienced a broken relationship with a family member or friend because of dishonesty? The Bible encourages forgiveness and restoration. Consider these passages: Matthew 5:23-24, Ephesians 4:32, and Genesis 50:15-21.

3. Luther almost loses hope when he realizes he can't control what happens to Portia and is powerless to save her. That's when Gath speaks truth into his life and says:

> "If you believed in God, you'd realize that He can use even the most out-of-control situations and bring about good. Who knows if Portia is in Deadwood at this specific time for this specific reason? You need to start praying and believing that there's a God who can turn the world upside down on its head if He chooses—and He doesn't need you or me to do it."

In the Old Testament, Queen Esther found herself in a life and death situation but moved forward, believing she was right where she needed to be "for such a time as this" (Esther 4:14). Read her story in the book of Esther and consider: What are the unfair situations she faced? Through them, how did God use her to save her people?

Even today, God can use people—He can even use *you* right where you are. Sometimes, we may not understand His ways, but we can trust the truth of Romans 8:28 that He does work all things together for good for those who love Him and are called according to His purpose.

4. Gath tells Portia to get her "go-bag" before meeting him at the station. Maybe you've never heard of a go-bag, also called a bug-out-bag (BOB). In my family, each of us always kept one on hand. Even today, you'll find a backpack in my car trunk.

What is a go-bag? It's a backpack of essential items I'd need if I were stranded somewhere. Typically, it will include canned or long-term food items, water or an electrolyte drink, a change of clothes, basic toiletries, a flashlight, and other first-aid or basic survival gear. For a Florida girl who does a lot of traveling, I've never regretted having mine!

If you were to pack a go-bag, what would yours include?

5. When Portia is tempted to sink in self-pity, Orbit tells her, "You don't know everything. Do your friends a favor and stop thinking of yourself as a lost cause. Maybe you can do them some good." Even though Portia's situation looks bleak, she resolves to live in the present and do what she can.

Have you ever been tempted to forecast grief? In other words, do you worry about what-ifs or what-could-happen in the future? Living in the present is one of the greatest gifts we can give to ourselves and the people we love, because when we worry about tomorrow, we waste today (Matthew 6:34).

Kristen Hogrefe

ACKNOWLEDGMENTS

Coming to the end of a trilogy is a little like crossing the finish line of a half marathon. The only reason I felt amazing at that time is that I'd prepared and trained with friends. Others cheered me on, even though they may have secretly thought I was crazy.

I want to say a thank-you to everyone who made crossing this finish line not only possible, but truly unforgettable. My family has been my constant support, and some new faces have joined those ranks throughout this journey, including my sister-in-law Brooke. I also want to say a special thanks to my fiancé, James Parnell, for wanting to join this bandwagon and encouraging my writing.

Members of my writing family include fellow author Ashley Jones, my Word Weavers group, members of my book tribe (You know who you are!), and more recently, my colleague Maria Constantine whose family roots go back to Italy. At one point, I mentioned to her that my heroine travels to Italy in this final book and that in my dreams, I'd get to visit one day.

That's when she said, "You have to go! Want to come with me?" Long story short, she and I planned a spontaneous trip to some of the settings in this novel, and in a month's time, I found myself walking the streets of Orvieto and then mapping out Portia's entrance to the Port of Civitavecchia from just outside Fort Michelangelo. I can't thank Maria enough for helping make this dream a reality!

In another sense, Kelli Sorg (Make It Snappy) traveled with me this whole journey as well. She made brainstorming and creating the final cover perhaps the most enjoyable design session of all time.

The leadership and talent at Write Integrity Press also deserve my heartfelt gratitude. My editor Marji Laine championed this book and made the production process as seamless as possible. I'm also grateful to my primary editor Brittany Clubine who grasped the vision of Portia's story from the start and believed in it.

At the end of my half marathon, people asked me, "So, what's next?" I told them, "I'll keep running!" Those runs might be in my neighborhood, for my church's Hope 5K, another half marathon someday… who knows!

The same is true of my writing. Lord willing, I'll keep composing the stories He gives me and then watch where He takes them.

About the Author

Kristen Hogrefe is an award-winning author and life-long learner. Her desire to think truthfully and live daringly inspires her real life and fictional adventures.

Kristen also has the heart of an educator and mentor. She teaches secondary language arts for Alpha Omega Academy and served in youth ministry for several years. She is a motivational speaker for graduations and a workshop presenter at writers' conferences where she enjoys meeting students, readers, and other writers.

She currently serves as the president of an online writing chapter through Word Weavers International and teaches on the faculty of Serious Writer Academy, designed to help equip other writers in their publication journeys.

You can connect with Kristen through her website and blog at KristenHogrefe.com. She is active on Facebook, Twitter, and Instagram as well.

FROM THE AUTHOR

Hello, my friends!

Although I may never have the privilege of meeting most of you, I hope you know that I write with you in mind. I want you to feel like you've gone on an adventure, slipped into my characters' skins, and experienced their growth right along with them. On a deeper level, I hope you've learned something about human nature and even about yourself on the journey.

As an avid reader myself, I know that what I take away from the story may be different than what the author intended, or perhaps I connect with a secondary character instead of the protagonist. If that has been your experience with this trilogy, I think that's wonderful!

If you have a minute, would you share your thoughts about Portia's and her friends' story on Amazon or Goodreads? I so much enjoy seeing what my readers thought about these novels and what they took away from them.

Also, if you enjoy social media, I'd love to hear from you! You can find me online at KristenHogrefe.com and connect with my social media accounts from there.

Thanks for being part of this trilogy adventure! I hope we'll share more stories together in the future.

Live in abundance!

Kristen Hogrefe

The Rogues Series is Complete

Oppression, rebellion, patriotism, and honor blend together to create this unique dystopian thriller. Fans of *The Hunger Games*, *Divergent*, and *The Giver* will feel at home in this new world. Suspense, mystery, and unexpected twists will keep readers turning the pages, desperate to learn the whole story of Portia and her loved ones.

This award-winning, coming-of-age story tracks everyday high schooler, Wendy, through issues of love, loss, betrayal, pressure, and heartbreak. Family brokenness and accusations threaten to destroy any joy Wendy could have. Even traveling across the country doesn't help.

Follow Wendy as she struggles to overcome so much more than being known as a Bird Face.

Kristen Hogrefe

Thank you
for reading our books!

Look for other books
published by

Write Integrity Press
www.WriteIntegrity.com

Made in the USA
Lexington, KY
08 November 2019

56747936R00263